ON THE RUGGED HILLS

Book Two of The Serpent's Throne

Dan Ackerman

Supposed Crimes LLC • Matthews, North Carolina

For David

THE SKY above had barely started to grow dark but Ira still found himself hurrying to get home, an instinct left over from decades of having a curfew. A year had not broken him of that habit. He still paused at his door every time he wanted to leave his apartment, feeling like he couldn't go out without someone's permission.

He let himself inside and called hello to the landlady, who almost always had her door open.

She greeted him with a pleasant screech and a twitch of her wing. He'd picked up a handful of words in Ancient Greek, enough to know that she was fond of him.

As he started up the stairs, she called to him, "Garbage night," or at least, that's what he thought she said.

"Thanks, Mrs. Spiros."

She bobbed her head and went back inside her apartment.

Ira continued up to the fourth floor and pushed open the door to his apartment. He emptied his pockets on to the kitchen table. Half a dozen silver serpents clattered against the wood. One clinked against the other coins that had built up there.

Every night for a week or so he had dumped his pay on to the kitchen table, not knowing what else to do with it.

He sat and looked at today's coins.

One from Tycho, who had spilled all over Ira's back and hadn't helped wipe it up, either. One from Molly, who had wanted the use of his tongue, two from Astrid, who he worried might fancy him a little bit too much, and one from Kal, who had disturbingly enough called Ira by the name of his son when he'd come.

And one that he'd won in a bet with Selene, one of the other pleasure workers. He'd bet her that he could guess what street she'd grown up on and he had guessed correctly – Notch Street, in the outskirts of the Eight.

She'd been so sure that she'd covered up all the telltale signs, but she hadn't remembered to tug her sleeve down to cover the tattoo on the crook of her elbow. A spider, a dead giveaway that she'd worked for the pimp who ran out of that area.

He thought again of the look on Kal's face, first grunting and heaving with pleasure as he'd spilled over Ira's hand, his legs wrapped around Ira's waist, and then the contorted expression of panic that had come over him when he'd realized he'd groaned 'Lucas.'

Ira played with that coin, rubbing his fingers over the monstrous beast stamped into one side. He wondered if turning Kal away would mean that he'd start trying to get his son to fuck him.

Of course, Lucas was grown and could do whatever he pleased, but the idea sat strangely in Ira's belly. Even raised without a family, Ira knew some lines shouldn't be crossed.

A knock at the door pulled Ira out of his thoughts. He went over to open it and looked up at the tall, lanky figure that darkened his doorway.

"I told you, you don't have to knock."

Lucifer stepped inside when Ira opened the door wider. "I didn't want to be rude."

Ira went back to the kitchen table and looked at the coins, then at the Devil. "I want to pay my own rent."

The Devil shook his head, his fingertips brushing over one of the many tiny braids he'd woven through his ink black hair. By some miracle, he hadn't unwound them yet, or he'd redone them right before coming over. "There isn't any rent to pay."

"What do you mean?"

"You already own it."

Ira's eyebrows shot up of their own accord. "You *bought* this?"

Lucifer nodded. His shoulders had a bit of a droop about them and he didn't stand as tall as he usually did.

Ira sighed and looked at the coins. He pushed them into a neater pile, then went over to Satan, and wrapped his arms around the Devil's waist. "What's wrong?"

"I...I don't know."

Ira squeezed him tighter. "How can I help?"

In the back of his mind, it still felt like a ridiculous question. How could a whore help the Devil? It would have been one thing if Lucifer had been amorous and Ira had slid to his knees with that question on his lips, but the thought hadn't even crossed his mind.

Lucifer raked his fingers through Ira's curls, tilting his head back a little so that he could press a soft kiss to his mouth. "Tell me about your day."

"You don't want to hear about my day."

Immediately, the Devil asked, his voice full of worry, "Was someone—"

"No, no. I'm fine," Ira soothed. "It's just, I don't know. They all want the same thing every time. One always rubs my feet and one always kisses my wrist and one *always* wants me to call her momma." He rolled his eyes and took Lucifer by the hand, pulling him towards the sofa in the parlor. "What about your day?"

"Do I always do the same thing?" The Devil's eyebrows had knitted, his terrible reddish gold eyes squinted with concern.

"It doesn't matter what you do, I like you a fair amount more than them."

"Oh."

Ira tangled his fingers with the Devil's, ash-gray twined with milky white. "Don't you like me better than your other lays?"

"You know there aren't any others."

Ira nodded. He had known, but he didn't know how he felt about it. Even though they hadn't imposed any agreements of fidelity or exclusivity on each other, Lucifer hadn't been with anyone else.

Part of Ira liked very much that no one else put their hands on the Devil's skin or their mouth on his lips.

They both stayed quiet, settled in on the sofa.

"I went to the Third today."

"Oh?"

"I saw your brother," Lucifer confessed.

Ira's stomach dropped. "You do that from time to time."

"He asked how you are."

"I don't care how he is," Ira spat.

"He wants to see you."

"No."

"Ira."

"No!" Ira pulled his hand back, crossing his arms.

Lucifer made a face but said nothing.

"And maybe after that, I can go and see my parents, too! Ask why...!" Ira stopped himself, his throat going tight. He didn't know why he'd started but felt sure that he didn't want to finish the thought.

Lucifer reached out and toyed with one of Ira's curls. "I love you."

"What!" Ira squawked.

"I love you," the Devil repeated calmly.

"No, I heard you! But...I mean, *that's* how you want to tell me for the first time!"

"It might have been the first time you heard me but it's not the first time I've said it."

"Oh? When've you been saying it, then?" Ira challenged.

"Usually when you're sleeping." After a moment of thought, the Devil added, "Or when you're making that absolutely wonderful sound you make when you come."

A crooked half-smile crawled across Ira's face.

"But I wanted to make sure you heard me this time."

Ira really grinned this time. "And you haven't even taken me captive yet."

Lucifer smiled, his black teeth disturbingly stark against the pallor of his skin. He took Ira's hands and kissed his fingers. "What if I just ate you up instead? Swallowed you whole so we'd never be apart."

"Maybe later, I have plans for tomorrow." Ira had gotten used to these sorts of odd statements from the Devil.

"What are you doing tomorrow?"

"Figuring out what to do with all that fucking money!"

Lucifer's eyes went to the pile on the table. It must have seemed like a paltry amount to the Prince of Hell himself, but Ira didn't know what to do with it. His rent was paid, or, it seemed, nonexistent. He'd gone out and bought himself new clothes when he'd first started making money, so he didn't have to wear the same pair of breeches and two shirts he'd had since he'd stopped growing.

He quite liked the way he looked in trousers and suspenders instead of fashion that had died on Earth above ages ago.

"You could put it in the bank," Lucifer suggested.

Ira frowned; the idea had never occurred to him.

"Save it for something you really want."

"You always get me what I want as soon as I mention it!" Ira reminded, feeling spoiled and whiny.

Lucifer smiled just a little, one corner of his mouth tipped up. "Is that why you've stopped mentioning things to me?"

"Maybe. I don't know how to open a bank account anyway."

"I'll take you tomorrow."

Ira pressed a kiss to the Devil's cheek, glad for the answer he'd given. Ira didn't like to ask for help or admit how much he didn't know about being on his own. At work, he tried to play it off like those things were beneath him, always saying, "I'll have *him* take care of it for me."

"Thank you."

"You're welcome, love. Is there anything you wanted to do tonight?" Lucifer asked.

"I haven't had dinner yet."

"Do you want to go somewhere?"

Ira shrugged. He didn't but also didn't want to eat one of the paltry meals he cobbled together for himself. Cheese, dried meat, and bread, maybe wine or fruit. Things that didn't need to be cooked. He had only turned his stove on five times in the year he'd lived here, and he'd scared himself each time; pots and pans he never used filled his cabinets.

Lucifer stood and went into the kitchen, peeking through the cabinets and the ice box. "Love, you haven't got anything in here."

"There's bread and I think half a bottle of wine."

The Devil shook his head and came back over to the couch. He took Ira's hand again and pressed his lips to the small tattoo on his right wrist; the black ink barely stood out against the gray of Ira's skin, but he hadn't gotten it for fashion. It was meant to keep away the sort of poxes and diseases that came with his line of work.

So far it had worked, as had the contraceptive one on his hip.

"So you don't want to go out and there's nothing to eat in here," Lucifer mused, "I think we're stuck. Maybe I will eat you after all."

Ira shrugged and didn't look at him, embarrassed.

The Devil swooped down and scooped him up off the couch. "Or, I don't think it's too late, and fuck it if it is, I am the Devil, after all, we can go fetch some ingredients."

"I can't cook."

"Yes, well, I can. That's why we work so well together, Ira, dear.

I can cook and you can...I don't know, sleep at night without the screams of the damned echoing through your skull. It's called balance."

The Devil set him down.

"You sleep fine at night," Ira told him.

"Only when you're beside me."

Lucifer took him by the hand and Ira went, grinning like a fool.

They roamed the market, arms linked, with Lucifer holding up an item every so often asking, "What do you think?"

Ira shrugged each time, but the Devil didn't grow irritated or impatient.

Back at Ira's flat, Ira sat at the kitchen table and watched as the Prince of Hell peeled potatoes.

"Do you want help?"

The Devil pushed a small knife and a potato his way.

Ira picked it up and tried to peel off the skin in thin slices but ending up carving off a thick slab.

"You know, I don't know how we haven't done this sooner," Lucifer said.

Ira lopped off another large slice of potato. "You were. Uh. Well, you were having a rough go, there, for a while."

Lucifer hummed agreement.

"How is the little one doing, anyway?" Ira asked.

"Good, good, really," the Devil answered. "Still can't believe I've gone ahead and left my son in the care of a Reinhart, but...you know, Hiram and Phaedrus, they're what he needs. Loving, kind. *Stable*. And Hiram can keep him hidden."

After Mercy had met her unfortunate end, Lucifer had tried to keep the baby in Hell with him, but all sorts of unsavory things had come to try to kill or capture the child. Angels and Moralists and even a few traitorous creatures among the ranks of the Fallen.

The fact that Felix was hidden with Hiram Reinhart and Phaedrus Queen on Earth was a grave secret, one that Ira almost wished he didn't know.

"He'll be a year in April," Lucifer said, his eyes on the knife.

Ira touched his hand and gave him a smile. Lucifer had been ruined when he'd decided he couldn't keep his son in Hell. Too many things had come searching and he had given the little thing a bad fright once.

That had really done him in, making the infant squall like that.

"Better for him to be up there," Lucifer had announced. "He is half-human. Mercy would have wanted up him up there."

Ira hadn't known enough of Mercy to know what she would have wanted, and he hadn't known what to say to soothe Lucifer's distress. He still didn't.

They finished peeling the potatoes in silence. By the time they'd been chopped and set to boil, Lucifer had regained some of his good mood.

When it came time to eat, the Devil heaped more mushrooms than meat on his plate.

Ira inquired, "Have you got enough mushrooms there?"

"Yes."

"You sure you don't want more?"

Lucifer pressed his lips together and Ira grinned at him.

THEY WENT to the bank first thing in the morning, Ira clutching the bag of coins in his arms like a child with a piggy bank.

Lucifer swept through the place as though he owned it, bypassing all the other customers and counters. He went directly to the office of who Ira assumed was one of the managers.

"Your Highness," the demon squawked upon their entrance. He stood to give a bow. "What can I do for you?"

Lucifer put a hand on Ira's shoulder and brought him forward. "We'd like to open a bank account, please, Yage."

"Of course, Your Highness. Have a seat, please." Yage gestured to the set of chairs in front of his desk.

Ira sat, playing with the purse strings, and looked up at the Devil, hoping he didn't seem too pathetic.

Lucifer sat beside him.

"Now, what's the name on the account?" Yage asked.

Lucifer gave Ira a nudge.

"Ira."

Yage waited a moment, pen in hand, then looked up when Ira didn't say anything else. "Ira...?"

"That's it, just Ira," Ira said.

Yage glanced at Lucifer.

Some Hell-born demons had family names, others used patronym or something like it for their second name, and others still had titles. Ira had nothing, just three letters.

Lucifer leaned in to whisper, "You can call yourself whatever you like, but your given name—"

Ira pulled back, shaking his head. "No."

He was on his feet before he knew what he was doing. He walked out of the manager's office, through the bank, and out the door, his heart thrumming in his chest.

He heard, faintly, Lucifer calling after him.

People pushed past him to get into the bank, wealthy demons all of them, with glittering rings and silken clothes. He pushed back, through the crowd to the street, where he looked about, wondering where to go.

He had lived in the Ninth since he was barely more than a toddler but still didn't know the streets as he should have. His mistress had forbidden him from going too far from the Trade House. Even now, he traced the same routes between work, home, and the market.

When he looked up the street, he could see the fenced-in estate where the Devil's palace sat. His feet well knew the way there. He walked there when the Devil hadn't stopped by in a while, usually to have Imogen tell him, "He's been busy," or worse, "He's resting."

"Hey." Lucifer had caught up to him, putting a hand on his elbow. "Ira, love..."

Ira pushed the bag of coins into the Devil's hands. "I don't want to open a bank account."

Lucifer opened his mouth.

"And I *don't* want to you to tell me their last name."

Lucifer nodded. "Would you like to go home?"

Ira shook his head. "I've got to go to work."

"I'll walk you—"

"No, I know how to get there," he snapped and set off, though he wasn't sure where he was going.

He was stupid, he knew, and too bold with his Prince. He should have been grateful, he should have been at the very least respectful, instead of snapping at him.

He didn't know why the Devil bothered to visit him. He wasn't the handsomest demon to be found, bought or otherwise. He didn't know why the Devil cooked him dinner or loved him. There was nothing about him worth loving.

He could spread his legs or get on his knees, but that was it. He was useless and stupid and, as his mistress had always reminded him, worth very little. He hadn't earned much for her, he'd never had clients clamoring to come to him.

His own parents had parted with him for nothing more than a few months' worth of groceries.

And, like that, absorbed in the spiral of his thoughts, Ira was lost. He looked up and could see the faraway spires of the library jutting up above the roofs and recognized nothing else.

His breath quickened.

The houses were spaced far enough apart that he knew he had not wandered into the Eighth. It was the middle of the morning. Most demons would be at work by now, toiling to clean and prepare the souls.

He should have been at work.

"Lost?" came a slippery voice from his right.

He looked over to see a woman leaning against a doorway, her eyes raking over him. "No."

"Standing there looking around for the last five minutes, you *look* lost." She came down the steps. "And young."

He stood up straighter. Slim and short as he was, people always mistook him for a youth. "Born before the Wasting Plagues."

She laughed at that. "You *are* young. Where do you need to be?"

He tried to keep his back straight. "Just...point me towards Queen Street."

She grinned, her smile wide and toothy. "Nothing but whorehouses there, lad."

He shrugged.

She put her hand on her shoulder. "I can show you a good time."

He stepped back. "No, I...I work there. At Marius' house..." He hoped that dropping the name of the brothel's owner would buy him some safety. Marius was well respected throughout the Ninth.

At that, though, she took his face in her hand, squeezing so that his teeth ached. "I can put you to work, too, little thing."

Ira tried to step back but she kept her grip, sliding her hand down his neck and squeezing his shoulder hard.

From a sheath on her belt, she produced a knife and placed it to the thrumming vein in Ira's throat. "What's your rate?"

"I...I need to go, I..." He took half a step back.

She pressed the blade to his neck. "Your rate."

"A serpent...for, for an hour..." His eyes searched the street, but he saw no one.

"What a high-priced whore you are! I'll give you two bits for the use of your tongue."

He shook his head. "I'm not...I have clients there, I'm not looking for work."

She slid the knife up his throat, leaving a smarting line from the base of his neck to just beneath his ear. "Or you can do it for free."

He swallowed and squeezed his eyes shut. He hadn't gotten that sort of offer for a while now.

It was better to service her and get paid for it. At least he could make that choice, to give it or have it taken.

He nodded, his eyes still shut.

With a coo, she traced her tongue along the shallow cut on his neck, then along his jaw. "Pretty thing, too, how lucky you were to have gotten lost."

Her hand still clamped onto his shoulder, she brought him up the stairs and closed the door to her house behind them.

Her mouth tasted sour on his when she kissed him.

He pulled away. "I...I've..." His tongue ran over an ulcer on the inside of his bottom lip, left from when he chomped down on it during dinner. He dug his teeth into it to make it look angrier. "I've got sores," he warned.

She moved back a little.

He put a finger in his mouth and pulled down his lip to show the wound. "See?"

In the Eighth, no one would have batted an eye, but demons in the Ninth tended to be a little more fastidious. Going to an orgy with sores on her lips and between her legs wouldn't be fashionable, he knew.

"And what about on your cock?" she asked.

He swallowed.

"Go on, let's see it."

His fingers fumbled at his belt and he found himself, for the first time in his life, wishing for a blemish on his privates.

Once he was exposed, she gestured for him to move things around for her inspection. Free from sores, free from anything more than a single, thin scar on one side which he'd gotten climbing through a broken window when he'd been thirteen and not particularly wise.

She grinned and before she could state her approval, he asked,

"Do you have somewhere I can wash up first? Marius says it's good practice, before and after."

She looked a little taken aback by the question but nodded towards a washroom. He shoved himself back into his trousers and hurried towards it before she could change her mind.

Within he found a pitcher full of water and a basin. His hands trembled as he reached for the water.

He had no wish to bed this woman, for two bits or a whole serpent.

He spied a lock on the door and twisted it, sinking to the floor, his hands gripping his curls.

Someone at Marius' would worry when he didn't show up and some of them knew enough about his personal life that they would tell the Devil he'd gone missing.

Whether Lucifer would come looking for him after he'd stormed off was up in the air.

The woman rapped on the door, scaring his heart into his mouth.

"One moment," he called.

He made himself stand, searching through the cabinets to find anything that might be of use.

He found nothing, though, and after another moment, made himself leave the washroom.

Lucifer would not be happy when he heard of this, Ira knew; he would be angry that Ira hadn't stood up for himself and that terrible form he took would rear its head.

That stretched-out, spindly beast with its gaping maw and talon fingers.

Ira had a single card to play and wondered if it would work.

The woman had put her knife away.

"I'm not looking for work," he told her, making himself stand up as tall as he could.

She grinned. "We've been over this—"

His voice shaking, he threatened, "If you make me, I'll tell our Prince, I'll go right to his palace—"

She cut him off with a laugh. "As though the Devil cares what happens to some lost whore."

"He'll care if you do it to me. He'll come and rip you to bits, shove your meat and your bones down his throat because I asked him to."

She drew her knife again and approached. "Then you won't be

leaving and—"

"And if you kill me it will be worse! You know what he's done to others who have displeased him, what he did to Mylas last year! We all saw him eat those traitors from the last coup!"

She paused her advance. Watching the Devil gulp down those unlucky bastards had been a gruesome sight, even for the denizens of Hell.

"I'm a whore, but I am *his*."

While she considered his threats, he moved toward the door, edging around her. His nerve held for only a moment and when he was close enough to reach the knob, he lunged for it and broke into a run.

He sprinted towards the spires of the library and ran all the way there. He stumbled inside the door and made such a commotion that everyone looked at him.

He drew himself together as best he could and marched towards the stacks. He had taken refuge there often as a youth and he knew which sections did not have heavy foot traffic. His mistress had allowed him trips to the library, thanks to Nial's encouragement.

Once on the fourth floor, in the back corner, he crumpled to the floor and pressed his knees to his chest.

He didn't know how long he'd been sitting there but eventually, a quiet, amused voice interrupted his solitude. "I thought I might find you here once you'd had time to cool off. I asked them to point me towards the most adorable but distraught demon who'd come in recently."

He looked up to see the Devil above him, smiling.

"I didn't mean to upset you about the names..." Lucifer's eyes fixed on the cut on Ira's neck.

As soon as Lucifer's face soured, tears began to stream down Ira's cheeks.

The Devil crouched in front of him, his long body folding. "What happened, darling?"

Ira shook his head and wiped his face with his sleeve.

Lucifer's spidery fingers caressed Ira's cheek. "Tell me."

"No."

"Why not?"

"You'll be angry." He pushed the Devil's hand away.

"Never with you."

Ira shook his head again. "I'm late for work."

"Love, look at you, I'll take you home. Marius will understand."

"No. I'll go to work," Ira insisted.

"Ira."

"I'll go to work." Ira made himself stand, even though his legs felt like they might give out and his heart had not yet settled comfortably in his chest.

Lucifer stood at the same time and followed him out of the library. He trailed behind Ira until they reached the pleasure house that Marius owned.

When Ira entered, Selene came up to him and pulled him into a hug, enveloping him with her wonderfully fat, soft body. "Ira!"

"Is he mad?" Ira asked in a low voice. His eyes flicked towards the bar behind which Marius could almost always be found.

"No, we were worried!" Selene assured. "Molly came to see if you were in, too."

He nodded. He'd have to make it up to her.

"What happened your neck?"

He put a hand to the scabby cut. "Just a scratch."

Lucifer went over to the bar and slid behind it like he belonged there. He approached the pander and put a hand on his arm, then leaned in to whisper something in the demon's ear.

Marius numbered among the Fallen, though his sandy brown skin made him appear more human than a lot of them.

While Selene tried to get an answer out of Ira about the scratch on his neck, the two once-angels conferred in hushed voices.

"Did *he* do it?" Selene whispered.

Ira pulled his eyes away from the two behind the bar. "He?"

"Our Prince."

"No, no, of course not."

Lucifer left Marius, giving the other Fallen a clap on the shoulder and a fond smile. He came back over to Ira and kissed his cheek. "I'll come back to see you later if you don't mind."

"That would be fine."

"I'll see you soon, love."

Ira nodded.

When Lucifer had left, Marius called, "Ira, come here!"

Ira approached the bar, his stomach twisting. He hadn't been late yet and didn't know what repercussions it would have.

The pander asked, "Are you alright to work today?"

"I'm fine."

"Tell me if you aren't."

"I'm fine."

Marius brushed a hand over his tight, close-cropped curls. "Listen, Ira...we've all been in a bad place at work, it's a profession that can get a little dicey."

"I told you, I'm fine."

The Fallen gave him a hard look, his topaz eyes boring into Ira's dark ones. Marius had not always been a pander; he had started his career as a whore, too, in the ancient temples of sacred prostitution.

Finally, Marius sighed. "Well, if you aren't, you know where the door is. Take it easy today."

Ira nodded. Being told to take it easy was more tolerable than being asked if he was okay or not.

Selene slipped her arm through Ira's and said, "I'll keep an eye out for him, don't worry." She took Ira by the face and pressed a kiss to his cheek.

Marius gave them both a smile, then shooed them away.

Selene picked up a customer soon enough, which left Ira to wait around on one of the couches.

The first customer that approached Ira was someone he'd never been with before. A someone who, with slippery words and sticky hands, made it clear that he intended to have Ira's ass and have it well.

The idea didn't sit well with him, not now, not today.

Once he would have made himself; he would have gritted his teeth or bit his tongue to get through it.

The man flashed a coin in front of Ira's eyes. "What do you say?"

The coin did nothing to change his mind. He had a whole pile of glittery coins at home and nothing to spend them on. "No, I...I'm not for that today, maybe a different time," Ira told him.

The man's faces contorted hideously, one mouth snarling as the other sneered.

"If you don't like it, you can talk to the pander. There's plenty of others."

The man barely got two steps away before Georg slid up to him and put an arm around his waist, promising the use of his body however he wanted.

The next who came for Ira was Reggie, a harmless old creature who never wanted to anything more than wash Ira's feet and rub them with fancy skin creams while he played with himself. Sometimes, when Reggie felt adventurous, he liked a bit of dirty talk or a little help stroking his cock.

Reggie would be perfect.

WHEN THE sky had started to grow dark, Satan entered Marius' house. Ira knew this not because he'd seen him, but because the whole place quieted as it only did when their Prince walked in.

Lucifer came right over to Ira. "Can I walk you home?"

"Ohh, two days in a row you've come to visit me. Should I be flattered?"

The Devil stared down at him with those eyes, red and gold and just awful, and Ira felt immediately bad for having teased him like that.

Lucifer hadn't been well of late. People whispered that he'd gone mad, lost his grip on reality. They even whispered that things might be ripe for a coup.

Ira knew better. The Devil had been deeply melancholy and maybe more out of touch than usual, but he remained perfectly capable.

"You can walk me home," Ira amended, standing and checking his pockets for the two coins he'd collected that day. He twined his fingers with Lucifer's as they walked. "Thank you for checking in on me."

"Maybe I just wanted to see you."

Ira glanced him at him, not believing it.

"Maybe it was a little of both," the Devil admitted. "Maybe I want you to tell me who put that scratch on your neck."

"Well, I can't, even if I wanted to."

"Mm, well."

They walked up to Ira's apartment together.

Once inside, Ira realized that someone had stocked his kitchen.

"I hope you don't mind," Lucifer said.

Ira peered into the cabinets, finding things like sugar and flour, things he didn't know how to use.

"I used the key you gave me," the Devil said. It sounded like a reminder that Ira had given him permission to come and go, a request not to be cross.

"I don't mind, dear, of course not."

Satan smiled and entered further into the kitchen. He beckoned for Ira to come over and gestured to the oven. "I put a chicken in to roast."

"You haven't got to take care of me."

"But I want to."

Ira shook his head.

Without warning, the Devil wrapped his arms around him, pulling him close and onto his toes. "I want to do it because when you hadn't seen me in a while, when I couldn't get out of bed, you came to ask about me. You walked all the way to the palace and once you knew I couldn't come out, you asked to come in."

"It isn't much of a walk."

Lucifer pulled back and ran his thumb along Ira's jaw. "You sat with me and talked to me and that's worth at least three roast chickens."

Ira cracked a smile.

Later, after they'd sat down to share a meal and a few cups of cold white wine and after they'd moved from the kitchen to the sofa in the parlor, Lucifer asked again what had happened to Ira's throat.

This time, Ira doled out his encounter in bits, his tongue loosened by the wine. When he realized he had started talking, he wished he hadn't and tried to trail off. The Devil had prompted him to finish and, once he had, at looked at Ira over the rim of his cup, paused halfway through taking a drink.

Satan brought the cup away from his mouth.

"Then you found me in the library." Ira stared into his wine.

Lucifer reached over and placed a light hand on his arm. "Ira, love, can you look at me?"

Ira raised his eyes.

"I'm proud of you."

Ira frowned.

"What you did was difficult and very brave."

"No, I didn't..." He shook his head. "I ran away."

Lucifer didn't argue. He picked up the bottle of wine that rested between them on the couch and tipped more into his cup, then offered the last of it to Ira.

Ira nodded.

Lucifer offered, "We've got another bottle if you want to get drunk."

Ira shook his head. "No, not too much, I'd like to be able to fuck you later if you're game."

"Goodness, you really are resilient, aren't you?"

Ira didn't know what to say to that, so he took a drink.

People often thought that whoring had a to be a lot of fun, and sometimes it was; sometimes his clients liked to get him off as much as they liked to get off themselves, and sometimes, his climax was incidental, a byproduct of what happened.

But more often than not, he was on his knees or slipping his tongue between some woman's legs, or he was being had by some careless man who hadn't been rough, no, but who came and left without caring if Ira had finished, too.

And now, Ira found, what he really liked was to wind his fingers through the Devil's hair while he kissed Ira's belly, and to watch his eyelashes rest against cheekbones and hear his sweet, breathy moans while Ira was as deep inside of him as he could go.

He liked the way Lucifer would press a kiss to the back of his neck. He liked how easy it was to let the Devil slide inside of him, no worrying if it would be good or not, no praying that he would be careful.

"I would be a mess," Satan confessed.

"Luci, darling, you're always a mess."

He paused, his drink nearly at his lips. "My wife called me that."

Ira immediately felt stupid. He had hoped to be endearingly bold, maybe sort of flirty, with the use of his nickname. He'd heard it before, on the lips of some of his favorite Fallen, of his sister-in-law, but had never uttered it. "I'm sorry," he whispered.

Lucifer shook his head. "I like it better from you."

"You do?"

"A thousand times." Lucifer set his glass on the floor beside the empty bottle of wine. He leaned over to Ira's side of the sofa and kissed his throat, his fingers working at the buttons on Ira's shirt.

He kissed his way down his throat and across Ira's collarbone, leaving a trail along his ribs, his belly, but pausing at the waist of his trousers.

No, not pausing, Ira realized, teasing.

The Devil undid the fly on his trousers and slid them down a little, his fingers wrapped in the straps of Ira's suspenders. He ran his tongue along the tattoo on Ira's hip, his touch barely there.

"Go on, then," Ira urged after a bit, hard and excited, yearning for any kind of contact, hand or mouth.

The other man had tugged Ira's trousers down around his thighs, leaving him exposed, and had kissed all around, nibbled carefully at some tender skin, but that was it.

Lucifer glanced up at him, grinning. "Don't be rude or I won't do it at all."

"You will, don't pretend you won't," Ira told him, smiling as well. "They tell us all about what a terrible monster you can be, how wrathful you are, but..." His breath caught in his throat when Lucifer circled his tongue around the tip of Ira's cock.

"But what?"

"But they don't tell you that the Devil is...ohh!" he cried when Lucifer took him into his mouth.

Ira couldn't keep his thoughts together any longer. He couldn't recall what he'd been trying to say. He could only think of the pressure of Lucifer's tongue, the slide of his lips, and the pleasant heat of his mouth.

When he started to get close, when he couldn't keep his hips still, the Devil pulled away and asked, "Did you still want to have me or...?"

"Your mouth," Ira begged, "Let me come in your mouth."

Lucifer kissed him first, before returning his lips to Ira's length. Ira wound his fingers in the Devil's hair, glad to have something to hold, wondering how much longer he could last so that this would never end but also wanting desperately to spill now.

When he did come, it was a rush of heat and need and bliss, something that lit up his whole body and utterly cleared his mind for a few seconds.

The next thing he knew, the Devil had nuzzled against his throat. "So what don't they tell you about the Devil?"

"That he's a proper fiend when it comes to sucking cock," Ira told him, "That he's thirstier for seed than he is for blood."

Lucifer snorted and pressed a kiss to Ira's throat. "And I am *very* bloodthirsty."

Ira put his arms around Satan's neck. "Carry me to bed, I want to lie down."

"Oh, so *bossy*." Lucifer lifted him and brought him to his bedroom.

With half-closed eyes, he watched the Devil shed his clothes and sat up to do the same. When Lucifer started to undo his braids, Ira reached over to help, working his fingers through the mussed plaits.

They settled into bed together, skin against skin, not sleeping but sleepy.

"Do you know what I would like to do?" Lucifer asked into the crook of Ira's shoulder.

"I can go again soon," Ira mumbled, half-awake.

"No, shh, not that."

"What?"

"I'd like to have a day off together. A whole day."

"Do you have days off?" Ira asked. Days when he could not move didn't count.

"Parts of them. Sometimes. I'm sure I could scrape together a whole day if I put my mind to it," Lucifer assured.

"Not until you sort out that...oh, that rowdy bunch of workers in the Fifth."

"I really shouldn't tell you as much as I do."

Ira yawned. "I'm not a gossip."

"No, dear, you've been trustworthy."

Ira nestled closer to him. He could go again now if Lucifer wanted, or he could return the favor. He hadn't even offered, he realized. "Did you want anything?"

"No."

"I must be the worst whore in Hell..."

"Ira."

"Hmm?"

"You know that isn't what you are to me. Your work is your work but...we're us."

"We are us, yes, grammatically I think it holds up," Ira agreed, but when he sensed that the Devil wanted something more, he said, "I will admit, the fucking has become sort of...incidental to rather than the cause of our time together."

In the back of his mind, Ira knew that sex had ceased to be

Lucifer's primary reason for visiting him long before he'd stopped working at the Trade House.

"I like it, though," he told the Devil. "This...What we have between us. It's easy and comfortable and I still think that maybe someday I'll want us to only be with each other."

"Imagine all the time you'd have to read!" Lucifer teased.

Ira had to agree, adding, "And no one coming around trying to fuck me in the middle of a chapter, either!"

Satan kissed him once more, then closed his eyes and pulled the covers up higher. He had dropped off to sleep in no time, giving Ira the chance to study the lines of his face.

They spent a cozy series of nights and mornings together, four in a row. On the fifth morning, Ira woke when he felt a light kiss pressed to his temple.

"Love, I've got to go."

Ira stretched and propped himself up on one elbow. The Devil had already dressed; Ira glimpsed Imogen through the open bedroom door, her arms crossed as she leaned against the arm of the sofa.

"What's wrong?" he asked, knowing that if Imogen had come to fetch him, things couldn't be going well.

"Some careless creature in the First was lax with locking the doors last night."

Ira sat up further. "Souls have gotten out?"

"That's what they're telling me." Lucifer kissed him once more. "I've got to go."

Ira nodded and swung himself out of bed, walking him to the door. "Don't be a stranger."

Lucifer nodded and walked out, Imogen in his wake.

Ira watched them disappear down the stairs, then retreated into his apartment when he realized he'd been standing stark-naked in the hall. He didn't want to give the neighbors the wrong impression.

Working in one of the nice brothels in the Ninth didn't have the same stigma as working the streets or taverns in the Eighth, but it did give people the impression that he was willing to do anything, anytime, for the right amount.

He couldn't get back to sleep, so he washed and dressed then bought something to eat on his walk to work.

He arrived before those who rented rooms upstairs sauntered downstairs and the others who came from their own homes rushed in.

At first, he didn't notice Marius at the bar, seated in one of the stools with his head bent over a ledger.

He cleared his throat, not wanting to startle the Fallen.

Marius glanced over. "What's one thirty-two plus ninety-seven?"

Ira thought, then replied, "Two twenty-nine."

Marius's pen scratched against the page of the ledger and he gestured for Ira to come sit at the bar next to him. "Drink?"

Ira shook his head. "Bit early for that."

"Yes, well, when dealing with sums..." Marius trailed off with a sigh and returned his eyes to the ledger. "What's got you in so early?"

Ira shrugged.

"Do you need money?"

"No. Just couldn't get back to sleep," Ira explained.

"Ah."

Ira scanned the sheets of scratch paper covered with arithmetic.

Marius must have seen him looking because he admitted, "He didn't give me a head for sums."

"Do you want help?"

"Oh, Christ, do I." Marius pushed the ledger towards Ira.

Ira's eyes skimmed down the columns. Who had earned what, who elected to pay two bits out of every serpent they earned to the house, and those who agreed to play the flat rate of three serpents at the start of each week.

Ira reread the names of the earners and flipped back a few pages. "Do I charge the most?"

"No. Travys and Helen charge a serpent as well. Sometimes two."

"Oh." Travys and Helen were beautiful creatures, well regarded in their profession and in society. They had been trained in pleasure work as an art, they hadn't come by it as a necessity. "Oh."

"What?"

Ira shook his head. "I just...I didn't think I rated that high."

"Well, you are his favorite," the Fallen reminded.

"Is that why they come to see me?"

"You're also very pretty," Marius told him. "And diligent."

Ira turned his eyes back to the numbers, jotting down a few sums at the bottom of the page. Marius had turned a tidy profit this week.

"There's plenty more to do if you'd rather play with numbers today."

Ira's head jerked up. He hadn't noticed Marius slide behind the bar; he hadn't notice anyone else come inside, but the parlor had filled. "Sorry, what?"

"I've got months of those. And other things."

"Months?" Ira's eyes flicked to the top of the page. He'd been doing the books for a week that had ended months ago.

Marius shrugged and poured a golden spirit over a tumbler of ice. He pushed it towards Ira. "Tax seasons soon. I shouldn't let things build up but...zounds, I hate that shit."

Ira returned to the numbers, shaking his head at the pander.

Each time a client came for him, Ira left behind the ledger and returned to them after he'd washed up until Marius took them away around midday.

"No need to work two jobs," the pander told him and pushed another drink his way.

Ira wondered if he'd end up with a bill for these drinks later. The other workers had warned him away from drinks that seemed free, but Ira had swallowed dozens of drinks since he'd started working here and none of them had ever been applied to his weekly fee.

He wondered if Lucifer had something to do with it.

He sighed and turned to look out over the parlor. Lucifer probably had something to do with everything, really.

Molly came to sit next to him; she put a hand on his arm and told him, "I missed you the other morning."

"I'm sorry, Mol, I was running a little bit late."

"We were all aflutter worrying about you."

He smiled his best smile at her. "Well, here I am, whole and sound. Would you like to me to make up for the worrying you did?"

He wrapped his fingers around her wrist, let his thumb caress the tender skin. He leaned in to press a careful kiss to her throat, right next to her ear, which he knew would remind her of the feel of his tongue on her earlobe.

"I'll be extra nice to you," he promised.

She trailed her finger down the buttons on his shirt and hooked one foot around his ankle. "I think I'd be able to forgive you."

He took her by the hand, leading her to one of the rooms set aside for these things, making sure he doled the right about of kisses and touches so that her interest wouldn't cool between the parlor and the room.

Once the door closed behind them and she had placed a coin on the table next to the bed, he pressed a harder kiss to the crook of her shoulder, nipping a little bit, knowing she liked that.

With caresses and plenty of kisses, he slipped her out of her clothes, though she made no move to help him shed any of his.

She probably wouldn't. Molly hadn't ever wanted him inside of her like that.

"Cock I get plenty of at home, what I want is that mouth of yours," she told him when he asked what she wanted today.

She had wed for status and bedded her husband to ensure she kept it.

He rolled up his sleeves and unfastened the first few buttons on his shirt for ease of movement. He kissed the swell of her hip. "Maybe you should bring your husband some time, I could teach him what to do."

She laughed, then shushed him. She gave his head a gentle but insistent push, so he swept his tongue along the folds of her quim.

It garnered the moan he had expected. He continued as he always did with her, pressing kisses to her thighs every so often so she wouldn't come too fast. He knew, too, when she would start to get impatient and when that moment started to approach, he started to work in earnest.

She came with a gasping cry and a buck of her hips.

Ira sat back, looking up at her as she lay sprawled out, one leg dangling off the side of the bed, her hand tracing between her chest and her navel. She didn't like it if he tried to kiss her afterward, so he went over to the basin in the corner to wipe his face and rinse out his mouth.

He came back to sit beside her, traced a finger over her warm skin and she gave his leg a pat. He bent his head to kiss her rounded belly, but she pushed him back.

"No, I've got to go, once was all I needed."

He straightened up and ran his fingers along the seam of his trouser leg.

"It was funny, though, about teaching my husband. I might take you up on it."

He gathered up her clothes and handed them over.

She was dressed and out before her hour had even ended so he flopped on the bed to wait out the timer.

He must have fallen asleep because the next thing he knew Selene was shaking him awake.

"Ira, come on, we need the room," she whispered.

He pushed himself up and looked over to see that she had a plainly amorous client with her. He hurried out of the room, muttered an apology, and pocketed the coin Molly had left.

Marius grinned at him when he went to sit at the bar.

"What?"

Marius touched his own cheek to indicate location. "You've got indents on your face."

Ira sighed.

"It'll be the next big thing, better than dimples," the pander teased.

"Pour me a drink, why don't you?"

"Only cause you asked so nice."

What Marius pushed in front of him had bubbles and a pink tinge. Ira didn't know what he'd been given; he usually didn't drink much at work. Maybe a single drink at the end of the night, but never three drinks in one day.

"What is this?"

"Vodka soda with a splash of pomegranate."

He nodded and slurped it down faster than he should have. When that sticky-fingered man from earlier in the week came and proposition him again, Ira went with him, his tongue heavy and his head light.

For a coin he didn't particularly want, Ira let the man take him from behind; Ira's only participation in the event was to make sure the man's cock was properly oiled. As the man walked out as Ira pulled his trousers back on, he regretted doing it and he took off early that night.

When he entered the building, Mrs. Spiros squawked, "Ira, that you?" so he popped his head into her apartment.

"Did you need something?"

She twitched on wing towards a small package on her table.

"Came for you."

He scooped it up and found it heavier than its size indicated. Books, he knew right away. "Thanks."

As he walked up the stairs, he broke the wax seal on the note to find the spidery handwriting he expected.

I'll be busy for a few days, I don't know how much we'll see of each other. Hopefully, you'll like the books as much as you like my cooking.

Thinking of you,

Luci

Seeing the note signed with the Devil's pet name sent a warm thrill through Ira. He had never signed any of the notes he sent with that name before.

Inside his apartment, Ira tore open the package to find a volume of poetry by someone with the ridiculous name of Digby Mackworth Dolben and a novel by E.T.A. Hoffman. Lucifer had a weakness for human writers; he hadn't ever voiced such an opinion but almost all the books he gave to Ira had been written on Earth.

Ira settled onto his sofa with a hunk of bread, some cold meat from the icebox, and the book of poems.

After a few poems, he got up to add a glass of wine to his dinner and nodded off with the volume resting his chest and a slick of drool down his chin.

The next day he arrived at work on time and tried to resume his usual pliant sobriety but found himself in an irritated mood.

When Astrid came in and right over to him, he had to stifle a groan. She slid right up next to him on the sofa, her hand finding its usual perch on his thigh.

He marked his page in his book. "Hello, darling."

With wide, blue eyes that made her look sweet and lovely, she stared at him for long enough that he wished she would blink. "Could we go somewhere quiet?"

She had her sketchbook and charcoals in hand.

"Of course, that's what they pay me for," he said, trying to remind her that their time together was bought.

On the way upstairs, he left his novel with Marius, not wanting anyone to paw at it while he was gone.

She left her coins on the table by the door and had her mouth on his before he could even acclimate to the room. She had her hands in his trousers before he had even gotten hard; she caressed him and slid to her knees.

He wished she wouldn't do it with such servility, like she

worshipped his cock, like it would send floods and rain fire on her village if it were displeased.

Once he'd gotten hard, she pleaded for him to fuck her; he obliged, of course, and when he came, he was even glad to have done it before a weird melancholy settled over him.

He tried to be cordial as she pressed kisses to his shoulders.

"I can go again, if you like, or use my mouth," he offered without any desire to follow through.

She shook her head, her finger tracing a circle on his chest. "Can I draw you?"

He nodded.

"No, don't move, just like you are right now, that's how I want you to look."

He did his best to not to move at all.

She grabbed her sketchbook and pencils and settled in on the bed beside him. He got a pleasant view of her tits while she drew, smearing charcoal on her face and her eyebrows knitted together.

She always wanted to draw him. She must have had dozens of these sketches by now and he didn't know why she wanted so many.

He turned a little on his side. "I don't know what you need me for, you've got to have my face memorized by now."

She looked up, set aside her sketchbook, then arranged him back to how he had been. "Don't move."

He tried not to sigh.

She drew him for the better part of an hour. "The university is having an art show."

"Is it? Are you in it?" he asked.

"Yes."

"Oh, that's good. Are you selling pieces?"

"I don't know. If someone makes me an offer, I'll take it, of course." She put down her pencil and paper, then leaned in and pressed her mouth to his throat. "You are a gorgeous thing."

"I bet you tell that to all the boys."

"There aren't any other boys." She kissed along his shoulder and he wished she wouldn't. "I don't want anyone else. Just you."

He didn't know how to respond and scrambled for words. "If all my customers liked me as much as you do—"

She pulled back. "You're too good for this place."

"No, Marius runs a good house! You should have seen the last place I worked," he told her, an easy grin spreading across his face. He liked Marius, he liked the way he ran his business and, more than anything else, he liked that he could do as he pleased.

She protested, "But letting people use you all the time!"

"Aye, well, they've paid for it," he reminded uneasily.

She shook her head. "I hate to think of what they do to you. Their hands all over you..."

He looked at the hourglass on the table and wished it would chime already. "Astrid, darling, you haven't got to worry about me."

"I do, though. It turns my stomach."

"Aren't you going to show me the drawing?"

Before she could answer, the gentle tinkling of the hourglass's alarm told them their time was up.

He hurried into his trousers then handed her the clothes she'd cast aside.

"I'll be back to see you," she promised.

He wondered if he had seemed too desperate and eager for clients when she'd first started to see him. He gave her a kiss goodbye and went to the bar to retrieve his book.

"Oh, there's our muse," Selene teased. She put an arm around his waist and pulled him in for a hug.

"Bet she hangs all those drawings right above her bed," Marius said.

"Or glues them to a pillow!" Selene laughed.

He shook his head and scoffed. "Lunch?"

"No, I couldn't," Selene said, "Billy was just in, fed me so much cake I'm fit to burst."

He nodded and glanced over at Marius, who had already gone to the other end of the bar to serve a customer.

"Do you ever get bored?" Ira asked Selene.

"I've got a deck of cards."

"No, not...I mean, of this." He gestured vaguely around the room.

"What, making a living? I've got mouths to feed at home."

He nodded. Selene cared for her mother, who had delicate health, as well as two little ones.

"Besides, it's as good as anything else. I can't imagine slaving away all day to whip the skin off some stupid human soul."

With that, he could heartily agree. "I don't know how they do it. The screaming would drive me mad."

His parents' home had been on the last street of the Eighth before it became the Seventh. He had, lying in bed at night with his brother beside him, been able to hear the souls there, shrieking and wailing all the time.

His brother had hated the screams, too. He had clung to Ira with shaky hands, his eyes squeezed shut.

"It drives them all mad!" Selene declared. "Drives *him* mad most of all."

He knew by the emphasis in her voice and her nod towards the door that she meant the Devil. She almost always referred to Satan as just *him*, as though she were afraid to say his name, afraid for anyone to know she'd been gossiping about their Prince.

"He's not..." Ira shook his head. Maybe the Devil struggled sometimes, maybe he could get lost, but he wasn't insensible. "He isn't mad."

She shuddered like she'd walked through a cobweb. "I don't know how much he pays you, but it isn't enough. I see him, and I understand why his wife's been missing."

Ira wanted to say that Lucifer didn't pay him, but that felt like oversharing. To say 'he loves me' felt childish, naïve, and more than that, it felt like bad business to accept affection instead of coin.

He looked at the time. "I do need something to eat, though. I'll be back."

He left his book behind the bar and went for a walk, not just because he was hungry but because he wanted to. He took a long lunch most days, usually going back to his apartment to eat and take a bit of a nap, especially if his night before had run late.

Sometimes the Devil would come by Marius' to take him to lunch. Sometimes they would eat in public together and on the following days, Ira would get a spike in business.

Amazing what people wanted to do just because the Devil had done it too.

On the fourth day that he hadn't seen hide or tail of Satan, Ira stopped by the palace in the morning.

Imogen answered, a foxy smile on her face. Her smile worried him; he didn't think she had any bad intentions, but she had a reputation for liking the blood of pretty boys.

And, as everyone always reminded him, he was pretty and didn't look particularly mature.

"Is he in?"

The butler answered, "No, sorry, Ira, he's been busy in the First. Home late and leaving early."

"Did that many get out?" he asked.

"They've got them all wrangled now. The souls in the First are soft sentences anyway, but he's got this idea that they were let out on purpose."

Ira raised his eyebrows. "Oh, that's...Who would be that stupid?"

She nodded. "Once he ferrets out the idiot who's done it, he'll be back in your bed, don't you worry."

He smiled.

"I'll tell him you stopped by."

"Thanks." He took a step back. "And, uh, tell him I like the books."

"I will."

Disappointed, he headed to work and arrived early enough to find Marius at work with the ledgers again.

"You should get an accountant," Ira suggested.

Marius wheeled around. "Shit, you scared me."

"Sorry."

"What about you?" he asked as Ira approached the bar to fish out the book he'd stashed there.

"What about me what?"

"I'll set you up at my desk in the back," Marius proposed.

Ira tilted his head, not sure if he wanted to take Marius up on the offer or not.

"You can be my bottom bitch," the Fallen offered, half-joking.

The words fell on Ira's ears like magic, though; it sounded like an excellent idea phrased like that. Managing finances for the pander would lend Ira a bit of prestige, give him a reason not to see as many clients. He nodded. "Sure."

A grin lit up Marius' face. "You aren't joking, are you?"

"No, course not."

The Fallen wrapped an arm around Ira in an unexpected embrace. "Oh, what a relief to hear you say that. I thought my eyes would go on strike if I kept it up."

"Maybe you need spectacles."

Marius shook his head. "No, I can see them but the numbers, uh...well. They move."

"They move?"

"Mmm." Marius scooped up the ledger and gestured for Ira to follow him into the back room.

Marius cleared piles of papers off his desk and piled them on another table in the corner next to the bookshelf. Once he had cleaned off the desk, he plopped down the ledger, and gestured grandly to the chair. "All for you."

Ira grinned and laughed when Marius pressed a kiss to his cheek and gave his shoulder a squeeze.

The numbers fell into place easily; every so often, someone would come back to tell him that a certain client was looking for him.

Selene came back at one point, to bring him lunch and to tease him about thinking he was too good to suck cock now.

At the end of the night, he let Reggie play with his feet and walked home trying to think of what he wanted for dinner. He felt confident and bold until he burned the living shit out of a panful of potatoes.

He settled for his usual bread and cheese and enough wine to soothe his ego.

He spent another day balancing the books and considered taking a client, just out of habit.

"His taxes are *always* incredibly poorly done. I hope you can do better," came a soft, slippery voice from the doorway.

An unexpected surge of joy bubbled up into Ira's chest. He had stood up and come around the desk before he'd even taken in how haggard the Devil looked. Even noticing that didn't give him a moment's pause. He threw his arms around Lucifer and squeezed him tight, letting out a pleased hum.

He thought the Devil would tease him, but instead, he wound his arms around Ira and returned the embrace. "Oh, love," Lucifer sighed, kissing Ira's curls. "Would you believe that I haven't slept at all this week?"

"Imogen mentioned you'd been busy."

"Not a wink."

"You do look like shit."

He had circles under his eyes and the hollows of his cheeks had grown hollower, bordering on gaunt. His hair had only been messily woven into a single braid. He had stains of some sort crusted onto his clothes.

Ira noted, "And you sort of...well, you're a little ripe."

"I came right to see you."

"What if I took you home and gave you a bath and tucked you into bed," Ira proposed, brushing his fingertips over Satan's cheek. "And we could get crumbs all over your sheets and Marlow could try to eat off my plate."

"I might not let you leave," Lucifer warned.

"You will."

"Someday I won't."

"Dramatic." Ira wove his fingers through the Devil's and led him out of the brothel.

He brought the Devil to the bathroom in the palace, lighting candles and dribbling scented oil over the water. Lucifer leaned against the wall until Ira started to undo the buttons on his shirt and trousers, slipping him out of his clothes.

"I should be more excited," Lucifer apologized.

"No, love, you're beat. A bath and a meal and a good night's sleep and then you can be very excited in the morning." He shed his own clothes and stepped into the bath, bringing the Devil along with him. "You can be so excited that we'll take turns and have each other both ways."

"Both? Are there only two?"

"Three seemed excessive for first thing in the morning."

Lucifer cracked a grin at that. He all but melted in Ira's hands during the bath, with long, slow sighs passing his lips. He had knots in his back, in his shoulders, even in his thighs. Ira wondered what he'd gotten up to in the First Precinct.

When they'd retired to bed, Imogen sent up the cook with bread and stew.

Marlow, a black cat with a white splotch on one side, did try to steal out of their bowls. Once she'd stolen the piece of meat she wanted, she spent the rest of dinner nestled between the Devil's arm and his side.

After the cook had come back up for their plates, Ira curled himself around Lucifer and nudged his arm with his nose.

"What?" Satan asked.

"Nothing, I missed you is all."

Lucifer worked his fingers through Ira's curls, kneading his scalp. "In the morning, you'll have to tell me how Marius talked you into doing his books for him."

"Before or after we've had each other?"

"Well, I imagine after. I imagine that gone so many days from your side I won't be able to contain myself any longer."

Ira scowled and pulled back. "Why do you always make fun like that?"

"Why do you always think I'm teasing? I missed you, Ira, love. I missed you like...uh. Bugger, I don't know, I missed you a lot." He wrapped his arms around Ira and pulled him close to his side, burrowing them beneath the covers.

The Devil dropped off to sleep in an instant, leaving Ira and Marlow to stare at each other. The cat did not like Ira. Even after a year she would still hiss and swat at him sometimes.

By the time the morning came, Lucifer had pressed himself against Ira's back and Ira woke when he kissed the base of his neck.

Ira stretched and made sure that he pushed his ass up against Lucifer's cock. If every client could send this content and lazy roll of heat through him, he would never give up whoring. He turned so they were facing each other.

"Oh, I was having fun the other way."

Ira instantly went to turn back but the Devil caught him around the waist and kissed him.

"*That* was teasing," Lucifer said.

"Sorry."

"Tell me what you did while I was working."

Ira told him everything, down to the burnt potatoes, and Lucifer listened like it was an epic tale, not a rundown of a few days in a whorehouse.

"What about you?" Ira prompted.

"Just crawling through the First looking for souls—"

"How many got out?"

"Um, I want to say…three hundred or so."

Ira's eyes widened. "That's a lot."

"Biggest breach we've had in a while," Lucifer agreed.

"It sounds like more than just someone forgetting to lock the door on their way out."

The Devil nodded. "It was. But the First, well, it's soft sentences and everyone starts there, which means a high staff turnover and sometimes you get, hmm…these groups of neophytes who all come in together and think they know what they're doing better than we do. They put their heads together and start with this talk of *if I was the captain* and all that."

Ira nodded and knew he was getting more information than anyone other than Imogen and the Precinct captains. "So…?"

"So." Here Lucifer sighed, rubbed his eyes, and rolled on to his back. "So then Ulster, captain of the First, right? He gets wind of these malcontents and decides *not* to tell me about it."

"Why not!"

The Devil heaved an even larger sigh. "Because of the fainting spells."

"Oh, but, love…" Ira wanted exactly the right words but couldn't quite grasp them. "You haven't had one in months."

Without looking at Ira, he admitted, "I had one a few weeks ago."

Ira hadn't known that. Immediately after he'd been poisoned last year, Satan fainted a lot, at first several times a day, then at least once a week, but now it only happened every few months. Ira had thought he'd had a nice long stretch without one, but apparently, he'd been wrong.

"Don't look at me like that," Lucifer admonished.

"You didn't tell me."

"Because it upsets you."

"Yes, well, wouldn't you be upset if your...!" Ira had started the sentence with intensity, but he lacked a word for what Lucifer was to him. More than a client, certainly, and even more than a lover. "And besides, it doesn't *upset me*, I just want to know you're well."

Marlow walked across Ira to settle on to the Devil's chest.

"So Ulster didn't tell you," Ira prompted.

"He tried to deal with them himself. He cracked down hard but...not hard enough and not the way I would have done it. They let the souls out in retaliation."

"Oh. Did you...?"

"Exiled," Lucifer said with a casual wave of his hand. "Out beyond the walls, never to return under pain of consumption."

Ira nodded. He dared to reach out and stroke Marlow, but she glowered at him and let out a low, dangerous growl.

Lucifer scooped her up, rolled so he was sitting on the edge of the bed, and deposited her on the floor. "None of that, he's my friend, you'll have to get used to him."

Scooting closer, Ira came up behind him, letting his legs settle on either side of Lucifer's hips. He put his arms around the other man's shoulders and asked, "When did you faint?"

He shook his head and kissed Ira's arm. "I think last night you said we could have each other both ways. I wasn't clear on what that meant, would you like to elaborate?"

Ira sighed. He rested his forehead against the Devil's back. "If that's what you want, I'll lay on my belly right now and you can have me like that. I won't ask for a bit or even a penny, either—"

"Don't."

Ira pulled away and Lucifer turned to look at him. "Well, do you want me to be your whore or do you want me to love you?"

Lucifer stared.

Ira's throat tightened up. He hated this part of their relationship. He didn't know where he stood, not at all; he didn't know what he was supposed to do. He had never been in love, no one had ever been in love with him. "Tell me what to do."

"You hate when I do that," Lucifer reminded.

"But I don't know how to do this." Ira rubbed his hands over his face. "Whatever it is that we're doing."

The Devil knotted his fingers in his hair, starting to braid it, as he always did when he was anxious or thinking hard. "What you've been doing has been exactly right."

Ira shook his head. He didn't know what response he had wanted. "I'm sorry."

Lucifer gathered him into an embrace. "No need. I'm pleased as punch with what we have. I will take whatever you're willing to give me."

Nestled against him, feeling safe folded up in his arms, Ira's worries from before felt silly. "I...I don't know, Lu. It's so different."

"Oh, are you calling me Lu now? That is different, no one's ever done that."

"No one ever?" Ira asked.

Lucifer elaborated, "Well, maybe someone has but not like this. Not so with so much skin against mine, not with such fetching curls and such a pretty mouth."

Ira snorted.

"I wasn't *just* trying to distract you before, I did wake up feeling sort of...affectionate."

"Where did you faint?" Ira asked.

"In front of all of them. One of the captains' meetings. It's...you know, only happens twice a year and I've got them *all* gathered at the round table. I stand up to get a drink and halfway there, I just...crumple. Imogen says I looked like someone had dropped a lot of wet rags. So now they're all in a titter."

Ira kissed him. "See, that wasn't so bad. Now, here's my plan, tell me if you don't like it. I think what I'd like to do would be first with our mouths—"

"Our?"

"Yes, I'll spill in yours, you'll spill in mine. Our."

"And that's first," Lucifer said.

"Yes, that, then a bath and *then*, this is all assuming you don't have anywhere to be..."

The Devil confirmed, "I don't."

"I'd like you to fuck me. For a long time."

"Ah." Lucifer nodded wisely. "That's why we'd start with our mouths. Good thing one of us does this for a living, I'd be lost without you."

"Better than spiking your tea with chasteberries."

Lucifer let out a surprised laugh. "Did Imogen tell you that! God, she can be a *beast*." He put his mouth to Ira's throat and nipped gently.

It didn't take much for either them to spill the first time and didn't take long in the bath before they started to get frisky again. It was a fun, if not particularly cleansing bath, that ended with Ira half-toweled-off and on all fours, waiting, his stomach fluttering, for the Devil to enter him.

Lucifer slid in slowly and only halfway, his hands holding Ira's hips firmly, not letting him push back to take the other man's cock in deeper.

"Tease," Ira panted.

With his fingers lightly moving over Ira's shaft, the Devil asked, "Did you want something more?"

"I want you to really fuck me."

He moved in a little deeper, his hands loosening on Ira's hips so that Ira could thrust back, taking him all the way in.

The Devil had him gasping and moaning in no time. More than that, he had Ira feeling certain that this was what he wanted, without a single doubt.

When Lucifer came, he did so with a breathy series of swears that sounded so reverent and ecstatic that it brought Ira to the edge, enough that he spilled not long after.

"Oh," the Devil murmured.

"Oh what?" Ira hadn't quite come back to himself yet, his skin flush and his cock still twitching.

"Oh, I've got a nosebleed." Lucifer stood with a hand cupped against his face. Blood had spattered down his chin and throat, disturbingly bright against his white skin.

"Are you alright!" Ira scrambled to find him a towel.

Lucifer nodded and took the washcloth Ira had handed him, pressing it to his nose. His voice slightly muffled, he explained, "It happens sometimes after I've...uh, after I've changed shape a lot."

"Oh. Were you doing a lot of changing in the First, then?" Ira asked, then realized it was a stupid question.

"Mmm." The Devil perched on the edge of the bathtub, pulled the washcloth away, and touched his nose. He returned the cloth when his fingers came away bloody. "The university is having a student gallery in a few weeks."

"So?"

"So as a patron, my attendance is...expected, if not required."

Ira waited.

"I had sort of wanted to ask you to go with me. I didn't know if you'd be interested."

"Of course, sure, that...it could be fun."

Ira had never been to anything like that before, but he'd

looked at lots of reproductions of well-known works in large, glossy library books. He didn't know why Lucifer had picked now, of all times, to invite him, but Ira had come to understand that the Devil's thoughts came and went, slipping over each other and often not quite concrete.

"YOU'VE GOT blood on your shirt," Selene told him.

Ira looked up from the ledgers to find her leaning against the doorframe.

She gestured to the cuff of his shirt. "Right there."

He glanced down. "Oh, no, that's jam. Uh, I think it was strawberry."

She made a face. "Isn't that *fancy*? Strawberries. They don't even grow down here, you know."

He shrugged.

"I guess it does have its perks, being our Prince's kept man."

"Don't start with that," he warned. He didn't want to hear how unsettling she found the Devil.

"I came back to tell you Tycho's looking for you."

"Thanks."

"Should I tell him you'll see him?"

Ira weighed his options, then nodded. He might as well go and see what he wanted. When he walked out, Tycho beckoned him over.

"Never thought I'd have to ask to see you," the man told him.

It took a lot of effort not to frown. Tycho always said things like that, little ribs that built up over time. "Sorry, I've been—"

"Doing the books for your pander. I heard. I didn't figure *you* for that," the other man sneered.

"I've always been good with arithmetic."

"And always reading, too. What a little scholar." Tycho brushed his hand over Ira's cheek then pinched it hard.

Ira jerked back. "What did you want, anyway? Just to chat?"

Tycho's brow knitted. "Considering that you're a whore, I'd imagined I was going to fuck you, ludicrous as that might sound."

Ira shifted. He'd snapped at Tycho, but he hadn't meant to.

"You are still a whore, aren't you?"

"Yes."

Tycho gave him a push towards the stairs. "Then let's go."

Ira went. He stumbled when Tycho shoved him into a room and started to feel unsure when the other man closed the door.

Without a single word, Tycho moved Ira over to the bed, giving him a hard push so he fell onto his belly.

"Hey," Ira protested.

Tycho kept a hand pressed to Ira's back. "I'm going to teach you not to talk back." His fingers raked down Ira's suspenders and he jerked down Ira's trousers. "Because I don't come here to have whores talk back to me, especially not little trashy ones who ride the Devil's coattails."

Ira tried to sit up but Tycho didn't move back.

Instead, he hissed, "Someone should have taught you better manners."

Ira did have better manners. He knew not to snap at the customers or to keep them waiting. He knew how to flirt and make them feel wanted; he knew how to do what he was told. He knew how to relax so it wouldn't hurt as much when someone wanted things rough.

He felt himself slipping into that faraway place, a quiet spot in his mind where he could take refuge unless things went badly awry. He closed his eyes, took slow breaths, and gripped the sheets.

But still, a whimpering sort of grunt escaped him when Tycho tried to plunge inside of him and missed, his cock jabbing just below where he'd aimed.

The jolt of pain made Ira realize he couldn't settle into that quiet spot anymore. This would be as bad as it had ever been.

"Stop."

Tycho didn't stop. He grabbed Ira by the back of the neck and pressed his face into the mattress. "You'll thank me after—"

"Stop it!" Ira's mind scrambled. "You didn't pay, you can't if you haven't paid."

Tycho gave Ira's neck a final shove. "Ah, there's the money-grubbing tramp showing his face."

Tycho pulled back a little to rummage through his pockets.

"On the table, put it on the table..."

When the other man moved away and had his back turned, Ira slid his fingers along the edge of the headboard, searching for the rune there. He'd never needed to use it before, but Selene had shown it to him on his first day.

His voice cracked when he whispered the spell to activate the alarm.

After that, he yanked his trousers back up and realized that Tycho, when he'd jerked them down, had caused some of the buttons on the fly to pop off.

"You'd better—" the other man began.

Ira shook his head. "No, I won't do it, I won't let you."

Tycho grinned a horrible, toothy smile like he'd been waiting for Ira to say that exact thing. He grabbed Ira by the hair and dragged him close. Ira could feel his breath, hot and moist, on his neck when he crooned, "I thought you were such a good boy, Ira, I thought you knew how to do your job."

"If you hurt me—"

He barked a laugh. "You think I'm afraid of that milksop who sits the throne?"

The door opened and Marius, along with the three broad and burly demons employed for this exact purpose, entered. "Let the lad go," the pander advised.

Tycho looked at the four of them and must have decided that teaching Ira how to be good wasn't worth the trouble. He didn't let Ira go so much as he tossed him. He did it hard enough so that Ira cracked his temple on the corner of the bed.

After that Elle, the fiercest of the guards, grabbed Tycho and marched him out. He went without fighting but the other two guards trailed behind him just in case.

Ira had seen that procession before but had never been the cause of it.

Marius came over and knelt beside him, his fingers brushing aside a few curls. "Oh, you'll have a bruise there for sure, lovey."

Ira lurched to his knees, trying to stand, but fell back, trembling all over.

"Shh, hey, take it easy." The pander put his hands on Ira's shoulders. "You're alright."

"I'm sorry. I am, I should...I know better than to make customers angry, I should have let." His voice hitched. "I'm sorry, I am, I can do better." He pressed his hands against his face, unable to stop the tears. "I'm so sorry."

"You did the right thing."

Ira shook his head. He couldn't stop thinking about how wrong things had gone, what he should have done instead, how he shouldn't have made him mad, how he should have let him do what he wanted.

Marius looped an arm around his shoulder and helped him stand. Once he'd gotten to his feet, Ira pulled away and dashed for the washbowl on the side table. He threw up what little bit was left of the toast and jam he'd had for breakfast.

When his stomach settled, he rinsed his mouth with water from the pitcher. Still weak and shaky, he let Marius lead him downstairs. A few people stared, but most of them turned their eyes away, embarrassed for him.

Marius brought him back to the backroom and settled him into the fat, cozy armchair by the bookshelf. He left and returned a few minutes later with a towel full of ice. He placed it in Ira's hand and then, when Ira didn't move, took his hand and pressed it to his temple.

"It's gonna swell up." Marius took the chair from behind the desk and brought it over so he could sit next to Ira. "Our Prince will be mighty displeased."

Ira pulled the towel away from his head. "Don't tell him."

"Well, someone's going to tell him." Marius gently returned Ira's hand to where it had been. "Hold that there. He's going to find out. Better he hears it from someone he likes."

Ira sighed. "He'll be angry."

"Of course, he will. *I'm* angry."

"I didn't mean to make a fuss."

"Shit, Ira, you're not stupid," Marius declared. "No one's mad at you, you've got to know that."

Ira shrugged.

More gently, Marius assured, "No one is mad at you. You did the right thing. I promise."

"Mmm."

"So, listen, I can you walk you home—"

"No, I'm fine. I can work."

Instead of arguing, Marius said, "If you're going to stay, then I don't want you taking customers."

Ira shook his head.

"No, none of that. I don't even know if I should let you do the books with that bump on your head. I'd like to take you home, really."

Ira adjusted the towel a little.

Marius sat back, his hands resting on his thighs. "About the books—"

"I think they're all right, I don't think I missed anything," Ira rushed to say.

"No, not that. I think, well, you've been missing out on taking clients cause you've been doing that for me. Eight a week, I think that's a fair rate for bookkeeping. And I'll waive your fee for taking clients."

Ira thought of the useless bag of coins he had shoved into one of his cabinets. He recalled how he'd earned eight serpents in a single day once when he'd first started and he'd run himself ragged trying to please his new pander. Eight fat, stupid coins that he didn't know what to do with.

He nodded.

Marius grinned. "Wonderful." He glanced over at the stack of ledgers.

"It'll be nice, I guess, for a little while, to do something else," Ira ventured.

"Only a little while?"

"Well, it won't take me more than a few months to get through them and then, you know, I'll keep doing the weekly numbers for you if you want..."

"Oh, Ira, lovey, I've got lots of things that I need you for. I've got all sorts of horrible invoices with their wiggly little letters," Marius shared. "No. As long as you want it, I've got paperwork for you."

"I..." Ira adjusted the towel full of ice. "Maybe it's what I need."

Marius nodded, his eyes solemnly fixed on Ira's. "I think so."

"It's...it's not a bad line of work. I do like it," Ira insisted.

"But you don't have to do it if you don't want to."

"I don't know, I won't give it up altogether I don't think," Ira said.

"I'm not telling you what to do, but can I give you some advice?"

Ira nodded.

"You've been hurt, lad, and a lot. And you've got no reason to keep doing this; you don't need the money. If you don't need to do it and you don't *want* to do it...why keep it up?"

Ira couldn't stop his fingers from running over the leather fastener of his suspenders. "It's...it's."

"It's what you've always done, I know. It was what I did for a long time, too. And then it wasn't fun anymore. I didn't like it. So I quit before things got bad for me."

He opened his mouth but had no words.

"You don't have to tell me anything. I just...I feel better for saying it, knowing that you've heard it." Marius reached over and gave his shoulder an affectionate punch. "I'll be at the bar if you need me."

"Thanks."

The Fallen stood, stretched, and left.

Ira didn't know what to do after he had gone.

Selene came back with a book for him and dropped it on his lap. "Not as good as the ones your friend in the palace sends."

"You're wonderful."

She wrapped up him in a hug, pillowy-soft and safe. She kissed his cheek, then left him alone to curl up with the book.

He stayed there until lunch time came and Lucifer stopped by. He entered the back room and paused in the doorway. "Marius says you've got something to tell me."

Ira marked the page in his book and set it on the desk. "Just a kerfuffle with one of the clients."

"Would you like me to—"

"No," Ira answered immediately.

"Then what about lunch?"

"Yes."

He offered Ira his hand and helped him to stand when he took it. "You've got blood on your sleeve."

"No, it's jam. Remember?"

Lucifer frowned for half a second, then clarity came across his face. "Oh, you're right, you're right."

With their hands linked, they walked back to Ira's apartment for lunch, which turned into lunch and a nap.

Ira woke with a start and saw that it had already gotten dark outside. He gave Satan a push. "Hey."

"Mmm?"

"It's night time."

"Oh." Lucifer peered out the window. "I suppose it is."

"Shit."

A small bit of light appeared in the Devil's hand and he left it to sit in the air as he pushed back the hair from Ira's face. "Who did you kerfuffle with?"

Ira pulled back.

"You're right, sorry, with whom did you kerfuffle?" Lucifer amended.

"It doesn't matter."

"It does."

"I don't want you to do anything."

Lucifer waved a hand and the light disappeared. "What if I promised not to kill him?"

"Or anything else," Ira insisted.

"Or anything else," Satan vowed. "Except maybe ruin his life. Just a little bit. But only a little, I promise."

Ira could accept that compromise and Lucifer could have found out who it was anyway, so he said, "Tycho."

"Brahe? The astronomer?"

Ira frowned. "No, I don't think so. What's an astronomer?"

"Sorry, Earth joke."

"Promise you won't do anything really bad to him."

"He's going to be demoted, that's for sure." Lucifer leaned in for a kiss.

Ira said, "He called you a milksop."

Undeterred, Lucifer pressed his lips to his mouth and told him, "That is a popular opinion these days, I'm afraid. Imogen is concerned."

Ira nestled into his arms. "Do you think they're…I mean, it's happened before, do you think they'll revolt?"

"They might try."

Ira tightened his arms around him. "And you, Lu, they won't be able to *do* anything, will they?"

"I always claw my way back out of the ground eventually."

A shiver crawled up Ira's spine. "Don't say things like that."

Neither of them spoke for a while.

"I was supposed to go back to work."

"No, you weren't," Lucifer told him.

"What do you mean I wasn't?"

"Well, I don't think Marius had a runner come to fetch me all the way from the Third because he wanted me to bring you back to work," Lucifer said.

Ira put his hands on the Devil's chest and pushed away from him. "He sent someone to get you!"

"Should I not have come? I was worried."

Ira pulled farther back. "I'm fine. He shouldn't have bothered you."

Lucifer straightened up. "I'd like to clarify something between us."

Ira nodded, trying to ignore the discomfort in his belly.

"When something is amiss with my health or my mood, you express concern and I appreciate it. It means a lot to me to know that you care whether I am well or not. Do you feel differently?"

"No, that's...that's not what I meant."

"Because your well-being is...I don't know how to say this without being a little overbearing, it is incredibly and deeply important to me that you are safe and well. If something happens, I want to know and I want to be there for you," Lucifer explained.

"It's just a bump."

"That is not what I'm talking about, darling, and you know it."

Ira sulked, "He didn't even get it in."

"Ira, I have found you *bleeding*, with your insides—"

"I know!" Ira hated to hear his past injuries recounted. He hated to think about them, let alone talk about them.

"And you told me you were fine then, too," Lucifer finished. "So I don't believe you when you tell me you're alright."

"It doesn't matter."

With his terrible eyes fixed on Ira's face, the Devil warned, "This is going to catch up with you someday and the harder you try to stave it off, the harder it's going to hit you."

Unable to abide that thought, Ira got to his feet and moved away from the sofa. "Maybe you should go."

Lucifer stood, his long body unfolding. He did it so smoothly and coldly that Ira thought he would keep going up, that he would double in size and stretch out until his mouth gaped and his fingers were talons, until Ira would be able to see the jut of bones all over his body.

"If that's what you want, then I'll go."

Ira dug his teeth into his tongue.

"I would like to say one more thing, though, if you don't mind."

He couldn't form any words, so he shrugged and didn't make eye contact.

"I don't know what's been done to you, not the whole extent of it, and I don't know what that woman who ran the other house told you, but...Ira, dear, can you look at me?" Lucifer asked gently.

He shook his head. If he looked up, he would cry. He shouldn't have cried about something as stupid as this and definitely not twice in one day. Others had experienced things twice as bad and never shed a tear.

"No? Well...I'd like you to understand that none of the things that happened to you were ever your fault."

But they had been, that much had always been clear.

"Did you really want me to go? I'd feel terrible leaving you like this."

Ira took half a step forward, knowing what he wanted, where he wanted to be, but feeling that he shouldn't have dared. He tried to say something, but the word came out as no more than a throaty rasp.

"Did you...love, did you say 'don't' or did you call me a cunt?"

A laugh jumped out of Ira's mouth, ragged and ugly. He looked up to see an astounded sort of smile on the Devil's face. "I said *don't*."

"Ah."

"Don't go, I...." Ira let out a breath and ran a hand through his curls, ruffling his hair. He went to the kitchen and put the kettle on.

Lucifer joined him, lingering a short distance away until Ira gestured for him to come over. When he approached, Ira put an arm around his waist and rested his head against his chest. "Thank you."

"Hmm?"

"I know I'm dense sometimes," Ira said.

"Are you? I thought I was the dense one."

He shook his head.

"Yes, and you're the one who loves to read and is apparently good with numbers as well. Balance."

"You like to read, too," Ira pointed out.

"Shit."

"Maybe that's why we're good together."

Lucifer pressed a feather-light kiss to Ira's temple. "It's probably one reason but I can think of a thousand reasons to love you."

Ira could only name one reason anyone had ever expressed any affection for him. "Start with one."

"That you knew I fancied you before I did."

The statement sent a small flutter though Ira's chest and he felt bold enough to ask, "What else?"

"That you always want to share with everyone."

"And?"

Lucifer grinned. "That you didn't know what an astronomer was."

"And you still haven't told me."

"Someone who studies the stars."

"Why would we have astronomers, we haven't got any stars! You had me feeling all kinds of stupid," Ira scolded.

The kettle whistled and before Ira could do it, Lucifer took it off the heat, whispering that he hated that sound.

Ira took down mugs and tea leaves. "That's only three reasons."

"That you've kept all the notes I've written you and that you bought a box just to keep them in. That's five."

Ira poured water into both mugs, then took his over to the kitchen table. Lucifer followed; he didn't keep listing reasons why he loved Ira, but he did let his legs sprawl under the table and settle his feet against Ira's.

Ira still couldn't fathom that their Prince did these kinds of things and that he did them with a nobody like Ira.

"I think it's started to rain, do you hear that?" the Devil murmured.

Ira cocked an ear towards the ceiling and thought he could hear the patter of raindrops against the building.

"I hope the Second doesn't flood again..." Lucifer sighed.

"I don't think it will, it only does that when it's been really raining for a while. What was it, three years ago? Four? When we had storms for a week straight?"

"I've got to do something about it one of these days. Put in some more drains. Should have left that part undeveloped, really..." Lucifer sipped his tea. "Maybe..."

"Hmm?" Ira prompted when he'd gone quiet for too long.

"No, I was thinking about the other city."

"What other city?"

"Promise not to tell?"

Ira nodded. "Promise."

"On the other side of the Empty Plains, there's a mountain range. If you're cross that range, you'll find a city nestled in a valley."

"Bullshit," Ira blurted.

"I was shocked, too. About four centuries ago, I exiled hmm, maybe, two hundred or so malcontents. They weren't, you know, extremists but they were irritating. Turns out about half of them survived and they made their own little settlement."

Ira shook his head.

"I know, I couldn't believe it either! I have to say I was impressed. I'm excited to see how that's going to all play out. They've got this *adorable* attempt at an oligarchy going. Very ancient Rome, I just love it."

"You are mad, aren't you?" Ira asked.

"Probably."

"It's founded by exiles, what if they hate you!"

"No, no, dear, don't worry, I've got my puppets in their government," the Devil assured.

Ira shook his head again, letting out a sigh.

Lucifer reached across the table and rested his hand on Ira's wrist. "And I've got tunnels full of explosives beneath them should the situation ever become dire. Gave me nose bleeds for days, that did."

"I wish He'd made you a little sturdier..." Ira said then immediately wished he hadn't, hoping Lucifer wasn't offended by the idea.

"Oh, I wasn't made for half the things I end up doing." Lucifer shrugged, then boasted, "The fact that I do them anyway should be a testament to my will and fortitude."

"I'd hate for anything to happen to you."

The Devil gave no answer and Ira wished he would.

In the middle of the night, after they'd settled into bed and Ira had curled himself up in the sheets, content and hazy and close to sleep, Lucifer gave him a nudge.

"Hm?"

"I shouldn't have said what I did before," Lucifer said, then clarified, "About things catching up with you. I should have found a nicer way to say it."

A little more awake, Ira opened his eyes to find that Lucifer was propped up against the headboard staring at the wall.

"No, you said it fine. I hate hearing things like that is all."

"I know."

Ira rolled so he could nestle up to Satan. "Luci?"

"What, dear?"

It wasn't any of his business, but he wanted to know, and he thought that Lucifer would share with him. "You say things like that and it sounds like you know…like you know because you've been there."

The room filled up with quiet and Ira could hear the patter of rain against the building. He feared he'd made the Devil angry.

Then, after a long stretch came Lucifer's voice, low and hesitant, "Sometimes you let a person do things to you because it's what they want, you let them do it because they like it so much and all you want is for them to be happy."

Ira sat up, losing that cozy feeling he'd had before.

Lucifer continued, "But it's not even that. They'd be happy without doing those things, but you wouldn't be with them if you said no. You let them do whatever they want to you because you're afraid that if you don't, they'll be gone. And you'll be alone again."

It didn't feel like the Devil had shared a story, it felt like he had sliced himself open because Ira had requested it. He shouldn't have gone poking at things.

"But then she leaves you anyway."

"Lu, I…I didn't…" Ira didn't know what to say. There were things words couldn't soothe. "I didn't mean to pry."

"No, you weren't prying. And it's…you should know. You should know because if she came back, I don't know what I would do. I don't know if I would go crawling back to her as soon as she glanced at me."

Hearing Satan's voice quiver sent a lance of fear through Ira.

"Because I think I would. I think I'd let her do all those things to me again. I think would want her to stay and I think I would…I would ask her what I did to make her leave, what I had to do to make it so she never left again."

"You wouldn't," Ira told him. He reached for Lucifer's hand. "You wouldn't because she doesn't deserve you."

He heard the rustle of sheets and a bit of movement in the darkness of the room. Lucifer had shaken his head or nodded, Ira guessed; his grip on Ira's hand had tightened and his breathing came in wet little snuffles.

"And you won't because I love you and I won't ever tell you that you need to be more to deserve me." Ira wanted to continue, "You won't do it because I want you to be mine and not anyone else's. Especially not hers," but he didn't.

He didn't know he felt about the idea and he certainly didn't think that bringing up this new surge of possessiveness while the other man was crying about his wife would be appropriate or helpful.

"Fuck," Lucifer whispered.

Ira wrapped his arms around him. He buried his face in Ira's shoulder, his face slick with tears. Ira thought he heard him mutter, "Fucking Christ," but couldn't be sure.

In the darkness, it all felt surreal. In the morning, he was almost sure it had been a dream, especially because he had woken up alone. The flakey crust of salt the Devil's tears had left on his skin told him it hadn't been.

He got out of bed, decided it was too cold and wrapped his covers around his shoulders before he headed out into the parlor. At first glance, things seemed normal, then he noticed that all the books that had been left in various places around the room had been moved to the bookshelf.

He peered at the bookshelf and saw that they'd all been alphabetized. He found Lucifer standing in his newly immaculate kitchen cooking eggs and bacon.

"Did you..."

Lucifer looked over.

"Thanks for making breakfast."

"I tidied up a little," Lucifer admitted, somewhere between sheepish and casual.

"Thanks for that, too."

"Come sit."

Ira sat and the Devil put a mug of tea in front of him, followed by a heaping plate of food, which included more mushrooms that Ira would have taken for himself.

Lucifer settled on the other side of the table and took up his fork.

They ate for a few quiet minutes until Ira cleared his throat, took a sip of his tea, and asked, "Are you...darling, are you feeling better?"

"I didn't, ah, I didn't mean to get so maudlin. I hope you can forgive me."

"I'm glad you told me."

"I know I get dramatic sometimes, I don't want you to think that she was awful to me. Things weren't that bad."

Ira pursed his lips but didn't point out that relationships that 'weren't that bad' didn't make a person weep in the middle of the night years after they'd ended. Instead, he scooped up a forkful of mushrooms and shoveled them into his mouth, then pointed with his fork to Lucifer's plate. "It's really good."

The Devil nodded and pushed his food around his plate.

"What?"

"I...well, I don't want to upset you."

"What?" Ira repeated.

"I was in the Third yesterday, I ran into your brother. He asked how you were."

"You know I don't care, why do you keep bringing him up?"

"Because I told him I'd let you know he was asking about you," Lucifer answered.

"What's it matter to you, anyway, what you told some bastard in the Third you'd do?" Ira grumbled.

"I do like Eodus, you know, and anyway, I told him I would, and I have."

Ira stopped to consider what he'd said. He hadn't ever fathomed that Lucifer knew his brother as anything more than a subordinate, some mewling worker he ran into occasionally. He took another bite of food, glad for the salt of the bacon and the pleasant chew of the mushrooms.

He was not who he had been a year ago. Things had gotten better. Maybe it was time to let his life expand a little further outside his carefully guarded realm of books and pleasure work.

Hesitantly, Ira asked, "Do you think I should meet him?"

Choosing his words carefully, Lucifer replied, "I think that if I were you, I would have missed him, even if I was angry."

Ira shook his head and tried to swallow a bite of food past the lump in his throat.

He didn't remember much more than snippets and bits of feelings. He remembered that having a brother had been having a constant companion, down to the bed they'd shared. He remembered what it had been like to sleep alone for the first time, to have no one to play with anymore. He remembered how much he had wanted to go home.

"Fine," Ira huffed.

Lucifer looked up from his plate. "Hm?"

"Fine, tell him I'll meet him."
"I will."
"But you've got to promise to come with me."
"I promise," the Devil assured.

"SOMEONE'S HERE to see you," Selene announced from the doorway.

Ira looked up from the ledgers, then shook his head. "I don't want to take any clients."

The only clients he'd seen in the past few days had been Reggie because the poor thing was harmless, and Astrid because she had caught him on his way back from lunch and he hadn't wanted to upset her.

"I don't think she's here to fuck you," Selene told him and stepped aside to let Imogen past.

"Decidedly not," the vampire assured him. "I'm here to bring you over to the tailor."

"Why?"

"Because the art gallery is a formal event."

"I've got plenty of suits."

"And they've got a bit of wear and tear," Imogen reminded him. "And some stains."

He considered that he'd just had to resew the buttons back onto the fly of his favorite pair of trousers. He wondered if the Devil considered him shabby. "Did he send you?"

"No, he's gone above to deal with some contracts and visit a few people."

Ira sighed. "I don't..."

"Yes, you do, come along. You agreed to go with him, you must have known you'd have to dress up," Imogen told him. She came over to the desk and lifted Ira up from his seat, her hand firmly grasping him by the elbow.

She led him out of the brothel to a street he'd never visited before. He glanced up at the sign and recognized the name as one of the finer places Hell had to offer, where the highest-ranking demons bought their jewels and silks.

The vampire must have sensed his hesitation because she put an arm around his shoulders and pulled him close. "Don't you think he'll be thrilled to see you dressed up? I think he'll like it so much your clothes might not survive the night in one piece."

Ira felt himself blush at that. It gave Imogen the chance to pull him down the street and into a tailor. Here people hustled him into and out of a lot of different clothing and marked them up with chalk and pins. Imogen watched and made the occasional comment.

By the end, he had tried on dozens of trousers, shirts, and jackets. Some of them had made Imogen nod and others had been whisked off of him after she gave a small shake of her head. He ended up disoriented and barely protested when she had the bill sent to the palace.

"The clothes should be at yours in a few days," she informed him. "What do you think, something to eat? You've got to be hungry."

He shook his head. "No, I...I've been gone for a while. I should get back."

She rolled her eyes and walked him back to work. They passed by a shop that smelled amazingly of roasting meat and he stopped to stare. She gave him a nudge towards it and didn't even tease him when he caved and bought something.

She dropped him off at Marius' house with the assurance, "He'll be by to pick you for the show but don't be surprised if that's the first you see of him. You know how Earth takes it out of him."

When the clothes arrived, he thought it must have been a mistake because he received a stack of boxes. Each of them contained a complete three-piece suit with shirt and tie to match, in a variety of colors, including the requisite neutrals and a few in rich, deep tones like emerald, ochre, and burgundy.

Another box contained several pairs of shoes and suspenders and had a note pinned to the top.

They're all the same cut of suit. I know how fond you are of them since your time on Earth. The shop does have your measurements now if you ever want to expand your wardrobe.

On the day of the gallery, he dressed in the black suit, feeling that it was the most formal color, and a crisp white shirt that had no jam stains on the sleeves. He did, however, choose a green tie instead of a black one.

He felt incredibly sharp and well put together, enough that he wished for a full-length mirror the same as they'd had at the tailor's, instead of just the small one above his sink.

He dashed over to pull open the door when someone knocked and couldn't help but grin when he saw the Devil. "Is that a tiara?"

"It is not."

Ira's grin grew wider. "How badly did Imogen have to bully you to make you wear it?"

"Not as much as she had to in order to make me wear the rest of it."

Lucifer had dressed in something formal and elegant; his normal loose, black trousers had been replaced with ones that skimmed along his legs and had been tucked into boots. His shirt was not so old that it had been worn to thinness and it did not threaten to slip off his shoulder like his shirts normally did, half-buttoned and a size too large.

There was something about the cut of the pants, the delicate drape of the shirt sleeves and the upright collar that struck a familiar note, but Ira couldn't quite place it. He reached out to run his fingers over the line of silver buttons that ran down one side of Lucifer's vest.

"What?" Lucifer asked.

Ira looked up at him, unable to stop grinning. He'd never seen him wear a crown before, even one as delicate as the circlet nestled among his braids. "You look like our Prince tonight."

"Are you saying I don't normally?" Lucifer pretended to be insulted.

"I'm saying that if you had dressed like this the first time I saw you, I would have believed that you were the Devil."

Satan twined his fingers with Ira's and brought them to his mouth, leaving a light kiss on his knuckles. He kept an arm around Ira's waist as they walked, his spindly fingers gripping Ira's hip the whole time.

The gallery had been set up throughout several rooms in the university, rooms with high ceilings and lots of windows, which made Ira think that these were rooms set aside especially for functions such as this.

When they entered, at first no one noticed, but soon enough a quiet rush went through the crowd. There came no announcement of who had arrived, but those gathered all knelt or bowed, some of them touching their heads to the floor. They remained like that until their Prince's voice, whisper-soft, requested, "Rise."

Only Ira hadn't knelt. He had kept his arm around the Devil's waist.

After everyone had resumed what they had been doing, Lucifer moved towards the statue in the center of the room. It depicted something that was either abstract or a monstrous beast, Ira couldn't tell.

People took turns coming over to their Prince, greeting him and making small talk to which Ira paid no mind. Instead, he contemplated the statue, deciding that it was a fen crow and the cat that hunted it.

Or maybe it was a tree, he really couldn't tell.

A round-faced young man stood next to it and Ira came to understand that this was his sculpture.

Ira caught his eye and when he had his attention, asked, "Is it a tree?"

"A what? Is it a tree?" the sculptor asked.

Ira nodded. He gestured up to the highest bits of the sculpture, that he guessed to be branches or wings. "Sort of looks like a tree."

"Haven't gotten that one yet." He sighed. "It is meant to be seen from above...I told them this wasn't a good place for it..."

"Maybe at the bottom of the staircase or something," Ira suggested.

The sculptor sighed and moped away, not encouraged by Ira's suggestion.

He looked around and spied a table covered with rows of wine glasses. He ran a finger along the inside of Lucifer's wrist and the Devil stopped mid-sentence to look at him.

"What, darling?" Lucifer asked.

"Do you want a drink?"

"Please."

Ira went and took two glasses from the table. He felt like he had stolen them.

On his walk back, he spied a familiar set of pale blue locks. Glad to recognize someone, he detoured over to the painting she stood beside. "Hey, Molly! Hi!"

She turned to face him and at first, she frowned like she didn't recognize him.

Maybe she didn't. They hadn't ever seen each other outside of the brothel before, he realized.

Recognition broke on her face and with it came a look like she'd found a maggot in her breakfast. "What are *you* doing here?"

The man at her side, who must have been her husband, glowered at Ira.

He couldn't fathom a reason for their displeasure. A quick glance around showed pleasure workers on the arms of a few other people. In a far-off corner, he saw Helen, who came from a well-respected family and likely had been invited in her own right. Georg might even be here too, if he could bother to do something other than drink and fuck.

Ira glanced back at the Devil, who had moved away from the statue but still chatted with a few people. "He brought me."

"Our Prince?" she asked, making it sound unreasonable.

He nodded.

"I'm sorry, how are the two of you acquainted?" Molly's husband asked.

"Oh, well, when I worked at the Trade House he used to hire me but—"

"No, you and my *wife*," the man growled.

"I, um." Ira looked over at Lucifer again and felt better when the Devil caught his eye and made his way over. "Well."

Satan ran his hand along Ira's back and took one of the wine glasses. "Come on, love, I hear there's a very interesting exhibit in the back room."

As Lucifer pulled him away from Molly and her husband, Ira thought he heard the word 'whore' hissed by her husband.

"How do you know Romila and Walt?" Lucifer asked when they'd gotten a distance away.

"Molly hires me sometimes."

Lucifer looked delightedly scandalized by that. "Molly! No one's called her that in *years*. Must be trying to relive some of her youth in your arms."

Ira shrugged and took a swallow of wine. "What's in the backroom?"

"I don't know, Rema wouldn't tell me, but she seems to think I'd like it. Insisted I go."

The name Rema he recognized. "She's a captain, isn't she?"

"Of the Fourth. Lovely, efficient, couldn't ask for more. You'll probably end up meeting all the captains tonight."

"I will?"

"Unless you plan on passing the time by upsetting all your clients' spouses," Lucifer said.

Ira looked around. He saw a few more faces that he recognized from Marius' house. He waved to one. "You'll think they'll be upset?"

Lucifer glanced at him. "Forget I said anything."

"Lu," Ira pressed.

"Married people who visit brothels are usually looking for something discreet and free of emotional entanglement, not a jolly hello at high society events."

Ira looked down and kept his eyes trained on the floor.

With a reassuring squeeze, the Devil told him, "There's no way you could have known."

"No, what a miserable whore I am, not even knowing that I'm supposed to be a secret. You think someone would have mentioned."

"People are stupid, Ira."

He couldn't shake the feeling that he wanted to cry. He hadn't ever been under the delusion that Molly, or any of his clients, could be counted as friends, but he had expected to get as much recognition as the assistant at the stationary shop or the fishmonger at the market.

His stomach twisted when he wondered what would happen if Lucifer's wife did come back someday. Would he become a secret for him, too?

"Love."

"Hm?" Ira barely lifted his eyes.

"I never said thank you for agreeing to come with me."

"Oh. Well. You're welcome."

"I didn't know if you would want to come…" Lucifer admitted. "I suppose it could be a bit of good marketing for you, you do look *wonderful* dressed up like that."

Ira bobbed his head. He could leave with two fistfuls of coins tonight if he wanted. He'd get plenty of offers tomorrow, too.

"Or, I…" The Devil cleared his throat. "I sort of hoped that it could be a kind of debut."

"A debut?" Ira wrinkled his nose, now too confused to feel

sorry for himself anymore. "What are you debuting?"

Lucifer's word tumbled over each other. "You. Rather, you and I. Together. As...as something...more official than, than everyone thinking that you're a kept man."

Ira stopped and frowned up at him.

Lucifer stopped as well. "I thought you might have...the gallery is a formal, public event and it's...it's not the kind of thing to which a monarch would bring a mistress or a—"

"Whore."

"Putting it aside as your occupation?"

Ira rolled his eyes.

"Because your work is your work," Lucifer reminded, "But I am not your client. And I was going to say, 'a casual lover'."

Neither of them said anything and neither of them resumed walking. They stared at each other and Lucifer shifted, then cleared his throat.

"Unless I misjudged," the Devil offered, then added, with considerable coolness in his tone, "In which case I apologize. I know I can be a little overeager in some endeavors."

He had pulled back physically as well, taking half a step back and wrapping an arm across his belly. He sandwiched one hand between his ribs and his arm and kept the other hand, the one with the wine glass, close to his face.

Ira hadn't ever seen this posture from him before. Once again Ira felt like the Devil had sliced himself open instead of shared something personal.

"What would be more official about it?" Ira asked.

Lucifer shrugged and looked everywhere but at Ira's face. "I don't know, I'm not saying we should start sending out Christmas cards together or anything."

Ira had no idea what that meant.

"I just...I want people to know that...that we are together. That we aren't just sleeping together but when we do, when you're beside me, I can finally sleep again. That I feel sick when I say goodbye and know I won't see you for a few days. I want people to look at us and understand that I would do anything for you."

"Oh." Ira looked at his shoes, then back at Lucifer. "I didn't know that going to an art show said all that about a relationship."

"Neither did I."

Ira stepped in and rocked up on to his toes, the only way he could kiss the Devil without him bending down or lifting Ira up.

Even then, Ira only managed to brush his lips. "But I sort of like the sound of it."

Lucifer's body loosened up; he lost the tight grip he'd had on himself and the hunch in his shoulders. He sipped from his wine glass and smiled, though it was a hair more nervous than his usual grin. He linked arms with Ira and they continued their walk.

"I hate to say it, you had me petrified for a few minutes there," the Devil admitted.

Ira wanted to say something quippy but pulled back. Not a minute ago the poor thing had been working so hard to hide the shake in his hands and he had looked ready to throw up. "I'm sorry, darling, I just had to catch up with what you were trying to tell me."

Lucifer smiled again, but this time it looked more confident.

Ira tilted up his chin and stood on his toes so that Lucifer would know he wanted a kiss; the Devil leaned in and obliged. "I do love you something awful," Ira told him.

IRA, AT first, had no idea why anyone had directed Lucifer to the back room. It was filled with small displays of student work ranging in quality from decent to excellent.

He didn't understand until he saw a larger than life painting of his own face, flanked by a smaller one of him, eyes closed, lounging nude across a bed. Interspersed with landscapes and bowls of fruit and sketches of models were at least half a dozen paintings of Ira. All of them were intimate and all of them showed more of himself to strangers than he ever had without getting paid for it.

Lucifer laughed. "Oh, holy shit."

"Fuck off," Ira grumbled. He had not even conceived of the notion that Astrid would be showing her work here.

"Oh, love, I'm going to buy the lot of them." Satan swooped down and wrapped his arm around Ira's waist, pulling him in close to kiss his cheek. "I'm going to paper my walls with them! Come, introduce me to this artist with whom you're so personally entangled."

"I didn't know."

"I can tell by the look on your face."

When Astrid saw him, her eyes opened wide and her jaw went slack. "Ira!"

"Hello, darling," Ira said, though without much feeling.

She glanced at Lucifer when he cleared his throat, then did

half a curtsey. "Your Highness."

Ira didn't think that Lucifer had been looking for a curtsey and he didn't even think he'd cleared his throat for her attention since he did it again then took a sip of wine. He didn't really seem to notice that Astrid had said anything to him; his eyes were fixed on a small painting on the wall.

"I didn't figure I'd see you here, Ira," Astrid said.

"Ah, well, they let me out sometimes," he joked.

She frowned.

He felt the need to clarify, "I have my own apartment, it was just a joke."

She didn't look amused at all.

"I, uh, I didn't know you'd have pieces here."

"I told you I was going to," Astrid reminded quietly.

He winced when he remembered that she had and tried to recover, "Well, I mean, I meant," he jutted his chin towards a painting where his own ass was prominently displayed, "I meant this kind of work."

Satan's fingers found a home in Ira's curls, raking through them so gently that a chill ran down Ira's spine. "You look so sad in this one." Lucifer tapped the frame with his wine glass.

Ira shrugged and stepped away. He thought the sketch for that one had been done on one of the occasions when, after he'd spilled, a peculiar sadness had settled over him. He didn't like the painting. He didn't like that there was hard evidence that he had ever looked so forlorn.

He turned his eyes elsewhere, to a painting of a pair of cats with one of the sprawled on its side, the other lounging on its back.

"Maybe he'd be happier if he worked somewhere better," Astrid suggested.

"As far as pleasure houses, you won't do better than Marius'," Lucifer told her, his tone conversational. "About this one." He gestured to one painting of Ira where he had a dreamy sort of look on his face.

"I meant somewhere that people don't hurt him," she said, but she gave it as a challenge instead of clarification.

Ira wished she hadn't said anything.

Lucifer's brow furrowed a little. "Have a lot of people been hurting him?" he asked. His tone and the worried glance he bestowed on Ira made it clear that he thought Ira hadn't been telling him something.

Ira shook his head. "No."

"They use him and leave him behind like he's nothing."

The polite way to tell Astrid to shut up escaped Ira. He tried, "I like the one with the cats."

"And that's different from what you've done?" Lucifer inquired in the softest of voices.

"The black one sort of looks like Marlow," Ira raised his voice.

Astrid fixed her eyes, huge and blue and loving, on Ira's face. He hated when she got that look on her face. The let-me-worship-at-the-shrine-of-your-cock kind of look. Then she turned her gaze to the Devil. With a frown and a note of hardness in her voice, she began, "When *we're* together—"

Ira dropped his drink and the glass shattered. The wine sloshed across the floor and Ira said, "Oh, shit, sorry," like he'd done it by accident. He put his hand on Lucifer's arm and tugged him away. "I'm sorry, I don't think I got any on you, we've got to find someone to clean it up."

"Wouldn't want anyone to slip," the Devil murmured.

Ira dragged him away from the spill.

Once they'd gotten out of the room, Satan assured Ira, "I wouldn't have done anything."

"Ah, no, it wasn't you. She makes me uncomfortable anyway."

"Oh?"

Ira nodded.

"So ask her not to come see you anymore," Lucifer advised.

Ira shrugged. "She's harmless, just..."

"Obsessive," Lucifer supplied, not without a hint of cattiness.

Ira shrugged again. He didn't want to be mean. Astrid has only ever been kind to him. "She's...she's got this idea in her head like, you know, like my other clients are awful to me."

"Sounds familiar somehow."

Ira shook his head. "No, darling, you were...you weren't like her. You...I don't know, it was just different. You didn't think my work was bad just because of what it was."

"And she does?"

"I think so. She always says things like I'm being used, that it makes her sick."

Lucifer reached out and put his hand on the shoulder of one of the waiters milling around the gallery.

The waiter froze up for an instant then he recovered enough to whisper, "Your Highness?"

"Dropped a glass," Lucifer said and nodded back towards the room.

The servant nodded and hurried away.

Lucifer slung his arm around Ira's shoulder and leaned on him a little bit. "It makes her sick," he stated.

"Mmm, that's what she says."

"Not sick enough to stop hiring you."

Ira shook his head. "I don't want to talk about Astrid."

"Fair enough, I don't really want to talk about her either. What should we do?" Lucifer asked.

"You should show me off."

A curious smile started to spread across Lucifer's face. "Oh?"

"In all the books I've read, when a rich man has a pretty girl on his arm, he shows her off. You're always telling me how pretty I am."

Ira had learned that from books, but he hadn't learned that even in Hell time spent in a brothel was meant to be a secret from one's spouse.

"Very pretty."

"And this is official now, isn't it?"

Lucifer nodded.

"What, officially, will I be to you? How should I introduce myself? Hello, I'm Ira, our Prince sleeps at my place sometimes? Hello, nice to meet you, he bought me an apartment?"

"My companion."

"Companion," Ira repeated, letting the word roll over his tongue.

"Yes. Have you met Ira? He's my very dear companion," Lucifer said. "Ira, love, this is Jarrod, he's the captain of the Fifth."

Ira turned to see a stocky demon with golden yellow skin offering his hand. Ira shook it, a little startled. He hadn't realized that Lucifer was actually talking to anyone.

"Nice to meet you. Ira, was it?" Jarrod said.

Ira nodded. "Yes, it is. Ira. Nice to meet you, too."

The Devil looped his arm around Ira's waist and brought him through the gallery like that, keeping good on his promise to introduce Ira to all the Precinct captains.

Some of them even conversed with him beyond polite small talk. At one point he'd talked to Ulster, a chatty man dressed in peacock-colored satin, for so long that his mouth grew dry.

"I, uh, excuse me, I need a drink. Do you want me to bring you one?" Ira asked.

Ulster shook his head and held up his still-full glass.

Ira made his way over to the nearest drink table and felt enormously pleased to see that the waitstaff had put out fruits and cheeses and little plates.

Before he could reach the table and fill up a plate with snacks, a hard hand closed around his upper arm and yanked him so that he faced Molly's husband.

"Are you fucking my wife?" the man demanded.

The question took Ira by surprise so badly he could only mutely shake his head.

"Why else would she know a whore?"

Ira shook his head again, getting his wits back to some degree. "No, I haven't—"

"If I even *suspect* that the babe isn't mine," the man warned.

"Uh." Ira tried to think. He put together how Molly had never let him spill inside of her. More than that, he didn't think he'd ever spilled when she'd hired him; he didn't even think he'd been undressed around her. He thought of the new roundness of her belly over the past few months.

"Oh." Ira stepped back, out of Walt's grip. "I can't. I can't do that, I've got this tattoo—"

Walt backhanded Ira hard across his left cheek. "I don't care what tattoos you've got!"

Ira stumbled back from the blow, for once more embarrassed than frightened.

He didn't know who Molly's husband was, only that he was rich and important and gave her status.

People had gathered around to stare, whispering and giggling.

Ira gave Walt a solid punch, not too hard, but right in the nose, enough to make the other man's eyes water.

The crowd gasped. Above their concerned murmurs came a laugh, smooth and rich. Everyone turned to look at their Prince. Even Walt, who had his hand clasped over his nose even though it wasn't even bleeding, looked.

The crowd parted for their Prince. The whispers surged, so many of them sure that Ira would be eaten or flogged at the very least.

Lucifer took Ira's face in one hand. When he smiled, a quiver went through the crowd. It was a horrible smile, to be sure, and one that often preceded a devouring. The Devil drew Ira up on his toes and, in front of the everyone, pressed his mouth to Ira's.

"Would you like me to kill him?" Lucifer asked.

"No."

"Have him flogged?"

Ira shook his head.

"What about taking a few fingers?"

With each question, Walt grew sweatier and more ashen.

"How about an apology?" Ira proposed.

Lucifer's eyes slid towards Walt and then he turned his head. "How about an apology?"

Stammering so much that Ira could barely understand him, Walt managed an apology. Ira would have been pleased, but it seemed that Lucifer was not.

"Again," Lucifer said, "Kneel while you say it."

"Lu," Ira breathed but the Devil pressed his fingers to the inside of Ira's wrist, a gesture of reassurance, once that asked for patience and understanding.

Walt dropped to his knees.

Lucifer tapped Ira's heel with the toe of his boot so that Ira put his foot forward.

"Apologize," their Prince ordered, "And be grateful my companion is more merciful than I."

Walt pressed his lips to the tip of Ira's shoe. "I'm sorry, I'm so sorry."

Ira pulled his shoe back. "I was in the middle of getting a drink."

Lucifer put his hand on Ira's elbow and led him to the refreshment table. He took two wine glasses and handed one to Ira. He went to pick off a few grapes from a platter but came away with the whole bunch by accident.

He cradled them in his hand and nodded away from the crowd.

Ira followed him to a staircase he hadn't noticed and up to a balcony that had been roped off. Lucifer stepped over the rope and gestured for Ira to follow him.

Ira did so with some hesitance.

There were no seats on the balcony. Lucifer settled against the wall, nibbling the grapes he'd taken.

He offered the bunch to Ira. "Hm?"

Ira plucked a couple from their stems.

"Sorry about the display. Sometimes these things need to be

done."

"Mhm."

A hint of worry crept into Lucifer's voice as he asked, "You understand, don't you?"

Ira reached over and caught Lucifer's earlobe between his thumb and forefinger, giving it a tender caress. In his very best purr, asked, "You are coming back to see me, aren't you? I'll be so nice to you if you do."

A brief expression of confusion passed over Satan's face only to be replaced by a crooked smile.

Ira took his fingers back and slipped a grape between his lips, suggestive and overexaggerated.

"Careful you don't choke eating it like that."

Ira giggled, accidentally biting the grape in half and clapping a hand to his mouth so he wouldn't spit it all over.

"Some monarchs would be incredibly offended if you compared political posturing to seducing clients," the Devil pointed out.

Ira shoved the rest of the grape into his mouth and once he'd swallowed, he said, "Most monarchs want to be called king."

Lucifer wrinkled his nose. "I *hate* that word."

"Alright, fine, you aren't king. But your wife was queen?"

He nodded.

"Princes and queens don't go together."

"It's my realm, they can go together if I want them to," Lucifer sulked.

Ira let his fingers run along the Devil's thigh, not because he hoped to be seductive but because he liked the feel of it. They picked at the grapes in silence until they were gone.

Lucifer said, "I don't have any plans tomorrow."

"None at all?"

"I made sure of it." He put an arm around Ira's shoulders and tugged him a little closer. He rested his chin on Ira's head. "I am sort of, mm, worn out after all that time on Earth and going back and forth."

"How's Felix?"

"Good. He's put on some weight. He was so small when he was born and even...even after a month, he was still so *tiny*. I thought I would break him just looking at him."

Ira recalled the babe, who'd been born too early. He'd been stick-thin; Ira had been afraid to even touch him.

Lucifer reached up to run his fingers through his braids and Ira took him by the hands so he wouldn't undo them. The Devil gripped his hands hard.

"I was afraid, you know, the whole time. I left Mercy and expected to come back to a fat, pink, squalling babe and...he was so small and so *quiet*." He scrunched up his face. "I thought he was going to die and the idea of that is...it's *monstrous*, abhorrent, that he could die and I would keep going."

"There wasn't anything you could have done." Ira didn't know that for sure. Maybe the Devil could have done a lot. "She couldn't have stayed down here. She didn't *want* to stay down here."

"I shouldn't have left her alone."

Ira reminded, "You can't stay on Earth, Lu, and you had no way of knowing her family was going to be looking for her."

"I should have kept a better eye on her."

"Lu! Stop," Ira insisted. "It wasn't your fault. Bad things happen, no one can do anything about it."

"They wouldn't let me go back."

"What?"

"The Parliament, when I found out she'd been killed, I tried to go back but..." Lucifer let out a hard breath through his nose. "I would have saved her...I could have if I'd had the guts to fight them."

"Luci, darling, you did what you could. You're the Prince of Hell, not of Earth and *not* of time. It's no good when people mess around with things that have already happened."

Lucifer didn't look comforted.

"And you found him a good home," Ira reminded. "With two people to love him. He'll be well and happy there. He'll be safe. No one will find him."

"I was so stupid."

"Stupid and hopeful aren't the same."

"It feels the same."

"I know, love." Ira leaned in to kiss his temple. "And you said he's doing well. That's the important thing, isn't it?"

"Yes. I just...I wish." The Devil shook his head.

"I know." Ira knew that Lucifer had wanted to keep the babe with him, a secret he had kept as closely guarded as who Felix's new parents were. "You did the right thing."

"I didn't deserve to keep him."

"Oh, love..." Ira sighed.

"I don't deserve you either."

"You do."

A few quiet minutes passed before the Devil asked, "Do you think we should go back downstairs at some point?"

"If you want to. You can really get a great view of the show from up here."

"Can you?"

Ira nodded towards the balcony.

Lucifer leaned forward a little, then a little more until he had scooted forward so his knees were pressed up against the banister rails. He remained like that for a few more minutes, his eyes grazing over the people below him.

Finally, Lucifer stood and stretched, linking his fingers and stretching his hands high above his head.

They returned to the event below but not before Ira slid his arms around Lucifer's neck and pressed a kiss to his mouth. "We are all so lucky to have you, darling."

ASLEEP, THE Devil did not look so monstrous. When he slept, the black of his teeth and the red-gold of his eyes was hidden; when he slept, Ira could believe that he had been an angel once, beatific and lovely to look upon.

And really, Ira considered, as he studied the curve of Satan's cheek, the angle of his jaw, as he memorized the way his too-dark eyelashes lay against his too-white skin, he was lovely now, too, sleeping or not.

"What did you look like?" Ira murmured, not even realizing he'd said anything aloud until Satan stirred.

"Hm?"

"Nothing."

Eyes still closed, Lucifer slipped his hands onto Ira's ribcage. "Don't make me tickle it out of you," he threatened.

"Before you fell..." Ira trailed his fingers through the Devil's hair. "Is this always how you've looked?"

His eyes opened. "Oh. No."

"You don't have to tell me."

"No, it's fine." He rolled to look at Ira. "I don't think I was so spindly. I think I was...slender. Slim hips and smooth thighs. A little trail of golden hair from here to here." He traced from between Ira's legs to his chest. "I was blond, too. Strawberry blond. It was so soft and pretty, tumbling waves...I loved my hair. God, I was so *proud* of it..."

Ira played with a lock of his hair, rumpled from sleep and waved because of the braids he kept it in.

"My eyes were...Junius says they were golden, like sheaves of wheat. And I had freckles. I remember those. I felt like a little sunlight god, all warm and gilded and...what?" he interrupted himself to regard Ira suspiciously.

Ira shook his head, unable to stop the wholehearted smile that spread across his face. "Nothing. I love you."

Lucifer sighed, the warm glow of nostalgia slipping from his face. "I thought I was so *beautiful*."

"You are beautiful, Lu."

The Devil didn't seem to hear him. "Of course, He knew that. Of course, He took it away...a little hefty on the symbolism, *really*. Literally trading light for dark. Ugh." He wrinkled his nose, made a sort of retching face. "Makes me sick. Makes me glad I rebelled."

"Not as heavy-handed as losing your wings."

Lucifer laughed, a deep belly laugh. "Ah, imagine if we'd had wings! He would have *loved* to take those away."

He rolled a little more, on to his side, and then he was crawling on top of Ira, his legs on either side of Ira's hips, his fingers combing through his curls. He put his lips just below Ira's ear. "Can I tell you a secret?"

"Always."

"I tell you all my secrets anyway, I don't know why. I open my mouth and they come pouring out as soon as you fix those doe eyes on me..." He nipped the lobe of Ira's ear. "I want to go home...I hate this place, I hate all of it. I didn't think He'd kick me out. I was such a brat, so spoiled and haughty. I want to go home, Ira."

Ira didn't know what to do with that information. It was a grave secret to be sure, that their Prince yearned for Heaven, a place all Hell-born things had been taught to scorn. He hated to think of his Prince wishing for the love of the Father who'd cast him out. It made his belly flip to think of Lucifer begging his Father to take him back.

"But you know what else?" He flicked his tongue against Ira's throat. "I hated it there more. I hated those stupid fucking angels and their stupid serene minds. I hated how they never wondered about anything. I hated the righteousness."

He pressed his hips against Ira, hard between the legs, his skin hot; Ira arched his back to push against him.

"I *despised* that goddamn boring fucking paradise."

He bit Ira hard enough to leave a little hickey, but without causing real pain.

Ira wrapped his arms around him and drew him in closer, hungry for kisses, needing the taste of his skin and the heat of his mouth.

The Devil ran his hands up Ira's arms and grasped his wrists, pinning him to the bed and locking his mouth over Ira's. He pulled back to whisper the same spell he always did at times like these, the one that would conjure lubricant. Once he had, he wrapped his hand around Ira's length, his caress firm and slow.

When Lucifer guided Ira inside of him, Ira could not help but groan. He didn't want to help it, either, he wanted this, he wanted this heat and urgency. He thrust hard, quick, not concerned with being gentle because the Devil had no gentleness in his touch, either. He was a thing made of need, they both were, twined together, hurried and demanding.

He left scratch marks on the Devil's back and when he spilled, the whole world fell apart and came back together in a matter of seconds.

Panting and shaking, Lucifer came, too, in time with Ira's final thrusts.

After that he crumpled, putting his forehead against Ira's shoulder, pressing a lazy kiss to his skin.

"So tell me more about your father," Ira prompted teasingly after his heart had settled and his head had cleared.

Lucifer chuckled. "He might have made me, but He *isn't* my father."

Ira grinned and turned his head to kiss the Devil's cheek. "No, if He was, you'd have started crying halfway through."

Lucifer really laughed at that, so hard that he rolled off to one side and wrapped an arm around his stomach. He settled after a minute and Ira put a hand on his waist.

"Have I told you how much I adore being inside of you?" Ira asked.

"You've mentioned."

"I..."

Lucifer prompted, "What?"

"No, it's silly."

"Ira, no secrets, I share mine with you," Lucifer admonished.

"You were only the third man I've ever been with like that."

"No!" Lucifer gasped, though Ira couldn't tell if the shock was real or feigned.

Ira nodded. "I told you, men who like being fucked don't hire me."

"Who was the first one?"

"Oh, his name was Alain. University student, so shy, he didn't have the nerve to flirt with his classmates. I think he picked me cause I was the least intimidating lad there."

"And the second?" Lucifer asked.

"Uri. He's so strapping and manly and everyone who hired him always wanted him to be pounding away at them, hard and fast and brutal. All that. He was one of my roommates and one day he's all...hot and bothered and I hadn't gotten much work. I ask him what's wrong, didn't you get enough today? You know, teasing. And he tells me how bad he wants someone to be inside him for once, that what he can do with his own fingers just isn't enough...Well, you know what happens when you leave two vital young lads together."

With a half-smile on his face, Lucifer purred, "I'm familiar with the result."

"It was a lot of fun until Mistress found out about it. Now he works at, mmm, that place three down from Marius. House of...Dreams? Sighs? He stops by sometimes, you know."

"I know."

"Cause you know everything," Ira said.

"If I want to. Or if people tell me."

"Who told you?"

"That little boy who works for Marius. He's not a *boy*, but he's so...immature. All pouts and simpers and eyelash flutters. Georg?"

Ira nodded. That sounded exactly like Georg.

Lucifer added, "Told me he'd be just for me if I wanted, that I could do anything I like to him."

Ira sat up, scandalized. "He did not! I'm going to have a fucking talk with him! That little shit."

Lucifer grinned. "Oh, possessive suddenly."

Ira felt his face get hot. "No," he protested, but then was compelled to admit, "Maybe."

"Hm?" The Devil looked surprised.

"Maybe a little. Maybe sometimes I think that..." He ran a hand through his curls and couldn't look at the Devil. "Sometimes I think that maybe it should be just the two of us."

Like he couldn't believe what Ira was saying, the Devil asked, "Do you?"

"Well, us and Reggie, I'd feel bad if I didn't let him give me foot rubs anymore," he tried to joke.

"Ira, love."

"No, I know, I'm trying to be serious, it's only..."

Lucifer ventured a guess, "You'd like to keep taking clients?"

"No, I don't, not really. I sort of feel like I don't want to tell you what to do," Ira confessed. "But I do. I want to tell you what to do a lot. I want you to be only for me."

"Tell me, then, tell me what to do. Tell me not to be with anyone else. Tell me I'm yours," Lucifer said and it sounded like begging.

"Will you be?"

"Yes. I will. A thousand times. Just for you."

Lucifer fixed his eyes on Ira's face and Ira could almost imagine them being beautiful and warm and golden, he could almost picture the tumbles of strawberry blond locks, he could almost see exactly where his freckles had been, like ghosts on his skin. In there, inside the Devil, lurking closer to the surface than anyone knew, was the angel he had been and would always be. A thing made to serve, made to love, a thing that had gotten lost.

"And I...I don't think I'm going to take any more clients. Not...not for now. Not for a long time. I need something else."

Lucifer gazed up at him. "I love you, Ira."

"I love you, too, Luci." He took the Devil's face in his hands and kissed him. "But will you promise me something?"

"Yes."

"Will you promise that if there *is* someone else you want to sleep with, that you'll talk to me first? And I'd tell you, too. And we won't be with anyone else unless we're both okay with it."

Ira had never felt this way before and he didn't know if it would last, but he knew that right now he wanted to make a world where there was nothing but him and Lucifer.

"I promise."

"If it's not too much to expect..."

"I already promised."

Ira folded himself up against the Devil, nestling in his arms. "I promise, too," he said, even though Satan hadn't asked him to promise anything.

"Do you know what this will mean?" Lucifer murmured after a

while.

"What?"

"You can't call yourself a whore anymore if you aren't taking clients."

Ira pulled back. "What's it matter to you?"

"*You're* the one always on about what a miserable whore you are, not me."

"Are you ashamed of it?" Ira asked. Sometimes question had floated around in his head but after last night, after Molly's husband had taken things so poorly, he needed the reassurance.

"Of course not, love, it's a perfectly valid line of work as long you're going about it the right way."

"And what's the right way?"

"Not being kidnapped or coerced into it, or, I think what I meant to say is that panders and madams should never stoop so low as to force people into the profession. It isn't the whores that are in the wrong."

Ira snorted.

"What?"

"You're always picking all this nuance out of things."

"I do habitually make contracts with people for items of some value." Lucifer swung his legs out of bed, then pulled Ira into his lap and stood with Ira in his arms. "We should clean up, we've got a lunch date."

"Have we? I thought you didn't have any plans."

"He Himself, the Prince of Darkness and Lord of Hell, who sits upon the serpent's throne has no plans. Lucifer, gutless and common thing that he is, has a lunch date with your brother."

"Oh."

"You did tell me to," he reminded.

"I know. I just...I didn't think it would be so soon," Ira said.

"No time like the present."

In the hall, as Lucifer carried Ira to the bathroom, they passed one of the servants and Lucifer said, "Gila, be a dear, change my sheets."

The woman bobbed her head. "Yethhhhire."

"She doesn't talk much," Ira commented as Gila ducked into his bedroom and Lucifer brought him into the bathroom.

"She's got a lot of teeth. I think it's hard for her."

Lucifer hadn't chosen the smaller bathroom they usually used, the modest, cozy one with the roomy clawfoot tub, but the big one that he had only brought Ira into once before.

It had a wide pool in the center, large enough for quite a few people, and a variety of other amenities, like a shower and sauna. Ira had always wanted to go back in, but the room had belonged to the Devil's wife and it had felt wrong to ask to go playing around in his wife's private space.

Lucifer set Ira down, went over to light the lamps, and then started filling the tub set into the floor. He adjusted the taps, checking the temperature of the water every so often.

It looked different than it had the last time he'd been in here. The vanity in the corner had been cleared off, free of all his wife's left behind items. When Ira looked closer, he thought that it was a different vanity altogether. A settee and a bookshelf had been added in the corner that didn't have a sauna or a shower.

"Changed things around a little," he noted.

Lucifer, who had been crouching beside the tub, looked over. "Hm? Oh." His face sobered a little and he slid from crouching to sitting, his legs crossed Indian-style. "Got rid of it all. Really got rid of it. In the trash."

"Oh."

"I thought..." Lucifer shrugged. "I thought maybe this could be yours. A space to call your own when you're here. If you wanted it."

Ira raised his eyebrows. "Been thinking on that for a while, haven't you?"

"About a year."

"Shit, Lu."

"Before you went to stay with Junius."

Ira approached.

Lucifer slid his arms around Ira's legs, pressing a soft kiss to Ira's thigh. "I didn't want you to come back. I mean. I did. I wanted you to come back so bad that I prayed you wouldn't. I *prayed*."

Ira combed his fingers through the Devil's hair. "You worry too much." He pulled away and stepped into the tub. He gave Lucifer's arm a tug. "Come on."

Lucifer entered the tub and wrapped around Ira, pulling him into his arms and onto his lap, both up to their chests in water. He kissed Ira's shoulder.

"I promised I wouldn't make you stay," Satan murmured, his lips skimming against Ira's skin. "I promised I wouldn't, but I don't want you to go home tonight. Will you stay with me for just a few days?"

"Might be nice."

"Yeah?"

"Yeah." Ira nodded. He looked around. "You haven't got any soap."

"Shit, I knew I'd forget something. I'm awful at things like this." Lucifer pushed his hand into the fabric of reality and pulled it back with a bar of soap clenched in his fist.

He handed it over to Ira with a boastful grin.

It was a neat trick, but Ira knew he hated doing it. He knew it had bothered him by the way he clenched his hand, once, twice, three times, afterward, to try to banish the crawling feeling it left on his skin.

Ira clarified, "I've still got to go to work tomorrow. Marius hates doing the books and it's almost—"

"Tax season. Yes. I won't lock you away from the world just yet, darling."

A DOOR had never looked so imposing. It was an ordinary door to an ordinary restaurant in the Eighth, a place where the workers who lived in that precinct could have a quiet meal.

With the lightest touch, Lucifer put his hand on Ira's back and urged him inside. Ira even made it ten paces inside before he stopped dead. He tried to leave but as he turned, Lucifer caught him around the waist.

"I don't want to know," Ira confessed, his eyes starting to smart.

"Know what, love?"

"I don't want to meet him and know why they kept him instead of me."

The Devil promised, "It won't be like that."

"It will."

"It won't because you'll meet him and remember that he's not the one who's got the Prince of Hell wrapped around his little finger," Lucifer assured.

A tentative smile began of its own volition. "Maybe."

Lucifer kept his arm around Ira's waist, a secure and guiding force through the restaurant. Ira kept his eyes peeled, not knowing if he would recognize his own twin, not knowing what he would look like after so many years.

He got his answer shortly when he spied another thin-limbed

and ash-gray demon sitting at a table in the corner. Instead of curls, he had straight, messy hair, and his face had a few slight differences, mostly in the nose and mouth, but he had the same dark eyes.

This other demon stood as soon as he saw Ira and rushed around to the other side of the table. He embraced Ira the way a parent might embrace a child that had gotten lost.

Ira hated it; he hated how familiar, how *normal* it felt. He pulled away, shrinking against Lucifer, who had started chatting with the young man who accompanied his brother.

When he realized that this man, with his peachy-pink skin and fluffy brown curls, was not Hell-born or one of the Devil's bastards, not a vampire or a demon of any sort, Ira couldn't help but gape.

He'd heard that there was a human that lived in the Eighth. Selene always told him if she'd seen him when she was out doing the shopping or when she went to a show at Dreams of Eulalia. Ira had never figured that he would show up with his brother, though.

"I can't tell you how much, well, maybe I can, I don't know, I-I know you didn't really want to meet," his brother began, but Ira couldn't really follow.

Ira had slipped away from the moment a little, the way he did sometimes with a bad client, and noticed the human elbow his brother.

"Oh, and this is Jack," Eodus said.

"Jack Callahan." The human offered his hand for Ira to shake.

He shook his hand. "Ira."

"Nice to meet you, really," Jack said, giving Ira a winning smile, a lot of dimple.

He tried not to stare too much at the smooth, white scars on each of his cheeks, symbols that Ira recognized from his schooling. *Refuge. Citizen.*

He glanced up at Lucifer and wondered what sort of deal this man had made with the Devil.

"Let's sit, at any rate, I'm hungry," Lucifer said, moving his arms in a vague, sweeping gesture towards the table.

They settled in around the table.

Eodus went silent.

Ira didn't have anything to say either.

Lucifer and Jack kept up a hearty conversation though, talking mostly about Jack's place of employment and his boss, who was Lucifer's sister-in-law.

Ira sighed.

"I, uh," Eodus began.

Ira raised his eyes from the tablecloth. "Hm?"

"I didn't know."

"Didn't know what?" Ira asked.

"That you were alive. If I had...Ira, if I had, I would have looked for you, I would have."

Ira shrugged. He didn't know what else to do. He had never thought his brother was dead, but he hadn't gone looking for him.

Eodus told him, "I'm so sorry."

"For what?" Ira took his hands from the table and put them on his lap, getting the feeling that Eodus would reach out to touch him if he didn't.

He hated that he wanted his brother to take his hand. He hated that he wished he'd let that hug go on for longer.

"For what happened. That I didn't know. That...that all this time I should have had a brother, that *you* should have had a brother."

Eodus started to wring his hands and in a horrible flash of clarity, Ira remembered a little boy wringing his hands like that, wringing them so much he ran the risk of breaking a finger.

"Wasn't your doing, I figure. No reason to be sorry." Ira nodded towards Jack. "How'd you two meet up, anyway? You go up to Earth a lot?"

Eodus shook his head. "No. Well." His cheeks darkened and he glanced furtively at the Devil.

Lucifer rolled his eyes. "Oh, for fuck's sake, Eodus, you can't think I don't know about Vani running people up. Or did you ask Yatha? She's a little less intimidating."

"I used to sneak up sometimes," Eodus admitted. "I went to the circus. That was it, really. I knew as soon as I saw him."

One corner of Ira's mouth tugged up. "Never been to the circus."

That garnered Jack's attention. "You should! Oh, it's something else, really."

"I don't think there are any down here," Ira admitted.

"I could take you up, dear, if you wanted to go," the Devil offered.

"Maybe." He shrugged.

"Your Highness, we didn't notice you come in," came a wheedling voice from the left of the table.

Lucifer sighed audibly. He didn't turn towards the demon who had sidled up to them. "If I'd wanted attention, don't you think I'd have done something to get it?"

The creature shrank. "I'm sorry, my Prince, we, I..."

The Devil tossed the interloper half a smile. "Just here for a quiet lunch is all. No need to fuss."

"Of course, I'm sorry, of course." The owner of the restaurant bobbed and bowed away.

Not five minutes later, though, two waiters brought out plates of meats, cheeses, and breads that they hadn't ordered, as well as wine that paired nicely with the spread, but that also hadn't been ordered.

"You know what," Jack said after they'd all had a few bites.

"What?" Lucifer asked.

"No one makes beer down here."

"Sure, they do," Eodus said.

Jack shook his head. "No, not real beer. It's all sweet."

"On Earth, they add a bittering agent to the beer. Hops. That sort of stuff," Lucifer said.

"And the beer on Earth is horrible!" Eodus pointed out. "Tastes like piss."

"Oh, you drink a lot of piss, then?" Jack challenged.

Ira reached over and pushed his fingers between Lucifer's. He wanted to leave and never come back, even though a thousand questions raced through his mind, a thousand things he wanted to know. His world did not need to be any larger than it was now. He had work and he had books; he had Lucifer. He did not need a brother.

"It's salty," Ira muttered.

"What?" Jack asked.

"Piss. It's salty. The beer on Earth wasn't salty."

Lucifer snickered, covering his mouth with the back of his hand, but couldn't control himself. He dissolved into giggles, until he gasped, "I'm sorry, but he's right."

Eodus examined a piece of bread. "So. You've been to Earth?"

Ira nodded. "Sure, I mean, I wasn't that impressed. What about Hell?" he asked Jack. "You like it down here?"

"It's, uh...the sky is something, isn't it! But, you know." Jack gazed at Eodus briefly and took him by the hand. "I'd like it less if I'd died and come here, I bet."

"One would hope," Lucifer said.

"Lots more *stuff* up there, though, isn't there? Trains and Coca-

Cola...we haven't got things like that," Ira offered, feeling bad that he'd had nothing to say about Jack's home realm. He'd given a poor answer because Eodus had been the one to ask. "Or the ocean."

Lucifer stopped making a little bread and cheese sandwich for himself to look up and say, "There's an ocean."

They all frowned at him.

"Well. It's not...it's not made of water, I don't think. Hell only has so much land and if you go far enough, you'll come to this beach, it's...it looks like its covered in volcano ash, softest sand you've ever felt."

All three had their eyes fixed on him.

"And you'll think it's water, you'll even take off your boots and your furs and wade in. At first, nothing, then it's cold, biting cold and you want to get out, you know you really should, but it's too cold to move. Your legs don't work."

Ira reached over to put a hand on Lucifer's thigh. The Devil took his hand, his fingertips pressing into Ira's palms.

"But you start to feel warm again, it's spreading up through your body all over so you're...melting. Oozing into the water, up to your waist, your chest, your chin...and close your eyes and..." He went quiet.

"And?" Jack prompted.

"And then you're on the beach again. The others have dragged you out. Somehow. It didn't affect them the way it had you." Lucifer still had that little sandwich dangling limply between his fingers. He set it down and wiped his hand on his trousers. He cleared his throat. "So we've got an ocean. I don't know how far it goes. To be honest, I'm not keen to find out."

The Devil took in a big breath of air, almost like he'd forgotten to do it for a while, then turned around in his seat. He flagged over a waiter and ordered more food and drinks for the table. He kept his grip on Ira's hand.

"Eodus has a cat," the Devil told Ira. "Her name is Pumpkin."

"Oh." Ira looked at his brother. "Uh. Is she orange?"

"No. White. But she's round."

"And you know, I saw a white pumpkin once," Jack said, "I think it was...we were at a farmer's stand in Connecticut. Me and Brigid made a great jack-o'-lantern."

"Is that the thing with the face?" Ira asked. He thought he'd read about it at some point. He'd spent hours haunting the library as a youth and had acquired incidental knowledge of many things.

Jack nodded. "You lot don't do many holidays here, do you?"

"Zero, actually, considering the root of that word is *holy*," Lucifer pointed out. "But there is the Revel."

Ira grinned and Eodus nodded.

"The what?" the human asked.

"Oh, Jack, you've...how long have you been here, have we not had one?" Lucifer asked.

"Not in three years," Ira informed him.

"*Really*," Lucifer murmured. "Hmm."

Jack asked, "What's the Revel?"

"No more than once a year the denizens of Hell will revel but only when it has been declared by he who sits the serpent's throne," Eodus recited.

Just as he'd learned it in school; Ira had learned the same thing, though he'd learned it from the bookkeeper before Nial instead of in a schoolhouse. It was one of the Charter Edicts, a handful of rules that governed the citizens of Hell.

"Has it really been three years?" Lucifer asked. "I swear I meant to have one."

He had meant to have one, Ira knew, but Felix's untimely birth and delicate health, coupled with the subsequent killing of Mercy and the pursuit of the babe by angels and Moralists had extinguished the idea.

Ira emptied the rest of the wine into the Devil's glass.

"Why no more than once a year?" Jack inquired.

"Oh, because I used to declare them all the time and they'd last for days and nothing got done," Lucifer explained, "Ever. Had one that lasted nearly a whole year once. *That* was a debacle. Thus, limits were required."

"Gee."

"But stick around, we'll have one eventually," Lucifer assured.

Their food arrived, a spread of dishes that came with little plates and spoons with which to serve themselves.

Ira and Eodus reached for the spoon that Satan had shoved into the bowl of brussels sprouts at the same time and both pulled back.

Ira stared at the sprouts, tantalizingly speckled with bits of bacon and garlic, and decided he didn't care about being polite. He grabbed the spoon and shoveled some on to his plate. He pushed the handle of the spoon towards his brother when he was done, though, the smallest display of manners he could manage.

Lucifer had heaped mushrooms and wild rice onto his plate.

Ira reached over and speared a mushroom. He popped it into his mouth as the Devil scowled at him.

"If you wanted—"

"I didn't," Ira said, grinning up at him, his chin tilted proudly. "I just wanted that one."

Lucifer let out a hard breath through his nose but leaned in to kiss him, exactly as Ira had hoped he would do.

Ira liked to do things that no one else would dare to do, things no one else could do if they wanted to keep all their fingers.

Lucifer kissed him once more and Ira pulled back before it became three kisses, then a dozen. Before they caused a scene.

"You work in the Third," Ira stated after he'd filled his plate and taken a few bites.

Eodus nodded.

"How is that?"

His brother's eyes darted towards Satan before he answered, "Loud."

Ira nodded. "I remember at night..."

Eodus began to say, "Ma would..." He shook his head.

"What?" Ira prompted even though he didn't want to hear a single thing about his mother.

"She wished I wasn't so soft is all." Eodus pushed some food around his plate. "But after Pa took off—"

"Took off?" Ira asked.

"Sure, I mean, he wasn't home much and then after a while he just wasn't home at all. He lives out on Teak Road now, I think. Ma did as best she could."

Ira chewed, thinking. Reevaluating, really. "Have I..." he began but thought better of it.

"What?"

"Any other, you know, long lost brothers or sisters?"

"No."

Ira snagged a piece of bread and used it to sop up some of the bacon grease that lingered on his plate. "You read at all?"

"A little."

"Oh?"

"Mostly just news dispatches and things like that."

"Oh." Ira didn't know what else to say. "What, um, so what do you do for fun, then?"

"I play cards a lot. Bit of chess here and there, but I'm not any good at it."

"You're getting better," Jack offered through a mouthful of squash and chickpeas. "You know what! There would be four of us if you ever wanted to get together and play bridge."

Ira had nothing to say to that offer. He looked to Lucifer only to find him beaming like a madman and tickled pink by the idea.

"I used to play, me and the other boys would play on Sunday when everyone else was at church," Jack continued. "Not...not that it was much of a church."

Ira shook his head. He didn't know what counted as a church or didn't.

"It was just the tent that the pastor set up, but we weren't exactly welcome."

Ira couldn't help but glance at Satan again, his nose wrinkled. To the table in general, he said, "Figure I don't know a lot about churches or who's welcome there. Probably not demons, I guess."

Lucifer reached over to caress his earlobe. "Oh, a tame little Hell-born thing like you? They wouldn't even know what you were."

"He is gray," Jack pointed out.

The Devil snorted. "Mm, nothing in that book they like so much about being gray."

A look of melancholy came over Jack's face and Eodus slid his hand across the table to cover the young man's.

"It's a stupid book," Lucifer told Jack, insistent and reassuring.

The human shrugged half-heartedly. "Some parts aren't so bad, you know. Being good to your neighbors and taking care of the poor. When times got lean there was usually some nice church folk in town that would hand over a couple cents when we went begging."

Lucifer seemed ready to argue, but he kept his mouth shut.

No one spoke.

Ira took the bottle of wine and topped off Jack's glass. He didn't look like a man who needed a drink, he looked like a kid who needed his mother. "You work at Siobhan's, don't you?" he asked, even though he knew the answer.

Jack nodded, then straightened up. "Yes. I do."

"I don't think I ever saw you there."

"Trapeze always goes last," Jack told him.

"I've only been a few times."

Eodus said, "He's a wonder to see, really, you should go."

"I keep telling him he'll like it. Who wouldn't beg for a glimpse of Jack in those stockings?" Lucifer teased.

The young man blushed and took a sip of his wine, not looking up at the Devil. When he'd put his glass back, he turned his eyes to Ira and asked, "What about you? What do you do for work?"

The question took him by surprise. He didn't think anyone had ever asked that and it made him realize how few people outside of the realm of pleasure work made up his social circle. "I work up on Queen Street."

"Oh, is that...? I don't know where that is," Jack admitted.

"It's in the Ninth, it's where all the brothels are."

"All the nice brothels," Lucifer corrected.

Jack's eyes had gotten wide. "Oh."

"Mostly these days I do the books for Marius."

"You..." Jack looked to Eodus, his face crawling with concern and unasked questions. "I'm sorry, I didn't know," he told Ira, "I wouldn't have asked."

Lucifer began to speak, but Ira said, "No, it's not like it is on Earth, I don't think. It's not, uh, shameful? Like it is with humans."

The stigma in Hell came not from the act of whoring but from the class of whore to which one belonged. Maybe it was like that on Earth, too, Ira couldn't tell from books or from his brief stay above.

"But weren't you...I mean, your parents, they..." Jack fumbled, then shook his head, and firmly stated, "You know, it isn't my business."

Ira instantly understood where Jack had misjudged his life. "No, Mistress ran a brothel, to be sure, but she didn't put me to work until I was old enough."

Lucifer huffed at that declaration, which he always did. "Fifteen-year-olds should be playing with themselves and with each other, not being paid to suck off grown men," he had grumbled once when Ira had pressed him as to why.

Now, the Devil maintained, "Youth is for learning. For those spirited indiscretions. Not for working."

Ira didn't know about that. He'd done plenty of learning in his youth. He took a swallow of wine and went for one last scoop of food, scraping up what remained at the bottom of the bowl of brussels sprouts.

"I really would like to play bridge, no one else wants to play," Jack said. "I guess bridge clubs are a little tame compared to what everyone else gets up to at night around here."

"I'd love to play bridge with you, Jack, darling," Lucifer

assured, giving Ira a nudge. "What about you?"

"Maybe, yeah, if you want. You'll have to show me how to play."

Jack beamed, showing those dimples again. Ira, until that moment, had never realized how appealing he found dimples.

The meal wrapped up and Lucifer tugged on a waiter's sleeve, saying, "You can have the bill sent up to the palace, Imogen will take care of it."

When they parted ways, Eodus threw his arms around Ira again.

Ira stepped back almost immediately. Judging by the look on Eodus' face, he thought knocking him on the jaw would have had less effect on his brother. He could let perfect strangers ejaculate inside of him, but he couldn't let his brother hug him.

"I..." Ira began.

"Well..." Eodus trailed off.

Ira held out his hand and Eodus shook it with both of his, holding on for a long time until they were no longer shaking hands but holding them. Ira had, without thinking, clamped his other hand on top of his brother's.

"It was good to see you."

Ira took his hands back. "Sure."

"I hope it won't be the last time."

Unable to shake the feeling that Lucifer would drag him along just so he could play whatever card game Jack had invited them to play, he conceded, "Probably won't be."

Eodus touched him one last time before they parted, a pat on Ira's upper arm.

On the walk home, Ira kept his arms crossed across his chest and his hands sandwiched in his armpits. "What about that book?" he asked.

Lucifer glanced over at him. "What book? Do I owe you one?"

"No. I mean that Earth book, the uh. The good one?"

The Devil squinted at him, then realization dawned on his face. "Do you mean the Bible?"

"That's the one! Can't believe I forgot the name. Shit, they talk about all that stuff enough in the books you bring me. The Lord Almighty and all that shit." Ira couldn't help but roll his eyes.

Things that lived in Hell, apart from some of the Fallen, had little respect for angels or God.

"There is a bit of a preoccupation," Lucifer agreed. "What's your question?”

“Why’d it make Jack look so sad?”

“Ah, well, that is a question whose answer requires a lot more reading.”

“Give me the short version,” Ira said.

“That book has got rules. Lots of rules.”

Ira knew about rules, knew about following them and what happened if he didn’t. He uncrossed his arms and took Lucifer by the hand.

“Lovely, armpit hands, that’s what I wanted,” the Devil noted.

Not particularly wanting to know, Ira asked, “Are they harsh rules?”

“The thing about those rules is that people can get enthusiastic about enforcing them, even when it’s not their business, even when breaking them doesn’t do anyone any harm.”

“Mm.”

“Even when they’re rules written by men and not by God.”

“And, what, acrobats or circuses or playing bridge is against those rules?” Ira guessed because he knew nothing else about Jack Callahan.

“No,” Lucifer answered cagily.

“What then?”

“I don’t want to tell you.”

Ira tugged on his hand. “You tell me everything, all kinds of secrets, you won’t tell me about a book I can go get from the library?”

“There aren’t any Bibles in my library.”

“Lu, come on!” Ira whined.

The Devil sighed. “You remember that party Junius took you to? The one on the rooftop.”

He nodded.

“Secret, right? Clandestine in a way that sort of made you wonder what exactly was going to be happening there.”

“Sure.”

“And what did happen?” Satan asked.

“Drinking. I threw up on that fellow’s shoes.”

“They were all men who were inclined towards other men in some way, were they not?”

“Seemed like it, sure,” Ira said, not able to see where this conversation was headed.

“The way in which many on Earth interpret statements from

that book makes it so that such things are illegal."

"What things?"

"Being inclined towards men."

"Then how does anyone have babies!" Ira protested. "And a lot of them are having babies, fucking *millions* of humans are swarming around up there."

Lucifer sighed, then cracked a smile. "No, love, not...It's about men who are inclined towards men."

Ira couldn't help wrinkling his nose. "That's a sort of specific thing to make a rule about. Are you making fun?"

"No."

"Shit, Lu, don't ever bring me back, then, if that's what passes for a rule up there."

The Charter laid out a dozen or so basic and sweeping rules that allowed for interpretation, a booming lawyer population, and fascinating court cases. There wasn't a rule in Hell saying who a person could bed apart from the first Edict which read: *No creature in Hell will couple with any other creature who has not yet matured.*

Ira had heard that the Edicts had been created specifically for that cause, that it had been the first and only edict for centuries until the walls had been built and the Devil and his followers had started to put down roots.

He'd heard that the first Edict had been made after the first babe had been born in Hell. The other creatures had all crowded around it, the story went, and the Devil had been one of the gawkers. One of the Hell-made demons had been too curious.

The stories ended there. Curious or forward or handsy, no one knew, because it had happened so long ago.

"I asked what now." Lucifer's voice caught Ira's attention, louder than usual.

"Oh, sorry, I was thinking. I don't know. I thought it was your day off. We already fucked and we just ate so I don't think that's a good idea on a full stomach." He leaned against Lucifer and gave his belly a pat. "You might as well have a baby in there."

"I think I'd be a worse mother than I am a father."

"I don't know, isn't there something about instinct that kicks in?" Ira asked, then wished he hadn't.

Not with Felix so far away and not the way things stood between Lucifer and his other children, especially Elisa.

"I don't think I'd be a good father either," Ira confessed. "Babies, they...they're so *loud* and squirmy and I'm always just afraid

I'll do something wrong." He couldn't stop rambling. "Not that it'll be an issue, you know, I've got that tattoo, so even if you were a woman—"

"Sometimes I'm a woman," Lucifer murmured.

Ira put his arms around the Devil's waist and pulled him closer, not sure what to make of that. Sometimes Lucifer said things that didn't make sense to Ira; he wasn't sure if it was because the Devil understood something Ira didn't or if it was because he just wasn't making sense.

They walked along, hip-to-hip, through the Eighth and back up to the Ninth, with no specific destination in mind.

Their walk took them back to the palace and ended with them in the Devil's study. Ira settled onto the chaise longue after he'd plucked a book from one of the shelves.

The Devil stood in the middle of the room, looking around.

"Do you want to come sit? I can make room," Ira offered.

"Uh."

"Lu, you're just standing there, it's making me nervous."

"I'm just thinking," Lucifer mumbled.

"About what?"

"Do you want this room, too?"

Ira assured, "You don't have to give me anything."

"I want to."

"You already gave me the whole apartment. And the bathroom. Which, believe me, I will come up here just to use," Ira said. "Whether you're home or not."

Lucifer smiled.

"You look tired."

"I feel, uh, sort of...gone."

Before Ira could ask what that meant, before he could find a ribbon or scrap of paper to mark his page, Lucifer had crumpled to the floor, his head smacking against the carpet with a sickening thump.

IRA RUSHED over and knelt beside him. He turned him on to his back; he ran his hands over his face, down his neck, and let them rest on the Devil's chest.

"Lu."

He hadn't seen him faint in a while and had to remind himself that no harm really ever came of it, other than a bump or a scrape. One time he had knocked out a tooth and even that they'd been able to put back in.

"Darling, come on, now," he whispered.

He splayed his hands over the Devil's heart and felt the usual steady beat, though maybe the cadence was a little off.

There was nothing to worry about. The Devil always woke up. Always. And he was never out for more than a few minutes.

After an achingly long time, which hadn't more than four minutes according to the clock but had felt like hours to Ira, Lucifer stirred.

Ira let out a breath and pressed his forehead against the Devil's. "Oh. Love. Scared me."

"Mm." Lucifer raised one hand and his fingertips barely grazed Ira's cheek before his arm flopped back down to the ground. He let out a groan.

"I'll bring you to bed."

The barest movement of his head indicated that Devil

protested the proposal.

"Yes, love, I can carry you, you're nothing but skin and bones anyway."

"No. Thrup," the Devil threatened.

Ira waited, having learned the hard way not to take those promises lightly. He didn't relish the idea of all those mushrooms barfed up onto his trousers.

Several more minutes went by until Satan tried to sit up. He did no more than tip his head forward, but Ira took the effort as consent to be moved.

Ira gathered the Devil into his arms and made it to the bedroom without dropping him.

Marlow made a mad dash for the bed, galloping over and catapulting up on to it before Ira had even managed to pull the covers down.

He did his best to avoid depositing the Devil directly on top of the cat, but she made it almost impossible. He pushed her out of the way and got a swat across the back of his hand for his trouble. As soon as he'd lain the Devil down, she was right there, burrowed into the crook of his arm.

"How are you feeling?"

Lucifer shook his head minimally.

Ira sat on the bed and took one of the Devil's hand into his own, unable to stop his eyes from finding the scar that ran across the meat of his palm. The mark still held some of the greenish-black discoloration that had resulted from a cut with a poisoned blade.

Angels always came to Hell with poison on their blades, afraid they wouldn't make it back to Heaven without it.

It hadn't killed the Devil and it wouldn't. He couldn't die, at least not in the permanent sense, but it had done him some damage.

"Annoying, really," was the phrase Lucifer used to brush aside the matter, or sometimes he would call it, "Inconvenient, certainly."

"Should I get Imogen?" Ira asked.

Lucifer gave a small shake of his head.

"What, then?"

Satan tugged on Ira's hand, his pull as light as a breeze.

Ira settled beside him on the bed, to Marlow's displeasure.

Within minutes, Lucifer had drifted off to sleep, his eyes fluttering behind the lids, his breathing calm and even. Ira couldn't help but place his hand over his chest, making sure he could feel his heartbeat.

Marlow glowered at him, making a low growl in the back of her throat, her ears laid back.

"I'll put you out," he warned her.

She stopped growling and he'd thought he'd gotten through to her, but she hissed and swiped at his face.

He grabbed her by the scruff and tossed her into the hallway, not presently inclined to be nice.

She dashed for the door and he had to slam it so she wouldn't get back in.

When he returned to the bed, he found a smirk on the Devil's face.

"*Hates* you," Lucifer accused.

"Shut up. Go back to sleep."

Ira went to lie back down, not tired, but not wanting to leave him alone either.

Outside the bedroom door, the cat yowled. Ira knew she would be sticking her paws through the gap under the door.

A long while passed without either of them falling asleep. Lucifer slid his fingers through Ira's curls, then let his hand rest heavily against the side of Ira's head.

"Can't sleep," he admitted.

"Imogen can make you something to help."

He shook his head. "Your brother."

"What about him?" Ira asked, not bristling but definitely confused.

"You tell me."

"Oh."

A single finger poked into Ira's scalp, a prodding reminder to share his thoughts when he'd been quiet for too long.

"I don't know, Luci, I don't. He...I. I imagined him having this life, with two parents and a warm bed and plenty to eat. I didn't think he'd be there telling me that our father had taken off or anything like that. But I guess trading a child for food probably means you aren't such a good parent."

"Mhm."

"Just goes to show," Ira said.

"Show what?"

"The grass is never greener."

Lucifer hummed a wordless agreement.

"And besides, I wouldn't want to end up working in the Third.

Or any of the precincts, really. I don't think I'm cut out for soul work."

"Maybe not."

Ira scowled. "Ugh, go to sleep. I ran out of things to say!"

Lucifer smiled. He knotted his fingers loosely in Ira's curls and put a smidge of pressure on the back of Ira's head.

Knowing what he wanted, Ira scooted closer and pressed his lips to Satan's forehead. He stole a kiss, too, for good measure, and thought of all the cozy, warm mornings they'd shared over the year.

"I never thought I'd like anyone as much as I like you," Ira told him.

"Oh?"

"Sure, I mean, I had all these clients, you know, I'd been with lots of people. I'd even had that fling with Uri—which was fun, but that's all it was. But I'd never...you know, I'd never *liked* anyone. There's the feeling you get when you want to fuck someone, you know the one, almost like a stomachache."

Lucifer nodded.

"But it was never anything else. I'd started to think that maybe I just wasn't meant for that. Lots of people aren't. Lots of people never find someone they really want to be with."

Most relationships in the city came together out of convenience or necessity. A lot of people kept their relationships open and considered them semi-permanent, at best. Nearly all marriages were performed for political or financial gain, or as a way for rutabaga farmers to get a healthy start on the next generation.

Ira hadn't ever seen himself practically involved in anything more than something casual and even then, he had doubted that he would have ever come across a person he could love.

"I wanted to, though, and Mistress always said it was because she let me read too much. Too much of that *human garbage*, that's what she always called it, even when I told her that Queen isn't human."

Lucifer shook his head. "No."

"No what, Lu?"

"It isn't human. The concept."

"No?" Ira asked.

"It's divine."

"You mean love."

The Devil nodded. "That's why I left it out." He closed his eyes, but opened them and continued after a few seconds, "When I started making things down here. I left it out, that bit that craves love."

"But...?" Ira prompted, thinking of Lucifer alone among a horde of demons that couldn't love.

"But it happened anyway."

"How?" Ira knew he shouldn't have asked; he shouldn't make the Devil tax himself.

"Beda. She was one of the Fallen, among the second. And there was a woman. Hell-born. Rithys." Lucifer paused. "And, sometimes, if you give someone enough love, well, they learn to give it back."

"That sounds like a lot of giving."

"Children."

"Hm?"

"It's what we do to children. Have you ever..." Lucifer stopped to catch his breath. "How children start? Squalling little beasts."

About a thousand questions swirled around in Ira's mind, all of them ephemeral and half-formed. Maybe another day he would try to put all his thoughts together and press for answers about the history of Hell, of how things had been outside the legends.

Disturbingly enough, questions about the future, *their* future, had bounced around in Ira's head lately, too. He didn't like it. Idly contemplating a relationship had been one thing but knowing what to do with it was turning out to be entirely different.

"Not how I imagined today," Lucifer mumbled.

He'd wanted a day off and gotten it; he must have done a lot of rearranging and the rest would be spent recovering bed.

"I'll be here tomorrow, too," Ira reminded.

"Work," the Devil reminded. "And lying around with me." He yawned. "Can't be any fun."

"I do come back from work, you know, at a pretty reasonable hour now that I'm not waiting around for clients. Go to sleep."

He thought the Devil would protest, but he nodded his head and closed his eyes. When his breathing had evened out, Ira went back to the study to get the book he'd started, and then down to see Imogen.

He rapped on the doorframe of her open door to gain her attention.

"Yes?" she asked without looking up from the paper in front of her.

"He's fainted again."

She started to stand.

"No, no, he's in bed now. I got him all settled in."

She sat back in her chair, pressing her hand to her eyes, then pinched the bridge of her nose. "Thank you for telling me."

"Imogen?"

She took her hand away and looked up.

"He's okay, isn't he?"

"He can't die."

Ira shook his head. "That's not what I asked."

With a sigh, she leaned back in her chair. She folded her hands across her ribs, resting them just below her breasts. She looked at Ira for a long time, her flint gray eyes fixed on his face.

He shifted under her gaze.

"You love him."

He nodded.

"So I know you wouldn't tell anyone about any of this."

"The fainting? No, I wouldn't," he promised.

"Or anything else. Not a single word."

"Of course not," he assured the vampire.

She seemed to accept his answer. "I'm worried about him but more than that I worry about what those other monsters might do. They're a rowdy lot. All he needs is time to recover, I think. A bit of peace, a decade where no one guts or poisons or chokes the life out of him. But what do they see?"

Ira knew where she was headed. "I know there's always that rough bunch but, you know, the rest of us..."

"What?" she prompted.

He didn't know how to explain the mixture of fear and respect most citizens had for the Devil. "We're in awe, I think. Most of us wouldn't want to cross him but...Demic brags that it's his shop the Devil visits and Georg is always fawning over him, saying how handsome he is." He shrugged, thinking of how Selene always thought the Devil was doing something bad to him, how Tycho had called the Devil a milksop. "There's people who have got their grievances but...I mean, you can't please everyone."

She nodded.

He scuffed his foot against the carpet.

She assured him, "No, it's important to know."

"But you think he's going to be okay."

"If he can rest," she confirmed.

"And if he can't?" Ira didn't foresee a restful future.

"Then he'll stay this way. Maybe. I don't know."

Imogen always seemed to know what was going on and to hear her admit that she didn't worried Ira.

She gestured for him to sit in the chair in front of her desk. He did so, uncomfortably reminded of the times when he had been called into Mistress's office.

"I don't like coups, attempted or otherwise," Imogen told him. "It's a mess if they fail and it's a trying time for palace staff if they succeed."

Ira couldn't imagine that rebellious demons were gentle captors, especially not to the staff of the monarch against whom they had rebelled.

"I'm not trying to frighten you…"

He raised his eyebrows when she didn't finish. "Might as well give it your best shot."

"It's not a secret that he's fond of you. Less so after last night. If they're looking to rub salt in his wounds after a successful revolt…" She shrugged. "You would be a tempting start."

He tried to grimace like he was shocked, but her statement didn't surprise him. "I'd like it better if things didn't come to that."

"Makes two of us, doesn't it?"

"So what do we do?"

"Help."

"How?" he asked.

A grin bloomed on Imogen's face, a concerning vampire smile that would have terrified Ira if she'd ever come in as a client, or if he'd strayed into a back alley to find her smiling like that. "I'm his butler, everything I do helps."

"And what about me?"

"You're his companion, aren't you?"

He nodded.

"So you help, too, by virtue of what you are." She straightened up in her seat and leaned towards Ira, resting her elbows on her desk. "But you do have the power to be incredibly *unhelpful*."

He swallowed. "I'll do my best."

"I hope so."

He nodded, then stood. "Anyway. I'm going to go check on him."

"I'll send Oris up in a little. Make sure he eats."

Ira hurried back upstairs and found Lucifer still sleeping soundly.

IRA ARRIVED at work early, which he always did, so maybe he wasn't early anymore, maybe it was his new version of 'on time'.

Marius grinned at him when he walked in.

"What?"

He grinned wider.

"Marius."

"Nothing, sorry, glad to see you is all."

Ira wrinkled his nose and headed to the back room. He became aware that Marius had followed him. Before Ira could look back and ask what he wanted, he saw the painting hung behind the desk.

"You didn't," Ira breathed.

"No, *I* didn't, of course not, Ira," Marius said. "Do you *always* look that sad when—"

"Get rid of it."

"It was a gift from our Prince! How could I!" The pander hadn't stopped grinning. He put an arm around Ira's shoulders. "And you look lovely, really. I can see why Lucifer likes you so much."

Marius pulled him closer and Ira, who had never worried about Marius before, started to worry.

"Don't get flustered, Ira, you're not my type," the Fallen

assured. "Generally not inclined towards the male form...in any of its variations! And I did a lot of trying to make sure...though there was that one fellow in Budapest..."

Marius took his arm back and headed towards the door. He paused and glanced back. "You're bound to get a lot coming in today with how public you two were last night."

"I don't want to see any of them."

"None?" Marius raised his eyebrows.

"I'm not taking clients. For a while."

"At all?"

"At all," Ira confirmed.

Marius smiled again.

"He didn't make me," Ira felt the need to say.

"I didn't imagine he'd make you do a thing. He is...no. He isn't. But he was. And he might be again. With some of us." Marius had gotten that same far away, remembering things look in his eyes that Lucifer did sometimes and walked away without explaining or elaborating.

Ira settled into his desk and pulled out his current ledger. He kept glancing back over his shoulder, though, unsettled by the portrait behind him.

He went out for lunch with Selene and she demanded to know all the details of what had happened at the art gallery. He handed them over sparingly, playing up what he knew she wanted to hear and keeping the more personal tidbits to himself.

"I guess it isn't all bad, then," she told him.

"What isn't?"

"Being his pet. All new clothes? How many suits was it?"

"I'm..." He sighed.

"What?" she asked, her head tilted to the side.

"I'm not his pet."

She made a face, a face that said she thought he was simple and being used. She always thought he was being used. "Hon, we do what we have to do to get by." She put a reassuring hand on his, her soft, warm fingers wrapping around his.

"I'm in love with him."

Her mouth formed into a perfect O and her eyes went wide. Her hands flew up to cradle her cheeks.

"He's not my client, he hasn't been for a long time. He stays at my place and I stay at his and he cooks me dinner sometimes."

She shook her head and crossed her arms knowingly. "Ira, rich men, they're—"

"No." He hadn't meant to cut her off, but the word had jumped from his mouth without his consent. He couldn't bear the look of pity on her face. "I didn't tell you because I want advice. I told you because I want you to stop thinking that he's doing something bad to me. He isn't."

"Would you tell me if he was?"

He nodded.

She gave his hand another reassuring squeeze. "Make sure you do."

They didn't speak of Lucifer for the rest of their meal.

Back at the brothel, they found Astrid waiting outside, her sketchbook and pencils clutched to her chest.

Selene raised her eyebrows and gave Ira a knowing look, then went inside, leaving Ira on his own.

Astrid rushed over to him and took one of his hands in her own. "Ira."

"Oh. Hello."

"Can we talk?"

He nodded. "I think that would be best."

She followed him inside, still holding his hand. He almost brought her to the back room but thought better of it when he recalled its newest decoration. He led her to one of the rooms upstairs but left the door open.

She closed it anyway.

He sat on the bed and she sat beside him, putting her hand on his thigh.

He pulled back, turned to face her, and crossed his legs Indian-style. "It's about us," he began.

"At the gallery, I didn't mean...he didn't do anything to you, did he?"

He shook his head.

"You looked so scared."

"No, it's not like that. About us, Astrid—"

"We could—"

"I'm not taking clients anymore," he snapped, unable to keep it in any longer.

She stared.

"It's just us, now. Him and me. And nobody else."

She looked at him like he'd ripped the heart out of a child in front of her. "Ira, you don't have to do this."

"I *want* to do this. He's good to me."

She shook her head. "What about us?"

Tears had welled up in her eyes, he could see them glittering in her blue, ingénue eyes, threatening to streak down her pale pink cheeks at the sound a harsh word. He didn't have the heart to say, "There is no us," so he told her, "We can be friends."

She clutched her art supplies closer to her chest.

He gave her a smile, his nicest one, and offered, "You can still draw me if you want. For free, even."

"He'll let you?" she asked, her voice low and conspiratorial.

He nodded. "He doesn't *let* me do anything," he scoffed, then felt the need to explain, "I mean, I do what I want, I don't need his permission. Besides, he *liked* your paintings."

"He wasn't angry?"

Ira shook his head. "No."

"I can really keep drawing you?"

He nodded. "Not today, though, but...you're in one of the university residences, right? I'll send word when I'm free."

As she reached for his hand, she grinned. "You're too good, Ira, for all of this. Someday you won't have to anymore."

"I..." He sighed and ran a hand through his hair; he regretted it right away and wondered how badly he'd upset his curls.

Astrid combed her fingers through his hair, gentle and loving, and he wished she would stop touching him. "All fixed," she told him, her eyes fixed on his. Her fingers traced along his jaw and she cradled his face.

He stood up. "I have work to finish."

She blinked.

"I do the books."

"Oh."

He nodded and made for the door. "But I will send you a message, I promise. Or you can write to me here if you want. Marius won't mind."

"Can I visit?"

"Uhhh."

"I'll be quiet."

"Maybe." He didn't think Marius would care as long as he got his work done, but he didn't want her hanging around the back room all the time.

He opened the door and held it for her. As they walked back downstairs, he told her, "Georg is usually looking for work—"

"No." She sounded revolted. "I don't want him."

"Oh. He's a nice lad, just a little...boyish, I guess. Some people go for that."

"He's a slut."

Ira dug his teeth into his tongue.

"Sometimes I think he *likes* being a whore."

Georg did like being a whore, he liked it a lot. He liked it so much he wore the word like a badge of honor. He'd come across the trade as a natural extension of his inborn passions, which was to say, Georg liked to fuck and he'd figured he might as well get paid to do it.

"I'll see you," Ira mumbled, hurrying away and towards the backroom, where he could take some solace in the simplicity of arithmetic.

He scowled at the painting and thought about getting a sheet or a curtain to hang over it.

Seeing Astrid had soured his mood and he wished he hadn't offered to let her draw him again. There was something about her face, heart-shaped and delicate, and her youth that tugged at his heartstrings when he saw her.

Before it had even started to grow dark, he told Marius he was going home and got no resistance. They hadn't agreed on any formal hours, but Marius seemed to trust him, though that didn't stop Ira from always asking if he could leave for lunch or go home for the night.

At the palace, Imogen tasked him with getting the Devil to eat.

He made a tray in the kitchen, bread and soup, and brought it up to Lucifer's bedroom.

He found the Devil lying on his side, moving too much to really be asleep. "Stop pretending."

"I'm not *pretending*," Lucifer said, "I'm *trying*."

"Imogen says you have to eat."

"I'm not hungry."

Ira blew a raspberry, having no argument as to why he should eat if he wasn't hungry. He came over to stand beside the bed. "Sit up."

Satan propped himself up on some pillows.

Ira settled the tray on the Devil's legs and sat on the edge of the bed. "You've got to eat something."

"I don't *have*—"

"I'll make a deal with you..."

Something sinister flashed across the Devil's face and his mouth started to split into that awful grin. "You don't want to make deals with me," he rasped, his tongue flicking out to wet his lips.

Ira hadn't given the phrase much thought but wished he'd chosen his words more carefully. "Eat something."

Without sounding like himself and with those horrible eyes fixed on Ira's face, the Devil asked, leaning towards Ira, "What's in it for me?"

Greed had twisted up his features. Ira worried that he'd stirred something in Lucifer that he shouldn't have.

Unable to make his voice strong or loud, Ira whispered, "What do you want?"

Lucifer's face softened and he sounded more like himself when he proposed, "A kiss."

Ira nodded. "Fine. But eat first."

Satan ripped a piece from the bread and dipped it into the soup. He did this with about half the loaf, then moved the tray aside and wrapped his spidery long fingers around Ira's arm, leaning in close.

His lips barely touched Ira's when he took the kiss he was owed. Ira knew he would think twice before he uttered such a phrase around the Devil again.

Neither of them spoke as Ira ate his half of the bread and soup. The Devil barely looked at him.

It wasn't until after Ira had returned the tray to the kitchen and come back upstairs that the Devil said, "Normally I'm better about these things."

"I." Ira wanted to say it was fine, but it had been unsettling. "You just need your strength back."

Lucifer nodded. "Do you think..."

"What?"

"How was your day?" Lucifer asked.

"Uneventful, mostly."

"Tell me about that mostly part."

Ira approached the bed, at first unsure, but there was no trace of that part of the Devil anymore. He sat next to him, then scooted closer and rested his head against Lucifer's shoulder.

"What?"

Ira shrugged.

Lucifer gathered him up into his arms and pulled him on to his lap, stronger than Ira had expected considering that he'd spent the day in bed. Satan gave Ira a tight squeeze and kissed his temple. "What?" he asked again.

"Astrid came by is all."

"And," the Devil prompted.

"And I told her I wasn't taking any more clients."

"How'd she take that?"

Ira sighed. "I ended up telling her I'd still let her draw me."

"You know you don't have to do that."

"I know. It's, well, she's harmless, really," Ira assured. "She just...I bet she's lonely, is all, I bet she'll forget all about me soon enough. You know how it is to be young. Things flare up and die down."

"I was never young like you were young. I was always...uh. My body never had that disequilibrium of maturing. I had to adjust to being corporeal but once I had, it was fairly stable."

"So then trust me for once," Ira proposed.

"I always trust you."

"I meant let me be right this time."

"It's not about letting you be right—"

"Shhh, stop. She's harmless. It's just a few drawings," Ira told him. "And!" He pulled out of his grip. "Speaking of drawings."

Lucifer grinned. "Where'd Marius put it?"

"In the back room."

"Perfect." The Devil's grin widened.

"I hate it."

"How could you hate such a magnificent work of art? I'll buy you one to hang in your bathroom if you want."

"No."

"What if we commissioned one of me? You can put it in your apartment so you won't have to miss me when I'm busy," Lucifer teased.

"Mm, what could paint and canvas do for me when I'm missing something made of flesh?" Ira asked. He nestled into Lucifer's lap.

"More than this flesh could do for you right now, I'm sure."

Ira, amused by the idea of trying to get off with a painting, couldn't help but snort. He kissed Lucifer's cheek, then his nose. "I'm perfectly pleased with your flesh at it is."

"Let's agree not to say the word flesh anymore tonight."

"Flesh."

"Ira."

He twisted so his breath would be hot and moist on the Devil's ear and whispered, "Flesh."

"Really, don't be fresh."

"Why, what are you going to do to me?" he teased, giving Lucifer's earlobe a nip. "If that *flesh* of yours is so impotent right now..."

In one smooth movement, Lucifer had leaned forward, flipped Ira onto his back and pinned his wrists to the bed, straddling him before Ira's senses had time to process.

Ira stared up at him, knowing he must have looked particularly cow-eyed. His nerves found an unusual stasis between fear and arousal.

"This is about it if we're being honest," the Devil admitted, his arms shaking slightly. He let go of Ira's wrists and settled back against the pillows.

Propping himself up on his elbows, Ira proposed, "I could use my mouth."

Lucifer gave a small shake of his head. "No, love, thank you, though."

"You sure? I'll be gentle with you, darling, like it's your first time," he cooed, half-joking.

With a snort and a smile, Lucifer shook his head again. "No, but why don't you come help me take a bath? Imogen offered but I thought we might have more fun."

Ira raised an eyebrow. "What sort of fun?"

"Not the amorous kind," Lucifer clarified.

"Mmm, what if I'm feeling a little amorous?" Ira asked, unable to shake the heat that had settled in his belly.

Lucifer sighed and Ira decided to give up the chase. He sat up and put an arm around the Devil's ribs, helping him out of bed.

He didn't think Lucifer needed as much help as Ira gave, but he wanted to be close to him. Instead of the small bathroom, Ira brought him into the larger bathroom, the one that was his.

He hadn't adjusted to the idea yet, that something in the Devil's palace belonged to him. He stripped the Devil of his garments and started to fill the tub, dribbling oil onto the surface.

Lucifer kept his hand braced on Ira's shoulder as he climbed into the bath. "Are you coming in?"

"Impatient," Ira clucked as he stooped to untie his shoes.

Once he'd undressed, he slid into the water, unable to keep his hands from the Devil's skin. He hugged him from behind, his hands sliding from Lucifer's waist to his hips.

"If you're going to feel me up, could you do it with soapy hands?"

"Am I bothering you?"

"I'd hate to disappoint," Lucifer confessed, his voice unusually small.

Ira wrapped his arms around Lucifer's waist and kissed his shoulder. "I want to be close, that's all, I'm not asking for anything else. Hand me the soap, I'll wash your back."

Once Ira had helped him scrub and wash his hair, he wrapped him up in a towel and brought him back to bed.

"Where's Marlow?" Ira asked when the cat didn't immediately skulk out from somewhere.

"She's mad at me."

Ira couldn't check the noise of disgust he made. "She's a *cat*."

"Aye, but dead things never come back right." Lucifer perched on the side of his bed and used his towel to wring the water out of his hair.

"Should have left her dead."

"I can't say you're wrong."

Ira climbed on to the bed and settled behind him, comb in hand; he gathered up the Devil's hair and started to comb it. Once he had it free of knots, he split it into three parts and wove it into a neat braid. He'd gotten good at simple braids over the past year, though he hadn't yet mastered the intricate ones the Devil preferred.

"Ready for bed?"

"I could actually eat," Lucifer said.

Ira gave him a slight push.

"Yes, I know." He pointed to the settee. "Grab my robe, we'll go to the kitchen."

"You're a monster," Ira accused.

Lucifer turned and snagged him by the waist, then kissed his cheek. "A hungry monster." He nibbled at Ira's neck and shoulders using more teeth than strictly necessary. "Better feed me or I'll gobble you up."

Ira was tempted, and tempted badly, to let the Devil keep nibbling. "You'd miss me when I was gone."

"Enormously. Your absence would be a chasm in my life, a gaping new wound that would burst open with the slightest prodding for centuries to come, one that would grow putrid, festering and *hurting—*"

Ira pulled away to get his robe, disturbed by the abrupt change from silly to morbid. "Shit, alright, let's get you fed, then."

When Lucifer grinned, not a wide and terrible one, but a sweet, almost shy one, Ira realized the shift in mood had been accompanied by some self-awareness.

A WEEK went by without word from Astrid and Ira had forgotten, for the most part, that he'd agreed to anything.

He was comfortably settled at his desk after lunch when Marius came by with a note in his hand.

The pander tossed it, and Ira's pay for the week, onto the ledger Ira had open. "Since when do you get mail delivered here?"

Ira opened the letter and skimmed it. "Since I didn't want to give Astrid my address."

"Ah."

He reread the letter more carefully.

"I thought you weren't taking clients."

"I'm not."

"Are you seeing her personally?" Marius ventured.

Ira shook his head. "No."

"Hmm, well, it isn't my place to say anything, but I've got advice if you want it," Marius told him.

Ira looked up and considered the set of his mouth, the crinkle at the corners of his eyes. "What's your advice?"

"Don't. Cut her off and do it yesterday. Clients who like you that much." Marius nodded towards the painting. "Don't take 'let's be friends' very well."

"I felt bad."

"She's a client, Ira. She paid for what she got and she got what she paid for. You don't owe her shit."

Ira shrugged. "She'll get bored soon enough, I bet."

"It's your life," Marius said as he left.

Taking little comfort in those words, Ira read the letter a third time. Finally, he took out a piece of paper and wrote her back, offer to meet up with her tomorrow afternoon for a few hours. He asked if the university had a studio they could use, then scratched it out and wandered out to find Georg.

He spied the younger man with his clothes half-off, as they always were, made eye contact, and called, "Hey," but got ignored.

"*Hey*, Georg, you little shit," he called, loud enough so the whole brothel turned to look at him.

Georg, a scowl firmly etched on his shapely lips, turned towards him. "What?"

"Come here."

He slunk over, his arms crossed over his chest, bare except for the unbuttoned vest. Georg came into work looking like any other respectable university student, usually trousers and some kind of sweater or cardigan, but by the end of his night, he ended up barely dressed or in someone else's clothes altogether. "What?"

"You go to the university, don't you?"

Georg shrugged. "Sometimes."

"Fuck off, you take classes."

"Sure, fine. What do you *want?*" the younger man asked.

"Is there an art studio?"

Georg wrinkled his nose. "Course there is, where would all the art students go otherwise?"

Ira nodded.

"That was it?" Georg asked.

"Yes."

"Haven't you ever *been* to the university?"

Ira hadn't, apart from the art show, which he didn't think really counted. He shook his head.

"Shit." Georg looked him over, his beautiful face twisted up. "I guess it's true."

Ira crossed his arms, hating that look. Georg wasn't that much younger than Ira, a decade or fifteen years at the most. "What's true?" he asked, feeling stupid and small.

"That the Devil's pet *is* just some common whore. I'd heard you used to work at that..." Georg seemed to pause for effect, to pick his words carefully. "*Establishment* run by Lilia Gotes."

"The Trade House was *clean*," Ira protested. Being clean had been important to his mistress.

"I heard you were *owned*."

It had never occurred to Ira that he should have been ashamed of that. It had hurt to know he had been sold and it had been shameful that he hadn't been a good earner for his mistress, but until Georg, with his haughty, beautiful face and his lovely, sneering mouth, it had never embarrassed him that he'd belonged to someone.

"Is it true?" Georg prodded.

"Is it true you earned your first bit sucking your brother's cock?" Ira snapped. "Is it true he used to give you candy to do it, that's how young you were when you started chasing him?"

Right away, Ira felt awful for asking. Before the tears of shock had even welled up in Georg's eyes, Ira knew he'd gone too far.

Georg shoved him, not hard, though Ira wouldn't have held it against him if he'd knocked him across the jaw. "He *didn't*, take it *back*."

"I'm sorry."

Georg gave him another push, his face contorted. People had been paying them some mind before but now they openly stared.

Ira took him by the arm and pulled him into the back room. Making a scene like this didn't do much to boost business and it wouldn't do Georg any good for his clients to see him all ugly and crying.

"I didn't mean it," Ira assured as soon as the door had closed.

Georg had yanked his arm back. "Well, I did, you are just some piece of trash from the Eighth. Your parents didn't even want you, I don't know what our Prince is doing slumming it with *you*," the lad screeched.

Ira couldn't work up the right level of irritation to go with the insults. "I didn't mean it about your brother."

"You don't have any right to talk about him."

"No, I figure I don't."

"He was *never* like that."

Ira nodded. People said a lot of things about what had happened between Georg and his older brother, postulated about why it was such a touchy subject.

Of course, it didn't help that Georg's brother had been bludgeoned to death by a little girl's father a few years ago. The brother had been entrusted to watch over the daughter of a family friend, something he'd done countless times. Whatever the parents had found when they'd come back, they hadn't liked. The parents hadn't elaborated much on what had displeased them so much and obviously, the brother hadn't been around to defend himself.

"I'm sorry, I shouldn't have said anything," Ira offered.

Georg rubbed his eyes. "He wasn't," the lad insisted.

"I believe you."

Ira poured Georg a glass of water and handed him a damp handkerchief. "Go on, fix your face, no one's going to want you looking like that. You've ruined your makeup."

Georg snorted and wiped his face, clearing away the smeared lines of kohl and the color on his lips.

Ira made him take a drink of water, then took the handkerchief and scrubbed at a stubborn smudge on Georg's cheek. "There you go."

Georg sipped the water. "I shouldn't have called you common."

"It's true, I guess."

The younger man let out a sigh.

Ira leaned against his desk, grasping one elbow with the opposite hand. "Rumors are a nasty business, Mistress never liked them."

"She really made you call her that?"

Ira nodded.

Georg rolled his eyes. "I've got lots of rumors about her if you want them."

"No. I try not to dwell."

A little bark of a laugh escaped Georg's lips. "I feel like dwelling is *all* I do."

It didn't feel proper to ask what he dwelled on, so instead, he suggested, "It helps to talk."

Georg wrinkled his nose. "Sure, cause I've got *so* many friends that are dying to hear about how hard *my* life is."

The lad, when he wasn't working, had an almost constant escort of other young demons of various genders. "You've got friends."

"I've got money and people who like to spend it. That's not the same as friends."

Unable to keep a smirk off his face, Ira teased, "Oh, that sounds *really* difficult, having money and an entourage."

Georg stiffened and didn't appear to understand that Ira had meant things good-naturedly. His mouth contorted and he made for the door, but Ira grabbed his wrist before he could go.

"I wasn't trying to be mean."

Georg pulled his arm back. "Fine."

"If you ever want to talk, I'm back here all day."

The lad didn't appear to know what to do with that offer, looking aberrantly innocent for a moment. "Uh. Sure."

He left after that and Ira returned to his letter to Astrid, which he amended to say that they would meet at the studio at the university, telling her any time the following day would work for him.

He snagged a runner and sent it to her. Before the end of the day she had written back, giving him the hour of her choosing.

She'd picked a time in the evening and he sighed when he saw it. He'd hoped she'd have chosen an earlier time, so it would be over and done with as soon as possible.

He crumpled the letter up when he realized that he didn't even know how to get to the university on his own, or how to find the art studio from there. He would waste at least an hour wandering around the Ninth trying to find it.

Lucifer came by not too long later and found Ira sitting at the bar, the crumpled note tossed on the counter beside his drink. "You come here often?" the Devil inquired lamely, a silly smile on his face.

"Ugh."

"Sorry, I didn't think it was that bad of a joke."

Ira saw that Georg, as he always did, had fixed his eyes on the Devil and started to scowl before he recalled that he'd made Georg cry today. "Sit," he told Lucifer.

"I also know 'speak' and 'roll over'."

"Just sit down, Lu," Ira snapped.

Lucifer took a seat at the bar. "What's that?" He gestured to the crumpled letter.

"Nothing." He looked away and caught eyes with Georg. He nodded for him to come to the bar without being sure why he wanted it. Maybe because he felt guilty for making him cry or because he found himself wanting to know more about him. Maybe for no other reason than to make Georg come see up close what Ira had, and Georg hadn't been able to get.

Georg approached, staring at Lucifer like he'd spotted something magnificent.

Lucifer raised an eyebrow and leaned in to ask Ira, "Should I order a drink or what?"

"Do whatever you like."

"What's got you so grumpy?" he asked but Ira gave no response.

Georg lingered nervously near them. "Your Highness," he said with a small bow.

"Master Schreiber," Lucifer greeted him. "How are your parents?"

Georg visibly blushed, which took Ira by surprise, considering that he'd never displayed an ounce of shame before. "Fine, thank you."

"Give them my regards."

"I will, sire."

Ira frowned and Lucifer explained, "The Schreiber family runs the records office of the library."

"Oh." Ira had known Georg came from money, just not what type.

"Have for, hmm, ten generations?"

"Eleven," Georg corrected meekly.

"And your parents hope you'll make it twelve soon enough," Lucifer said.

Georg bobbed his head. "When I've finished my studies."

"You're promised to...which of Ulster's daughters?"

It struck Ira as a bizarre conversation to have in a pleasure house.

"Amaranth." Georg had started to rub his thumb over a series of runes that showed plainly against the paleness of his peachy-pink skin.

Popular opinion attributed that skin tone to the mixed ancestry of Georg's family, inherited from when his grandfather had married one of the Devil's earthly great-great-granddaughters. Having a smidge of royal blood was not much of a boon when it came with a lot of humanity.

"Not a bad match," Lucifer appraised.

Georg nodded again.

Ira wondered what had happened to the lad who had been all coquettishness and insinuation earlier in the day, the one who'd flirted with the Devil on so many occasions. Perhaps because he was not propositioning Lucifer as a worker propositioned a client but instead speaking to his monarch as any citizen might.

Ira slugged back the rest of his drink and told Lucifer, "Georg doesn't have any friends."

"Neither do you," Lucifer reminded.

"I have you!"

"Ah, 'friends' is a bit of a weak description for what we are, don't you think? And, you know." Lucifer gestured between Ira and Georg. "This is a pretty odd way to make a friend. Would you like to come out to dinner, Master Schreiber?"

"I'd be honored," Georg answered.

"Ira?"

"I don't care what he does," Ira huffed.

"What has gotten *into* you?" Lucifer demanded, giving Ira a bit of a poke in the ribs.

"Nothing." He stood and headed towards the door, trying to look like he didn't care if either of them followed.

Once outside, though, he stopped to glance back and found them exiting Marius' right behind him. Lucifer had a bemused sort of irritation scrawled across his face and Georg looked worried.

The Devil caught up to him and took him by the hand. "Did you have somewhere particular in mind you wanted to eat?"

"No." He knew he was being short without any reason to do so and felt deeply relieved when Lucifer kept a hold on his hand and lead him to a restaurant.

Once seated, none of them said much. Lucifer rearranged his silverware briefly, then looked to Georg and asked, "How long until you've completed your studies?"

"Ah...it's three more years to complete this program on the histories, but I think, if my parents will let me, I'd like to take another round of courses on manuscript preservation after that."

"Smart."

The lad's eyebrows shot up. "You think so?"

"Sure, we've got a lot of old fucking manuscripts. That would be a part of the College of Magics, though. Are you good with magic?"

"A fair hand," Georg said eagerly. "You really think it's a good idea?"

With half a laugh, Lucifer inquired, "What, do you want it in writing?"

"To my parents, if you can!" Georg quipped, then seemed to realize he'd been too forward.

Unable to keep quiet any longer, Ira was compelled to ask,

"Your parents don't want you to take more classes?"

"No, they want me to make babies."

"Uh." Ira's eyes flicked to the plainly exposed contraception runes tattooed on Georg's forearm. "Well."

Georg rubbed the tattoo. "I'll have to get it scraped off."

Ira grimaced sympathetically. "It isn't my business but, uh, you don't seem thrilled by the idea."

"I like the job I've got now, and I don't think Mother's going to retire anytime soon. I don't know why they're in such a rush...I mean, I do, I'm the last one now that...well. Anyway." He picked up his glass and took a sip of water.

"You can tell them I approve, if you'd like," Lucifer offered, then pushed the basket of bread from the middle of the table towards Georg.

Georg took a piece of bread but didn't eat it. It was odd to see him fully dressed and not in the process of shedding anything. In his trousers and cozy sweater, with shoes that he probably hadn't had to shine himself, he looked like he belonged in a classroom.

The rouge on his lips suggested otherwise, a bold color faded from so much kissing. That made it look like he'd been servicing the teacher for a better grade on an exam.

"So what was that letter?" Lucifer asked, fixing his gaze on Ira.

Ira shrugged. "Nothing." He wanted to leave it at that, but Lucifer had always been too willing to share. If Ira could be privy to his political and personal secrets, then he should share something as meaningless as this. "Just. Figured out when I'm going to be seeing Astrid."

The Devil said nothing. He leaned in and pressed a kiss to the top of Ira's head.

When their drinks came, Ira snatched his glass quicker than he should have. The swallow he took was too big and hurt going down. He sulked through most of the meal, his mood soured. He continued to empty glasses of wine, hoping it would put him a pleasanter state of mind.

All it did was make him nosy.

"What'd your brother do?" he asked after he'd gotten bored of running his fingers around the rim of his empty wine glass, bored of waiting for a refill.

Georg choked on the sip he was taking. He'd had less to drink than Ira and probably wasn't in a sharing mood.

"Ira," Lucifer clucked.

"Rumors have got to be, uh, they've. They start somewhere. Right? Don't they?"

"Not always," the Devil said.

"But who comes house. Home. And thinks well, better just bludgeon this bastard to death?" Ira jabbed the table with his finger. "So what'd he do? And what's his name, anyway?"

Lucifer leaned back in his seat and steepled his fingers. He probably disapproved. He didn't like rudeness and Ira hadn't ever been this drunk around him.

"Hansel," Georg whispered, then cleared his throat and pronounced, "And he didn't do anything. He would never have done anything. To anyone."

"He did *something*." Ira caught eyes with the server and gestured for another drink, which he received and sipped right away.

"Love," Lucifer counseled.

Ira ignored him and kept his gaze trained on Georg, one eyebrow cocked.

"Hansel was...he was an innocent, all the way to his core. I know, it sounds daft, a Hell-born demon being innocent, but he. He fed all the stray cats and he always knew how to make you laugh and he got along well with children. They loved him and he loved them."

"Sounds suspect."

"He *didn't* do anything to them."

"Ira, really," Lucifer sighed.

"What!" Ira protested.

"Hansel didn't have any interest in fucking anything. Ever. Not men or women, not me or...*cats* or children," Georg said, his voice rising in pitch and trembling somewhat.

Remembering how little it had taken to make Georg cry before, Ira knew he had to pull back, but realized it was too late.

"So you'll all say what you want about him, that he fucked me or that he fucked that little girl, but you'll be bastards for it! Go ahead, ask me if he liked being blown or fucking me more, ask me—"

"Georg."

"If I could even walk before he started fondling me—"

"Georg!" Ira shouted.

The lad stopped, his cheeks flushed bright red and streaked with tears.

"Making a spectacle of yourself," Ira mumbled.

"He was sleeping."

Each word clattered like a stone in a bucket.

Georg continued, "We'd gone swimming in the Elde. We were staying at one of the river houses, friends of ours owned this really lovely one and they'd invited us to come visit, and we swam for *hours*. We were exhausted when we got back to the house. Especially Rhea."

Ira hadn't had any idea that Georg had been around for the incident. He would never have thought to bring it up if he'd suspected. His tongue sat in his mouth, heavy and useless, and he couldn't think of anything to say to fix the absolute assholery in which he'd engaged.

"We fell asleep, just for a nap. We knew everyone would be back in time for dinner and thought Rhea'd be too cranky if we kept her up any longer."

"I..."

"Except!"

Ira felt lightheaded; he took a drink of his wine anyway.

"Except we didn't bother getting dressed. What was the point? We'd been swimming together all day, and we were brothers and she was just a little girl. He'd been changing her diapers since she was born."

"I'm really sorry."

"*I* should have known better. I should have *told him* to get her dressed, to put on some trousers. Except Hansel, he was so...he lived in this other world, telling him things like that would have been like telling a cat."

Ira glanced at Lucifer, who had a quiet, rueful look on his face, one that asked 'what did you expect?'. The Devil produced a handkerchief from out of nowhere and handed it over to Georg.

"I think I'd like to go home," the lad whispered.

Lucifer nodded and stood, putting his hand on Georg's back and leading him out of the restaurant.

As they left together, Ira heard the Devil say, "He wasn't a bad fellow at all, your brother. Do you still live at home? I can come in and talk to your parents about the preservation classes if you'd like."

"No, at one of the residence halls."

Ira downed the rest of his wine, threw too much money on the table, and left. He started to walk home and ended up hunched over on all fours in some alley, puking his guts out. He threw up so much and so hard that when he woke the following afternoon, he found that he'd burst a blood vessel in one eye.

"You look like shit," Lucifer observed from the bathroom doorway, thoroughly scaring the life out of Ira.

He whipped around. "Fuck *off*! Fuck! I didn't know you were here!"

"I thought I should check in on you. And I cleaned the sick out of your kitchen sink."

Ira scrubbed his hands over his face. "I'm awful."

Lucifer said nothing, didn't assure him that he wasn't or give any suggestions for how to make it right.

Ira stared at him and tried to think. "I threw up in the sink?"

Lucifer nodded. "Are you hungry?"

He shook his head.

"Tea?"

He nodded.

Lucifer left the doorway and Ira could hear him in the kitchen. He washed up a little bit and changed out of his shirt, which he discovered had a dribble of vomit down the front. He'd have a real bath later, but for now, he needed something to make him feel less like dying.

"I'm a horrible person." He mostly collapsed into his usual seat at the kitchen table.

"What had you drinking like that?"

"I don't know."

Lucifer put a mug of ginger tea in front of him, set a plate of dry toast in the middle of the table, then sat across from him. "If I were you, I do some introspection, since the result doesn't seem to be satisfactory."

"I'll introspect when I can think without it hurting."

The Devil stretched his arm across the table and gave Ira's hand a pat. Ira grabbed onto him before he could take his hand back.

"I'm sorry."

"You gave me no offense," Lucifer answered calmly.

"I must have embarrassed you."

Lucifer squeezed his hand. "No, love, you've got no amends to make with me. Georg, on the other hand."

"I know."

But he couldn't do anything now, not with his stomach hungry, empty, but still threatening to revolt, with his head pounding, with his skin greasy and sticky all at once. He sipped his tea and tried to gather his strength for his time with Astrid.

Once Ira had bathed properly, Lucifer gave him a kiss and said, "I do have things to do today. It will be a late night, too; you should eat without me."

He thought briefly, then reached over to fix a crookedly fastened buttoned on the Devil's shirt. "We'll meet back here, though?"

Lucifer nodded his agreement, took another kiss, and then left.

Ira sipped ginger tea until his stomach had quieted and ate once it had. After that, he headed over to Marius', hoping to catch Georg and give the best apology he could.

He didn't see the youth on the floor. He approached Marius, at his usual station behind the bar. "Is Georg in?"

"With someone right now, I think," the pander told him. "What are you doing here on your day off?"

Ira shrugged. "Thought I'd talk to him."

"You look like you had a rough night."

He shrugged again. "Figure I did."

The Fallen held up a bottle of clear spirits and offered, "Hair of the dog?"

Ira threw up in his mouth a little bit and shook his head as he swallowed it back down. "Water?"

Marius set a glass of water on the bar and Ira took a sip, swishing it around in his mouth the get rid of the throw-up taste.

"What do you want with Georg? Didn't think I'd ever see the two of you heading out to dinner together."

"I owe him an apology."

"Throw up on him?" Marius guessed.

"Something like that."

He nursed his water, waiting for Georg.

When the other demon did appear, he looked radiant, with flushed cheeks and bright eyes, his coppery hair wonderfully tousled. As soon as he saw Ira, that look soured. "What?"

"What I did was shitty and I shouldn't have done it and I apologize."

Georg crossed his arms. "I should have expected as much from a piece of trash like you."

"Georg, really," Ira insisted, forgiving all the bitchiness in his tone, "It was awful of me. I'm sorry."

"Fine." He didn't sound like he meant it.

Ira fidgeted, running his hands through his hair. He nodded towards the bar. "Buy you a drink? You can call me trash as much as you want."

Georg shook his head, his hair swaying slightly. "No, thanks. I'm heading out."

He made for the door and Ira followed him.

Georg looked back. "I said no thanks."

"No, uh, just. I'm leaving, too. I have to go over to the university," Ira explained, scanning the skyline of the city, trying to remember which way he needed to go.

He saw the spires of the library but that didn't help; they weren't near each other, at least, not as far as he knew.

"How...?" he began, almost too embarrassed to look at Georg.

Georg had already started walking away, but he paused in his tracks and raised an eyebrow. "What?"

"Do you know how to get to the university?"

"Yes."

"Do you think you can tell me?"

The younger man heaved a sigh and gestured for Ira to follow him. "If I wasn't already headed that way, I'd let you get lost."

They walked in silence for several streets, until Ira worked up the courage to ask, "Do you have class?"

"No."

"Oh."

Georg must have taken some pity because he explained, "I live there. And I'm meeting up with some friends."

"I thought you didn't have friends."

"I'm meeting up with some bottom feeders."

"If you don't like them—"

"I didn't say I don't like them," he snapped, then looked reticent. "It's just that none of them give two shits about me."

"Uh."

Georg told him, "You look like shit, you know. What happened to your eye?"

"I threw up."

Georg smirked. "Astrid will be disappointed for sure."

Ira hadn't thought of that.

They reached the cobblestone walkway that denoted the end of the street and the start of the university campus. Georg pointed vaguely. "Studios are over there, in the art building."

"Studios?"

He nodded.

Ira took a hesitant step towards the half dozen buildings, unsure as to which one would be his destination.

Georg scoffed and headed off the way he'd tried to send Ira. "So is it a thing for him, for our Prince? Pathetic wretches who need hand-holding?"

"Uh."

"Cause he was proper sweet with me last night, walked me home and everything. I've offered to let him have me however he liked at least three times and hardly any interest, but as soon as the tears started...!" He let out a little chuckle, his tone light.

Ira had forgotten that the Devil had walked Georg home and started to wonder if he should suspect anything.

"And look at you, can't even get around your own precinct!"

"I..."

"What?" Georg asked.

"He didn't...I mean. Lu, he and you?"

"What, worried I'll whisk away your meal ticket?" Georg asked, clearly teasing with a bit of a laugh in his voice.

Ira's guts squirmed worse than they had when he'd woken up and he wondered if he'd throw up again. "I love him."

Georg sobered right away. "You what?"

"I love him."

Pity softened the youth's sharp features. "That's awful, I'm sorry."

"Why's it awful?"

"I mean...well, come on, Ira, he's got a real wife and everything. Hell already has a queen, even if she's absent. You don't think he's...it isn't anything serious, you've got to know that."

"No."

"He takes lovers all the time. None of them last. He's just waiting for her to come back."

"He isn't."

Georg evaluated Ira. "You really think that?"

He nodded.

"You *really* think he'd stay with you if she came back?"

Ira wasn't sure, but he nodded anyway because if Tabitha returned, he wasn't about to let Lucifer go back to her with nothing more than a whimper and some tears. "He loves me, too."

"Sure, but love is..." Georg gestured vaguely. "Love isn't. It doesn't get you anything. It's not binding."

"You've never been in love?"

"Why bother!" Georg scoffed. "Not when I've only got a few years before I have to buckle down and donate as much seed as I can to the cause of making more Schreibers." After a moment, he added, "With my wife. And just my wife."

"Lots of people have open marriages."

"Not Amaranth, apparently. It was a term of our engagement. Once we're married, it's to be us and only us."

"Ah."

"She's had some issues with bastards weaseling into the family fortune, so I figure it's understandable why she wants to avoid those."

"There's lots of ways not to make babies," Ira pointed out.

Georg shrugged. "She's the only one who'd have me after that business with Hansel, so we take what she offers."

"Even if your brother had..." Ira began but bit his tongue.

"Even if he had," Georg prompted, opening the door to a building with more windows than walls.

Ira stepped inside and glanced around the sprawling building, wondering where he'd find Astrid. "Even if he'd fucked you or that girl, you've got money and looks and I assume some skill in bed. You've got prospects for a career, too, haven't you?"

"Maybe you should quit bookkeeping or whoring and start up as a matchmaker for families who've pissed off important people."

"Who was the girl's family anyway?" Ira asked.

"Her grandfather, Roth Yage, manages the—"

"The bank."

"Ira!" called a voice.

Both young men turned towards the source, finding Astrid peeking out from one room at the end of the hall.

"I thought I heard someone come in," she said, grinning as she exited the room. She looked over Georg with a bit of a puss on her face. "Two, I guess."

Ira wanted to be anywhere but here. He shoved his hands in his pockets, recalling her dislike for the other whore. "Georg, uh—"

"Was just *dying* to know about Ira's little artist. Your painting is *all* the rage at the brothel. None of us knew that Ira had such a pretty cock to go with his pretty face," Georg said, slinging an arm around Ira's shoulder. "Who knew it'd be *you?*" he sneered, looking over Astrid with familiar distaste.

Ira blushed.

Georg continued, "We should all be so lucky to have our Prince keeping us *and* an artist flattering us. I do think you were a little kinder to him in that painting than you needed to be."

Astrid looked livid. Ira supposed he deserved the jibe.

"I could model for you, you know, I've got the bone structure for it," Georg offered. "And the body! Not skinny like him!"

Her mouth opened and Ira knew she would decline the offer, though Ira didn't want to be alone with her.

Georg, without waiting to be asked, stepped into the studio, his arm still around Ira. He pulled Ira over to the couch in the middle of the room. He, with soft but insistent hands, pushed Ira onto the couch and slipped onto his lap.

"What about the two of us!" he said with a laugh.

She frowned at the sight.

To Ira, he whispered, "The way she stares at you gives me the creeps."

Ira swallowed.

"Do you want me to stay?" Georg asked, his voice still too low for her to hear.

He gave a small nod.

Georg grinned at Astrid. "What do you think? Should we take our clothes off? You can take your clothes off, too, if you want."

"No," she replied, her voice flat.

"Well, aren't you supposed to pose us?" Georg prompted.

"Get off him."

Georg frowned.

She softened her tone a little. "I want him reclining."

She guided them into the pose she wanted, occasionally using her hands to mold them when they couldn't do it on their own. In the end, she had Ira reclining on the couch and Georg seated on the ground beside him with one of Ira's hand resting languidly on his shoulder.

"*Don't* move."

Georg moved almost immediately, and she came over to rearrange the way his legs were sprawled.

"What about talking?"

She ignored him, retreating to her easel.

Ira could hear the scratch of her pencil on the paper soon enough.

"I sort of wanted to take my clothes off," Georg confided to Ira. "You've really given up the trade?"

"For now."

"Tycho is a bit of a rough customer, I can see that being a turn off for a while," Georg admitted.

"It's not just that...Don't you ever get bored?"

"Not yet."

"Give it another decade or two," Ira said.

Georg raised an eyebrow. "A decade? When you'd start?"

"Fifteen."

The youth seemed to be doing some math in his head.

"I'm older than I look," Ira clarified to help him out.

"Must be." Georg let out a bored sigh. "How'd you meet our Prince?"

"Everyone knows that already."

"Everyone knows that he went a brothel and you were there. That he got all big and scary over it. Then he took you away and you wound up at Marius'."

Ira wanted to shrug but checked the urge. "That's about it."

Georg rolled his eyes. "There's got to be more to it."

"Why?"

"Because he's our Prince! He doesn't dally with common whores at second-rate—"

"Hey."

"But very clean brothels," Georg amended. "He's...He is splendid and wonderful and terrifying. What was he doing with you?"

Ira couldn't blame Georg for his disbelief; he hadn't believed that the Devil had come to trade for him either. "He's the Devil, not some spoiled Hell-born brat from the Ninth. He does what he likes."

"You're moving too much," Astrid said.

Ira didn't think they had been. He glanced at Georg, making eye contact and raising an eyebrow.

"How much time does this take?" Georg asked when they had all be silent for nearly a quarter of an hour.

Astrid sighed. "You can go."

Georg popped right up off the floor and stretched. "Good, cause my ass was starting to go numb." He grabbed Ira by the wrist and tugged him off the couch. "Come on, my friends have been waiting for ages."

"Oh, I..." Astrid looked at Ira, pencil still in hand, those blue eyes wide and innocent.

"You can write to me," Ira called to her as Georg pulled him out the door.

"What do you mean she can write to you?" Georg scoffed.

"I just. I don't know. She was a client..."

"*Was* being the important word there." Georg looked him over with a critical eye. "Anyway, are you coming out?"

Ira didn't know where they were going and he didn't know if he should drink again after last night, but he didn't have any other plans for the evening. "I could."

"But you have to promise not to be a complete bastard this time."

"I will only be a little bit of a bastard."

Georg grinned and Ira could see why he had so many customers. He linked arms with Ira, all transgressions apparently forgiven between the two of them, and brought him across campus to a drinking establishment that Ira guessed to be a popular gathering place for students.

Outside the bar stood at least half a dozen young demons, people Ira recognized as part of Georg's group of friends.

They clamored to know where he had been, some worried, some complaining about the wait.

Georg brushed them off, instead nodding and saying, "This is Ira. We work together. Or did. Do we work together?"

"I still work there," Ira reminded, "I'm not doing the books for free."

Georg nodded his agreement and untangled his arm from Ira's. He ushered the group inside and headed over to the bar.

The group followed, swarming around him and putting in their orders, though none of them offered any coin.

Ira hung back until they'd cleared out, then ordered a vodka soda. "Mostly soda, if you don't mind," he told the bartender.

The bartender didn't seem to mind, mixing the drinking with just a dash of alcohol. "You on his tab?" she asked, nodding towards Georg.

He shook his head, placed a coin on the bar, and waited for his change.

Georg glanced back as Ira pocketed the coins. "You can go on my tab."

"I guess, but what have I been sucking all these cocks for if not to buy my own drinks?"

One of Georg's friends countered, "Wouldn't you suck them so you *don't* have to buy your own drinks?"

Ira couldn't work up a response to what must have felt like a clever question to her, so he sipped his drink.

The group found its way to a table in the back and crowded around with one person electing to sit on a lap instead of a chair.

They fell to discussing a variety of things they didn't like, including their classes and several people.

Georg chimed in occasionally with a snipe or off-color remark.

"I think I hate Professor Rias," a young woman in green said.

"She's not so bad," Georg protested, the first kind thing he'd said since they'd sat down.

"No one cares about poetry anyway, you just need to get the credit and get out," a friend advised.

"What kind of poetry?" Ira asked.

They looked at him. "Uh. General stuff, I guess. Why?"

"I do some reading," he said. "Lu got me this book of poems by—"

"Lou?" the green-clad young woman interrupted.

He nodded.

"Not Loucayn Tillman," she giggled as though the name should mean something hilarious to him.

"Uh. No. Lucifer," Ira corrected, then wondered if he'd said too much when the entire table turned to fix their eyes on him.

He sipped his vodka soda.

Several people asked him questions at the same time, and he

looked to Georg, who rolled his eyes and shrugged. "So he's fucked our Prince, he's a whore, he's fucked a lot of people," Georg said with a lot of disdain, maybe too much; his attempt to discard the topic didn't work.

"You fucked him, or he fucked you?" a young man with bright red curls asked, leaning across the table to catch Ira's answer.

"Well, we were fucking each other," Ira answered, intentionally misunderstanding the question. He had never liked the way some people made judgments based on who was doing the receiving or penetrating, as though they could divine so much from it.

"Kind of hard to fuck by yourself," he added after a moment.

"What's he like?" the girl in green asked.

"I hear he turns into a cat," said a demon of indeterminate gender.

"A cat!" another crowed.

"I've never seen him turn into a cat," Ira told them mildly. If Lucifer could turn into a cat, then Marlow would really give him a run for his money.

"Then you've been to the palace?" the demon with no apparent gender and incredibly green eyes asked.

"Visya, *no one* goes to the palace," someone sneered.

"All the captains go to the palace. The staff go and—"

"Whores fuck in brothels, not in princes' bedrooms," sniggered that same someone, a boy with two horns jutting from his temples.

Visya scowled at the horned boy.

Ira felt the need to say, "I've been to the palace." He made sure it sounded quiet and self-assured instead of like bragging.

"I *doubt*—"

"Doubt it as much as you want," Ira interrupted, unable to stop thinking of how silly the youth's horns looked, spiky and garish, not curled and elegant like others he had seen. "But ask me if I care what you think and you'll probably be disappointed."

The group let out a collective laugh at the horned boy's expense.

Visya put their hand on Ira's to get his attention. "Is it true what they're saying about him?"

"Depends on what you're hearing," Ira replied, knowing that he'd entered dangerous territory a while ago and now threatened to say too much, or say exactly the wrong thing.

"He's sick?" Visya asked, voice laden with concern.

Ira shook his head confidently. "No, that's nonsense, he's not sick."

"I hear he's gone mad," said the girl in green.

He couldn't help but sneer at that. "Look around you. Is this a realm run by a madman? If he were mad don't you think we'd have rivers of blood instead of running water? Don't you think he'd be dining on your gristle instead of steak and mushrooms?"

Visya grinned at his answer. They, or maybe she, Ira couldn't be sure, said, "One last question."

"Fine," he agreed.

"I heard there was a baby in the palace not so long ago."

He shrugged and did his best to feign disinterest, to cover up the quivering in his gut. He wondered how she'd heard that. "Not that *I* ever saw. He's not exactly paternal."

Visya looked disappointed. "Ah, but could you imagine? A new little prince or princess. Wouldn't that be something?"

"No luck if Ira's the one he's fucking," Georg teased.

"Garris had a baby last year and he'd have your guts—" the youth with red curls began.

"Aye, Rogg, he did and Garris can whelp as often as he wants but I know that what Ira's got between his legs *isn't* for birthing babies," Georg shot back.

Ira finished his drink and wondered if he should risk another one, considering that he hadn't eaten much.

Home and dinner called to him and would be a smart choice.

"I should get home."

"One more drink," Georg insisted and when Ira started to hesitate, he said, "On me."

"Fine," Ira agreed and went up to the bar with Georg.

They both ordered and Ira left the requisite number of coins on the counter.

"I said—"

"You can owe me," Ira told him.

Georg could barely look at him and swished the cherry in his drink around by the stem. "Who even says you're invited out with me again?"

Ira had the odd impulse to kiss him, though it wasn't accompanied by any sort of lustful stirrings.

Instead of kissing him, Ira told him, "Your friends are awful."

"They really are."

"So what kind of poetry do you like?"

"Oh. I don't much. But Rias teaches other literature classes."

Ira rolled his eyes, took a sip of his drink, and asked, "So then what kind of books do you like to read?"

"I love those trashy ones you can pick up for a penny—"

In excitement, Ira reached out to grasp his arm and demanded, "Do you read *The Butcher's Wife?*"

Georg put his hand over Ira's. "Yes! What about *Adventures of Lazlo Corbin?*"

"Every issue."

Beaming, Georg confided, "You'd think I was reading the Bible the way my mother screeches about them. Like she thinks being trash is contagious. She would *die* if she ever knew..."

"What?"

Georg shook his head and stepped back.

"What, go on," Ira urged, giving a reassuring smile. "When am I ever going to see your mother?"

"She doesn't know where I work."

Ira raised his eyebrows.

"She thinks the people I see are flings, you know, just a lad sowing his oats before he settles down, I guess. If she knew...or Amaranth! Shit, I'd be dead."

"Georg."

"I know! I know." He looked at the floor. "Fucking is one thing but for the next Master of Records to be taking coin for it, that's something else altogether."

"Is it?" Ira asked.

"It would be just as bad if I was laying bricks or...working in a shop or on a farm. It's the record office or the university or, if you're not in line for any of the important positions, you can elect to work in one of the precincts."

"Oh." Ira wrinkled his nose. "You know, maybe my parents sold me cause I'm too stupid to understand any of this, but there's all these rules I didn't know about and they're hard to keep track of."

Georg smiled a little.

"Oh, fuck, you know what?" Ira asked after a minute.

"What?"

"If your parents are important and all that, I might actually meet them."

"Uh."

"So it's good you told me," Ira pointed out, thinking of his gaff with Molly.

"When would you see them?"

He straightened his back and told Georg, "We are official, Lucifer and me. I'm not a kept man, he's not my client. I might run into you at events."

"I'll have to start going to them."

"We can coordinate."

Georg smiled. "Official, huh? I might have sounded like an ass asking if he was going to leave you for his wife. I'm surprised I didn't hear about it."

"I met all the captains."

"I'll be sure to ask Ulster about it, then, next time he's over for dinner."

Ira finished his drink, set the glass on the bar, and said, "Make sure you tell me everything he has to say."

"I will."

"I really have got to go now," Ira said, even though he had nowhere else to be. He longed for a bit of quiet and an early bedtime. He wanted to fall asleep and wake up with the Devil in his arms.

Without thinking about it as much as he should have, he slipped an arm around Georg and brushed a kiss against his cheek, not sure why he wanted to touch the lad as much as he did. He pulled back and Georg seemed just as nonplussed as Ira.

Ira took his leave, heading towards the spires of the library, then making his way home from there, even though it must have been an incredibly indirect route.

He should have made more of an effort to get to know the precinct but after he'd gotten lost storming out of the bank, the idea made him shudder.

IN A small, neat house in the Eighth, where the streets were narrow and the houses touched, Ira ran his fingers over the spine of a large white cat and tried not to look at his brother.

It had been Lucifer's idea to get in touch with Eodus and set up a night to play cards as they'd discussed. Ira suspected the Devil wanted to do this more because he liked Jack than out of any desire to play cards.

Right now, Lucifer and the acrobat chatted, both of them animated and laughing like old friends. Eodus sulked next to the stove, frowning at the tea kettle. Ira couldn't be sure, but he assumed that his brother worried about the Devil's intentions with Jack. Ira counted the worry as pointless. If Lucifer wanted the acrobat for his own, surely he would have taken him already.

Ira guessed, though he likely wouldn't have shared the thought, that Lucifer liked Jack simply because he was human. Even after more than a year in Hell, the smell of Earth still perfumed the lad's skin and his eyes still held bits of sunlight when he laughed. Humanity had some essential quality to it that Ira hadn't been able to define when he'd been among them.

Maybe it was because their species had been cultivated over millennia by the Almighty, instead of cobbled together by the Devil. Maybe in a million years, or two or five, demons would grow to be more like their counterparts on Earth above.

He scratched behind the cat's ears and wondered if calling demons and humans counterparts would upset Lucifer; he wondered if the first demons made in Hell had been imitations of angels or if Lucifer had wanted to make something entirely different.

"Love?"

"Mm?" Ira glanced over.

"Are you going to play cards or just bother the cat?" Lucifer asked.

"Oh, Pumpkin doesn't mind!" Jack insisted. "I don't think anything bothers her, not even when I roll over on her sometimes. She just sort of...oozes over a little."

Lucifer put his arm around Ira's shoulders, his fingers brushing against the back of his neck, and pulled him in closer. He placed a kiss on his temple. "Do you know how to play bridge?"

"No."

"Come have a seat, we'll go over the rules."

Eodus remained by the tea kettle until it whistled.

Two minutes into an explanation of the game, Ira was reasonably sure he wanted nothing to do with bridge; he soldiered through only because Lucifer seemed so enthused.

"Ira."

"Hm?" He tried to refocus himself.

Lucifer nodded towards Eodus, who was trying to set a mug of tea in front of him, but Ira had propped his elbows on the table, taking up most of the surface where tea could be set.

He sat back in the chair. "Sorry."

He burned his tongue on the tea when he tried to sip it even though he had waited several minutes.

When Jack and Lucifer finished explaining, he assured them he understood, even though he didn't, and partnered with the Devil while they played.

He passed most of his turns because he wasn't sure what he was doing.

"Your turn," Jack reminded.

Ira put down a card and no one told him he was wrong.

"You want a cookie?" Jack offered.

"No, thanks."

"You sure?" Jack held out the plate a little bit, showing an attractive array of butter cookies in delightful shapes.

Ira snagged one and took a nibble.

Jack passed the plate over to Lucifer, who took several, all of them disappearing down his throat in the blink of an eye. Ira wasn't sure he'd even chewed. He grinned when he saw Ira watch him, his black teeth glinting.

When Ira didn't return the smile, the Devil's face sobered. "What?"

Ira shook his head, not knowing how to express the alienness of what he felt. The world around him felt infirm and he didn't want to look at Lucifer any longer. He stood. "I, uh. I'll be back in a second."

He walked out, not daring to stray too far from the house. He wanted something to do with his hands and ended up picking at the skin around his nails.

After a few minutes, Lucifer poked his head out. "Love, are you alright?"

He shrugged.

"Do you want me to go away?"

He shook his head.

Lucifer came to stand beside him and Ira leaned against him. The Devil rested a hand on his shoulder then kissed his hair. "What's wrong?"

"I don't know." It felt like a lie. "I hate seeing him."

"What do you hate about it?"

"It...I feel like." He sighed, frustrated, and wrapped his arms around Lucifer's waist. He buried his face in the Devil's shirt, thankful for the feeling of the worn silk. "I had this book once and...there was a client trying to trade for me, but I was in the middle of a chapter. I asked him to wait and...Mistress didn't like that. She tossed the book in the fire and I had to take the customer anyway. It feels like that. It feels like seeing the corner of the cover poking out from the ashes."

"Oh, love."

"*Don't* feel bad for me."

"I don't pity you, Ira." The Devil stepped back, his hands resting on Ira's shoulders.

Ira looked up at him.

"I admire you."

"For what?" Ira sneered, not able to check his contempt. What had he ever done worthy of admiration?

"Because you're brave and strong and through all of it you've stayed soft-hearted."

"Pathetic is what it is."

"No," Lucifer assured.

"It is. All my life I let people do whatever they want to me, there's nothing admirable about that."

"Ira, dear, I can't make you love yourself, but I do think you're wonderful and I hope someday you'll understand why."

"Because I let you fuck me, too," Ira told him.

Even as he said it, he knew it wasn't true. He hadn't ever tried to start a fight before, but he'd never had anyone with whom he could safely pick a fight. He'd been one of the smallest whores at the Trade House and if he'd given his mistress or customers a hint of lip, he'd have been whipped for sure.

Lucifer didn't take the bait. "Do you want to go home?"

"No."

"Would you like to come in?"

Ira huffed, "Bridge is a stupid game."

"We don't have to play bridge." He ran his fingers down Ira's arm and took his hand. "Come inside, love."

Ira unhappily allowed the Devil to pull him along.

Jack smiled at him, his pretty blue-hazel eyes filled with warmth, no malice or judgment. "We've got a checkerboard if you want," he offered. "I've had about enough bridge for one day."

Ira shrugged.

Jack scooped up the cards and slid the deck back into the box. He put a hand on Eodus' arm and asked, "Can you check the closet?"

"I...I don't know, maybe we should just go," Ira said.

Jack's face fell. "Oh. Well. If you want to go..."

Eodus had paused on his way to the closet, standing uncertainly with his hands dangling near his chest. He started to wring his hands.

Lucifer waited, his face a neutral mask. He leaned against the sofa, examining his nails.

Ira snagged the cards from Jack's hands and tapped them out of the box into his hand. "Beggar-my-neighbor?" It was a game he knew well.

Jack nodded.

Ira gestured for Eodus to come over, started to shuffle, and told his brother, "You can play the winner. Are you amenable to that?"

Eodus nodded.

Ira won against Jack and end up matched against his brother. He started to deal, splitting the deck into two piles, and kept his eyes on his brother's nervous hands. He wanted to do something to quiet his nerves but didn't know what to do. He couldn't figure out why his twin was so anxious in the first place.

"What's got you all worked up?"

Eodus looked up, eyes wide and his lips somewhat parted.

Ira hated looking at him, he hated meeting his eyes and knowing what people saw when they looked at his own face. "Every time I see you, you look like you're about to have a breakdown."

"I worry, is all," Eodus admitted softly.

"Worry about what?"

"Everything." He pulled his cards closer and made them into a neater stack. "Mostly that you'll hate me."

Ira wanted to tell him that he did hate him, but it wouldn't be fair and it wouldn't be true. He wanted to hate his brother; it would be easy to hate him, to fill up that empty space in his life with seething anger and hard resentment. "I don't."

"You should."

Since the delusion of missing out on a quiet and cozy family life had been dispelled, Ira didn't envy his brother. "How do you figure?"

"If I hadn't been born, you wouldn't have been sold."

Ira raised an eyebrow and had to ask again, "How do you figure?"

"You're older. By a few hours."

Not for the first time, Ira wondered how their parents had decided which of them to sell. If they'd had a favorite, if one had shown more promise, if Ira had been an irritating or troublesome child, or if they'd just drawn lots. Even being older by just a few hours, Ira should have been the beneficiary to all his parents' possessions.

"Is there money?"

"What?" Eodus asked.

"Money or property or family heirlooms," he clarified. "Things to be inherited."

"Uh. A few things. Ma gave me some things for the kitchen when she got herself new ones and there's the tub. That was Old Pop's. This was his house, too, but I bought it from him."

Ira didn't know who Old Pop was but figured he had to be a grandparent or something farther back. He didn't figure a bathtub was worth inheriting, not when he had his own apartment with plumbing. Not when he had a bathroom the size of this kitchen, and then some, that was just his in the Devil's palace. "Don't want 'em, anyway, I've got enough of my own stuff."

"Oh."

"Besides, I don't..." Ira struggled to get out what he wanted to say. He placed a card face up in the center of the table, on top of the cards that had already been put there. "I don't think you had it as good as I'd thought."

"Things were fine."

"Things were fine for me, too, except when they weren't. I guess that's how it is for everyone, really."

Eodus ogled at him, then turned his eyes to the cards in the center of the table. As he placed his card, he told Ira, "I wish we could go back."

The only response Ira had was harsh, so he held his tongue.

Ira lost the round and Lucifer switched out with him. While the other two played, Jack tugged on Ira's sleeve and nodded outside. Ira followed him out, thinking he must need help with something.

The youth rubbed the back of his neck. "Uh. About Eodus."

"What about him?"

"It isn't my business to say anything."

"Say it anyway," Ira urged.

"He's really been having a rough time since he found out you were alive."

"Oh." Ira didn't know what Jack could want from him. "I, uh. That's too bad."

"I'm sorry, I'm not...I appreciate it, you coming out to visit and everything," the young man told him. "You didn't have to and I can tell you don't really want to, but thank you."

That Jack thought he'd visited out of some sense of altruism was too much and he tried to dispel it by saying, "It was Lu's idea."

"But you came anyway. It means a lot to him."

Ira shrugged.

"I, uh. Hmm. Growing up, I didn't see much of my family either."

"No?"

"No. They." Jack paused for a long time, his brow creased. "I didn't lose them or anything, we were in the same circus and everything. But when I went to Shanley's tent it was like I became someone else. Except no one told me. I would run up to my sister or my pa and they'd look at me like some kind of stray."

"Mm." Ira searched for something to say but came up with nothing.

"Shanley was the fellow I trained under," Jack clarified.

"Oh."

"When he came for me it was like they all knew something I didn't. Like I'd gotten sick and they didn't know how to tell me I was going to die. I didn't understand why I had to move into his tent or why it was such a bad thing that he'd come to see me. At first, I thought it was because they were afraid I'd get hurt on the tight rope. I told my ma that we were careful, that we had nets and everything so we wouldn't break our necks. She told me it would be better if I did."

"Was it because of the Bible?" Ira guessed.

Jack smiled and even as sad as that little half-smile was, he still looked sweet. Ira wondered if that was what Georg's brother had smiled like because he couldn't imagine a lustful thought ever stirring behind such an innocent face.

"It was. I think. None of them ever told me outright that it was about sodomy, but I figured out that when they said unnatural, that's what they meant. One day I was their son, a few days later I wasn't. I don't know. But anyway, I guess I know what it's like to feel like you missed out on something. That's all I was trying to say. I know it isn't the same."

"I know what you meant."

"It would be good to have a family again." Jack let out a chuckle. "Or just a few friends. There aren't a lot of folks around here that care for me."

"No?" Ira had thought Jack would be sought after, a rare jewel for the Hell-born to gawk at.

"No. I guess if you spend all day punishing humans you don't want to sit down for drinks with one. Not that they're cruel to me! But I'm the human, I'm never Jack anymore."

"What about at Siobhan's?"

"Oh, the girls are lovely, they really are. But they're their own little family and I, you know, I haven't been there that long and they've known each other for decades."

"Lu likes you."

Jack laughed. "Lucky for me he does! I never would have stood a chance against Shanley."

Ira tapped the side of his shoe on a bit of cobblestone that jutted out from the road, then said, "We should get back in."

Inside they found Eodus on the verge of a nervous breakdown, stuttering and stumbling over his words.

Lucifer had leaned back in his chair, a grin on his face, as he watched the lesser demon try to communicate that the Devil had been cheating at cards without being accusatory.

"Lu, they're not going to invite us back," Ira warned.

"I didn't know there was anywhere in Hell where the Devil needed to be invited," Lucifer said, not taking his eyes from Eodus.

"No, no, of c-course not, my Prince, you're—"

"Lu!" Ira scolded.

"What?"

"Quit staring at him."

Lucifer took his eyes from Eodus and fixed them on Ira, his face fleetingly drawn and serious before he smiled a softer smile than the wolf-grin he had fixed on Ira's twin. He beckoned Ira over. Ira went and Lucifer folded him into his arms, pulling him onto his lap and kissed his temple.

"Are you hungry?" the Devil asked.

"I could eat," Ira said, glad that Lucifer's appetite had started to show its face again. He put one arm around the other man's neck and rested his head against his. "What do you want?"

"Oh, I don't know, whatever Oris has cooking will do, I'm sure. It's about time for us to head home anyway. My self-restraint is not what it should be—"

"Lu."

"And your brother would be a treat."

"Come on," Ira scolded.

"Or Jack, though I think I would be heartbroken..." Lucifer let out a hefty sigh, tightening his grip on Ira and nestling his face in the crook of Ira's neck. He took a deep breath and sank his teeth into Ira's flesh, harder than he normally did.

Ira pulled out of his arms but kept a grip on his hand, worrying that it felt a little thinner and longer than normal. "Then let's go."

They exchanged a series of goodbyes and thank-yous. Ira would have left it at that, but he forced himself to give his brother a hug. He couldn't not, after what Jack had said. Eodus squeezed him tight and didn't seem so nervous for a moment.

"We'll get together soon," Ira told him.

"Can't wait!" his twin declared with a genuine smile.

While they walked home, Lucifer kept his fingers firmly twined with Ira's, leading Ira to ask, "Do you have to hold my hand so hard?"

"Yes." The Devil swallowed. "I do."

Ira squinted up at him. "Lu..."

"Yes, dear?"

He didn't want to think that the Devil's mouth looked a little wider than it normally did or that he seemed to stand a little taller, but Ira couldn't help but ask, "Should I be worried?"

"No."

"Are you sure?"

"Yes."

Ira didn't ask again; he didn't say a peep for the remainder of their walk back to the Devil's palace. He didn't think he wanted to stay the night but didn't know how to extract himself from the situation.

Instead of heading towards the kitchen when they'd gotten inside, Lucifer pulled Ira into a kiss before they'd even left the antechamber. He pulled him up onto his toes and pressed him against the wall. He nipped Ira's ear and then his throat; his fingers found a home in Ira's curls so that he could tilt Ira's head back, exposing his neck.

Ira tensed, expecting the Devil to use more teeth than he did. He expected him to draw blood and didn't know how to tell him to stop. He closed his eyes and bit his tongue as Lucifer unfastened the buttons on his shirt, untucking it from his trousers and dropping to his knees.

They weren't a yard away from Imogen's office and any of the staff could wander in at any moment. At least two cats watched from the stairs.

"Lu," he tried but his voice got caught in the phlegm in his throat, so he cleared his throat and tried again, too loud this time, "*Lu*."

"What, darling?" the Devil asked without looking up, his thin fingers unfastening Ira's trousers.

"I thought you were hungry."

"I am. Starving."

"Lu," he insisted and it felt like a whine.

"Yes?" Lucifer pressed his mouth to Ira's belly, sending a quiver of longing and fear through Ira.

"You're scaring me."

At that, the Devil hesitated, lifting his gaze. With his eyes trained on Ira's face, he breathed, "I know," and sounded exhilarated. He swallowed and licked his lips. "Let me. I'll have you shaking in no time." He pressed his forehead to Ira's hip and ran his fingers down Ira's legs, gripping his thighs.

Ira dug his teeth hard into his lip, hard enough that he would draw blood if he kept it up. His heart pattered in his chest. "I."

Lucifer looked up again. "What?"

"I don't know."

"Do you want me to stop?"

"Please."

Lucifer moved back, going from kneeling to sitting. His eyes still had that hungry quality; as Ira put his clothes back together, he felt the need to run.

"Love, come here," Lucifer said as Ira edged away from him. The Devil hadn't averted his eyes yet. He hadn't even blinked.

Ira shook his head.

"I won't hurt you."

It felt like a lie.

Lucifer closed his eyes finally and rested his hands on his thighs. He sucked in a breath and let it out slowly. He repeated, "I won't hurt you."

Ira believed him that time.

His face had grown softer. His eyes had lost that predatory fixation. "Will you come here, please?"

Ira approached, trying to tuck in his shirt but feeling unsteady.

"I'm sorry. I am. I shouldn't have." He offered his hand.

Ira wanted to take it, wanted to be safe in his arms, but couldn't make himself.

"It's...darling, it's just a game. It's." Lucifer cast his gaze to the floor. "The other day. After the art gallery."

"What about it?"

"I had you pinned to the bed, for just a second and, well, you seemed to respond favorably. I thought maybe you would like this."

A wave of heat, then cold, ran through Ira. He had been so stupid.

"I got carried away, I apologize."

Ira shook his head, feeling small and worthless.

Lucifer started to stand but Ira shrank back, not able to check the reflex. At that, Lucifer returned to his sitting position, legs crossed Indian style, his palms resting on his knees.

The Devil didn't move, not an inch; it wasn't the stillness of a coiled snake, but something vast and patient. Ira knew he wouldn't move until he'd been given leave, or until Ira approached him.

It had been weeks since they'd been together, weeks since the Devil'd had the energy for anything more than a few kisses. The first time he had tried anything and Ira had soured his advances.

"I'm sorry," Ira whispered.

"No need."

"I got scared is all, we can if you want," Ira told him and hated himself when he added, "However you like."

"No, dear, that's alright. I'd like you to come a little closer and sit with me if you don't mind too much."

Ira took a few steps forwards and sat across from him, mirroring his position. A few inches separated their knees.

Lucifer still hadn't budged. "Would you like to talk about anything?"

Ira shook his head, not able to look at him.

"Can I?" Lucifer asked.

"That's fine."

"It isn't an excuse, only an explanation."

"Sure."

"I've been feeling better lately. More...vital, I suppose. Hungrier. When these things come back to me, the sensations get a little out of hand. And sometimes, uh. Signals get crossed. I am usually able to control myself at times like this." Lucifer turned one hand to be palm up and extended it slightly towards Ira, not a request, but an offer. "I did think it might be fun to play around a little and I had no intention to do you any harm."

Ira eyed his hand. He wanted to take it but something nagging in the back of his mind stopped him. "But you knew you were scaring me."

The Devil nodded.

"You liked it."

"Yes."

"You liked scaring me," Ira repeated.

"I like a lot of things. If I had thought you would be genuinely distressed, I wouldn't have proceeded as I did. I have no wish to do you harm, physical or emotional, but I cannot change the nature of what I am."

"Why do you always talk like that?" Ira demanded, hating the artful flow of words.

"I cannot change the nature of what I am," Lucifer repeated. "I have my desires, same as any other person, and I cannot change them. But I promise that I'll never expect you to participate in them if you don't want. And if I'm ever doing something you don't like, tell me to stop and I will."

Ira picked at the seam of his trousers.

"You know I mean that, don't you?" the Devil asked earnestly.

"Figure you do."

"Darling, I'm sorry. Could you not pick at that, please? I'm sorry, I know they're yours..."

Ira stopped picking at the seam.

"Just..."

"No, I know," Ira told him. Sometimes certain things bothered Lucifer, things that shouldn't have but did in a way he couldn't explain, like when something broke or spilled or when books were shelved out of order. Normally his fastidiousness didn't show its face so plainly.

They sat on the floor for a while, neither of them speaking or moving.

Imogen exited her office, a bundle of letters in her hand, and peered at them. "So are the two of you done? Because I have to send these and I didn't want to interrupt..."

Lucifer turned his eyes towards her. "Imogen, really."

"Well, do you want your bills to get paid or not!" she huffed.

"Do you think anyone is going to come collecting debts?" he inquired.

She closed her eyes. "Sire, I...I'm only trying to do my job, I didn't mean any disrespect."

Lucifer looked to Ira as if to ask if he were ready to move. Ira stood and Lucifer followed suit.

Imogen edged around them on her way to the door.

"Probably should eat dinner," Ira proposed.

"Would you like to stay? Imogen can walk you home otherwise."

"I can get home on my own if I want," Ira snapped. He made his way towards the kitchen, helping himself to what Oris had on the stove.

To the bespectacled chef, he said, "Go away."

Oris scurried off into the servants' quarters.

He set two bowls on the kitchen table, old ghostwood so dark it had gone black. He rifled around in the drawers to find spoons then tossed them onto the table.

They clattered against the wood and Lucifer flinched at the sound.

Halfway through his bowl of lentil soup, Lucifer began, "Maybe..." then never finished.

"Maybe what?"

"Maybe the next time I go to visit Felix you could come with me."

"You don't have to bring me," Ira told him.

"If you don't want to come..."

"He's your son."

"And you're my companion. We are, or, we could be...that is to say, the two of you are my family. I know you haven't got any relation to each other," the Devil said.

"I'm not your family. You've got a wife already."

"Oh."

Right away, Ira regretted the harshness in his voice. "I just meant—"

"No, I understand. You're right. Neither blood nor law binds us. I forget how literal these things are for demons."

"Lu, I just meant to say that he's your son, it's not my choice if I'm going to meet him."

"I understand."

"I should go home." Ira started to stand.

"I wish you wouldn't."

"I think I should. Before I say anything else."

"Or before I do," Lucifer agreed gloomily.

"I'm sorry, Lu. I think in the morning..." Ira sighed. "It feels like a lot happened. We should sleep on it."

"You're right, dear."

Lucifer walked him to the front door. "I've got several things that need seeing to in the morning. I don't know when I'll be free next. It might be a few days. There were a few things that got neglected while I wasn't feeling well."

Ira nodded.

"I love you."

"I love you, too." Ira headed down the steps but glanced back to find the Devil watching him, his face fraught. He doubled back and hugged him. "I do, Lu, I love you."

Lucifer put a hand on Ira's cheek and kissed his forehead. "I'll write."

"You better."

THE NOTE came, as it always did, with a gift. This time it was not a book, but a jar made of glass. It appeared to be empty.

Ira set the jar on the couch beside him and broke the seal of the note.

I remembered I could make these. I always used to think they were pretty. I hope you do, too. Save it for when your spirits need lifting.

Thinking of you. All my love,

Luci

Ira peered into the jar again and saw something faint and shimmery swirling inside. He contemplated opening it now, half out of curiosity and half because he wasn't looking forward to his engagement this evening.

He was supposed to meet up with Astrid at the studio in the afternoon. She hadn't written to him, but they'd run into each other at the student bar Georg frequented.

The youth had almost begged him to come out. Ira didn't think, proud as he was, that Georg was capable of real begging, but he'd taken Ira by the hand and insisted, "The rest of them are *so* boring. And I owe you a drink."

Three drinks later, Ira had been in a friendly mood, so when Astrid had come in and spotted him, he'd readily agreed to model for her again.

Now his mood was less friendly, but the obligation remained.

He dressed in one of his older suits, knowing there was no need to dress up when she'd just ask him to take his clothes off anyway.

He successfully navigated his way to the studio at which they'd met last time. He poked his head inside and found her setting up an easel.

"Hello, darling."

She turned to look at him, her face lighting up, a grin spreading across her dainty features. "Ira."

He couldn't help but return her smile. Maybe they could be friends. Maybe he needed to go into this with a better attitude. He entered further into the room.

She hugged him and he allowed it.

"I'm glad you came alone this time."

"Oh, well, Georg was curious. Everyone likes your painting."

"You mentioned." She nodded towards the stool in the middle of the room.

He headed over.

"You can put your clothes on the table," she said, pointing.

"Don't you ever want to draw me with my clothes on?" he joked.

One corner of her mouth tipped up.

He perched on the stool once he'd stripped down.

She approached and adjusted the way he sat, her small hands dancing over his skin, lingering a little longer than he liked on his thigh. At one point, he thought she was going to kiss him so he turned his head.

She retreated to the easel.

"I haven't got a lot of friends," he told her.

"Hmm?"

"But, you know, I'm trying to get out more. That's what people are supposed to do, right?"

She sniffed, "I would have thought our Prince would keep you busy."

"Oh, uh, well, he's got his own stuff to do a lot of the time."

"Does he?" she asked.

"Sure, he has all kinds of things he needs to do."

"Like what?"

"Oh, you know, princely duties and all that. The souls, the captains, the workers. His affairs on Earth."

Her face appeared at the side of the easel, as it did from time to time. "Is he around a lot?"

"I don't know, what's a lot?" Ira mused. "Sometimes it's a couple of days in a row, sometimes it's a couple of days apart."

"Do you get lonely?"

He shrugged. "I, uh, not really. I...I do a lot of reading."

"I can't imagine."

He waited for her to elaborate, but she didn't so he prompted, "Can't imagine what?"

"Being left behind all the time."

Ira hadn't ever thought of himself as being left behind by Lucifer. Satan was an important person with important things to oversee.

"What about you?" he asked.

"What?"

"What do you do? Or are you single-minded in your pursuit of art?"

"I go to classes."

"For art, I bet."

"Yes, for art, how else would I become a better artist?" she asked, sounding almost upset.

"What do you do for fun? And don't say art!"

"Then I won't say anything," she sniffed.

He stayed quiet, sure he had offended her. Sitting for so long gave him time to think about what he would do later, what he might make for dinner, and when he might see Lucifer again. He wondered what they would do when they saw each other next. He wished their last meeting had gone differently. Lucifer had called him family and he should have let that terminology stand.

He should have taken the Devil up on his offer to go to Earth and see Felix. He should have understood then what Lucifer had been offering.

The sound of voices interrupted his thoughts and he looked over to see a cluster of students coming through the door.

Astrid turned to look at them, a hand going to her mouth. "Oh. I thought..."

Ira chuckled at the look of pure surprise on her face, on that of the students.

An older gentleman approached and informed them, "Studio Six is having some issues with the plumbing. We'll be moving our class in here."

"I'm sorry," Astrid said.

Ira shimmied into his clothes, not concerned with the

audience he'd gained, but a little worried about Astrid. She looked absolutely on the verge of tears.

"Come on, darling, there's got to be another space," he urged. "I've got to say, my legs could do with a stretch."

"All the other studios are being used."

"Then let's grab a bite to eat. Are you hungry? I am, we've been at it for ages." She looked ready to refuse so he said, "My treat."

"You don't have to."

"I haven't got any other plans." He put a hand on her arm.

She gathered up her supplies and said, "I've got to put these away."

He laughed at the idea of going out to lunch with such a large drawing pad. "I sort of figured. Want me to carry something?"

"Thank you."

With the burden split between them, they headed to her room in one of the student residences. She let him into the room and nodded towards one of the beds. "You can just leave everything there."

He placed her things on the bed as she set down her share; their hands brushed. She seemed to think more of it than he did, her already pink cheeks darkening.

"Are you blushing? Darling, after the things we've done together," he teased.

She wrapped her fingers around his and he realized he misinterpreted the flush in her cheeks.

"Oh, I, Astrid." He took his hand from hers. "I'd like to be friends, really, but that's it."

She nodded. "I'm sorry, I just. I'm used to what we had."

"Yeah, but that was business, you know. Come on, let's eat."

She brought him to a small restaurant filled with young people. As she searched for a table, he spied some of Georg's friends, the boy with garish spiky horns and Visya. He waved to them and they waved back, gesturing for him to come over.

He tapped Astrid on the shoulder. "I know them."

She wrinkled her nose and shook her head. "Whoremongers, both of them."

"And that makes you what, exactly?" he challenged.

She had no answer for that and followed when he headed over. There weren't many other seats available and he'd rather have shared it with them than strangers.

"What's that saying?" Visya asked, "Like a bad penny?"

Ira grinned. "That's me."

"You just missed Georg."

"Oh, too bad." He'd come to genuinely like Georg, as well as Visya, though the fondness may have been aided by the merriment of drinking slightly too much on most occasions they saw each other.

"We're heading out," the horned boy told them.

"But there's a party tonight," Visya said, putting a hand on Ira's arm. "You should come."

He had no plans for the rest of the night and without a glance at Astrid, he agreed to go. "Sure, where?"

"At Ransom Hall."

He nodded.

Once they'd left, Astrid told him he shouldn't go.

"Why not?" he asked.

"It will be a mess."

"Probably, but aren't parties supposed to get messy at this age?" he asked. He didn't know, not firsthand, what parties at the university were like, but he'd heard clients at the Trade House swapping tales of wild carousing. "It's a bit of fun."

She pursed her lips.

"So you aren't coming?" he asked.

"No."

"Astrid, come on, if you don't like it, we can leave," he promised. Maybe a party would do her some good. Maybe she could meet someone else, someone who would be unattached and interested in her. Maybe if she got a few drinks in her, she would worry less about who went to whores or worked as one.

She shook her head.

"Well, then, will you at least walk me there? I don't want to get turned around."

"Fine."

He thought about borrowing a pen and paper from someone so he could send a note to Lucifer but resolved to do it in the morning instead. The Devil was bound to be busy now and might not even be in Hell presently.

Astrid brought him to the residence hall with a scowl on her face and he tried once more, "Are you sure you don't want to come in? Even for a little while."

"No."

"I don't know, I think you're being too hard on them."

"I...! A bunch of spoiled brats and their groupies? You can't *be* too hard on them."

"They're nice," Ira insisted.

"Probably because they know who's keeping you."

He huffed. "Or because they like me."

He could hear the clamor of revelry even from outside.

She crossed her arms, as though her judgment could get him to change his mind, as though her opinion meant anything to him.

"Come in or don't," he warned, reaching for the door, "It doesn't matter to me."

He went in without waiting for her and found the common room on the first floor flooded with students and their laughter.

Someone pointed him towards the table littered with half-full bottles of wine and spirits.

He glanced back to see that Astrid had followed him in.

As he made himself a drink, someone threw their arms around him. "Darling!" Georg greeted him. "I heard a rumor you might show up."

"How could I resist?" He gestured around to the wild array of bodies. "What's the occasion? Should at least some of you be studying?"

"No, end of the semester, we've got to use all this up or risk bringing it home with us." Georg took him by the hand. "Anyway, come upstairs, it's quieter."

He went and Astrid followed, her arms still crossed.

"Why's she following you around?" Georg whispered into Ira's ear.

"I kind of goaded her into coming."

"Ugh, Ira, she's awful."

"She isn't."

"Just cause she's pretty doesn't mean she isn't awful. She's so...she thinks she's better than everyone."

"You two should get together then," Ira suggested.

"Fresh!" Georg laughed.

The common room on the third floor had fewer bodies and enough room for them to find a seat.

They settled on to a couch with Astrid sitting next to Ira. He offered her a sip of his drink when he saw she didn't have one.

"Or I've got some chilled white wine, if my lady prefers," Georg teased. "From Earth-grown grapes, of course, nothing but the finest."

She shot him a dirty look.

Georg rolled his eyes and confided to Ira, "I swear, sometimes I wish I'd agreed to marry into any other family."

"No other family would have you!" Astrid hissed.

"Shh, don't. Be nice," Ira insisted. "Would it kill you?"

Neither of them said anything, until finally, Georg said, "It wouldn't kill me, but it might kill her."

"I'll tell them, I swear, I will," she threatened.

"It isn't any of your business," Georg warned.

"Stop," Ira demanded. "What are you even on about?"

"He's engaged to my cousin," Astrid informed him.

"Ah." Ira took a drink. "Well. That's between them, isn't it? Do you like poetry?"

She frowned at the abruptness of the question, but he'd been desperate to change the topic. He didn't want to get involved in their family intrigue, especially not if it involved shaming Georg because he'd decided to work.

"Some of it, I guess," she answered.

"Oh, Ira, hang on," Georg said. "Rogg, tell Ira that poem."

A young man with red curls came over and Ira felt sure that he recognized him.

"What poem?" Rogg asked.

Georg waved one hand in a vague gesture. "There once was a whatever..."

"It's not a poem, it's a limerick."

"Well, it rhymes, doesn't it? Anyway, go on, tell him."

Rogg took a breath and recited, "There once was a young lass named Sally, who loved an occasional dally. She sat on the lap of a well-endowed chap crying, 'Gee, Dick, you're right up my alley!'"

Ira cracked a smile. "Not exactly what I had in mind."

"It's the best you'll do with this crowd," Astrid promised.

Georg huffed and reached out to brush his fingers through Ira's curls. He'd plainly already had enough to drink, his eyes shining and his lips swollen as though he'd been kissing someone not long ago.

Ira twisted to face him, tired of Astrid and her negativity. "Do you want to play a game?"

"Always."

Ira fished a handful of pennies out of his pocket and tossed them on the table, setting up an empty glass on the other end.

"Oh!" Georg cried, "I know this one." He expertly bounced

two pennies into the glass but missed on the third one.

Uri had taught him this game, though they'd had to use buttons instead of coins, and they had played frequently until Mistress had decided they couldn't anymore. Things had never gotten out of hand, but she had never trusted the two of them together after she'd found out about their affair.

Astrid watched with her nose turned up, but Ira managed to goad her into playing after a few rounds.

Visya was the first one to sink three pennies in a row and crowed, "New rule! Anytime Ira calls someone 'darling' he has to drink."

The crowd erupted in laughter, most of them having been around when he'd been out drinking with Georg.

"That isn't fair!" Ira protested.

"Sorry, darling," Visya said with a grin.

The next two rules followed suit. He could not call anyone 'dear' or 'love' either.

By the end of the game, he'd ended up saying things like, "Georg, darling, fucking shit, get me a drink, though, I've finished this one."

"You still have to drink," Rogg taunted.

"I know, I can't, this one's empty!"

Rogg passed him his own glass and Ira swigged from it, wincing at the overly sweet drink.

Georg brought Ira the drink he'd requested, sinking down on his knees to hand it to him, because Ira had long since given up on sitting on the couch. Too many people had crowded around to play the game and he had slid onto the floor to make room for them.

"It's mostly soda and juice, I promise, because you're, oh, if you keep drinking like this you're going to start getting mean again," Georg giggled, taking Ira's hand and squeezing it.

"I won't, I promise. I won't," he insisted, "Because I like you now."

"Ohhh, lucky me, our Prince's man *likes me now*."

"Shh, stop, don't." Ira sipped his drink. He couldn't taste much alcohol, but he hadn't tasted much in his last few drinks either, though he was sure it had been there.

He leaned closer to Astrid, who had stuck close to his side all night. Now she put an arm around his shoulders, and he allowed it, not thinking any more of it than he did of the way Georg now lay his head on one of Ira's thighs.

"Your turn," Visya told him.

Ira shook his head. "I can't."

"Yes, your turn!"

He took a coin, hucked it without any aim or effort, but managed to make it into the glass anyway. He missed the next one and drank.

The game petered out after a few more hours. People wandered away to their own rooms, or the rooms of friends, or passed out in corners.

Georg said, "You aren't going to...you can't walk home."

"No," Ira agreed. He didn't know if he could even walk out of the building.

"You can stay here."

"Yeah." He nodded. "Yeah, we'll stay here."

Astrid said, "Come on, we can go to my room."

"The couch," Georg insisted. "Blankets?"

Ira nodded and hauled himself up onto the couch. He opened his arms to Astrid.

"Ira, come on, we can go back to my room," she said. She tugged on his outstretched arm to get him to stand. "I didn't drink that much, I can get us there in one piece."

He shook his head. "I'm tired, I want to get some sleep."

She didn't look pleased, but she joined him on the couch.

Georg brought him a blanket. He ruffled Ira's hair and bid him goodnight.

Astrid curled up in his arms.

Ira asked, "Aren't you glad you came?"

"Yes."

He closed his eyes, his whole body pleasantly warm and light. He wondered where Lucifer was, if he was in bed like he should have been or if something was keeping him up. He nestled his face into the arm of the overstuffed couch and drifted off.

Something soft and sweet brushed across his neck and he licked his lips, thinking of how feather soft the Devil's kisses could be.

Maybe tomorrow he would visit the palace and see what Lucifer was up to. Busy as the Devil was, he might have a little while to spare, especially when it had been so long since they'd been together. Maybe if Ira stayed the night, they'd have time for something before dinner, or in the morning before he had to go out again.

A pair of lips pressed against his.

He opened his eyes, frowning. He tried to sit up.

"Shh," Astrid whispered, her hands sliding inside his shirt, already half-undone from the night's festivities. She crawled on top of him, the weight of her body far more than it should have been considering her frame.

"I..."

"Shh, they're sleeping." She covered his mouth with a kiss, cutting off the protest he wanted to give. She pressed her hand between his legs, finding him somewhat erect.

Her fingers undid the fly of his trousers and she caressed him, getting him hard. He put his hand over hers and tried to stop her, but his hands felt clumsy, not part of his body. Somehow it seemed important that they stay quiet. He didn't want to disturb anyone and didn't know how to extract himself from this without upsetting her or causing a commotion.

Her mouth was warm and her fingers were sweet, the right amount of pressure. She cupped the head of his cock with her palm, giving a gentle squeeze. He tensed, not knowing what to do as some base part of him yearned for more.

They had done this a dozen times and he knew how warm and slick her quim would be around his cock. He knew how lovely it would be to spill inside of her.

"Astrid, I don't," he managed, his head fuzzy, but she ignored him.

"He doesn't need to know," she promised as she straddled him.

He didn't know when she'd shed her underclothes, but like that she guided him inside of her even as he tried to tell her not to. When he pushed her hands away, they were back a second later and when he turned his mouth from her kisses, she pressed her lips to whatever skin she could find.

"Stop, stop it," he said, knowing his voice had gone high and shaky, not able to stop the tears from dribbling down his cheeks or the pleasure he felt as she rocked her hips back and forth, coaxing him towards climax.

He wanted her off him, but she was too close, his legs were tangled in the blankets and his trousers.

The world went quiet, his ears ringing, he couldn't think past the heady mix of alcohol, of confusion and yearning.

"*Don't*," he insisted as she continued.

He moved beyond confusion then, his throat growing tight and thick with phlegm. She didn't notice his tears, she didn't notice anything until he had gone soft and slipped out of her.

"Ira." She moved back a little, looking at him for the first time. "What's wrong?"

He shook his head.

She reached between his legs again. "It's fine, I think this happens sometimes, especially if you've been drinking." She gave him a smile.

"Don't!" he shouted, pushing her hand away. "Stop it!"

She frowned. "I..."

"Stop touching me!" He couldn't control the volume of his voice.

She didn't move away from him until he had lost what remained of his composure, breaking down into ugly heavy sobs with snot running out of his nose.

"Go away!" His words came out as a scream.

People started to stir. Someone lit a lamp.

Astrid was gone, like she'd never even been there, like the whole thing had been a shitty dream.

He couldn't reign in his crying.

"Hey," came a voice he almost recognized. "Hey, you're Georg's friend, right?"

He continued to sob, unable to do anything else.

"Uh. Are you alright?" the stranger asked.

He pulled his knees to his chest and hid his face, wrapping his arms around himself. Dimly, he knew he heard more voices but didn't know what to do about it. He hadn't meant to wake anyone up.

"Someone find Georg."

Ira knotted his fingers in his hair and tried to find quiet. He couldn't pretend to be anywhere else. He couldn't breathe.

"Ira!" Georg exclaimed softly. "Hey, darling, what happened?"

He shook his head.

"Alright, alright, shhhh," Georg soothed, putting a hand on Ira's shoulder. "Come with me."

Georg put an arm around him and took him, blanket and all, into a dimly lit room and sat him on a bed. "What happened?"

"I don't know," was all Ira managed but couldn't even be sure that he'd communicated that clearly. "I don't, I don't know."

"Alright. You're alright, love, you are."

Georg pulled Ira into an embrace, making soft soothing noises until Ira had cried himself out.

With a damp handkerchief, he wiped Ira's face, then offered him a drink of water. Ira accepted and clutched the glass like he needed it to live. His hands shook as he tried to sip from it.

"Where's Astrid?" Georg asked.

The glass clinked against his teeth and he spilled water down his chin. His breath started to hitch and he thought he would start to cry again.

He didn't want to cry anymore because his face hurt and his throat had gone raw; even his ribs ached.

"I...she."

"What?" Georg inquired softly.

"I don't know. I think." His throat closed and he shook his head.

Georg rubbed his back. "Alright, that's fine, you don't have to say anything. What about something more comfortable to wear, huh? Better than suspenders."

Ira nodded. He wanted to be out of these clothes; they smelled like her and worse than that he could feel the dampness the encounter had left on them. He didn't know if he'd come or not. He didn't want to know.

Georg left his side and returned with a set of thin, soft pajamas. Ira yanked off his shirt and felt Georg staring, no, trying not to stare, at the fly of his trousers. He had not refastened it and he had remained exposed this whole time, his cock limply poking out.

He ripped off all his clothes, throwing them onto the floor, and pulled on the pajamas. He wanted a bath. He wanted to go home. He wanted Lucifer.

But Lucifer wouldn't want him. Ira had been the one to say they shouldn't be with anyone else, to ask before having sex with someone else, and he had been the one to break that rule, too.

"Ira," Georg breathed.

He shook his head.

"I'll take you home in the morning, I promise, but I'm...I drank too much, I..."

Ira nodded. He'd drank too much, too, and it would be stupid to go out this drunk into the night. Anything could be waiting for them, especially when so many partygoers would be making their own way home.

"Do you want to be alone?" Georg asked.

"No."

"You can have the bed, I can—"

"No." He reached out for Georg's hand. He didn't want to be alone. Not here, not in this place he didn't know, a place full of strangers.

Georg nodded.

Ira sat back down on the bed but couldn't make himself lay down.

Georg sat beside him and wrapped him in a blanket, rubbing his back.

Ira couldn't stop the same handful of thoughts from chasing each other in his mind. "I didn't mean to," he confessed to Georg.

"You didn't do anything wrong."

But he had. He had insisted she come out to the party. He had too much to drink. He had stayed on the couch with her. He hadn't done enough to stop her. He should have screamed, he should have pushed her away.

"Try to sleep."

Ira nodded his head.

"Close your eyes and just...try not to think about something else."

"I can't."

"Hansel used to tell me this story when I was little, about a cat and a little girl. It was...this little girl had a cat, she'd found it when it was just a stray, skinny and starving and sick. But they were poor, and her parents said she couldn't keep it, that they couldn't feed it. Every night she would split her dinner with this cat, feeding it until it grew sleek and fat. It slept in her bed and she would tell it all her secrets, all her hopes."

Ira knew this story. The cat started bringing the girl gifts, the things for which she'd wished. In the end, she came to suspect that the cat was their Prince in hiding after a terrible coup.

"She murders the usurper," Ira mumbled.

"Don't ruin the fucking story, Ira," Georg scolded, then resumed, "Anyway, so the cat brings her a bag of coins."

Ira tightened the blanket around his shoulders and tried to keep his breathing even, focusing on Georg's words. Soon enough, exhaustion and drink pulled him back under.

GEORG WALKED Ira back to the Inverness, even though Ira told him he'd be fine on his own.

"I don't know, if you're as hungover as you look, I'm not sure you'll make it down the stairs," Georg had teased, his smile only half there.

Relief had washed over Ira. He hadn't been ready to face the world alone and he didn't know if he could have found his way home unmolested. He felt small and shaky and that made him look like someone who deserved to be accosted, even in the Ninth, though the harassment would surely be milder than if he'd been in the Eighth.

Georg had accompanied him inside and now wandered around Ira's parlor. He ran his hand over the back of the couch and went over to peer at the bookshelf. "I don't think I've heard of half these authors and I like to consider myself pretty well read."

Ira paused his trek between the sink and the stove, the tea kettle in his hand. He looked where Georg looked. "Humans."

Georg ran his finger over the spine of one book. "I..."

"What?"

"My grandmother was mostly human," Georg said.

"It shows."

"But she had a little of the Devil's blood in her, too, you know. I don't think it's even enough for me to say I'm related to our

Prince."

Ira put the kettle on the stove harder than he meant to, his body going weak all of a sudden.

"You alright?" Georg asked.

"Mhm. I, uh."

"You want me to stick around or...?"

"I, uh. I'm going to have some tea and a bath, you don't need to stay for that."

Georg nodded. "I'll tell Marius—"

Ira yelped, "Don't!"

"I'll tell him you're too hungover," Georg finished. "See you tomorrow?"

Ira nodded.

Georg headed towards the door, then turned back and came over to the kitchen. He put his arms around Ira. "Take care of yourself, darling, really."

"Sure."

When Georg had left, Ira sat at the table and lost track of time until the kettle started whistling.

He looked over at it and forgot having put it on at all.

He made himself tea and sipped at it for a little while until the need for a bath overwhelmed him.

In the bathtub, he sat without washing until the water got cold.

He forced himself to wash his hair and his skin then crawled into bed. He didn't sleep but didn't exactly feel awake either.

In the morning, he made it to work somehow, not sure how he'd gotten there.

"Still hungover?" Marius asked.

Ira frowned.

"You're late."

"Didn't know I had hours to keep," Ira snapped.

The pander frowned and Ira went to the back room.

He stopped dead when he saw the painting hanging behind his desk. Before he'd realized how he felt, before he even had time to think about what he was doing, he snatched a letter opener from his desk and stabbed it into the painting. He cut the canvas to ribbons with such fervor that he tore it from the wall, snapping the frame and throwing it against the floor.

When there was nothing left he could do to the painting, he threw the letter opener and kicked the chair with a shout.

He stood there, his toes smarting, and swayed, looking around the room for anything else that might need to be ruined.

Marius entered the room, looked around, and promptly declared, "What the fuck, Ira!"

"I *hate* that fucking painting."

"And what did the wall ever do to you!" Marius demanded.

Ira turned to see that he had left gouges carved into the wall. He had to reach out for the desk, gripping it to stay upright. Shame rolled through him and he had to sit.

Marius went over, stepping around the remains of the painting, to run his fingers over the gouges. "Shit."

"I'm sorry," Ira said, the words coming out unbidden, the same as the tears that burned his eyes. He scrubbed them away before they could spill. "I am, I'm so sorry, I just, I *hate that fucking painting,* I hate it so much."

Slowly, Marius said, "I thought you and your artist were on good terms."

Ira shook his head. "No."

"Does that mean when she comes looking for you I shouldn't tell her that you're in?"

Bile leaped into the back of his throat. "Is she here?"

"She came in earlier looking for you. Seemed to think it was important. Looked upset."

"*Don't* tell her," Ira begged.

"Maybe you should go home. Cause you look awful."

Ira shook his head. "No, I need to be here. I need to do something."

Marius pursed his lips, then sighed. "Alright, well, do you think you could pick this up?" He gestured towards the ruined painting.

Ira nodded. He bent and gathered up the broken frame and the tattered canvas. He shoved them into the refuse bin in the back, glad that it would get covered with scraps from the kitchen and unsalvageable rags from the brothels, glad that at the end of the week the sanitation crew would shovel it up and bring it to be sorted into one of the landfills outside the city.

He did his best to clean up the gouges in the wall, smoothing the rough edges as best he could. It was useless, though; it needed plaster and a new coat of paint.

Georg came to check on him in between clients a few times. The third time, he asked, "You want me to send a runner?" with his eyes fixed on the ruined wall, same as Ira's were.

"What?" Ira hadn't even noticed him come in.

"The wall?"

"Oh. Uh." He hadn't really been looking at the wall, instead gazing with his eyes unfocused and his mind entirely elsewhere. "Yeah. Yes. Please."

"Have you eaten anything?"

"Uh. No."

"Well, let's do that, too." Georg came around the side of the desk and tapped Ira on the arm. "Come on."

"I'm not hungry."

"No, but you've got to eat."

Ira shook his head. He didn't want to eat.

"Please."

The pleading note in the younger man's voice pulled Ira a little closer to reality. Georg's face was drawn tight, his perfect mouth curved in the most beautiful expression of worry Ira had ever seen.

"You've got..." Ira started but didn't know how to finish because the thought had been fleeting and mostly untrue.

He had intended to tell Georg that he had Lucifer's eyes, but it wasn't true. They were honey-colored instead of that horrible reddish gold and had a different shape entirely. He didn't look anything like the Devil, but there was something about the look on his face that reminded Ira of their Prince.

"What, darling?" Georg asked.

Ira shook his head and stood.

With the barest amount of pressure, Georg touched Ira's back and led him out of the brothel.

They settled into a table in the back corner of a nearby restaurant.

As he ripped a piece of bread into tiny bits, only occasionally eating a piece, Georg said, "About the other night."

Ira shook his head. "I don't want to talk about it."

"I just. I'm not clear, uh, I'm not clear on what happened and I don't want to assume anything..."

"I drank too much," Ira spat, "Did something stupid."

Georg grimaced. "You were so upset, though, I just...I want you to know that, well, Ira, if you want to talk, I'm here."

"I *don't* want to talk about it."

He didn't even want to think about it. The memory of that night felt distant, as though he'd watched it happen to someone else, or as though it had been a dream. He recalled enough to know that he hated the way it made his guts squirm. He hadn't meant for things to go that far; he hadn't wanted to do anything at all with her.

But somehow, he'd ended up there, inside of her and wanting more, aching to spill. He hadn't wanted it, but he had liked it.

He tightened his hand around the mug of tea he'd ordered with his lunch, hoping the mint would bring him a little clarity.

"Can I say one more thing and then I won't bring it up again?" Georg asked.

"I figure I can't stop you."

"I don't think you did anything wrong. I *know* you didn't. Whatever happened, you haven't got to feel bad about it."

Ira took another sip of his tea. Georg was wrong, but he was young, and Ira suspected, he was just as sweet as his poor bastard of a brother.

His suspicions were confirmed when Georg pushed a hunk of bread towards him and gave him a smile, touching Ira's hand for a second. "So tell me about your human authors."

"What?"

"You've got all those books, I always used to see you reading. Figure I've got some cultural heritage there, right?"

"Not something many Hell-born would own up to."

Georg smirked, knowing well that humans an amusement but never really people in the eyes of most of Hell's citizens. "Ah, well, everyone wants to go to Earth and play around with God's favorite toys, must explain why I've got so many admirers. Anyway, tell me about your authors. Who's your favorite?"

Ira shook his head. He couldn't think of anything. "I don't know. I. Um, there's this novel I'm reading now. Trying to read, anyway. It was written for children, it's about a girl who gets swept up in a cyclone."

"A what?"

"It's, uh, it's a type of windstorm they get up on Earth. It, hmmm, it brings her to another world."

Georg raised his eyebrows. "Like to one of the Otherworlds?"

He shook his head, then said, "Sort of, actually, it isn't a fairy realm, though, it's...it's over the rainbow."

"The *what?*" Georg asked.

"It's. Like stripes of colors in the sky. After it rains."

Georg laughed. "What?"

"I think they only happen on Earth. Or places with a sun, I

guess. Lu tried to explain it to me once, something about how the light hits the water. I didn't see one when I was up there."

"You've been?" Georg exclaimed.

"You haven't? I thought rich kids like you snuck up there all the time."

"No, I..." Georg shook his head, a pink flush creeping over his face. "I, uh, I almost did once, but I was too scared."

"Scared?"

Georg nodded. "There's so many of them! We're only one city...a big city, sure, but there's how many of *us*? A million between the Eighth and the Ninth *and* all the farms and shitty little villages out beyond the walls. They've got cities with more people."

"I only saw a little bit."

"Was it horrible?"

"No." Ira had to think. "Some of it was, though, but some parts were nice. You should go."

"You should take me."

Ira shook his head. Georg had said it with the spirit of adventure, but Ira only wanted to go home.

He didn't. He went back to work but wasn't particularly productive.

The next day was better. The next day he managed to get some work done and didn't take a knife to anything. Slowly, days went by and he found comfort in the arithmetic. Numbers tended to behave themselves and Ira never pursued mathematics to the point where numbers started bending in impossible ways.

Someone came to repair and paint the wall. Ira did his best to pretend nothing had ever been there. He tried to ignore the trace of paint fumes as he scratched his answers at the bottom of the ledger.

Selene came in, knocking on the door as she opened it. "Our Prince is here to see you."

He broke the pen nib on the page. "Tell him I'm not here."

She raised her eyebrows. "I already—"

"So tell him I went out already. Tell him you were wrong, that he just missed me." He could not stomach the thought of seeing Lucifer, not now, not when his choices were to lie or to admit what he had done.

"Are you sure?"

"Yes."

She made a face but went anyway.

Lucifer didn't come to the back room and he didn't come back that night either. When Ira went home, Mrs. Spiros gave him the thick, heavy package that had come for him.

He brought it upstairs with him and opened the note.

I'm sorry I missed you today. I'll try to find some time tomorrow to stop by. Things are slowing down.

Thinking of you,

Luci

Ira couldn't make himself open the package.

Ira had spent several days pretending to not be at home or at work, roping his coworkers and his landlady into the lie. He knew eventually the ruse would break; one could not avoid the Devil forever, but Ira had opened to avoid him for a little longer.

Lucifer sat on the stoop of the Inverness, his long legs sprawled over the steps, his wrists on his knees, his hands dangling. He looked discarded.

Ira thought of the skinny cat in Georg's bedtime story, wondering for the first time if it was rooted in truth.

When he saw Ira, he stood.

Ira almost turned around.

"I wanted to talk," Lucifer said.

"I don't have anything to say." He went inside and hurried upstairs but glanced back to see the Devil on his heels.

"Ira, please."

"What!" Ira snapped, turning around when he reached the landing. "What do you want?" he demanded, his stomach roiling.

Lucifer approached, coming to stand on the landing with him. "I want to know what's wrong. You...I sent you a note and I didn't hear back."

Ira moved away, fishing out his keys and opening his apartment. "There wasn't anything to say." He went inside and almost shouted at Lucifer for crossing the threshold.

"Imogen says you haven't stopped by at all, either."

"I didn't know I had to."

Lucifer stared at him, his eyes wide. His lips were parted the slightest bit and Ira could see that angel beneath his skin again, lost and confused and wanting to be loved. "Have I done something wrong?"

The question felt like a punch. He hadn't done anything, not a thing, he hadn't been the one who had broken his own rules and he hadn't been the one who'd almost spilled doing it.

First Ira's hands shook, then his eyes stung. "No."

"You...do you still want to see me?"

With the empty wretchedness of the past few days, where his only comfort had been shuffling numbers, Ira couldn't imagine sending him away. It had been one thing to keep a distance but seeing him had proved to be another matter. "Yes."

"Are you upset? Do you need help?"

"I'm sorry."

Lucifer's frown deepened.

Ira came unraveled, blubbering, "I am, I'm so sorry, I didn't mean for it to happen, I really didn't!"

"For what to happen?"

"Astrid, we were at a party and it was just...it was only going to be drawing but we ran into these friends...and I *swear* but I couldn't, she wouldn't stop."

The Devil went still and quiet and Ira knew he had to be livid.

"I said I wouldn't, but I did! I'm sorry, please, I really am."

"Did she hurt you?" Lucifer asked.

Ira shook his head, but he wanted to say yes. It hadn't hurt, he'd even liked it, he'd felt *good* inside of her. "I'd had a few drinks and-and I *told her*. I did."

Lucifer came closer and moved as though he would touch Ira, then stopped.

Ira wished he would close the gap. Ira couldn't do it, he didn't deserve to. "I'm sorry."

"You don't have to apologize."

"I promised I would tell you first! That we'd agree on things like this."

The Devil took another step forward and spread his arms like he was offering a blanket to a freezing man. "You can come here if you'd like."

Ira huddled against him, his shoulders hunched. He pressed

his face into the soft, thin silk of the Devil's shirt and pulled in a deep breath.

As he wrapped his arms around Ira, the right mix of firm and careful, Lucifer told him, "I am not upset with you, Ira, it wasn't your fault."

"It was," Ira insisted.

"It wasn't. I swear it wasn't," Lucifer soothed. "You didn't do anything wrong."

"I'm sorry."

"I love you."

A harsh, ugly sob tore out of Ira's throat; he hadn't meant to let it out, he shouldn't have been crying like this, not when Lucifer was the one who should have been upset. "I'm so sorry."

"You didn't do anything wrong, dear."

"But—"

Lucifer interrupted calmly, "I would know if you had."

"What?" Ira pulled back slightly, unable to process that statement. He had not been prepared to have the matter so abruptly removed from his control.

"I am Satan, I do generally know the state of one's soul," he explained as he wiped Ira's face.

"Have I got a soul?" Ira whispered, his voice hoarse.

"Ahh, maybe I've said too much," Lucifer mused. "If it is a soul or not, I cannot say, but there is that intangible thing within you that makes your life more than the life of a common beast."

Ira stared up at him. All his thoughts had evaporated, every mewling apology and wretched memory.

"Would you like to tell me what happened?"

Ira shook his head and a few more tears slipped down his cheeks.

"Would you like me to kill that horrible woman?"

"No. Don't. I. I don't want to think about her. Ever."

"There is a legal precedent here if you're worried about looking like you've gotten special treatment," Lucifer informed him. He used his sleeve to wipe away the last of Ira's tears and probably some of his snot; it made Ira feel like a child.

Ira shook his head. There weren't any Edicts about grown folks bedding each other.

"No creature in Hell will impose their will on another creature, through violence or coercion," Lucifer quoted. "That one has a lot of interpretations, but we do find it coming up in a lot of the court cases dealing with matters such as this."

The Third Edict was used to weasel out of arranged marriages; it was how workers with terrible contracts won their freedom and how children could separate themselves from unworthy parents. Ira didn't see how it applied to him.

"She didn't..." Ira shook his head. The encounter had not been violent or coercive, Ira had experienced enough to know what those things looked like. "Let's just. Let's not talk about it. Ever. Let's forget. Can we pretend that it never happened?"

Lucifer combed his fingers through Ira's hair. "Whatever you like, love. But first I need a promise."

"What?" Ira asked, sure that he would be asked not to break his word again.

"Tell me if you need anything. You don't have to tell me why, but tell me what you need me to do, or not do."

Ira nodded.

"Promise. The whole thing."

"I promise I'll tell you if I need something."

"Wonderful." Lucifer embraced him again. "Did you look at what I sent you?"

"The jar?"

"The book," the Devil clarified.

"Oh. No, I didn't."

"You should, go on, get it. I never do get to see your face when you open these things. I really thought you'd like this one."

Ira retrieved the gift and tore off the paper to find a thick, hardcover book, wider and longer than most books. It brought to mind a text or manuscript and when he opened it, he found that each page had a glossy black-and-white image.

"They're photographs," Lucifer told him. "Landscapes and architecture. No portraits, but, well, I thought they were beautiful. I thought you might want to give your brain something else digest." He reached over and skimmed through a few pages, then opened it to an image showing a vast expanse of flat land covered in tall grass. "That's Kansas. I know you couldn't quite picture it."

Ira stared down at the page. The image looked more real than any painting he'd ever seen. He touched it, half expecting it to have texture. "What type of spell is it?"

"It isn't. It's a photograph, uh, the light burns an image onto this film...I think. I was never good with the sciences. Anyway, isn't it marvelous?"

Ira nodded, going to sit on the couch and turn through some more of the pages. He'd studied about a dozen before he remembered his manners and cried, "Oh! Thank you!"

"You're welcome."

Lucifer hadn't come to sit next to him, instead standing to the side of the couch, almost as though he were peering over Ira's shoulder to look at the book.

Ira didn't think his eyes were on the images.

"What?" Ira asked.

"I missed you."

"Come sit."

The Devil settled into the couch. Ira scooted closer to him, spreading the book over both their laps.

As he turned the page, Ira asked, "Have you been to all these places?"

"Probably not all of them, but a lot of them."

Ira nodded towards the current photograph of a crack in the Earth. "Here?"

He nodded. "Sure, plenty of times. There's, uh, several peoples used to make their home in and around this area. I would visit sometimes. Just looking, really. They weren't of the Abrahamic persuasion."

"What?"

"They didn't believe in me. It's nice sometimes, to just be a visitor instead of the Devil," he confided. He put an arm around Ira's shoulders and pulled him closer to kiss his hair. "I missed you terribly, I really did, and I hate the way we left things."

Ira had almost forgotten entirely how things had ended last time they'd seen each other. It felt so far away and stupid. He set the book aside and wrapped his arms around the Devil. "You can stay, can't you? For tonight, at least."

"Yes." He put both his arms around Ira.

"And tomorrow?"

"I need to sort some things that cropped up while I was on Earth, but it shouldn't take long. Just a few things in the Third and, uh, someone in the Fourth has a soul that's…unusual, to say the least."

"Hm?"

"Can I tell you a secret?"

"You always do," Ira reminded dutifully.

"I know, I should really stop before someone tries to get

information out of you..." Lucifer mused. "But about the soul, it's...not human."

"You mean like one of yours?" The Devil's half-human bastards did sometimes come to Hell after they died if their actions and beliefs allowed it.

"No, not one of mine, it's fey, I think from the sound of it. Anyway, I'm not sure how it got here or if it needs to stay, but I'm not worried."

"That's good, at least, that you're not worried."

"It is nice, to worry about one less thing," Lucifer admitted. He kissed Ira's temple, then nestled his face into the crook of his neck. He let out a long sigh and tightened his arms. Half a word slipped out of his mouth.

"What?" Ira prompted.

"I don't want to be overbearing."

"Go on."

"I don't like being away from you this much. I know it's been standard for us, days apart, a few nights together. Notes and lunches. But I don't know, love, I. I know what I want, and I know it isn't what you want. I don't know where to go from here."

"What is it, exactly, that you want?" Ira asked.

"I want you with me. Not all the time, obviously, but the idea of...of maybe having one bed, that's our bed, not yours or mine, has its appeal."

Ira burrowed a little further into his arms, curling his legs up so his whole body was situated as close to Lucifer as he could get. "You've always wanted that."

"That's true."

"The palace will always just be yours," Ira pointed out. "And I like my apartment."

"I know you do. I know."

"It isn't that I don't love you," Ira vowed.

"No, I understand, I do, especially considering how long you spent sharing a room." The Devil let out a sigh.

"It will work out, Lu."

He expected the Devil to make one of his vaguely threatening statements, the ones where he expressed the desire to hold Ira captive or consume him whole, but instead he said, "I'll do whatever it takes to make it work," in a quiet, serious voice.

Ira wondered if it was hyperbole or not. He wondered if it applied to hypotheticals in which the Devil's wife returned. "I'm not looking for much."

"I'm looking for everything," Lucifer told him. "That's why I'm scared. I don't want to ask for too much."

"You haven't."

"I will. I know someday it will come to that."

"I don't think so." Ira shook his head and closed his eyes as that far away feeling started to inch over him and eat up all the space in his mind. He had no right to take this offer and throw it away; Lucifer had offered him so much more than he deserved.

They stayed like that on the couch for a while. Ira didn't feel entirely himself and he suspected that Lucifer didn't feel quite right either. Silence filled up the room, punctuated by the sounds from other apartments and Mrs. Spiros' far away screeches.

Ira played with one of the buttons on the Devil's shirt. "Did you see Felix?"

"Oh!" Satan exclaimed softly. "That reminds me. Oh, it's at the palace, don't let me forget. I picked up some of those terrible serial novels you like so much while I was up there. Something about Mars and a man who lives with apes. Phaedrus thought you might like them."

"Phaedrus Queen?" Ira asked, not sure who else Lucifer could be talking about, but also not sure why Phaedrus Queen would bother to recommend books Ira would like.

"I can't for the life of me think of another person I know named Phaedrus. I mean, the philosopher and the fabulist are both dead," Lucifer informed him. "And Felix is well. A year come and gone. Can you believe it?"

"No. How is he?"

"Good. Well. Both. He isn't used to me, but I visit too much as it is. Every time I go, I put him in danger."

"Lu, don't be morbid," Ira scolded. "You're always on about what a good mage that Reinhart is. I'm sure Felix is as safe as anything."

"He is a good fucking mage. It really irritates me."

Ira smiled, losing some of that far away feeling but couldn't entirely shake the disquiet that had hung over him recently. "How do you do it? All of this."

Lucifer seemed to understand what he meant, because he answered, "Sometimes I think I can't. Sometimes I absolutely know I can't. And then I see you or Felix and I feel that I can again. Or sometimes Imogen makes me do it anyway." He smiled a little. "But other times I really can't, and I stay in bed. Or someone slits my throat and buries me sixty miles outside the city and I have to walk the whole goddamn way back."

Ira didn't know what to do with that answer. "Were you ever a cat?"

"I've frequently been a cat. People take more kindly to cats hanging around and watching than they do to grown men. Or women. Or children or dogs. Being a bird works as well but I am *terrible* at being a bird."

"How can you be terrible at being a bird?"

"I hate flying."

Ira had to echo, "You hate flying?"

"Yes."

"Why?"

"It's too high."

Ira turned to look at him, one eyebrow arched and a silly grin on his face. "Are you afraid of heights?"

"No." A moment later, Lucifer added, "I'm scared of falling."

Ira's grin widened.

"You would be too if you'd fallen as many times as I have."

"Maybe you shouldn't fall so much."

"People always push me off of things," the Devil admitted, crestfallen. "It usually kills me."

Ira leaned in and gave him a kiss. "I would never push you off of anything."

"I'll hold you to that." He returned the kiss, gentle and quick.

Ira stretched a little. "So then that story about the cat and the little girl..."

"Which story would that be?"

"The girl takes in the cat and it's the Devil, but he's stuck, bewitched by the usurper. And the girl kills him."

"She kills the cat?" Lucifer asked.

"No, she kills the usurper."

"I don't know that one," the Devil said. "You should write it down for me. I'll send it to Junius. It would have him in stitches."

"How is June? Have you seen him?"

"I haven't," Lucifer answered, somewhere between cagey and morose.

"He's a good sort, you should. And I know he wishes you would visit him more."

"I don't know."

"Why?" Ira asked. "It hurts him more that you stay away than it would if you finally tried to sleep with him."

"Uh."

"I guess you probably wouldn't sleep with him, though, I bet you would try to *make love* to him," Ira teased.

"No, I..." Color had crept into Lucifer's cheeks, impossible to miss against his pallor. He shook his head and tucked a bit of hair behind his ear.

"I wouldn't mind if you did," Ira said and meant it. He had no ill will towards June; he had even made a pass at him. He liked that June held the Devil in high regard and that he understood that even Satan could need gentle handling.

"No. I can't. I couldn't. With Junius, I would want more. I would never be able to leave it at just sex with him and it wouldn't work out between us."

"No?"

"He hates being in Hell and I can't stay on Earth. And missing him would be as bad as missing you."

Ira didn't think that's all there was to it and wasn't surprised when Lucifer continued, saying, "And I couldn't be the Devil and be with him. Seeing him makes me wish I'd never fallen, that I'd never even whispered a rebellious word."

"Ah."

"But if I hadn't fallen, then I wouldn't be the Devil. I wouldn't have made my demons. Without that, there would be no Hell-born. And, of course, you see where I'm going with this, don't you?"

"No," Ira said. Although he had his suspicions, he didn't want to voice them and be wrong.

"I am glad I fell, Ira, love, because if I hadn't then I never would have found you."

Ira rolled his eyes and wondered how Lucifer had ever gotten the nerve to call Queen's poetry sentimental. "Defying all of Heaven was worth it cause you get to fuck me?"

"Well, and I've got my own realm now and debatably infinite power."

"How can anything be *debatably* infinite? It's infinite or it isn't."

"You'd think that!" Lucifer agreed. "I think, really, it's that I can't die so I'm getting away with a lot more than I should be."

Ira studied him for a little while, marveling at the way he'd come back to life in the past few days. Even though he'd probably been worried about why Ira was avoiding him, even though he'd spent days working and he'd had to go through the in-between spaces to get to Earth, he looked good. His color was better, less gray than he had been, and the gauntness in his cheeks had filled in.

"Are we in for the night?" Ira asked.

"I think so."

He started to undo Lucifer's hair. "Good. I'm glad you're feeling better."

The Devil smiled, but then it slipped from his face.

Ira asked, "What?"

"Nothing."

"Darling," Ira insisted.

"I want to ask how you've been feeling but I didn't think the question would be welcome."

"I've been feeling *terrible*." Ira could admit that much. "I haven't been sleeping. I know it shows, Selene's been on about how I look sick."

"What if you went in late tomorrow?"

Ira shook his head. "No, I wouldn't want to upset Marius."

"I'll send him a message. A late morning, a few hours of extra rest, of someone looking after you. I'll make you breakfast and draw you a bath and I'll send you out into the world pampered and loved and—"

"Saved?" Ira interrupted, running his fingers through a braid to undo it, then taking up another one.

"Can you blame me? I can't leave you alone for five minutes without someone trying to do something awful to you."

"Twins are unlucky, you know that."

"Twins are not unlucky, that's a stupid thing to say. It hasn't got anything to do with you. It's them. *People* are awful, that's what it is," Lucifer grumbled.

Ira continued to shake out Lucifer's braids. He didn't know what to say; he'd been treated poorly and seen others treated worse too many times to have any rebuttal. It was easier to blame bad luck or to blame himself than it was to consider that so many people had such potential to be so cruel.

"At least I know..." Ira sighed and combed his fingers through the Devil's hair, making sure he hadn't missed any braids. "At least I know that I am safe with you."

Lucifer made a face. Ira expected him to say that it wasn't true, that someday things would go bad between them. He always had a dour outlook on the future, he was always sure he would do something awful. Instead, he gave Ira a quick squeeze and said, "Yes, that's one of the absolute truths of the universe, I can confirm that. You will always be safe with me. I was going to do a bit with our full names and titles, but it felt a little pompous."

"Does the universe have absolute truths?"

"Sure. Circles don't have corners, for example, and triangles always have three."

"Any absolute truths that don't have to do with shapes?"

"None that come to mind."

"Shit," Ira said, clambering out of his arms to stand up, "Shit, it's garbage night."

He hurried to take the trash out. Otherwise, it would be sitting in his kitchen for another week. By the time he came back, Lucifer had left the couch and Ira feared, irrationally, that he had left, but he'd gone no farther than the kitchen. He was rummaging through the cabinets and ice box.

"Do you ever buy food, or do you just wait for me to do it for you?"

"I never know what to buy," Ira admitted.

"You should have some initiative."

"Georg thinks that's why you like me."

"Because you don't have any initiative?"

"Because I'm pathetic." Ira went to the icebox and pulled out a bottle of wine, then took a mug from the cupboard.

His glasses needed washing, as did a good deal of bowls and plates. He had let things get away from him recently.

"Oh, well, I don't think you're pathetic at all, Ira."

"What about Georg?" Ira asked, bringing the mug to his lips.

"Nice lad. Bloody interested to see what happens with him and Amaranth. And I have to say, I like his initiative with preservation courses. Why? Are we upset with Georg?"

"No."

"Are we pleased with Georg?" Lucifer ventured.

Ira gave a half-shrug. "Usually."

"Good. I knew you'd like him. I wouldn't have flirted with him so much otherwise."

"You...! What do you mean?"

"Oh, perhaps flirt is a strong word. I made some eye contact, but just to get him to come see me. And I only told him maybe when he propositioned me."

"You said maybe?"

"Well, it was before you asked me not to."

Ira set down his mug. "Were you going to sleep with him?"

"Probably not. I mean. Maybe. It's always good to have options."

Ira pushed him. "You were going to sleep with him!"

"I might have."

"Do you want to?" Ira demanded.

"He is particularly handsome."

"Lu!"

The Devil started to grin.

"Are you fucking with me?"

"Maybe a little. But you'll never know how much or about which parts." Lucifer reached over and took Ira's abandoned mug of wine, taking a deep drink. "See, that's the way Satan really operates."

Ira poured himself another mug. "Whatever. Fuck him if you want. See if I care."

"Does this count as us talking about it beforehand?"

Ira scoffed.

"I think it does, I even think it counts as agreeing that I can. Those were the terms, right, to discuss and agree upon it beforehand?"

"Go away."

Lucifer finished the wine, set down the glass, and headed towards the door.

"Where are you going?"

Lucifer turned towards him, a look of feigned bewilderment on his face. "Well, you told me to go so I thought I'd go see what Georg is up to. Georg and that pretty mouth of his. And that ass, Jesus..."

"Lu, stop being mean."

The Devil returned to his side and put an arm around him, kissing his hair. "Don't worry, if I was ever going to fuck Georg, I would certainly invite you."

Ira wrapped his arms around the Devil's waist. He pressed his forehead to the Devil's chest and took a moment to appreciate the slow build of heat in his belly. He really had missed him. "Come to bed."

"I sort of wanted to eat."

"You can eat after."

"Oh." The Devil's eyes went a little wide. "Oh, you meant...I thought you meant to sleep. I didn't know if you'd…"

Ira stood on his toes and kissed him, then tugged him towards the bedroom, his hands grasping Lucifer's hips.

Once in the bedroom, his fingers worked at the buttons on the Devil's shirt.

"Are you sure?" Lucifer asked.

"Yes."

"I mean considering…" He trailed off, leaving his concern unspoken but hanging heavily between them. He swallowed. "Considering what happened at that party."

Ira flushed, first cold then hot. "I thought we weren't going to talk about that."

"Well, no, but I don't know, you seemed so upset. I don't want to make things any worse."

"No." Ira shook his head. He wanted things to be normal between them, as though he'd never made such a stupid mistake. "No, I don't…" He lingered in the memory too long and a little wave of nausea ran through him. "I don't want her to be the last person who touched me like that…I don't. I want to do something good instead, something that's right. I want to be with you."

"If you're sure."

"I am, Lu, really, I am. You're always so sweet with me and I want that right now, darling, I do," Ira insisted, teetering towards begging. "Please, kiss me and do it like you mean it, like you love me."

"Tell me to stop and I will," the Devil vowed.

"I know."

Lucifer leaned in to kiss him, hesitant at first, but then with more confidence when Ira responded. He undid Ira's clothes and brought him onto the bed, his whole long, lanky body molding around Ira's in exactly the way Ira had wanted.

Ira wanted to be wrapped up in him, enveloped. He wanted to be covered in his kisses and he wanted the scent of him to linger in his bed. He wanted to feel right again.

After the Devil had covered in him kisses and caresses, when he conjured lubricant, as he usually did, Ira stopped him from applying it to Ira's length. He wrapped the Devil's hand around his own shaft. "Like this?"

"Whatever you like."

Lucifer slipped inside Ira, slow, deliberate. Ira almost wanted to cry, not from fear or pain or pleasure, but from some other emotion that he couldn't name.

The Devil spilled inside of him.

Ira realized he hadn't finished, that he was nowhere close to finishing. He'd been somewhere else, only half-involved in the act. When Lucifer pressed a kiss to his stomach and then lowered his head to take Ira's cock into his mouth, Ira put a hand on his shoulder and gave it a gentle tap.

"Don't."

"No?"

He shook his head. "No, come back up here."

Lucifer slid back up to lie beside him, taking Ira into his arms and touching his forehead to Ira's. "What?"

"I don't know, I want you to hold me is all."

Lucifer nodded and continued to hold him; his long fingers skimmed over Ira's hip, sometimes slid down to his thigh.

"Your hand?" Ira breathed.

He wrapped his hand around Ira's cock and gave it a gentle squeeze. Ira let out a long sigh and pushed closer to him. He pressed his mouth to the Devil's shoulder, digging his fingers into his back and moving his hips.

In the end, it was less the Devil using his hand and more Ira fucking it, but the result was the same warm, sticky mess that usually ensued. He clung to Lucifer afterward, not caring about the mess or the hunger gnawing at his belly. He didn't want to be anywhere else. They existed like that for a while, him running his fingers through the Devil's hair.

"It's so long," Ira said.

"It always grows back."

"Hair does that."

"No, I mean, it always grows back. It likes to be long," Lucifer clarified.

"You mean it grows back right away?"

"Not right away. Wouldn't that be disturbing, though, if it did?"

Ira tangled his fingers in his hair. "It likes to be long," he echoed. "You say it like your hair has its own wants."

"The body does what it wants. I try not to argue too much."

"We should eat."

"Yes," Lucifer agreed enthusiastically. "We should eat."

IRA AND the Devil hand in hand walked through the Eighth, towards the outskirts. The Devil seemed somewhat anxious, though Ira hadn't yet puzzled out why. They had dinner plans with Eodus and Jack. Ira even had hope that things would go better than last time.

He had decided to give having a brother a try in earnest. The thought had come to him over breakfast with Georg the other morning. Georg had reached across the table to take him by the hand and tell him how much better he looked. They had twined their fingers together, their hands resting on the table as they talked.

He liked when Georg touched him, and he didn't really understand why.

Georg had sopped up a bit of yolk with his toast and said, "We should have been friends sooner. I missed this."

"Breakfast?"

"No, stupid, having someone around who isn't after something."

"Darling, if you know they're using you, why do you let them?" Ira had asked.

Georg had shrugged. "Because no one would spend time with me otherwise."

"I don't think that's true. You're likable enough."

Georg had glowed as if it were the sweetest compliment he'd ever been paid, even though Ira knew that several poets had written odes to his looks and to his unbridled enthusiasm in bed.

"You know what I like best, about you, Ira?"

"What?" Ira had taken the bait.

"You don't want to sleep with me."

Ira had snorted at that.

"It's nice, though. I mean, I like to fuck as much as the next fellow…Alright, stop giving me that look, *more* than the next fellow, but I do like a bit of something in between. I'd like to have a conversation that isn't just pillow talk."

A look of melancholy had come over him and he'd taken his hand back to rub his eyes, to brush away tears that hadn't fallen yet.

"What?" Ira had asked.

"Nothing, it's just. I miss Hansel. It's been two years, but it feels like yesterday."

"Oh."

Georg had shaken his head and smiled. "He would have liked you."

Ira had forced a smile, not knowing what to say or how to feel, finding himself thinking of his own brother. He knew that Georg would have jumped at the chance to have his brother back, that he would have been overjoyed to find that his brother had been missing instead of dead.

That night he'd asked Lucifer to get in touch with Eodus and Lucifer had feigned concern, checking his forehead to see if he had a fever.

Now Ira wondered if he should check the Devil's forehead because he'd been twitching at every shadow and noise as they walked.

"Is something wrong?" Ira asked.

"Yes."

The terseness of the answer sent ice through Ira. "What?"

"I don't know. I've got a bad feeling, though. Something's off."

"Do you need to go? Eodus and Jack would understand."

The Devil shook his head but looked around the Precinct like he expected to see something that would explain his unease, assassins in the alleys or gremlins on the rooftops.

Ira looked around too, his eyes skimming over the wall that separated the Eighth from the Seventh. Forty feet high and made of stone, the walls had two gates each, one in the center of the city and one towards the outskirts. Any citizen could pass freely into any district in the city and sometimes people would go to visit other districts to watch the souls be tortured, just for a bit of entertainment.

Ira couldn't recall seeing anyone scale one of the walls before and he certainly had never seen anyone do it nude and flayed of all their skin.

He elbowed Lucifer and nodded towards the sticky, sexless thing clambering over one of the parapets, coming from the Seventh into the Eighth.

Lucifer released his hand and bounded over to the wall, snatching the creature as soon as it smacked against the floor.

Ira followed at a distance, watching as Lucifer poked at the person, examining them, then whispering, "The Third, the Third, nothing to worry about from you..."

"Lu?"

Keeping a grip on the bloody figure, Lucifer turned to look at Ira. He stood taller and thinner, his mouth had grown wider. "Ira, dear, love of my life, can I ask you for a favor?"

Ira nodded, watching the Devil's shape change with immense unease.

"Open that gate for me and then go get Imogen."

"What should I tell her?"

Lucifer lifted the flayed person into his arms. "That I found a soul from the Third."

Ira hurried over to the gate; he hadn't recognized the thing as a soul. His hand shook as he went to pull open the smaller, person-sized door that most people used when going for a casual visit to another precinct. He glanced back and saw that he'd have to open the full gate, the one that was used to let in masses of workers during their commutes.

The Devil had grown towering and spindly, his mouth a gaping maw; Ira had never seen him get this large up close before. He'd only witnessed this full monstrous form once before, the last time their Prince had publicly devoured traitors.

Ira couldn't look away when Lucifer started to shove the flayed soul into his mouth, swallowing it whole. The world swayed and a wave of lightheaded nausea ran over him; his arms trembled as he pulled open the gate so the Devil could pass through.

He closed the gate behind the monster, then ran for the palace. He ran as fast as he could the whole way and when he stumbled through the doors of the palace, the first thing he did was throw up.

It was only stomach acid and he made himself swallow it as he compelled himself towards Imogen's office.

The vampire had already left her desk by the time Ira entered her office.

"One got out," he wheezed, grabbing her by the arm.

She frowned, then asked, "Do you know from where?"

He held up three fingers, his breath coming in heavy gasps and pants. He doubled over, kept one hand on her arm, and rested the other on his knee.

She nodded.

"He went already," he managed.

She headed for the door and he tightened his grip on her arm. She glanced back, one eyebrow raised.

"I can help," he told her.

She considered him for no more for two seconds, brushed her long chestnut hair over one shoulder, then nodded. "You can. Go get your brother, bring him here."

"Why?" He couldn't comprehend what Eodus could have to do with any of this.

"Because he works in the Third."

"Oh."

She left after that.

He stayed behind, trying to catch his breath, not looking forward to running all the way back to the Eighth.

He jogged that time, instead of a full out run, and slammed on his brother's door with the flat of his hand.

Jack pulled it open, his face already pulled tight with concern. "Oh." He glanced back into the house and, over his shoulder, Ira could see Eodus speaking to a demon with deep orangey-brown skin and narrow blue eyes. "You should come in."

He shook his head and gestured over his shoulder. "I need Eodus."

"Uh. Eodus!" Jack called.

Eodus came over and the blue-eyed demon trailed behind him.

"You have to come to the palace," Ira told his brother. "It's about the Third."

The blue-eyed demon blanched. "I should come, too."

Ira couldn't think of a reason to waste energy arguing, so he nodded and stumbled back into the road.

They walked back to the palace and arrived before the Devil

had come home. Ira collapsed into one of the armchairs in the parlor off the foyer and to the right of the staircase. The other three stood in a nervous circle until Ira urged, "Sit."

They did.

Once Ira had caught his breath and guzzled down the mug of water Oris had brought him, he pulled the armchair closer to the couch where the other three had settled. He tucked his legs underneath him.

"Now considering that we were supposed to be at Eodus' for dinner, I'm wondering what this fellow was doing there," Ira said with a glance towards the blue-eyed demon.

Jack and Eodus exchanged a look; Eodus began to wring his hands and Jack looked lost, so Ira turned his gaze to the stranger.

Once their eyes met, the demon offered, "Oh. My name is Elisha, I started working in the Third a few months ago, but...I think there's something going on."

"There's definitely something going on," Ira told them. "Lu caught a soul climbing into the Eighth."

They stared at him.

"A soul from the Third," Ira clarified.

"No," Eodus breathed. "Is he...?"

Ira let out a sigh. "He went there to round them up, I think, but if one got as far as the Eighth then..."

"Then they must be everywhere," Elisha concluded. He looked at Eodus. "We should go help."

Ira shook his head. "Imogen told me to bring you here. Well, not you, but Eodus. And if Imogen wanted you here then she has a reason." He looked over Elisha, then added, "And maybe you should stay here, too, Elisha. What do you think's going on?"

"The same thing that happened in the First," Elisha replied. "I think. I...I overheard some of the others talking about, uh, about stirring the pot."

"What pot?" Ira asked, his nose wrinkled.

"It's an expression that means to cause trouble," Eodus said.

"No." Ira clucked his tongue. "I know what the expression means, I meant what pot are they stirring? Why are they doing this?"

Eodus and Elisha exchanged a look.

"What?" Ira demanded.

"Some of the people who live in Eighth are, um. Well, you know how some of them are. Rough around the edges. Boisterous," Eodus said.

"And?" Ira prompted.

"And I think," Elisha said, "I think they're upset with our Prince."

"Upset might be an understatement," Jack pointed out. "I mean, the things the neighbors say."

"What do they say?" Ira asked.

Eodus and Elisha looked at each other, similar looks of guilt on their faces.

Ira turned his eyes to Jack. "Well?"

"They say that he's ineffective and sick, that he's weak. That he's gone soft. That he cares more about..." Jack hesitated. "That he cares more about buggering pretty whores and fooling around on Earth than he does about what's happening in Hell."

"He doesn't *fool around* on Earth," Ira protested. "Idiots."

Jack reached up to touch one of the scars on his cheek. *Refuge.* "It's because of me. A lot of it, anyway. They think I don't belong here."

"And, well, the rumors about him always being in bed," Elisha half-murmured. "People say that when he says he's on Earth he's really lying around in bed. That he faints all the time."

Ira shook his head. "No."

He didn't know how these people knew so much about the Devil's business. He had fainted in front of the captains, but Ira didn't think they were stupid enough to tell anyone. He knew that rumors about the Devil being bedridden hadn't come from him, or Imogen, for that matter.

He ran through the other staff in his head. Gila, Oris, and the two cat keepers, Holly and Marcia.

One of them had to be spreading rumors. He'd have to tell Imogen.

The sky grew dark and still the Devil didn't return. The four of them agreed to wait up for the others, but Ira fell asleep after less than half an hour.

Imogen returned in the morning.

Ira, as soon as he heard her come in, ran out of the kitchen. "Where is he?" he demanded.

"Among the souls, finding the strays," she answered, her voice raw and weary.

"Is he alright? Are you alright?"

She gave a nod. "I'm tired, Ira, that's all. He was fine when I left him."

"Did a lot get out?"

"Enough."

"Imogen," he whined.

"A lot, but not too many," she answered. "He...he came upon those who'd been releasing them. They were...drunk. Sloppy in their task."

"And?" he pressed.

"And the Third will be needing a dozen new workers."

"Shit."

She shrugged. "He'll be back when he's done. Did you bring your brother?"

"Yes, and another worker from the Third. Elisha."

Recognition flitted across her features. "Oh, the new made one?"

"Uh. Maybe. I don't know."

"I'll speak with them later. Keep them here, though, I'll be ready for them in a few hours."

He nodded.

She gave his shoulder a pat and headed into the kitchen, going through it into the servants' quarters.

When she reappeared, she brought Eodus and Elisha into her office, closed the door, and spoke with them at length.

Jack and Ira went outside to sit on the stairs leading up to the palace. They watched fat, lazy bees buzz between the flowers and pretty, pink little birds flutter around.

Ira liked the birds. He hadn't ever seen them anywhere else in Hell and he hadn't seen anything like them on Earth.

Jack agreed that he'd never seen pink birds on Earth. "And I've been a lot of places," Jack told him proudly.

A few minutes passed by as Jack talked about the places he'd been. He came back to the topic of birds eventually. "But, you know, I heard that in the tropics, Australia and Africa and South America, you know places like that, they've got parrots and budgies and those sorts of birds. I never went to the tropics."

Ira didn't know much about the places Jack had mentioned.

Hours passed and the sky started to grow dark again. Jack went in to eat with the other two, but Ira couldn't stomach the idea of food.

"I'll bring you something," Eodus had offered.

Ira had shrugged.

In a rush, all the little birds started to fly away. Ira eventually heard what they heard. The sound of footsteps, slow and heavy, coming towards the palace. He stood and saw the monstrous creature that was their Prince staggering through the gate.

Ira ran down the stairs to meet him.

The Devil stood as tall as four men, at least, but as Ira grew closer, he seemed smaller. By the time he'd reached Ira, he had sunk to his knees, the right shape and size again.

Ira caught him before he toppled over. He put Lucifer's arm around his shoulder and his own arm around the Devil's waist.

"Let's get you inside, love," Ira said.

"Let's."

Ira grinned to hear his voice.

Halfway up the stairs, he realized there was something different about the body in his arms. It was not the same as the body he'd held last. There was an odd narrowness to the waist. He wondered if it was a remnant of the shape Lucifer had taken.

He brought him inside and upstairs, shifting his grip to find that the Devil's hips were broader than he recalled.

Halfway up the stairs, the Devil put a hand to his nose and pulled it way smeared with blood. "Fuck," he mumbled.

"No worries, love, we'll get you cleaned up."

He brought the Devil to the smaller bathroom and sat him on the edge of the tub. He grabbed a cloth, wet it, and started to wipe up the bright blood spattered down his neck and throat while Lucifer held another to his nose.

Ira barely had to undo the buttons to remove the Devil's shirt, tattered as it had gotten from his shape-shifting. It fell right off, fluttering into the tub, hardly more than ribbons.

"Oh!" He pulled back, staring at the Devil's chest.

"Hm?"

"No, just...Lu, you've got tits."

Lucifer reached up and gave his chest a bit of a grope with one hand, the other still holding a cloth to his nose. "Ah, well, the body does what it wants."

"Lu," Ira whispered. He couldn't make his voice return to a normal volume and continued to whisper, "Are you a girl now?"

The Devil took the cloth from his face and grinned one of his wide smiles, put his hand on Ira's waist and roughly pulled him closer, between his legs. His nose still oozing blood, he kissed Ira, his mouth slick and his teeth glittering awfully. "It would be a lot of fun to find out."

Ira swallowed, his breath quickening, and stared down at him. At her.

"But no, I'm not a woman any more than I was ever a man. Or maybe it's that I'm as much as a woman as I ever was a man. There's nuance there, I think. The body does what it wants. I play along."

"Like your hair."

"Like my hair."

Ira could taste blood on his lips. "I..."

"Tell me."

He shook his head.

The Devil loosened his grip. "Did I frighten you again?"

"No. Yes. I don't know. It's..." He licked his lips. "You should rest."

"I should." Blood had streamed all the way down his chin, now, coating his neck and wetting his chest again.

Ira handed him a clean cloth and he pressed it to his nose. Ira wiped him down once more and washed him up a little. He could have a real bath in the morning, but now he swayed even as he sat.

Ira brought him to bed and couldn't help but stare when he tossed aside the remains of his trousers.

Lucifer grinned again and ran his own fingers through the hair between his legs as though he were checking to see what was there. "Oooh, the cock is gone too. This is what I get for changing shape so much; the whole thing starts to think it gets to do whatever it wants."

With that, he collapsed heavily into the bed. He reached out and grabbed Ira by the wrist, tugging him in.

"Sit up," Ira told him.

He pushed himself up and Ira arranged some pillows behind him; he could lie flat when his nose stopped bleeding.

"Just a few hours," the Devil vowed, "Then I need to take care of a few things."

"Are the souls all caught?"

"All of them. Only a few score out this time, lucky for me."

"Then you should really sleep."

"A few hours." He reached over a twined his fingers with Ira's. "And when everything's taken care of, we can do those things you're thinking about."

Ira averted his eyes. He'd been staring at the Devil's breasts again; they were barely there and when he lay flat, Ira was sure they would all but disappear. Two small swellings of flesh, nothing Ira hadn't seen before, but he had never seen them before on Lucifer. He wanted to know everything about them, but especially if the nipples, slightly larger and pinker than they had been last time he'd seen them, would respond the same way.

The Devil's fingers climbed up his thigh and gave Ira a weak squeeze. "We could find out now if you're so very curious."

"You've got a nose bleed," Ira pointed out. The Devil's grip on his thigh was tenuous at best, so he added, "And you need to get some sleep."

"I imagine you're right."

Ira took his hand. "What's got you in an amorous mood, anyway? You must be exhausted."

"I think I'm actually a little delirious if we're being honest."

Ira sat up with him until his nose had stopped bleeding and then he climbed into bed next to him. He hadn't slept well last night, curled up in the armchair, waiting for him to come home.

As soon as the Devil put his arms around Ira, he felt at home again; it didn't matter the shape he had. It was the same skin, the same mouth, the same hair. The same fingers that ran through his curls.

Lucifer nestled against him, his ass against Ira's groin, Ira's arm draped over his ribs, a position they'd slept in a hundred times.

Any hint of flirtatiousness went out of the Devil as soon as he laid down. His eyes closed and his body went slack as he fell into a heavy sleep.

BY LUNCHTIME the following day, the Devil had clambered out of bed with circles under his eyes, clothed himself in one of his robes and sat down with Eodus, Jack, and Elisha at the kitchen table.

Ira hovered in the hall between the kitchen and Imogen's office, not sure what to do or how to help. He hated to hear the things the other men related to their Prince.

After Lucifer sent the other three home, Ira went into the kitchen and put his arms around the Devil. He assured him, "Not everyone thinks that."

"I am soft. Softer than I should be. No one wants a coward for a king."

"No one wants a despot for a king!" Ira insisted.

He pulled out of Ira's arms. "Ira, love, I have a problem to solve and my solving of it may not be to your liking."

Ira perched on the edge of the table, his eyes trained on the Devil. "What do you mean?"

"I mean there will be killing. I mean I will be eating people and you are nothing if not tenderhearted."

Ira raised an eyebrow. "You see what you want to see in me."

"Anytime I offer to hurt someone who has done you harm, you refuse," Lucifer pointed out.

"That's because they're not yours to hurt. They didn't do

anything to you."

Lucifer tilted his head to one side. His eyebrows pulled together, and his lips parted slightly. His face had not changed as his body had, but now Ira realized how little he looked like a man. Or a woman, in that case.

"If I want justice, I'll go to the courts. If I want revenge, I'll buy a knife. What I want is to put those things out of mind because..." Ira had to stop to consider his words, to make sure he said what he meant. "Because worse than being hurt is having to think about them all the time. I don't *want* to waste my life pursuing people who've done me wrong, giving statements to judges so they can dole out some punishment or defend why I sunk a blade into someone. They aren't worth it."

Lucifer opened his mouth.

"But if someone hurts you," Ira continued, cutting off whatever the Devil had meant to say, "If anyone ever did a single thing to you, then I don't want justice or revenge or punishment, I want them ripped to little pieces, I want you to destroy them. Because you're my friend, my lover, my very dear companion, but more than that you are my Prince and you are so much more than I am."

"I'm both flattered and concerned by your statements."

"Why concerned?" Ira asked.

"I'm not worth more than you."

"You're my Prince," Ira reminded.

"Are the walls less important than the roof?"

The question seemed one born of a moment of madness. "What?"

"I'm the roof. You're the walls. Together we're a home."

Ira grinned like a lunatic and let out a giggle. "We're a home."

"It's a metaphor."

"Obviously." Ira couldn't stop smiling. "I'm interested in the choice of building here, though. It had to be a home; it couldn't any old building or, you know, a store or a temple or a *house*."

"You know how I feel about you," Lucifer pointed out.

"Knowing and understanding are different. I still don't know if I understand." Ira held out his hand and Lucifer took it. "Kill the traitors. All of them. Eat them in the public square."

"Goodness me."

Ira rolled his eyes and shook his head. He slid off the table and left a kiss on Lucifer's forehead, then headed towards the stove. He peered inside the stock pot, gave it a stir and a taste, then took down a bowl from the cabinet.

He set the soup in front of Lucifer. "You should hire someone who doesn't always cook soup."

"I've gotten used to it."

Ira seated himself on the other side of the table. "What are you going to do about the rumors?"

"Imogen is looking into it."

"Lu."

"That's her job, she's my butler. She manages the household staff. My job will be to root out whoever is organizing these little rebellions." Lucifer heaved a sigh. "Which will be more difficult considering that I got ahead of myself and killed those idiots in the Third last night." He put his hands over his face and groaned.

Ira leaned over and gave his shoulder a squeeze. "You should get some rest."

He shook his head.

Ira came around to the other side of the table. "Yes, come on, I'll tuck you in and everything."

Lucifer took his hands away from his face, his eyebrows knitted together. "Are you going somewhere?"

"I haven't been to work in days, I should at least show my face if I want to keep my job."

"He won't fire you."

"Love," Ira said with a roll of his eyes. "I'll be back for dinner, I promise."

The Devil gripped his arm. "Don't go."

Ira frowned, his amusement slipping away. "Lu." He tried to take his arm back but found that the Devil's hand had become a shackle. A curl of pain wound through his gut, nothing like the playful unease that stirred when the Devil kissed him too hard. "Lu, let go."

"I just barely have this contained and I'm not even sure about that. There are people out there who likely want me dead."

"I don't think anyone—"

"Stay here," the Devil's voice sliced through him.

"You promised."

Lucifer said nothing and didn't release Ira, either.

"You promised you wouldn't make me stay, you did."

"I'm trying to keep you safe."

They stared at each other, a few seconds stretching into an

uncomfortable length of time. The only thing Ira could think to say was, "Don't ruin it, Luci. You're tired and you're not thinking straight. Eat. Get some rest. I'll be back by dinner."

Lucifer regarded him for a while longer, his awful eyes locked onto Ira's face. Finally, he said, his voice breaking, "Promise you'll come back."

"I swear it."

The Devil released his arm and slipped his arms around Ira's waist, burying his face in his chest. Ira rubbed his back, his own throat tight; when he stepped back, Lucifer let him go.

He made it to Marius' house without being waylaid. Once he stepped through the door, Selene came rushing over to him to fold him up into one of her magnificent hugs.

"Oh, we all thought something terrible had happened to you."

From off to the left, Georg said, "We didn't all think that."

"Those of us with sense!" Selene snapped. "Where've you been!"

"With my brother."

"What brother?" she demanded, stepping back and holding him at an arm's length.

"Yes, what brother?" Georg echoed.

Ira grimaced. "Uh, well."

They both looked at him. A woman came up and slid her arms around Selene's ample waist, nestling against her. Selene said, "Not now."

The woman pulled back, looking offended, but Selene took Ira by the hand and brought him to his office.

Georg followed and so did Marius.

"I had started to wonder if you still worked here," the pander said, his arms crossed, though not in a huffy, angry way, but in a looser pose that indicated he didn't know what else to do with his arms.

"Sorry, no, I...Lu had some things to deal with and I was with my brother and, well, I just...I'm sorry, Marius, I am, I should have sent a message or checked in sooner. I'll catch up on this week's numbers tomorrow, I promise."

"I'll hold you to it. Now, what's this about you having a brother?"

"Oh, well, you know. We were twins—"

Selene gasped then breathed, "Oh, no *wonder*." She took Ira by the hand and told him, "No wonder such terrible things happen to you."

Ira tried not to grimace but didn't do a good job. "Terrible things don't happen to me."

Selene lifted her hand and held up one finger. "You were sold to that woman," she said and put up a second finger.

Ira had no desire to hear the worst parts of his life rattled off and counted on fingers. "They're not *terrible*," he protested.

The woman opened her mouth, but Marius interrupted, "Let's not go through the litany of Ira's fortunes and misfortunes. We were hearing about your brother."

The other three trained expectant eyes on him so he related the story of their separation and recent reacquaintance. When he admitted that he had spent a whole year avoiding his brother, he could feel Georg's gaze trained on him. He even suspected that he saw the glint of tears in his golden honey eyes.

That gold reminded him of the gold in Lucifer's eyes. He watched Georg rake his fingers through his coppery hair and wondered if the reddish tint came from Lucifer, too, if Georg's blood still held traces of what Lucifer had looked like as an angel. If that speck of ancestry would show its face even in a great-great-great-great-grandson.

Selene had a thousand questions about his brother and Georg had none. Marius had asked only one. "Identical?"

"Sort of," Ira had said and then had amended, "Mostly. Anyway, I only came to let you know that I wasn't dead and that I'll be back in tomorrow for the full day."

Marius gave him a pat on the shoulder. "Give my regards to our Prince."

"I will."

The pander left after that.

"What happened in the Third, do you know?" Selene asked. "People have been talking about all sorts of things. I know at least three people who've got someone who didn't come home."

Ira shook his head. He had no idea what Lucifer would want people to know and what he would be telling them himself. "I don't know anything about that, really."

"My uncle hasn't come home," she told him.

He shifted uncomfortably. "It's his business, not mine. I don't know what happened, I wasn't there."

"He's the closest to a father I ever had."

"Selene, I can't tell you anything, I don't know anything to tell," he insisted, looking to Georg for help, though he didn't know what assistance the youth could give.

Georg made a sympathetic face.

"His name's Pate."

"Selene, come on now, Ira doesn't have anything to do with any of that," Georg reminded. "As long as your uncle wasn't involved with anything...untoward, I'm sure he'll be home soon enough."

Selene shot Ira a dirty look. "Untoward? You mean like having *opinions?*"

"No, I mean like being stupid enough to let out those souls," he snapped.

"Don't," Ira urged.

"Not everyone is a sycophant," Selene hissed.

"Sycophant!" Georg cried. "That's a big word for a girl from the last street in the Eighth!"

"I'll take that over being a little shit who still suckles at his mommy's tit!"

Ira expected Georg to take offense, but instead, he sneered and laughed. "As if she didn't hand me off to a nurse as soon as I was born!" he spat. "Call me brother-fucker, too, while you're at it, you miserable—"

"Georg, stop. Leave it."

The younger man glared at Ira for a moment, then his look softened. "Fine." He came over and left a kiss on Ira's cheek. "Come find me when you're done slumming it." He trailed his fingers through Ira's hair as he left.

Ira grinned after him.

Selene scowled, muttering, "Little shit."

"You shouldn't be so mean to him."

"I don't know what's got you paling around with him in the first place. You never used to like him either," she reminded.

"He's nice to me."

"Cause he thinks he can get something out of you. Society types always want something out of you."

"And what do you want from me?" he asked. "Asking me about your uncle and all that?"

"I want my uncle to come home alive, not to get some petty favors from the Devil!" she protested.

"Innocent men don't need favors," he told her. "I really hope your uncle was innocent."

She shook her head at him.

He didn't know how to tell her that her uncle was probably already dead, that he couldn't do anything to help, even if he'd been inclined to plead her uncle's case. They stood and looked at each other for a while, until Ira broke down and shared, "My brother's buggering the acrobat at Dreams of Eulalia."

Her eyes lit up. "What!"

"Actually, I think the acrobat's the one doing the buggering," he corrected. "Not, I guess, that it matters. We should go see a show together." Selene hesitated, so he added, "I can get us in for free."

She lit up at that. "I'll never say no to a free show!"

"Tomorrow?"

She nodded and grasped his hand. "I love seeing those girls dance, you can't even imagine."

He gave her a smile.

He took his leave not too long after, recalling his promise to be home by dinner. On the way out, though, he passed by Georg flirting with a chubby lad and invited him to come out tomorrow, too. Georg only agreed to think about it.

In the palace, he found Lucifer sitting in bed with papers spread out in front of him, his robe cast aside on the settee. He had his legs crossed Indian style and his inky hair draped over one milk-pale shoulder. He looked over when Ira entered.

He grinned when he saw Ira staring at his breasts again, not for any reason other than he had forgotten about them altogether. "For someone who grew up in a whorehouse you certainly are fascinated with these."

"I'm sorry." Even to his own ears, his apology sounded hollow. He tried to change the topic, tried not to think about how he would have rather gone home than come here. "What are those?"

"Contracts that are due soon." The Devil gathered them up in his hands, her hands, whosever hands they were and set them on the bedside table.

Ira fidgeted and felt bad for wanting to leave. "Should I be calling you her now?"

"Her or him or it or them, none of them mean what I am," Lucifer answered, "No matter what the body looks like."

"Oh." The enormity of the statement disoriented him.

"Come here."

Ira approached the bed. Lucifer took him by the arm and pulled him closer, onto his lap so that he straddled the Devil. The position lacked the heat it normally had, this time providing something warm, something tender.

"What's got you worried, love?" Lucifer asked, cupping his hand around Ira's face.

"You came back different."

"No."

He nodded. "You did." He didn't mean to argue.

"Tits haven't got anything to do with who I am."

"What? No, I know. It's not about that." He took a lock of Lucifer's hair and let it run through his fingers. "I thought you weren't going to let me leave."

"Oh." The Devil glanced away, then admitted, "I almost didn't."

"I can't do this if that's how it's going to be."

"I warned you," Lucifer sulked.

"And I'm asking you to be better than that."

Carefully, Lucifer ventured, "What happened to not asking me to be more to deserve you?"

Ira shook his head. "It's not about deserving me. It's not about me loving you. I can't do it again, Lu, I can't go back to how it was. I don't want a curfew or a lock on my door or a list of places I'm allowed to visit."

"If I kept you here would you love me still?" Lucifer asked.

"I'll love you always."

"But would you hate me too?"

Ira admitted, "I don't know. I don't want to find out."

"I need to know that you're safe."

"I need to know that I'm safe with you."

Lucifer blinked several times, then let out a long sigh. "Strike a deal with me."

Ira shook his head before he'd even realized what the Devil had asked. He had tread on this ground once before and hadn't liked it.

"You haven't even heard my terms yet," he admonished. "I want you to be able to trust me on the matter. I want it squarely in your hands."

Ira considered the set of his face, not seeing any of that desperate hunger he had last time. "What are your terms?"

"That I'll never keep you here against your will," Lucifer offered.

"And my end of the bargain?"

"Nothing."

"I don't think deals work that way."

"You might be right. A favor, then."

Ira told him, "I don't like owing people favors."

The Devil's mouth twitched slightly, then he proposed, "Another kiss, then."

"I give you a kiss and you'll swear that you'll never take me captive?" Ira confirmed.

"Yes."

Ira nodded. "Then it's a deal."

"A deal," the Devil echoed.

Ira brushed his lips across the Devil's mouth.

He went back for another, firmer kiss. He combed his fingers through Lucifer's hair and knotted his fingers in it, tilting back his head, wondering if this changed body would like the same things. The Devil arched against him and let out a small cry, the same cry as always, and the answer seemed to be yes. He nipped the Devil's throat, then his earlobe.

Lucifer started to undo his clothes, his fingers working at Ira's shirt and trousers with haste. The shirt was tossed aside. Ira hated to pull away from his kisses to remove his trousers all the way, but did it anyway, as fast as he could.

He returned and pressed his mouth to the Devil's chest, first pressing a kiss to his sternum, then moving his mouth to cover one of the nipples, sucking gently at first. When Lucifer tangled his fingers in Ira's curls and pressed him closer, Ira caught the tip between his teeth, careful but firm.

Lucifer's whole body tensed at that.

Ira gripped his thigh, sliding his hand up, forgetting briefly that there was no cock to hold. His fingers found heat and wetness instead. He pushed a finger inside and Lucifer gasped sharply.

Ira pulled back, not sure what had gone wrong. "I'm sorry, I didn't..."

"No, love, it was only that I forgot how it feels." The Devil wound his arms around Ira, drawing him close so that they were lying down with Ira on top.

Like this, Ira thought, it looked almost as if he had no breasts at all. The flesh there was a little more pliant, he noted, then forgot to think about anything when Lucifer spread his legs. Lucifer wiggled so that they were hip to hip, so that Ira's cock was not yet inside him, but nestled close against the lips.

His fingers brushed down Ira's back, the tips of his nails barely scraping along the skin. The Devil moved his hips so they slid together, over Ira's shaft, the pressure almost as good as fucking. At least, that's what Ira thought until Lucifer slipped a hand between them and guided Ira inside, no need for any lubricant other than what had come from between the Devil's legs.

They moved together, need and pressure building inside Ira, and he thought, inside Lucifer too, because he kept drawing him in deeper and had his fingers digging into Ira's back as though he wanted more. Finally, he gasped and arched his back, his body going stiff and then slack a moment later, melting into the bed.

Feeling Lucifer come, the muscles within him contracting around Ira's cock, brought him to the edge. A few thrusts later, Ira had spilled and melted along with him, burying his face in the crook of the Devil's neck.

Lucifer's fingers played along his ribs, his chest moving shallowly beneath Ira. He let out a long breath then pressed a kiss to the side of Ira's face. "You know what's kind of nice?" he asked.

"What?"

"Less to clean up."

Ira shook his head, a smile growing on his face. He rolled off Lucifer and on to his side.

Lucifer pushed himself up and gathered the papers he'd set aside before. "Do you mind if I work?"

"No."

"It shouldn't take long."

"You can do what you need to do," Ira assured him. He scooted closer and pressed a kiss to Lucifer's thigh, some of the fine hairs tickling his lips. "I'm going into work tomorrow."

"I should go back to the Third."

"You should rest," Ira insisted.

"I will, but after I rest, I need to go to the Third."

"Not unless you get a full night's sleep. And you eat something."

Lucifer glanced his way, his lips pursed. "Remind me again how it is that you're allowed to tell me what to do but not the other way around."

Ira huffed. "I'm not telling you what to do."

"It sort of feels like you are."

"Fine, then don't listen. Go out and collapse in front of everybody. It won't bother me, at least, not until someone slits your throat and buries you and then comes to make an example out of me."

The Devil rolled his eyes.

Ira wanted to pinch him, but instead, he said, "I'm going to work tomorrow."

"You said that already."

"And I'm going out, too."

Lucifer tensed at that. "Where?"

"Siobhan's."

"Oh, good, that's safe enough."

Neither of them spoke.

Lucifer returned to his contracts, reading through them and scribbling down notes on a scrap of paper, then organizing them into an order that must have made sense to him. He folded some of them in half, horizontally or vertically, and folded down the corners of others, sometimes the top and sometimes the bottom. Ira thought about asking what the folds meant but didn't think it was his business to know.

"Should I be worried?" Ira asked.

Lucifer paused what he was doing and turned his gaze to Ira. "That's a sort of ominous question."

"Souls out in the First and the Third in less than a year."

"Ah, what's a year, anyway?" Lucifer asked. "Some arbitrary system of time I borrowed from Earth...imagine the shit-storm it would have been if I'd tried to make my own." But a moment later, his face sobered. "But maybe. Maybe don't be worried but be vigilant. Fear won't serve us here, but caution might."

"You aren't afraid at all?" Ira prompted, trusting the Devil to be honest with him.

"No. Not yet. But I am uneasy."

Ira sighed and kissed his thigh again. The Devil raked his fingers through Ira's curls in the same absentminded way he stroked the cat.

LUCIFER WENT to speak with the other workers in the Third and Ira went to work, then to Dreams of Eulalia; nothing of note happened in either place, except that Georg declined to go take in a show and Selene nearly fainted when she got to go backstage and meet the performers.

She had regarded Jack warily and Ira guessed that she hadn't ever been so close to a human before.

Afterward, she'd whispered to Ira that Jack smelled. "Not bad, not really...I can't put my finger on it."

"Sunshine," Ira explained.

"What?"

"Food from Earth has a sweeter taste. Imogen says that the blood of things that live up there is sweeter, too, even the rats. It's the sunlight that does it to them, I think."

Selene had then pronounced that maybe she should try to go up to Earth sometime, though it had sounded more like an idle fantasy than real intention.

By the time a week had passed, Lucifer had relaxed somewhat about letting Ira out of his sight. He had spent most of his waking hours conducting interviews with workers and captains of the precincts. He seemed to think he was unraveling things.

Ira had spent last night in his own bed because Lucifer had stopped by Marius' to tell him that he was absolutely exhausted, that he was just going to go home and sleep. "Or maybe die," he'd added.

Today, Ira wondered if he should check in on him or let him rest some more.

While he considered his options at the bar, waiting for a glass of water, Georg came up behind him and put one arm over his shoulder and another around his waist. He rested his chin on Ira's shoulder and asked, "Any way that I can still take you up on your offer to see a show?"

Ira leaned his head against Georg's. "You certainly may. When do you want to go?"

"Tomorrow?"

"I thought you were—"

"I was," he interrupted, "But Rogg and Visya are fighting and I can't stand it."

"What are they fighting about?"

"Who. Who are they fighting over," Georg corrected. "Her name is Mirella and she's incredibly attractive, but she's not worth squabbling over."

Ira bobbed his head in understanding.

"So you're going to be my savior."

"Fine."

A man came up and hooked Georg around the waist, pressing close and asking, "How much for the pair of you?"

Georg wrinkled his nose and tried to shrug him off.

"Don't go rubbing all over him and expect no one to notice," the man accused. "I can fuck you and you can fuck him. Or one of you can take my cock and the other can tongue my asshole."

"I'm not looking for that kind of work," Ira told him.

"I've had you before."

Ira frowned. "Before isn't now."

"And I'm leaving," Georg said, disentangling himself from the man's grasp.

"Pair of cock-teases," the man growled, reaching for Georg again.

Georg grabbed the man by the wrist, grasping so hard that his knuckles went white. "I said I was leaving and that means no, so you can kindly fuck off or you'll not be having me or anyone else unless they leave a hole for it in your bandages."

The man yanked his wrist back. He shot both of them a dirty look but slunk away.

"I'm headed to class," Georg informed him. "Tomorrow night, though, you promise?"

"I promise."

Georg beamed at him, as though nothing had happened, and kissed Ira's cheek, leaving with a bounce in his step.

Ira took the water and returned to his office, marveling again at how poorly some people took no.

He decided to visit Lucifer that night since he'd made plans for the following one.

When he arrived at the palace, Imogen gave him a terse smile.

He asked, "Is he...?"

"No, he's fine, I've just had to fire a few people, so we're shorthanded and I *don't eat* so I have no idea what the fuck I'm doing."

Ira didn't think he'd ever seen her so ruffled. "A few?"

"The cook and the maid."

He raised his eyebrows. "Oh."

"Oris was selling information, so he's been marched outside the wall. Gila, though, the poor idiot fell in with one of the rabble-rousers." She rolled her eyes. "We've got her and her lover in the dungeons now."

"Is he busy?"

She shook her head. "Letting them sweat for a while, so he's getting some rest. You don't need to look so worried, he's tired, not spent."

He nodded, thanked her for the information and headed upstairs. He found the Devil in his study, nodded off on the chaise longue with a book on his chest.

Ira prodded him awake and joined him on the chaise. He curled up on his lap and offered to read to him.

"No, that's alright, but thank you, love."

Ira rested his head on Lucifer's chest, then had to reach up and give it a poke.

"Rude!" the Devil accused.

"Where've they gone?"

"Back to wherever they came from," he said. "Why, will you miss them so terribly?"

"No."

"I can always grow some more. Big ones, this time, if you want," he offered, a silly grin on his face.

Ira chuckled, then shook his head. "No, however you are is

fine."

"You sure? I can make them nice and pillowy soft so you'll have someone where to rest your head at night."

Ira really laughed at that, unable to picture the Devil looking anything but comical with large breasts. "You're too skinny."

He nodded, conceding the point. Without the same note of teasing, Lucifer asked, "And...what about things between my legs? Not everything changes all at once, you know..."

Ira hadn't known and didn't know what to do with the information. "Oh."

"Is there a way that you prefer me?"

"However you are." Ira didn't mind repeating himself.

"I do have some control—"

The idea of Lucifer pushing his body to take a shape it didn't want made Ira uneasy. "I want you as you come to me, Lu, no other way."

He kissed Ira's temple and they stayed cuddled on the chaise. The Devil turned the pages in his book.

At first, Ira mistook it for a book of poems, but soon realized it was a saga of some kind, one long poem dealing with the misadventures of a demon named Thagor Bloodaxe. It told a lengthy tale that took place before the building of the wall and was required reading for older school children.

"What's got you reading about Bloodaxe and his Screaming Horde?"

Lucifer answered, "Something one of those bastards in the Third said."

"Which bastard? And what did he say?"

"The bastard who spat on me. She referred to the...uh, Craven Company? I don't know, she was screaming. But I thought it bore looking into."

"The Raven Company?" Ira ventured.

"That's got to be it. I didn't think Craven Company sounded very frightening."

"The Raven Company wiped out the Screaming Horde."

"And their motivation?"

"Bloodaxe raped the daughter of Willa the Voracious."

"Oh!" The Devil sat up straighter. "Oh, you're right, aren't you? That's why I added the Third Edict to the Charter, isn't it?"

"Maybe. How should I know?"

"You shouldn't." The Devil kissed him. "But you're a clever

little thing. Sound of mind and all that. One of us ought to be." He flipped through the book, searching, Ira assumed, for the part about Bloodaxe and Ola Willasdaughter.

When he found the page, he marked it, then declared, "I'm starving and lazy and Imogen is a terrible cook. Would you like to go out and get dinner?"

Ira nodded.

They went out for dinner at one of their usual spots. At one point at the end of their meal, Lucifer disappeared for a long time and came back with a weedy woman dressed in kitchen clothes.

"You know her?" the Devil asked, jerking a thumb towards the woman. "She says she knows you."

Ira glanced around, realized the Devil had to be talking to him, then looked at the woman. She did look familiar and he stared at her for a long time before he started to recall her. "What's your name?"

"Becka Hearthshad."

The name sounded familiar and he tried to imagine her looking hale and youthful. "Nial's daughter?"

She nodded.

"So you know her?" Lucifer asked.

"Sure, she used to hang around the Trade House sometimes. Years ago, though, when I'd just started whoring."

"Good sort?"

Ira shrugged. "Good enough, far as I know. And Nial never did me wrong if they could help it."

"Mm, alright." To Becka, the Devil said, "Go to the palace. Tell Imogen I sent you."

The woman asked, "Uh, begging your pardon, Your Highness, what for?"

"I need a cook. You clearly need a better job."

"Oh, I'm not a cook yet, sire, I just—"

"Better than a vampire who doesn't eat. She'll sort things."

The woman stared at him.

"Well, go on, unless you'd rather spend your life chopping onions and potatoes back there. Christ knows Lorden is never going to die."

The woman shook her head, then hurried out the door, almost running.

"Is that all the reference it takes to get hired in the palace?" Ira asked as Lucifer threw a handful of coins on the table.

"No. But Imogen will sort it. Besides, I'm not looking for a paragon, I'm looking for a cook."

Ira shrugged. It wasn't any of his business if Lucifer wanted to hire random women and he trusted that Imogen would send her packing if she proved to be unsuitable. "Maybe she can make something other than soup."

"Maybe. Maybe she won't go pawing through my mushrooms, either. I should have killed him."

"Why didn't you?"

"Ah, I like to imagine him foraging for food better than I like the idea of killing him. I wonder how long it will take before something poisons him."

Ira linked hands with him and tugged him towards the Inverness, which was closer than the palace. The Devil followed willingly, stopping every so often to kiss Ira. One time he pushed him up against the wall of someone else's house for several minutes, long enough to slip his hands down the back of Ira's trousers and make him moan.

By the time they reached Ira's apartment, they were both aching and Lucifer pushed Ira onto the couch before the door had even closed all the way.

He climbed on top of Ira and pressed a kiss to his neck as he worked at the buttons on Ira's shirt.

Before he'd even undone three buttons, Ira's mouth went dry and his heart started to hammer, not in the heady way it had before. He lost control of his breathing, couldn't take in enough air, and all he managed to do was whisper, "Stop." Lucifer must not have heard him because he had to repeat, "Stop, stop, please."

Lucifer pulled back, at first only a little, but then climbed off him entirely when he saw Ira's face.

"I just."

"It's fine," the Devil assured.

"I can't breathe."

"You're alright."

Ira shook his head.

Lucifer slipped onto his knees before him and took Ira's hands in his. "You are. I promise. Take a breath."

Ira tried, sucking in a shaky breath, but he was unable to find anything to steady himself.

Lucifer wrapped him up in an embrace. "I promise you're safe. I swear."

Ira wanted to believe him but couldn't. It took a long time for his heart to settle again, for his body to stop trembling, for his mind to stop racing. When it had, a wave of embarrassment rolled over him, making him cold then hot, unbearably so.

He pulled out of Lucifer's arms and went to the kitchen, not able to look at him.

"Love," the Devil called after him, still kneeling before the couch.

He didn't look back, pretending to search for something in the cabinets.

"Did you ever open that jar I gave you?"

He turned around, puzzled by the question. "No."

"Go get it."

He fetched it from his bedroom, where it had glowed faintly every night since he'd got it. He sat when the Devil gestured for him to sit on the floor.

With a wave of his hand, the Devil closed the shades without standing. He nodded towards the jar and urged, "Open it."

Ira twisted off the top and hundreds of specks of lights came tumbling out, whooshing all over the room then stopping to settling into fixed spots. One orb, pale silver and larger than the rest hung there, too, and Ira thought it looked familiar.

He reached out to touch one light. It guttered then came back to life.

Lucifer traced his finger between seven of the lights. "The Pleiades. Subaru. Matariki, Thurayya...a dozen names, a dozen peoples all looking up at the same sky." He pointed to another cluster. "The Heavenly Shepherd. The Giant. The Hunter. Mriga." He traced a few more stars. "The arm of a chief ripped off by the Thunder People."

Ira stared where he pointed, unable to take his eyes away for the better part of an hour. He didn't see any of the things that Lucifer showed him, but they enraptured him, nonetheless. There were no stars in Hell. He had to ask, "How come we haven't got any?"

"Because there's nothing else in our sky. Do you think there should be?"

"Hmm?"

"Would you like to look up at night and see stars in our sky? I'll hang them there, just for you, if you want."

Ira shook his head. "I think it would frighten people."

"Maybe it would delight them."

He shook his head again and wound his arms around the Devil, climbing into his lap. "I'm sorry."

"No need."

"I don't know what happened."

The Devil kissed his hair and tightened his arms.

Ira couldn't shake the feeling that he did know what was wrong, that they both did, but knew it would remain unspoken unless Ira was the one to bring it up.

"Maybe just one star."

"Just one?" Satan repeated.

"The only star in the sky and I'll know you put it there for me."

Lucifer grinned. "I'll be right back," he promised and with that, he was gone.

He didn't come right back. It took nearly an hour before the Devil reappeared and when he did, he had a slick of blood trailing from his nose down to his throat, soaking into his shirt. He still had a grin on his face and his eyes glittered. He grabbed Ira by the hands and pulled him over to the window. He jerked back the shade and threw open the window. He climbed out onto the ledge then pulled himself on to the roof.

He reached back down to help Ira up but Ira had already shimmied out and hoisted himself beside him.

"I didn't take you for a climber."

"I hid on the roof sometimes."

"You hid a lot of places," Lucifer said.

"Hard to get any reading done in a whorehouse, especially when you're a lad on the cusp of being a man."

Lucifer stared, the blood drying on his chin.

"Don't worry, Mistress always kept me away from them. That Edict was never broken in her House, she was careful to make sure of that at least."

"If you call fifteen fully mature."

"I'd stopped growing."

Lucifer chortled. "You certainly had."

Ira scowled.

The Devil pulled him close, then turned him. He pointed to the sky, his hand luminously pale in the darkness. A small light glowed in the sky, a pinprick that had never been there before.

Ira couldn't stop staring at that speck in the sky.

It twinkled.

"I've never made a star before," Lucifer admitted. "And I don't think I'll ever do it again."

"Overextended yourself?"

"No, I don't think so. It's not that. It's that I don't think I'll love anyone the way I love you."

"That's a weighty declaration."

"It's a weighty feeling." He sat down.

Ira sat beside him. He could not stop the same thought from repeating in his head. *That is my star.* Prince of Darkness and Lord of Hell, he who sat the serpent's throne had made it for him and no one but him.

They stayed on the roof for a long time, until the sky started to lighten, and the star faded. Ira nudged the Devil awake.

He sat up with a snort, his face and neck and chest still crusted with blood. "Hm, what?"

"It's morning," Ira told him.

"Oh, it is, isn't it?"

"Lu?"

"What?"

"The sun, on Earth, that's a star."

"Yes."

"What makes it light here, then, if we haven't got a sun?"

"I don't know."

"You don't know?" Ira turned to look at him.

"No. It was like that when I got here." Lucifer pushed himself all the way up and scrubbed at the dried blood with his sleeve. It made hardly any improvement. "I've got a theory."

"Tell me your theory."

"Hell is a place where the absence of the Almighty is the ultimate punishment. More than the torture or the cleansing, being away from Him is the whole point of this place. And I think, well, what communicates that better than getting rid of the light from the sky, the thing that makes life possible?"

"But we are alive."

"Well, sure, of course. He might be a bastard, but I don't think He's enough of a bastard to make me stumble around in the dark for all of eternity. Can't punish souls if you can't find them." Lucifer grinned. "But fuck God. Better to stay down here than get burned up by the horrible fireball of His."

Ira shook his head.

"God thinks my jokes are funny."

"I never know when you're joking."

He shrugged, then continued, "As for getting things to grow here, Junius and Lilliana took care of that."

"Lilliana?"

"Angel of agriculture and husbandry. Or, she was. Demon of agriculture doesn't have the same ring. She pretty much lives in the kennels now."

"She lives in the kennels?"

"Well, she's got a bedroom and everything, she isn't bunking with the hounds. Doesn't care for people, she tells me whenever I go to check in on her. I figure I should leave well enough alone."

Ira considered what he'd said for a while, then told him, "You should wash up. And I've got to get to work." He stood and stretched. "Do you ever think of writing these things down instead of letting people wonder?"

"No. Wonder is good. People ought to wonder about things. Imagine how stupid and boring you all would be if you didn't have anything to wonder about."

Ira looked at the sky one last time, hoping to catch a glimpse of his star, but the sky had grown too light for that. He would have to check again when darkness fell. He would have to point it out to Georg.

IRA BROUGHT Georg over to Siobhan's. They walked with his arm around Georg's waist and Georg's arm slung around his shoulders. The woman at the front counter frowned at them and he wondered if she recognized him; he didn't recognize her. Last time he'd come with Selene, a different woman had waved him in with a pleasant smile.

This woman continued to frown at them.

Ira approached and said, "Normally we have seats right at the front. I think they're reserved. For us."

She nodded. "Our Prince has seats reserved at every show."

"Good, well, we'll be using them."

She said nothing else and he headed inside.

"I don't think she likes you very much," Georg whispered.

"Like I give a shit." Ira shrugged.

He brought Georg over to their usual seats and ordered drinks from the serving boy that approached. Servers flocked to serve the Devil because there was the chance that he would drink too much and leave a pile of coins or gems behind as a tip.

After their drinks had come but before the first show had started, Ira spied Siobhan. He decided that, since she was on good terms with Lucifer and had always been friendly towards him, he should go over to say hello.

She smiled when she saw him.

He barely registered the woman beside her, slender and half a head taller than he was.

"By yourself tonight?" Siobhan asked, her eyes scanning the crowd.

He shook his head and nodded towards Georg. "I brought a friend."

Siobhan looked relieved at that, though he couldn't imagine why.

"This one belongs to that acrobat of yours, doesn't he?" the woman asked, her eyes flicking over Ira.

"No, that's Eodus. They're twins."

"Ah."

Ira tried not to frown too severely at the stranger; he and Eodus did look alike but being mistaken for his brother chafed.

"Then what's your name?" the stranger asked.

He got the feeling he didn't want to answer. "Ira. You?"

"Tabitha."

He wondered if that name would ever not leave a sour taste in his mouth. He made himself smile and shake the hand she offered. It wasn't her fault and it wasn't an uncommon name; he couldn't be rude to everyone who had it. "But anyway, Siobhan, I just wanted to say hello."

"Of course."

He headed back to sit with Georg.

The younger man asked, "Who's that?"

"Siobhan? She owns the place?"

"No, stupid, the other one."

Ira shrugged. "Said her name's Tabitha."

Georg's eyes went wide and seeing his reaction made Ira's mind start to tick.

"Tabitha, as in...?"

"I don't know." Ira couldn't help glancing back at the woman, who was still by Siobhan's side and appeared deeply involved in a conversation. If they were sisters, they didn't look anything alike. The woman looked too mild and pretty to be the one Lucifer talked about. He would have expected a wicked and terrible beauty. It couldn't be her.

The lights fell and Siobhan introduced the first act, taking the place of the usual master of ceremonies. He was out with gripe, she informed them. She thanked them for coming and stepped aside as the first dancers came out, two pale-skinned sisters who danced to haunting music.

After the first acts, Siobhan came back and announced with a grin, "And I would like to welcome one of our captains, Rema, of the Fourth. I know she hates it when I do this, so I made sure I did."

A voice came through the crowd, clean and cool, "And no introduction for your queen?"

Siobhan went from her usual green to paler, sickly shade of chartreuse.

Ira wanted to throw up. Georg grasped his hand, a gesture of reassurance and shared shock.

They all knew the queen of Hell had been around, that she was not dead or exiled, but she had not made any public appearances. No one knew where she had been or what she had been doing.

Someone near them, probably drunker than they had any business being this early in the night, called, "Ira, when'd you two get hitched!"

Everyone in the building seemed to turn and look at Ira.

Tabitha stood up and peered at him as well. She had a small smile on her face, amused or irritated, Ira couldn't tell. When she made eye contact, his skin crawled, though she'd done nothing menacing.

Ira didn't know what the appropriate reaction would be, but he felt that the safest one was to flee. He got up, still holding hands with Georg, and hurried out.

They didn't run, but their pace was anything but leisurely. By the time they made it back to the palace, both were winded.

Imogen, in the foyer with one of the cat keepers, looked them over, stopped her discussion about hairballs and asked, "What now?" as they hastened through the door.

Ira shook his head.

"Have more souls gotten out?"

"No, no," he assured and saw the tension melt out of her shoulders. "Where is he?"

"In the kitchen."

They went together and found Lucifer, looking wan and tired, but better than he had been, making tea in the kitchen.

"What's got you two looking so bothered?" he asked.

Ira didn't know what to tell him or if he even should, but Georg blurted, "Your wife was at the show."

"Oh." Lucifer's eyebrows drew together, and the corners of his mouth turned down. "She can do as she pleases."

"But she called herself the queen," Georg insisted.

At that, the Devil's face smoothed into a mask. He stood, took Ira's left hand, then started to push up his sleeve, turning his hand palm up. "This might sting."

Ira frowned. "What might sting?"

Satan didn't answer.

At first, Ira was only concerned, but he grew afraid when the Devil dug a fingernail into his arm, carving a symbol. Ira tried to take his arm back, but he couldn't. It was more than the strength of the Devil's hand holding him still; something else rooted his feet to the ground, something Lucifer was doing to him as surely as he was slicing into Ira's flesh.

Lucifer carved a series of runes into Ira's skin; blood spattered onto the kitchen floor.

Imogen appeared in the doorway. When Georg tried to intervene, she stopped him.

Finally, the Devil released his arm.

Ira pulled away, shrinking against Georg, not sure if he was angry or terrified or if he was going to be sick.

He felt like bees had taken up residence under his skin and in his lungs and nose and mouth. He couldn't quite think.

The Devil opened his mouth but before he could say anything, he fainted, his head cracking against the kitchen tile, blood pouring from his nose.

Imogen went right over to Lucifer.

Georg brought Ira over to the kitchen table, made him sit, and gave him a clean rag to press over the cuts on his arm. Ira knew the younger man was talking to him, too, but couldn't process any of it.

"Don't move him," Ira warned. The warning was overdue and no one had tried to move Lucifer, but it was all he could think.

Imogen glanced over. "I know. What was he doing?"

"I don't know."

She had blood on her fingers. She kept bringing them half-way to her mouth before she realized what she was doing.

Ira tied the rag around his arm and went to kneel beside Lucifer, turning his head so the blood from his nose wouldn't dribble down his throat too much.

After barely a minute, he stirred. He blinked up at Ira. "Sorry."

"What did you do to me?"

He shook his head and Ira knew it meant he couldn't speak

that much yet.

Finally, when he was able to sit up and made it to the kitchen table, when Imogen had put a mug of tea in front of him, *and* when his nose had stopped bleeding, he said again, "I'm sorry."

"What did you do?"

"I gave you...I gave you part of me."

"What part?" Ira had to ask.

Lucifer swirled his hand in the air. "The, uh, the, you know. The good parts."

"Luci, what the fuck are you on about?"

He tapped his chest and then Ira's. "The part that keeps this beating. The part that will keep you safe. I won't risk anything happening to you."

Ira touched his own chest, wondering what he meant exactly.

"Are you angry?" the Devil ventured, his voice barely there.

"I don't think so," Ira said, though some part of him recognized that he should be. He didn't think he had the emotional wherewithal to be angry right now. "You should have asked first."

Lucifer shook his head. "No. I would have done it anyway."

"Sire," Imogen said.

The Devil turned to look at her. "Yes?"

"What will we do about your wife?"

"Nothing," he replied.

"At all?"

He nodded.

"What about him?" she asked.

"Ira is safe now," Lucifer said.

"No, the other one," she said, her eyes on Georg. "He's seen everything."

"We trust Georg, don't we, Ira?" Lucifer asked.

"We do," Ira confirmed.

"I've incredibly good at keeping secrets," Georg insisted.

Lucifer reached over to take Ira's hand. "Will you stay here tonight? It doesn't have to be with me but...but shit, knowing she's out there..."

"I don't think he should know about this," Imogen repeated.

"He does, though, and it is what it is," Lucifer almost-growled. Softly, he asked, "Ira, will you stay, please?"

Ira nodded, not sure what else to do. He had too many questions to leave.

"Good. Thank you. Imogen, help me upstairs."

Imogen assisted him, leaving Ira and Georg to sit in the kitchen and stare at each other. Someone came to clean up the blood all over the floor and eventually Georg helped Ira wash the runes carved into his arm.

"He's made you undying," Georg pronounced when the marks had stopped bleeding and they could finally make out the shapes.

"What?" Ira stared down at the runes. They didn't mean anything to him, but he had never studied magic or ancient texts.

"Undying," Georg repeated. "Like he is, not just long-lived like most of us are. He must be worried about his wife."

Ira didn't know what to say. He didn't know how long his family lived or how old his parents were now. He had never known what the future had held for him in that regard.

Georg bandaged his arm. "That's the only one I know. I haven't the foggiest what the rest of them mean."

Ira nodded.

"Are you alright, darling?"

"Maybe."

Georg gave him a squeeze on the shoulder.

"He made a star for me." He wrapped his hands around Georg's.

George echoed what Ira had said, then followed mutely outside to look at the light twinkling in the sky above them. They sat on the front steps to the palace, not looking at the garden but staring up at the sky.

"It seems sort of serious," Georg pronounced after a while. "All of this."

"I think it is," Ira confided.

The other man snaked his arm around Ira's waist.

Ira leaned into his embrace. "I don't know anything about being in love," he admitted, his eyes closed, and his face turned inward towards Georg's neck. "I don't know what I'm supposed to do after someone makes a star for you."

"I don't think there's a precedent for this."

Ira brushed his fingers over the gauze binding his arm. "He gave me part of him."

He didn't know what to do with that, either. It was something he could never reciprocate, something he had never even fathomed. The feeling that had filled him up, that vibrating energy from before, had faded and now he felt empty and exposed like people could come and pick out whatever bits of him they wanted.

Georg admitted, "No one's ever given me anything."

Ira kissed him then, an odd kiss that was born of the desire to express Georg's importance more than it was to provoke longing. "I don't want to fuck you."

"I don't want to fuck you either," Georg proclaimed with a smile.

"I would like you to come to bed with me, though."

Georg nodded and didn't seem to think anything of it when Ira brought him up to Lucifer's room. The Devil had already fallen asleep curled on his side with his cat wormed beneath his chin.

Ira started to shed his clothes and wondered if he shouldn't, if Georg would think it too forward. The other demon tossed his clothes on to the floor without hesitance. They climbed into bed together, neither of them more than mildly curious about the other's body.

"You really are skinny," Georg mentioned, his fingers trailing over Ira's ribs.

"And what a lean Adonis you are." Ira ran his hand over his bicep, down to his forearm and wrist, where their fingers tangled together again.

The cuts on his arm stung and he still wasn't sure how he felt.

"What's an Adonis?" Georg asked.

Ira didn't answer; he nestled closer against the younger man and tried not to think about anything too much. It took him a long time to fall asleep, longer than it took Georg. He stared up at the red and gray pattern on the ceiling, wondering what he was supposed to do now, knowing that he was undying.

Knowing that Lucifer had done this to him without asking.

Ira woke alone in a room that smelled faintly of vomit. Marlow watched him from the bedside table, her eyes half-closed. He sat up and inspected his bandages. A few dark blotches had soaked through the gauze and he peeled it off to find the wounds crusted over and scabby. He poked at them, a line of five symbols going from his elbow to his wrist.

He should wash them, he knew, but he didn't get out of bed.

Minutes passed before the other two returned. Georg helped the Devil make his way back into the room. Lucifer had circles beneath his eyes and his hair, damp, had been combed over one shoulder.

Georg, flushed pink, wore one of the Devil's robes and couldn't quite look at Ira.

"I threw up," Lucifer announced, and Ira realized it must have been an explanation as to where they had been. "You slept through it." He unwound his arm from around Georg and instructed, "Go see Imogen about a candle or something to get rid of the smell."

Georg nodded and left, his eyes still on the floor.

The Devil managed to make his way back to the bed unassisted. "I'm afraid I might have overextended myself."

"Seems that way."

He took Ira's left hand and turned his arm so he could examine the symbols. "I had to do it."

"You didn't have to," Ira pointed out and took his hand back. "You *have* to breathe, your body makes you, your heart *has* to beat. You didn't *have* to carve up my arm."

"You're right." He sighed. "You are. I wanted to do it."

"Why?"

"Because...because I don't want there to be any confusion. About what you mean to me."

Ira scratched off a bit of dried blood from around one of the symbols. "You needed to make me more? Like you thought you needed to make her more?" He hadn't expected his voice to catch but it did. He clenched his jaw to stop his lips from quivering.

With his mouth half-open and his eyes wide, Lucifer sucked in a breath, then shook his head. "*No.* Love, never."

"Then what?"

"I am selfish and I need...I *want* to know that time cannot take you from me because I don't know what will happen if she comes for me. I don't know what she'll tell me to do and I don't know if I'll listen."

"And you want me to wait around for you if you decide you should be with her again."

"It sounds horrible when you say it like that."

"It *is* horrible."

"I didn't...Ira, love, you have to know I didn't mean it like that, I didn't mean to be horrible."

It wasn't often that real fear wrote itself so plainly on the Devil's face. Ira had seen it a few times and usually, it had concerned Felix. He might not have been desperately ill or on the brink of death, but Satan was unwell. He had spent too long doing too much and he had so much with which to contend.

"I understand," Ira told him.

"I don't know what I'm going to do."

"Comb your hair before it tangles."

Lucifer stared at him, frowning for a moment, but then he nodded.

"Would you like help?"

He nodded.

Ira retrieved a comb and worked it through his hair. He didn't think he wanted to be undying, but he did understand that it had been a desperate act.

"I should apologize to Hiram," Lucifer declared out of nowhere as Ira braided his hair.

"Oh," Ira said, not sure what Lucifer had ever done to Hiram Reinhart that warranted an apology. "I don't think you should do any traveling for a while."

"I feel less than wonderful," Lucifer conceded.

"You need to rest."

"As long as nothing terrible happens, that is what I intend to do."

He had to feel worse than Ira had imagined.

"I'd appreciate it if you stayed for a few days."

"I do have a job," Ira reminded. "But I will sleep here if that's what you want."

"Thank you."

Ira scooted back, done braiding. "I'm going to wash up." He stood and turned back the covers, nodding for Lucifer to get into bed. He kissed his forehead and tucked him in.

He encountered Georg, his arms laden with candles, on his way to the bath.

"Nothing happened," Georg blurted as Ira passed him.

"Hmm?"

"The bath. Nothing happened. I know the two of you are, you know. I know you're only seeing each other."

"Oh. I wasn't worried."

Georg's brow creased. "No?"

"No." He shrugged. "I don't think he'd make it halfway to getting hard with the state he's in, anyway. Maybe in a week or two, you can give it a go."

Georg shifted the candles in his arms.

Ira grinned at him. "Just make sure you invite me to watch."

The other man let out a nervous laugh.

Ira let himself into the bathroom. While he washed, he took extra care with the cuts on his arm. They would scar for sure, but now that they had scabbed over, they didn't hurt much more than either of his tattoos had.

He wondered if he should stay home from work for a few days, worried as Lucifer had been. He also didn't like the idea of encountering his wife alone, or of Lucifer being alone if she came to the palace. Maybe if he was healthy, Ira wouldn't have worried.

Once clean, he padded down to Imogen's office. "Can you do me a favor?"

"Probably."

"Will you have someone go down to Marius' and get the ledgers?"

She looked up.

"I think it would be better if I stayed with him for a while," Ira admitted.

"Even after he carved you up like that?" Imogen asked, an eyebrow raised.

"I don't think he really knew what he was doing. I mean. He knew what he was doing for himself, I don't think he realized he knew what he was doing to me."

She regarded him for a while but finally nodded. "I'll send a runner down. About your friend."

"Georg won't say anything."

The answer didn't satisfy her. "How well do you even know him?"

"I trust him, Imogen, I do. He loves our Prince," Ira insisted. "Besides, if people were already selling secrets, what difference does it make?"

She sighed. "Speaking of secrets, what do you know about that star?"

Ira grinned, he couldn't help it, joy bubbling up inside his chest. "It's mine."

"Well, next time he wants to give you a present, try to limit it to something that isn't cosmically significant, given that he's been passing out so often."

His grin turned sheepish and he left her office, wishing she hadn't scolded him but unable to regret asking for the star.

IRA BROUGHT the ledgers into Lucifer's study and took up residence there for a few days while Lucifer mostly slept. Georg stayed to keep him company, availing himself of the books in the Devil's collection; he would leave to go to class, but not to go to work.

During the evening on the third day, Georg stretched and sighed and declared, "Shit, I could use a good fuck, though."

Ira glanced over. "Then go to work?"

"Ugh, but it's such a long walk."

"I'm sure you could find someone to fuck you on the way over, then."

Georg smiled. "What about that butler? She keeps staring at me."

"I don't know if Imogen has sex. Do vampires have sex?"

Marlow leaped up onto the desk and Ira held out his hand; she rubbed against his knuckles then padded across the ledger and jumped off the other side onto a bookshelf.

Georg replied, "Some of them do; I know at least three people who've fucked a vampire."

"She doesn't eat, though. I think she might be a purist when it comes to these kinds of things," Ira noted.

"Too bad. I like the way she smiles."

"Oh, she terrifies me when she smiles!" Ira laughed.

Georg stretched again, letting out a low, desperate moan that would have had customers swarming around him. "I could really go for a good toss."

Ira contemplated sleeping with him. It would be fun, he was sure, and Lucifer wouldn't have minded, he was sure of that, too. Something stopped him from offering. Maybe because that awful incident with Astrid had happened too recently. Maybe just because he'd rather have had Lucifer join them and the Devil wasn't up for that. "You've got hands, haven't you?"

Georg rolled his eyes. "I think I'm going to go to work for a little bit."

Ira lifted the ledger he'd completed. "Then take this with you. Tell Marius it's the last one that he needs for his taxes."

Georg came over to take the ledger and left a kiss on Ira's cheek. "Want me to bring you anything?"

"No. Tell Marius I'll be in soon, though."

Georg nodded. "Visya promised that she and Rogg aren't fighting anymore. I might go out tonight."

"Ah, I knew I wouldn't be able to keep you to myself forever."

Ira made his way through a few more pages of his current ledger before hunger brought him to the kitchen. He checked on Lucifer and found him sound asleep. He encountered Imogen in the kitchen, making tea and putting together a tray that was surely bound for the Devil's bedroom.

"He's out like a light," he told her. "Been sleeping like the dead."

"Good," she said. "Better than having him up at all hours wandering around like he's lost."

Ira had never seen him do that and expressed as much to her.

She responded, "When you're here he's occupied with other things. He worries less."

A shadow fell across the kitchen.

They both turned to find a comely woman standing in the doorway. Ira almost didn't recognize her in the full light of day. She had light red hair and fair skin, not milk-pale like the Devil, but warm and glowing ivory.

She exuded a quiet calmness, but like a tap only turned on half-way, Ira got the impression that there was a lot of energy lurking beneath the surface.

He hadn't imagined her looking this way, sweet-faced and not at all threatening. He couldn't imagine her doing the things Lucifer had mentioned. He couldn't imagine her dainty hands leaving bruises on his skin.

"What does the Devil have to worry about?" Lucifer's wife asked.

Imogen stared at her, still holding a kettle in one hand and a mug in the other.

"You're the butler now, aren't you?" Tabitha asked.

Imogen nodded, set down the mug and the kettle, and gave a small bow. "I am, Your Highness. Is there something I can do for you?"

"As long as the bedroom is where I left it, I think I can manage. I hear he's been in for a few days."

Imogen nodded. "He's resting."

Tabitha clucked her tongue. Her eyes barely flicked over Ira. "Always getting himself into something," she sighed and turned away from them, heading upstairs.

Ira wanted to run ahead of her to warn Lucifer. Instead, he watched from the doorway of the kitchen as she climbed the stairs, sidestepping a cat.

She disappeared into the bedroom.

Ira reached for Imogen's hand. "I don't, I don't think he'll be pleased."

"She's the queen, it's her palace, too, isn't it?" Imogen asked, her voice calm as ever. Her grip on Ira's hand tightened.

After about two minutes, Ira couldn't stand it any longer. He let go of Imogen's hand and marched upstairs. Imogen hissed for him to come back but he ignored her. He entered the room boldly, though without a plan.

He lost his nerve right away.

Tabitha knelt on the bed, her fingers knotted in Lucifer's hair, her grip tight and his head tipped back. She leaned in close to him, almost on top, one knee planted between his legs.

Lucifer had the look of a cornered animal, his hands gripping the bedspread to his chest.

They both turned to look at him and Ira lost any words he might have had.

Color came to the Devil's cheeks.

Tabitha frowned. "I did hear that you were carrying on with someone," she drawled.

"Lu." Ira locked eyes with the Devil, who started trying to push his wife's hands out of his hair.

She released him, irritation plain on her face.

The Devil clambered out of bed, keeping his sheets bunched around his waist.

"A bath," he told his wife. "I ought to wash up...It's been so long, I don't want, well, you know, this isn't how I imagined..." He grasped Ira with a shaky hand, dragging him towards the door. "This one can attend me. Imogen. She's the butler, anything you need. I won't be long."

He yanked Ira out of the bedroom with him, jostling Ira's shoulder, and dragged him into the small bathroom. As soon as the door closed, he came undone, his whole body trembling. He clung to Ira when he slid an arm around his waist.

Ira could only think of the Devil admitting that his wife had choked him until he'd blacked out, that she'd left marks all over him, that she had bitten him till he bled.

"I'm sorry," Lucifer whispered, his voice thick. "Love, I'm so sorry."

"You didn't do anything."

"I can't."

He didn't elaborate on what he couldn't do but Ira had his suspicions. He urged, "Come on, darling, we'll get you clean. You'll feel better."

The Devil nodded mutely.

Halfway through the bath, he grabbed Ira's hand so hard it hurt. "*Don't* tell her about Felix."

"Of course not."

His nails, too sharp, dug into Ira's skin. "*Promise.*"

"I swear." He smoothed the Devil's hair away from his brow.

Lucifer nodded and loosened his grip on Ira's hand.

Ira inquired, "What about us? I mean, am I...are we still official? Should I relegate myself to being—"

"No," Lucifer didn't let him finish. "No, you're not anything less than you were before she showed up."

Ira nodded.

"I just have to figure out how to tell her."

Uncertainly Ira offered, "Lu, if you're in love with her still, I know I asked you not to be with anyone else, but I mean, she's your wife."

"I don't know. I need time. I didn't think she would come back, I didn't."

"I understand."

"God, she scared the *shit* out of me, I thought someone had come to kill me!" Lucifer gave a nervous smile.

"Well, it's been ages since someone tried to do that, I figure you're about due for an attempted assassination," Ira tried to joke.

It didn't lighten the mood. Lucifer sank lower into the water. "Poor Mercy..."

With a sigh, Ira trailed his fingers through the water. "Mmm. Poor Mercy."

After he had toweled off, Lucifer pulled Ira close. "She's going to try to scare you off once she knows."

"Scare me how?" Ira asked.

"Put you in your place. She always liked being the queen, being better than the rest. Whatever she might tell you, I do want you with me."

"Should I go?"

"I don't know. Not yet. I don't know if she means to stay...Or what she expects."

When he'd dressed, Ira followed him to the kitchen.

Upon seeing his wife, Satan became someone else. Not babbling and jumpy as he'd been before, but someone cool and bored.

She looked him over. "You look a little more put together. I thought you were about to have a nervous breakdown."

"I had sort of gotten used to being woken *without* anyone hurting me."

She grinned. "I'll show you what hurting's like later."

Lucifer rolled his eyes. "Not unless you've learned some new tricks while you were away." He settled into the seat across from her at the kitchen table, his movements all reptilian languor. Ira had seen him move that way before when he was doing his best to menace someone, or sometimes when he was a particular kind of amorous.

Imogen took Ira by the arm and led him out of the kitchen. Before he had time to protest, she brought him into her office and pushed aside a slat in the wall the two rooms shared. The view was limited, but the sound came through clear enough.

He thought of the times he and Lucifer had fucked on the kitchen table; it must have shown on his face because she whispered, "Don't worry, I don't like to watch things like that."

"When did you start bedding children?" Tabitha asked.

"Would you care even if he was a child?"

She didn't answer, instead saying, "Speaking of children, I heard a whisper that you've been corrupting the souls of little boys."

"One," he corrected. "Never trust whispers, they always exaggerate."

"I had kind of hoped you were getting back to your old self. What made you do it?"

"There wasn't anything else I could do with him. It wasn't part of any grand scheme if that's what you want to know. You aren't missing out on anything. My sights aren't presently set on the Citadel."

"Mmm. And what's this I hear about you being ill?"

"Exaggeration," he scoffed. "You get a couple of nose bleeds and people think you're ready to keel over."

Ira saw her make a sympathetic face. "You were always prone to those. Gobbling lost souls and retching them back up in what, where was it? The Fourth?"

"The Third," he corrected. "If souls ever got out under Rema's watch, I'd know end times were nigh."

Tabitha laughed at that, a deep mellow sound that made Ira wish he could have been the one to make her laugh. "Why don't you send away that child you're fucking and get a bottle of wine and make me feel welcome in my own home?"

Ira's stomach dropped.

"Send him where?"

"Christ, you don't let him *live here*, do you?" She sounded truly appalled.

"What difference does it make to you who lives here?"

"And when did you get so many cats?"

"I didn't get them, they come here." Lucifer stood and left her in the kitchen.

Ira turned his eyes towards the doorway, wondering if Lucifer would ask him to leave. He wondered if his wife would expect to share his bed, if she had come back to be with him. He wondered, dread coiling in his gut, if she was here to stay.

The Devil came into Imogen's office, his body still held with a coolness Ira hadn't ever witnessed before.

Imogen rushed to close the slot in the wall.

"Do you want me to go?" Ira asked.

He shrugged. "That's up to you."

"Lu," he begged.

"I won't tell you what to do either way. You're welcome to

stay."

Welcome, but not exactly wanted. "I should go to work anyway, I guess. Let them know I haven't died."

The Devil nodded his agreement.

Ira shouldered past him to leave and headed into his study to gather up the ledgers. He wondered if he should take the other things that had ended up here over the past year. He decided not to, half because he didn't want to go back into the bedroom, but also because it felt too final.

As he left, he saw the Devil head back into the kitchen with a bottle of wine in hand, a sparkling white he'd picked up on Earth the last time he'd been up.

Ira went straight to Marius', dropped the ledgers on his desk, then took a seat at the bar.

Marius appraised him and then poured him a drink. "Glad to see you here."

"I do miss the smell when I'm away for too long," Ira said after he'd taken a sip.

The pander laughed. "And you've been keeping Georg away, too."

"He's been keeping me company. Is he still here?"

"Went upstairs with a couple of girls a little while ago."

Ira nodded.

"That artist."

Ira groaned and took a larger sip of his drink. "What about her?"

"She did come around asking for you. She seemed worried when I said you hadn't been in."

He couldn't help the scowl that crossed his face. It wasn't Marius' fault and if he'd listened to the pander in the first place, he wouldn't have ended up where he had. "Well, keep telling her I'm not in if she comes back."

"She seemed awfully upset about something."

"Makes two of us."

Marius didn't ask any questions; he gave Ira a pat on the hand and went to talk to another customer.

Georg came downstairs a while later, his arms draped over the shoulders of two girls. When he spotted Ira, he expressed his surprise at seeing him out of the palace. "He's doing better then?"

Ira shrugged. "I don't know. I think." He looked around the brothel and didn't know who could be counted as loyal. "I'll tell you later."

Selene, when she was free, came over to Ira and embraced him, telling him that she had been worried about him.

"Nothing to worry about," he assured her.

"And I do miss you when you're away," she told him. "I miss you being out on the floor with me. No one else ever wants to make bets."

He grinned and they both looked at the girl who walked in. He leaned in close to Selene and whispered, "Looking for a woman. Older. My money is on Lana if she's available and Shay if she isn't."

Selene surveyed the girl for a while, then said, "A woman, yes, but young like she is. Helen if she can afford it, or Dianna. Five bits?"

Ira nodded.

The girl, however, didn't go right over to any of the workers but approached the bar. She ordered a drink and gripped on to it, her eyes darting around the room.

Georg leaned in and whispered, "I bet I can get her."

"No." Selene shook her head. "You can't bet and court, it's against the rules."

He pouted, but after a while of watching the girl, said, "I think I've had classes with her. My money is on her leaving before she makes a choice."

In the end, Selene won. Ira retreated to the back room after that.

At the end of the night, Georg offered to walk Ira home and pestered him with questions for the entire walk, especially after he found out that Tabitha had come to the palace.

Initially, Ira didn't want to talk about it, but in the end, it was all he could talk about. They stayed up late into the night, both lounging on Ira's bed, trading hypotheticals back and forth about what she could want and what Lucifer would do and what it meant for Ira's future as companion to the Prince of Hell.

"Did he really ask you to leave?"

Ira shrugged, thinking back. "No. Not really. Didn't ask me to stay, though."

"Are you going to see him?"

"He knows where I am if he wants me," Ira replied, fully knowing he had given a petty answer. He wanted to know that Lucifer would bother to seek him out. He needed to know. He had no desire to become so pathetic that he begged for scraps of affection. "Besides, she's been gone since before I was born. In my whole life, Hell's never had a queen."

"You mean you think she'll leave?"

"No, but maybe they have some catching up to do."

"What kind of catching up, I wonder?" Georg asked, his eyebrows cocked and a smirk on his lips. "Was she pretty?"

"You saw her."

"But not up close!" Georg protested.

"She's pretty."

"Not as pretty as you, I bet," Georg told him, reaching over to pinch his cheek.

Ira rolled his eyes. He wasn't as pretty as the queen. He didn't think Lucifer would put him aside entirely, but he did worry that the nature of their relationship would shift. What use did he have for a companion if his wife returned? He let out a breath through his nose.

Georg gave his hand a pat. "Maybe she'll leave again," the younger man suggested hopefully.

Ira could barely muster a smile. "I'm tired. Do you want to stay?"

Georg nodded.

They curled up beneath the covers, distance between their bodies until Ira draped an arm around Georg's waist and nestled close. "If he leaves me, you and I should get together." He hated having such a morose thought and hated more that he'd voiced it, but he wanted assurance that he wasn't disposable to everyone in his life.

Georg reminded, "You don't want to sleep with me."

"No, but I like you well enough and you're very handsome, I'm sure I could manage it."

Georg chuckled. "I do have to get married at some point, though. Amaranth wouldn't be keen on us staying together...but let's not get started on *her*."

"Let's not," Ira agreed, in no mood to hear about another wife who wouldn't want him around.

"And I honestly don't think he'll leave you."

"I hope not."

"Not to mention, we could sleep together anyway."

Ira butted his head against Georg's shoulder. "Go to sleep."

"You're the one that brought it up."

"Sleep."

Georg wiggled his ass against up Ira's groin. "I wouldn't be so opposed—"

"Shut up and go to sleep or you aren't allowed to stay over anymore," Ira threatened without any bite, too busy thinking that maybe he did kind of want to sleep with Georg. But only a little and only because his ass felt very nice pressed up against Ira's cock.

Georg ceased his wiggling but remained nestled close.

THOUGH THE Devil had been sighted in the city, Ira had not seen him for about a week. He had received a note letting him know that Lucifer was taking care of some things and expected free time soon. It was not signed it the usual way; it was not signed at all. If Ira hadn't known his writing, he would have no way to know that the person who had named him his companion had sent it.

He tried not to think about it too much.

Georg assured him that it wasn't anything to worry about. "Sometimes my parents don't speak for a whole month and they still seem to like each other," he'd shared, though it hadn't brought any comfort.

At the end of the night, when he'd finished with the books for that day, Ira sat at the bar, swishing his drink around so the ice chips tinkled in the glass. It gave him no insight and didn't improve his mood, but it gave him something to do.

A family affair occupied Georg for the evening. His grandfather's three-hundred-fourth birthday. He'd invited Ira, but Ira had declined. He didn't want to know what a high society family would think of their heir bringing him around.

While he swirled his drink and dangled his feet a few inches above the floor, too short to reach from the height of the barstool, Ira pondered.

He pondered the fate of Hell, which would probably be fine no matter what, and the fate of the Devil, would couldn't die but might not have been fine at all. He might never have been fine in the first place.

As he pondered, three men and two women walked in. He glanced over again and reevaluated; it was two men and three women. One of the women stood as tall as the men. Slender and plainly dressed in loose clothing, she stood apart from her companions.

The other four wore fine-woven cloth, glittering rings, bracelets that gleamed on their wrists.

He recognized Tycho and the corners of his mouth curled down. Lucifer had demoted him from whatever position he'd held, but he didn't seem to have suffered for it. He sneered just as much and dressed as finely as he had before.

One of the women looked familiar and Ira realized that it was because she bore an uncanny resemblance to Georg's friend Rogg, down to the bright red curls and heart-shaped face. A mother or older sister. Maybe an aunt or cousin.

They all approached the bar and ordered drinks. A man with sharp teeth told Marius, "We're looking to take a few home for the night."

"A few what?" the pander asked.

Sharp-teeth frowned. "Whores. Is there something else you have here?"

"And what kind of whores?" Marius asked, setting a drink in front of him. "We've got a variety."

A woman reached forward to pick up her drink and Ira glimpsed a bird tattooed on the inside of her wrist. "Clean ones."

"They're all clean."

Ira eavesdropped on them, bored by their requests for young, tender, pretty things. Society types always wanted someone helpless to terrorize in bed, someone who would mewl like a lost little kitten.

"What you got in the way of hermaphrodites?" the red-haired woman toyed with a pendant, a silver bird with glittering ruby eyes.

Ira sat up straighter and couldn't help but lean in, trying to get a closer a look, something tickling the back of his mind.

Something about ravens.

"Not my business," Marius said. "And I might not go about asking it that way."

The red-head didn't appreciate the suggestion.

Tycho noticed Ira looking and grabbed his face, his fingers

digging into Ira's cheeks. "Did you learn manners yet?"

Marius moved towards them.

Ira looked at the ring on his thumb, a raven's head, and said, "Yes," then added, "Sir," for good measure.

Marius paused.

Tycho sneered, "And what about that wretch that sits the throne?"

"He hasn't been around," he confessed, trying to sound meek and bitter and heartbroken all at the same time.

Tycho leered at him and tightened his grip on Ira's face, hard enough that his jaw opened due to the pressure. "And now you're back to grubbing for coins."

Marius frowned so Ira wound an arm around Tycho's waist and nestled close to him, right under his arm like a lost little lamb, the kind of thing he knew Tycho liked. "I'll do whatever you like," Ira offered.

"Good. He never should have gone parading you around. Maybe this time you won't forget what you are."

"Have a look around, see who wants to go," Marius suggested to the others.

Within a few minutes, they had gathered half a dozen other pleasure workers to accompany them to a gathering at someone's house. Marius made it clear to all the workers that they had no obligation to go and to really consider what kind of work they wanted. He laid it on especially thick with Ira.

People talked around service workers and when whores were involved, they tended to drink. If these people were involved in whatever had happened in the First and the Third, then Ira wanted to know more about them. If they weren't, then his evening would be wasted, and he'd have to service someone he didn't particularly want to service. He had made peace with doing that years ago, before he'd even turned twenty.

The group headed to one of the fine, towering houses on Camden Way. Some of the houses had been built when the walls had started to go up and it was easy to distinguish which sections had been built centuries ago and which had been added on as their family's influence and wealth had grown.

The woman with the bird tattoo produced a key and let them into the house. She led them upstairs and down a hall with thick carpeting and dark woodwork. Two maids in uniform bobbed at them as the group passed by, their eyes lowered.

The woman opened a door to reveal a sitting room that reminded Ira of the Trade House; not how it had been when he'd worked there, but what it must have looked like when everything had been new and luxurious, before the barter system had fallen out of favor. Settees and armchairs and thick cushions were scattered throughout the room.

Tycho collapsed into an armchair as though the weight of the world rested on his shoulders and his alone. He gestured for Ira to sit on the cushions piled at the foot of his chair. He didn't seem to expect anything else of Ira for the moment, so Ira scooted close and rested his head against the arm of the chair. The position that indicated he was waiting for permission and would be willing when the order came.

A different servant than the two they had passed in the hall came in bearing a tray laden with wine bottles and glasses.

Enough glasses for the five of them, and one extra, but not enough for the whores, Ira noted.

The woman to whom the house belonged stoked some coals in the fireplace and added more wood.

"Ugh, Hena, aren't you *warm?*" complained Sharp-teeth.

She shrugged and returned to lounging on the settee. She indicated that the girl she'd bought should bring her a glass of wine.

The girl obliged with shaking hands. She was young, maybe Georg's age. Ira figured she hadn't been at this long.

Or maybe she'd had bad clients, that could be enough to make anyone nervous.

The other whores followed suit, pouring drinks for their clients and listening with masks of polite boredom as the five of them spoke. They drawled on about the minutia of their day and wondered where their sixth member could be.

Ira tried to settle more comfortably on the cushions. He let his eyes slide over the others, memorizing their faces and listening carefully for names.

"Falco's an *hour* late, do we really need to wait around for him?" Red Curls asked.

"He's our easiest way in," said the tall woman, the one dressed in all black. She examined her nails, then raked them through her long, silver hair.

Ira didn't know her; if he'd seen her before, he would have remembered. She was exquisite, like a bit of light made into a person. Silver hair and dappled silver skin and eyes that glinted like coins. He didn't know for sure, but he would have felt safe betting that she had been an angel once, made in Heaven for some divine purpose.

She noticed him staring and started to smile.

He turned his eyes away.

Tycho gripped him by the hair and made him look up. "Don't forget who's paying you at the end of the night," he advised softly.

"Don't be ornery," the woman advised. "Maybe he's never seen an angel up close before."

"He's sucked the Devil off enough times," Tycho told her. He released Ira's hair with a shove.

The woman smiled wider and reminded, "But Lucifer *isn't* an angel anymore. He fell."

Ira checked his impulse to frown and kept his eyes lowered. Under his breath but not *too* quiet, he said, "It doesn't matter what he is, he doesn't come to see me anymore."

"Poor thing," she cooed. "That's what you get for thinking anyone means anything to him."

Tears sprang to his eyes; he didn't even have to fake it.

The woman left her seat and came to crouch beside Ira. She had taken one of the whores from Marius', but she'd hardly touched him. "He can't be any better at being a lover than he is at being a king. How long did you hold his interest?"

He was spared from having to answer when a man traipsed into the room, his posture and gait indicating that he'd already been drinking. He snagged a girl around the waist and pulled her onto his lap as he sprawled into an empty seat. With his hand snaked up her shirt, he declared, "Sorry about the wait," without sounding sorry at all. He glanced around. "Bit of a quiet affair."

The silver woman stood and poured the newcomer a glass of wine. "Oh, Falco, how could the party start without you?"

He took the glass and drank deeply. The girl in his arms squealed when he gripped one of her breasts.

From that moment on, the gathering took on a different tone. Cups were drained and filled, Falco's faster than the others, and those who had been bought for the night climbed on to the laps of those who had bought them.

Ira gleaned little else from the conversations around him, except that Falco worked as an assistant to one of the captains and that he considered his job incredibly boring. Falco preferred carousing and drinking to work and resented that his parents had decided that he was too old to do only that. They'd arranged for him to have a cushy job attending in one of the precincts.

The angel, whose name didn't come up, seemed to hold Falco's attention better than the girl on his lap.

Fingers dug into Ira's shoulder, yanking him closer. "It is rude to stare," Tycho scolded.

"Sorry." Ira lowered his eyes.

"You should worry about doing what I paid you for."

Ira thought about tossing the coins back in his face and leaving. Four bits and a few coppers, far below what he usually took. Tycho had commented on it, too, leering. Instead of leaving, he turned to face Tycho and slipped between his legs, his fingers climbing up the other man's thighs. "What would you have of me?"

"You can't be that stupid. What else can you even do?"

Ira didn't let his irritation show.

"Should I get some of my ledgers and watch you do arithmetic?" he asked, his lip curling. "How about some of those horrible human poems you're always reading?"

He didn't take the bait, but he knew that Tycho wanted him to; he wanted an excuse to say something nastier. Ira didn't give it to him. He unfastened Tycho's trousers. He wished momentarily that Georg had been working that night and then thought of Lucifer. He would have to go to the palace after this and share what he'd learned. He hoped the information would prove useful; he knew for certain that the Devil would want to know that there was an angel, a real one, here in Hell.

As he slid his tongue over Tycho's shaft, he reflected that Lucifer might already know. He might already know everything. Ira might be wasting his time, as well as being unfaithful.

For the second time.

That thought sent little tendrils of numbness and mild nausea through him.

He barely noticed when Tycho pushed him back and manhandled him so that he knelt on all fours. He couldn't bring himself to care when Tycho pulled down his trousers; he buried his face in one of the cushions while the other man fucked him, thinking that Tycho had only ever taken him from behind.

He wondered what that said about Tycho if it said anything at all.

He must not have been appropriately enthusiastic, though, because Tycho grabbed him by the hair and pulled his face out of the cushion.

"Ow," Ira muttered, his own words sounding far away.

"Are you crying?" Tycho demanded.

"I don't think so," Ira said, though his face might have been damp. "Would you like me to?"

Tycho didn't answer. When he finished, he left Ira kneeling on the ground and walked out of the room, maybe to piss or maybe because he couldn't stand the sight of something so pathetic.

Maybe he felt sad and empty after he came. Maybe he knew how fast he'd been and didn't want to give anyone time to make a joke at his expense.

Ira pulled up his trousers and tucked his shirt back in. As he adjusted his suspenders, another person, Sharp-teeth, else reached for him.

Ira stepped out of his grasp.

Sharp-teeth grabbed at him again.

"You didn't pay for shit." Ira gave him a shove.

The other man pulled him close. "Oh, come on, I won't even make you cry."

Ira disentangled himself. Sharp-teeth wasn't holding him too hard and he wasn't holding his wine well either. "I need to go clean up before we do anything."

"I don't mind a mess."

Ira kissed his cheek. "I do. I'll be right back."

Sharp-teeth grinned. Ira noted that his teeth were crooked, too.

Ira left the house and didn't pass Tycho on his way out. He made it halfway up the street before he felt compelled to look back, the feeling of being watched prickling over his skin. He saw nothing, though, and continued home.

The feeling persisted and he looked again.

He saw nothing. Again.

When he turned back around before him stood the angel. He danced back, a hand clasped to his chest, surprise knocking all the breath out of him.

She smiled at him, a sweet smile that made him want to trust her. He wondered if demons were supposed to feel this way about angels and if one of the Hell-made creatures would hate her on sight. "You've been scorned by your king," she told him.

He nodded.

"He is a foul thing."

"He said he loved me."

"He can't," she assured him. She touched his cheek with slim, delicate fingers.

He stepped back, not sure that he wanted her to touch him.

"He is a prideful beast and a false one. He cannot love you. He has no capacity for it."

"Are you really an angel?" he asked; he knew it was a stupid question right away. "I mean, shouldn't you be in Heaven?"

"I do as I wish."

"What are you the angel of?"

She didn't answer. "Do you hate him?"

The question rocked him. "I…"

"You know things about him."

He shook his head and insisted, "He didn't tell me anything."

"He didn't have to tell you for you to see things. Useful things."

"I don't know."

She reached out and put a hand on his shoulder. "When you wish to tell us the things you saw, return to Hena's home. We'll be glad for the information. We can pay."

He nodded and hurried away, wishing he was home, wishing there was someone waiting for him, someone that would be wondering where he had gotten to and if he was alright. Someone who would look for him when he didn't come back.

He made it home unmolested, though he jumped at shadows the entire time. As he washed up and sank into bed, he decided to send a note to the palace in the morning and ask Lucifer to come by.

He had originally thought to go visit, but he didn't know if Tabitha would still be there or if his presence would be unwelcome.

THE NOTE went off with a runner, but Ira received no response. He tried not to worry. Sometimes his notes got answered with an hour and sometimes they went unacknowledged until they had been heeded.

Georg arrived late in the morning and sat on Ira's desk, pushing the current ledger out of the day. He plucked the inventory sheet from Ira's hand. "That's a lot of spirits."

"I know. I'm surprised they're not all too drunk to fuck out there."

"Some of them are." Georg set aside the paper and let his legs dangle, his foot brushing against Ira's leg every so often. "I'm hungry."

"Lu might be coming."

Georg raised his eyebrows. "Might he? I thought you hadn't heard from him."

"I haven't. But I wrote to him. So he might come."

"Did he write back?"

"No."

"But he might come," Georg teased, a good-natured grin on his face. When he saw that Ira hadn't smiled, he held out his hand for Ira to hold, which he did. "Have you been sulking in here all morning?"

"I miss him."

"Of course you do." Georg hopped off the desk and tugged on Ira's hand.

"Where are we going?"

"Outside. Come on, if you're going to do nothing, do it out front with me." He put an arm around Ira's shoulder and pulled him close enough that they walked hip-to-hip.

They settled onto the bench out front; sometimes the workers would sit there on slow days and flash browsing customers, as much for fun as for business. Today, though, no one else sat on the bench.

"Did you read the last issue of *The Butcher's Wife?*" Georg asked, his whole body oriented towards Ira's.

Ira turned to face him. "Halfway through."

"The part with Iliana and Rosie?"

Ira grinned and rolled his eyes. "To die for!"

"That'll be me someday," he said.

"Maybe Amaranth will lighten up after a few years."

Georg snorted with laughter. "You should meet her some time and then you can tell me what you think about her lightening up."

Ira had never met Georg's betrothed, but he heard about her often enough. Georg's family often dined with their in-laws-to-be. Georg's attendance was, of course, required and the following day, Ira's careful listening and commiserating were required.

Georg nudged Ira's knee with his. "I thought about what you said."

"What did I say?"

"About us getting together. And what I said about Amaranth, about her not letting me."

"What about it?"

"Maybe she will relax. Or she'll get all the children she wants and forget about me. And maybe we'll still be friends—"

"Maybe!" Ira cried. "We will *definitely* still be friends."

"So maybe we could be...kind of friends, kind of lovers. Amaranth isn't keen on conversations. Well, not with me, at least. She tries, I try, but it's always a miss. And, well, I don't think either of us are much interested in the other in bed."

Ira told him, "The more you talk about it, the more this sounds like an awful match."

"So let's make it less awful," George proposed.

"I think Lu would get jealous if I didn't invite him."

A delighted laugh leaped from Georg's throat. "Then invite him! Shit, I think I'd be too awestruck to get it up."

"Oh, don't pretend! You'd be hard as a rock and finish as soon as he touched you."

"Would not!" the younger man protested.

"Ohhh, you *would*, you've been making cow eyes for ages."

"Shut up."

They grinned at each other for a bit, until Georg reached over and patted Ira's thigh.

"He thinks you're handsome," Ira informed the other man.

"I am handsome," he declared, proudly tilting up his chin, his coppery hair gleaming in the light of day. The look on his face dried up in an instant, though, when his eyes fixed on something behind Ira. "For fuck's sake."

Ira twisted to see what had upset him and found himself staring into Astrid's sweet, heart-shaped face. The day, which had seemed so beautiful a moment before, felt cold suddenly, the light breeze became a biting wind.

"Could you fuck off, though!" Georg cried.

"We need to talk," she told Ira, giving Georg nothing more than a dirty look. "About what happened."

"I don't want to talk," Ira managed.

"Please," she begged. "I know you were upset but—"

"But nothing!" Ira stood to face her. "I don't want to talk to you."

"Ira," she said, locking eyes with him, "Whatever he's done to you, there are people that can help."

Words failed Ira then. He could only stare.

She must have taken his silence as proof that she was right because she reached out to grasp his hand in both of hers, coming closer. "I know he's king right now and I know he frightens you—"

Vomit leaped into the back of his throat at her touch. "No."

"At the art gallery, you were so frightened you couldn't even keep hold of your drink! You looked *terrified*. Whatever he's done, you don't have to put up with it."

He yanked his hands back. The raised edge her ring snagged on his skin, leaving a scrape. He had never known her to wear jewelry but on her forefinger, she wore a raven's head, charcoal crusted in the engraved feathers.

"He's got you under his thumb—" she began.

"He hasn't!" he snapped.

"You don't have to lie for him."

"I'm not!" The urge to push her almost overcame him.

She reached for his hands again.

He stepped closer to Georg, pulling his arms close to his sides.

Georg stood then and put a hand on Ira's shoulder. He edged between the two of them, not fully in front of Ira, but poised to move.

"We can go somewhere safe," she offered.

He let out a bark of laughter. "I don't *want* to go anywhere with you! I don't even want to *see* you."

She ogled at him as if he had started to speak in a language she didn't understand.

"Ira—"

"No! Just stop, Astrid, there isn't anything between us."

She shook her head, tears coming to her eyes.

"You were a client and that's all. And now you're nothing, not even a friend."

She reached for him again.

Georg pulled Ira back and put out an arm to keep her at a distance. "Go home, Astrid," Georg advised.

"Stay out of this," she snapped.

"Go away," Ira told her. He nearly cowered behind Georg, terrified that she would touch him again. "I don't want to see you again. Ever."

"I love you."

"You don't!"

Ira had not noticed anyone come up behind her, too worried about where he would flee too if she wouldn't go away, what he would do if she continued to show up places where she knew he would be. A long, spidery hand appeared on her shoulder and they all looked up to find Satan looming behind her, tall and spindly.

"He asked you to leave," the Devil noted.

A dark blossom spread across her shirt. It started where Lucifer's fingers touched her shoulder. It took a moment to register that the stain blackening her blue shirt was blood, that his fingers were not on her shoulder, but needle-like talons digging into it.

Lucifer put his other hand on her other shoulder, digging those fingers in as well. He leaned down and put his mouth next to her ear, whispering something that Ira couldn't hear. Another stain appeared on her shirt.

When Lucifer released her, she stumbled, her face contorted and flushed, tears streaming from her face. She looked at them once, then ran.

"You didn't have to hurt her," Ira scolded, not upset, but knowing that it was the right thing to say.

"And she didn't have to come here. Yet here we are." Lucifer looked at Ira but seemed to be glancing right through him. His eyes flicked over Georg the same way.

"I didn't want you to do that."

"I didn't do it because I thought that you would want me to. I did it and she is lucky I didn't do more because I will pull her guts out through her throat if she comes near you again," the Devil stated, his voice as even as if he'd told Ira that the mugs were in the other cabinet.

His fingers, and they were just fingers now, up to his second knuckle, were stained red, dripping on to the ground.

"Lu!"

Ira's raised voice got no reaction. The Devil simply asked, "Yes?"

Ira sighed and rubbed his eyes. "You ought to come clean up, at least."

"I received your note."

"I didn't think you were here just because you missed me," Ira baited, opening the door and leading Lucifer towards the sink behind the bar.

Georg trailed behind them, his eyes wide.

Lucifer didn't take the bait. He didn't inquire about how Ira had been or say that he'd missed him.

Marius eyed the Devil, then Ira, but said nothing.

As the Devil washed his hands, Selene came over and checked Ira over for wounds, quietly asking him if he was alright.

"You haven't got to fuss over me, I am grown!" Ira snapped, pulling out of her careful examination.

As he dried his hands, Lucifer said, "Well, you're so hesitant to say when someone has hurt you that I can't blame her. Believing you when you say you're fine is like believing a drunk who says this is his last drink."

"But you never hurt me."

"Not yet."

It was not the answer Ira had wanted. He wanted Lucifer to say that he would never hurt him. He wanted him to do anything but look aloof and bored. In full view of everyone in the brothel, Ira slapped the Devil across the face, harder than he had ever intentionally hit anyone.

He didn't know why he did it and as soon as his palm connected with Lucifer's cheek, he regretted it, his guts turning to worms and other crawling, writhing things.

Maybe because he was sick of Lucifer saying that he was going to hurt him someday or because he hated when people assumed he already had. It could have been that he hated that Astrid had come to his place of work and that he was terrified that she would come to his home next. Maybe he had done it just because Lucifer's cool demeanor irritated him, and Ira was used to be struck when he irritated people.

Ira expected wrath, he expected vengeance. The Devil could have snapped him in half, ripped his throat out, eaten him alive, and Ira would have deserved it. He had raised his hand against not just his lover but their Prince. Mistress would beat him bloody, scars be damned.

He had to remind himself that he wasn't hers to beat anymore.

Someone, though. Someone should hurt him for this.

Lucifer stared at him, his face blank, and his eyes round like a child's who had never been shouted at before.

Then that look was gone.

If Ira had thought his demeanor was cool before, it was absolutely frozen now.

Ira thought of Tabitha, who had choked him and pulled his hair and drawn blood, and he wondered if being hit for no reason wasn't something new for Lucifer.

Not knowing what else to do, Ira walked out of the building.

Lucifer followed but said nothing. He didn't keep following him either. He headed towards the palace.

Ira didn't know if he should follow, if Lucifer would even want him to.

The Devil kept walking until he shrank into the distance.

Ira bolted after him and caught up as he was about to disappear through the gate to his estate. "Wait!" he called.

Lucifer waited, more statue than person.

"I'm sorry. I shouldn't have don't that."

The Devil turned to glance at him. "Yes, well. I'm told violent people do tend to inspire violence in others. And the things I've done to people, I must inspire so much violence."

Ira wanted to cry, hardness searing across his chest.

"The things people have done to you. The things *I've* done to you...And it was just a slap, hardly the worst—"

Ira cut him off, "No, it was *wrong*, don't make it seem like nothing."

Lucifer nodded.

"Aren't you angry!" Ira demanded.

"No."

"Lu, say *something*."

"Maybe you should go home."

The words shred him as easily as a fork shredded stewed meat.

"Maybe tomorrow you can tell me whatever you wanted to tell me."

He'd forgotten completely why the Devil had come in the first place.

Lucifer walked away.

Ira stood outside the gate to the palace grounds, not knowing what to do with himself.

He slunk back to the brothel, straight to the back room, and spent the entire afternoon and well into the evening hunched over inventories and invoices. Georg and Selene both came to speak with him, but he had no words for them.

At the end of the night, Marius entered, rapping on the door frame to gain his attention. "Time to go home."

Ira glanced up, then stared back down at the papers in front of him, shaking his head.

"Go. Home," the pander told him with steel in his voice.

Ira nodded, set down his pencil with shaky hands, and went home.

He did not know how things had gone so badly awry in such a short time. Hardly more than a week ago, things had seemed so good. There had been dissenters, yes, and the problem with souls getting out, but that had been it. Things between them had been going well, but now it could all be ruined.

He had not considered himself the sort of person prone to any sort of aggression beyond self-defense. Then again, he'd never had anyone to hit who wouldn't have given it back to him and twice as bad.

He had always been the smallest of the men at the Trade House. He had even been smaller than some of the women. Mistress would have whipped him hideless if he'd ever dared raise a hand to a customer, no matter how careless and rough they got.

At home, he took out a few sheets of paper and wrote down everything he had a learned from his time with Tycho, about the raven symbol, about Falco, and about the angel. He told him everything he could remember and even confessed that he had let the other demon have him. Maybe Lucifer would not want to see him again, but it was important that he knew what Ira had learned.

He sent the letter off first thing in the morning, as the sky had barely started to lighten. He hadn't been able to sleep for most of the night.

Lucifer didn't come by the next day or the day after.

DURING THE afternoon of the third day, Ira sat in the back room with no work to do. On days when he ran out of paperwork, he would go out and sit at the bar, an extra pair of eyes to look out for the workers or to manage the bar as best he could when Marius needed to deal with something more pressing.

Today he sat at his desk and did nothing. Georg had been come in to say good morning and had accepted Ira's mute nod as well as anyone could.

He didn't think anyone else would bother him, but Selene let herself in, pale as death and trailed by the Devil.

"He asked if you were in," she told him. "Didn't take no for an answer."

He nodded.

She gave his arm a squeeze and whispered that she would be right outside if he needed her. He asked her not to bother, but he knew she'd worry anyway.

Once she'd left, Ira stood to move towards Lucifer but stopped himself.

"Do you want to get something to eat?" Lucifer asked.

Ira didn't want to eat. His stomach had been off for days. "I'm sorry, it was wrong."

Just as cool as he'd been the other day, Lucifer told him, "I'd like to put it behind us."

"I can't. Not until know that things are right between us."

"They are."

"It doesn't feel right."

"Will you do it again?" Lucifer asked.

"Never."

"Then things are right."

Ira shook his head. It couldn't be that easy. "I never wanted to be this sort of person."

"I don't think you are. I think you've been given a lot of bad examples and that your life has been stressful lately."

Ira wanted to promise that he would never strike him again but had started to realize that his promises weren't worth shit, not when he'd broken the last one so readily.

"I got your letter. I'd like to discuss it. Here is fine if you don't want to eat anything." He seated himself across from Ira's desk and gestured for Ira to be seated as well. He produced the letter, folded neatly, from his pocket. He unfolded it carefully and placed it on the desk, adjusting and smoothing it until it lay flat and centered in front of him. He arranged several things around it, straightening pens and other stacks of paper.

"Lu."

"Yes?"

"Your wife, is she still at the palace?"

"Yes. I did build it for her. Well, her and all the children I thought we'd have, as much as that ever panned out."

Ira studied him, then pushed the paper out of alignment.

The Devil reached over right away to fix it.

Ira took a pencil from the jar on his desk and set it down; it hadn't been there for a second before Lucifer returned it to the jar.

"How has that been, her being back?" Ira inquired.

"I'm adjusting."

"And the two of you...?"

Lucifer touched his shoulder, then tugged at his shirt so it didn't show as much skin.

Ira stood and came around the other side of the desk, slipping his fingers under the collar and moving the shirt aside so he could see the circle of teeth marks left on his shoulder. "Looks like it hurt."

Lucifer looked up at him. "It did."

Ira took his hand back and leaned against the desk. Lucifer still met his eyes and what Ira had taken to be coolness showed itself as control. He was using everything he had to keep himself together and Ira thought he knew exactly how to unravel that.

What would happen if Lucifer lost control, he didn't know. Or want to find out.

"Tell her to leave," he advised.

"It's her home, Ira, I can't make her leave."

Ira put his fingers under Lucifer's chin and tipped it up, checking for finger-shaped bruises on his throat. He found none; Lucifer reached up to touch his own throat. Their fingers brushed each other, and Ira took his hand away.

"She usually only does that if we're fucking."

"And you haven't?" Ira couldn't stop himself from asking.

"No. Not yet."

Ira waited.

"I told her I couldn't. She seemed happy to laugh at that." Satan almost smiled, his mouth stretching ruefully. "I'd rather let her think I'm impotent." He glanced around the room then added, "I spent all of last night reorganizing my study."

Ira sighed and leaned forward again, this time taking Lucifer into his arms.

The Devil gripped him hard, his cheek against Ira's chest. "Tell me that you love me."

"I love you," Ira told him, rubbing his back.

"Please don't hit me anymore."

Ira could have wept. "Lu, I won't, I swear it. On my life, I do."

Lucifer nodded.

"I've never been so ashamed of anything in my life."

The Devil sniffled, but that was it.

Ira could feel the tension ringing through him; he was close to vibrating right out of his skin. He combed his fingers through Lucifer's hair, which had not been braided that day.

"I couldn't get it right," Lucifer confessed. "I tried a hundred times, but I couldn't get the braids right."

Ira stepped back. "Come home with me. Marius will understand."

"About the letter..."

"We'll talk about it at home. People are probably listening here anyway."

"Right." Lucifer stood, neatly folded up the letter, then exited the room.

Ira followed, stopping long enough to whispered to the pander that they had things that needed to be discussed.

They walked without touching, Lucifer two paces ahead the whole time. Whenever there were eyes on him, Ira noticed, he wound himself in tighter, cold and lazy and dangerous, like a snake that hadn't yet decided if it wanted to squeeze you to death.

Inside Ira's apartment, though, he straightened things fastidiously and even made like he was going to wash the dishes.

"That can wait, darling, really, we should talk about this angel."

Lucifer produced the letter from his pocket. He skimmed it, then confirmed, "You said she was silver?"

Ira gestured for him to sit and he did. Ira sat next to him, not close enough to touch. "All over."

"Did you get a name?"

"No. Sorry."

Lucifer nodded.

Not wanting to be useless, Ira said, "But she told me to come back. If I wanted to, uh, tell them what I knew about you. She said they'd pay."

Lucifer nodded.

Ira shifted. "And I think Astrid's involved with them. They all wear something with a raven on it."

"Back to that saga, again," the Devil mused. "The Screaming Horde and the Raven Company...But I haven't raped anyone. Literally or figuratively."

Ira went over to his bookshelf. He searched for the copy of *Histories of the Underworld* he knew he had, then pulled it from the shelf. He flipped to the third chapter, skimming through it, past the early descriptions of clan leaders and their warboys. He found the section on Thagor Bloodaxe under a heading titled "The Addition of the Third Edict." He flipped through to the end, to the part that detailed how it was Bloodaxe had come to gain the ire of the Raven Company.

He read, "Willa the Voracious was the hearthwife of Yanis Swordbreaker. Together they produced only a single child, Ola, that survived to adulthood. When Thagor Bloodaxe broke bread in the Swordbreaker camp, he took notice of Ola and offered to pay a hefty bride price for her. Willa refused and to appease the other man, Swordbreaker offered Bloodaxe one of the daughters from his other wife."

"Thagor refused. He was pig-headed, I think that's the only reason he made it through so many skirmishes. He was too stubborn to know when he was beat," Lucifer recalled.

Ira didn't know how he could remember people who had perished thousands of years ago. Ira scanned the rest of the paragraph. "Thagor kidnapped Ola and raped her, but Yanis refused to go after her. Kidnapping was still considered a legitimate way to get a wife, then, I guess."

"Or a husband," Lucifer added.

"Or a husband," Ira conceded. "When Yanis wouldn't go after Ola, Willa rallied the other women from the camp. They approached as defectors and slaughtered the Screaming Horde in their sleep. After that, they called themselves the Raven Company and went after the slaver clans."

"Did a thorough job of it, too, if I remember right."

"And what did you do?"

"My camp didn't take captives. We punished souls...and made sure that the others did, too."

"But about the Raven Company, what did you do about them?" Ira asked.

"Nothing."

"Were they punishing souls?"

"No, but they saved me a lot of trouble dealing with clans who cared more about warring than soul-cleaning."

Ira sat and thought for a while, studying the book and studying the Devil. "You aren't Thagor."

Lucifer blinked a few times, then his brow knitted. "Sorry?"

"You're not the rapist. You're the father who did nothing."

"Oh."

"That's what they say, isn't it? It's not that you're a cruel king, it's that you're an ineffective one," Ira rationalized, the idea coming together. "Petty, callow, worried about Earth and not about Hell." Ira consulted the history book again. "Look here, after she dealt with Thagor she went back to Yanis and offered to let him crusade with her."

"I don't know if the word crusade can be applied to anything that's happened here," Lucifer corrected, his tone pedantic. "Given its context."

Ira rolled his eyes. "Fine, then, she offered to let him join her campaign. And he didn't. So she killed him and when his warwife wouldn't join, she killed her, too, and took the rest of the camp."

Lucifer took the text and flipped through it. After a while, he set it aside. "And you said this was an angel?"

He nodded.

"And not one of the Fallen?"

"I don't think so."

"Mmm. That is what I like least about all of this."

"Why?"

"Because an angel..." The Devil sighed. "An angel might not kill me. An angel might have the capacity to do something worse. An angel could bind me."

"Bind?"

He nodded. "Instead of letting me die and come back to regroup, an angel might keep me captive, keep me weak and insensible. I'm afraid it wouldn't be hard to do at this point, either."

"No."

"If she is young and hale, Ira, I worry."

"Well, stop it. I won't let anyone do that to you."

A small smile grew on Lucifer's lips. "And how would you stop her?"

"I'd find a way."

"What do you know of killing angels?"

"They've got hearts, haven't they?"

Lucifer nodded.

"Then I'd take her heart. Would that work? They don't come back like you do. That Mylas fellow you killed is still dead."

"And how would you get close enough to take her heart?"

He shrugged. "I'd find a way."

The Devil didn't look convinced.

"I would!"

"You would try, I believe that."

"I spent my whole life learning how to get close to people, to figure out what they want of me and to make sure they thought they would get what they wanted."

"And if the angel *doesn't* want to fuck you?" Lucifer challenged.

Ira snapped, "I'm good for more than that!"

"You are, of course, you are. Let's not fight, love, let's not talk about this." He slid his arms around Ira and pulled him close. "Let's not let it get to that in the first place."

"That sounds better."

"I've missed you."

"I missed you, too." He moved in closer, curling up on Lucifer's lap. "I really am sorry, Lu. About...about everything."

"Oh, such a trespass can be forgiven, especially when you've forgiven mine," the Devil assured softly.

After a quiet minute, Ira shared, "I've been talking to Georg."

"Oh?"

"I told him if you left me that he and I should get together."

Lucifer snorted in amusement. "What I wouldn't give to see that."

"We'd let you watch."

The Devil's grip on him tightened.

Ira whispered, "I let Tycho fuck me," into the Devil's shoulder, hoping he wouldn't hear.

"It couldn't have been easy for you."

"It felt like nothing. I think it must have hurt but I didn't even realize it till I was sore the next morning."

"I wish you wouldn't let people hurt you."

"How else was I supposed to find out anything about them?"

"I'd rather have you safe and well than out spying for me."

Ira didn't want to know, but had to ask, "Are you upset with me?"

"No."

"You mean it?"

"Were I displeased, I would certainly make it known." He drew Ira closer and kissed him, his touch hesitant, somewhere between gentle and cautious. "I don't intend to let Tabby come between us, it's just that—"

"You never thought she was going to come back."

"I didn't want her to come back. It wasn't that I'd...you know, given up hope or anything like that. What we have is better. So I don't want anyone to come between us."

Ira grinned.

"No one but Georg and that tight little body of his."

Ira's grin widened. "He is nice to cuddle."

"We really ought to get him into bed one of these days."

Ira turned to straddle him, putting his hands to rest on the Devil's shoulders. "Could you even handle just one of us right now?"

"I haven't slept in three days so it's unlikely."

"Three days!"

"I did pass out face first into a sandwich the other day, so that was thrilling. Becka thought she'd killed me."

"For fuck's sake, Lu, isn't anyone taking care of you?" Ira stood and pulled him to his feet.

"Imogen's been hovering if that's what you mean," he said as he let Ira drag him into the bedroom and push him into the bed. When Ira released him to turn back the covers, he snagged by the arm and pulled him close so that Ira was on top of him again. "I didn't come here to be hovered over."

"You came here to discuss a bunch of malcontents who want you off the throne."

"And we've done that. Let's do something else. Let's do something fun. Let's do something that doesn't involve biting or hair pulling."

"I thought you liked it when I do that."

"That's because you're always so very gentle with me," Lucifer told him, raising his hands to untuck Ira's shirt. "Even when you think you're being ferocious."

"Lu, you should rest."

"When you've tired me out, I will." His fingers found Ira's skin. "Go on, get this off."

Ira shrugged off the shirt and looked down at Lucifer's hands, long and thin and so white against the charcoal of his own skin, splayed against his belly.

Lucifer wiggled his fingers inside the waistband of Ira's trousers. "And what about these?"

Ira unfastened the buttons on Lucifer's shirt and found several more bite marks. He brushed his fingers over them. "And what about these?" Ira asked.

Lucifer tapped one on his chest, a deep purple bruise around his nipple. "She gave up after this one. I thought she was going to take a chunk out." He half-smiled. "I wondered if she used to be gentler or if I used to be stronger, but...I think...I was excited because she was excited and I wanted her to do it because I wanted her to enjoy me. Now I just feel lost. I don't know how to tell her."

"Tell her to leave."

"I'm certain she'll be bored again soon enough." He wrapped his fingers in the suspenders that dangled from the waist of Ira's trousers. "If there was a way for you to keep these on..." he mused.

"The suspenders?"

"Mmm. I've always been enthralled by things like that."

Ira hadn't known that but felt that he should have. "What are your feelings on garters?"

He grinned. "It's been years since I've had to roll down a pair of stockings. I could do it with my teeth, you know. Or to leave them on! Isn't that something?" He let out a wistful sigh.

Ira made a shopping list in his head. Normally, he didn't have the patience for dressing up in silly outfits so that a customer could fumble with it, but Lucifer wasn't a customer and Ira didn't think he'd be fumbling. Ira liked the word he'd used, enthralled. He wanted the Devil enthralled with his thighs, pressing a kiss right above the top of the stocking. It would be perfect, he knew, to slip them on some time he knew Lucifer would be over and never say a word, not even when Lucifer had gotten him undressed. He could imagine the look on his face.

He swooped down to give the Devil a kiss then rolled off him and onto his back so he could take off his trousers and shoes.

"Shit, you're cute," Lucifer told him, going in to kiss his neck, then moving back to remove his own clothing. "You're almost too cute to fuck."

"Should I get dressed, then?"

"Absolutely not," Lucifer said and slid on top of him, kissing his neck again.

Ira put his hands on his shoulders and pushed him back, knowing exactly what he wanted to do. When he had the Devil on his back, he took his cock into his mouth as far as he could, then drew back to tongue the head.

The Devil cried out, a sweet sound somewhere between a whimper and a sigh.

Ira pulled back once more, this time to fetch a bit of oil so he could slide his fingers inside Lucifer. He returned his mouth to the other man's cock with his fingers still within him.

The Devil gasped and then he panted. Ira wanted to watch him, he wanted to see his cheeks flushed and his chest heaving, but he kept his head lowered until the Devil grasped the sheets and thrust his hips. He spilled into Ira's mouth with a moan that the people in the next apartment must have heard.

He slid up to lay on top of Lucifer and kiss the tip of his nose. "Not every day I can get you to be that loud."

"I'm sorry."

"Don't be."

Lucifer wrapped his arms around Ira. "I'm absolutely mortified, I have to say."

"Almost as loud as that time on the kitchen counter," Ira teased, "And they all came running. Do you remember the look on Imogen's face!" He reached for the blankets and pulled them up.

"Did you want me to...?"

"No."

"Good, because I'm exhausted." He kept his arms around Ira but turned onto his side. He nestled his face into Ira's shoulder. "Ask me again in the morning."

"I didn't ask you anything."

"I think I meant I'll ask you again in the morning."

"Oh. I love you."

"I love you, too. Heaps and bunches."

Heaps and bunches. Ira couldn't believe those words had passed his Prince's lips. *Love of my life,* he'd said that once too and Ira wondered if it was still true. It seemed inconceivable that after so many thousands of years that Ira could be *the* love of his life.

MORNING CAME and went before the Devil woke. When he did wake, he stumbled out into the parlor with Ira's covers around his shoulders.

Ira had sent someone over to Marius' to let him know that he wouldn't be in. He stretched out on the couch with a book.

"Want me to suck your cock?" Lucifer asked.

Ira chuckled. "Good afternoon to you, too." He nodded towards the kitchen. "Hungry?"

"Famished. I could eat a whole orphanage."

Grinning, Ira marked his page and headed to the kitchen. He put the kettle on for tea and rooted through his icebox to see what he could cook.

Lucifer loomed behind him, peering into the icebox. "First time I've ever seen this stocked without doing it myself."

"That's because I went out while you were sleeping." He reached in and pulled out eggs and a link of breakfast sausage, as well as a little basket of white mushrooms. He handed the mushrooms to Lucifer. "Want to take care of those for me?"

"If by take care of..."

"I do not mean to eat them raw and unwashed, it's disgusting. They grow in shit, you know that, don't you?"

Lucifer, the basket of mushrooms clasped in his hands and the blanket still around his shoulders, informed Ira, "I've had my tongue in your asshole."

"That's different."

"Not sure how," he muttered as went to the sink to rinse them.

"It's different because you love me."

"I love mushrooms."

Ira snorted and fished around for a cutting board and a knife, leaving it on the kitchen table for the Devil to use. "Are they the love of your life?"

"That's you."

Ira cracked a few eggs, then turned to watch him cutting mushrooms into perfectly even slices. "Do you mean that?"

"Yes."

"And what about the other people before me, were they the loves of your lives? Until things went bad and then they weren't anymore?"

Lucifer looked up. "Are you asking if I've loved you all equally?"

"I'm asking if you thought you loved them as much as you could love someone."

"No, of course not. I hardly even liked some of them. Why?"

"I like to know where I stand."

Lucifer sliced a few more mushrooms and Ira returned to the eggs. He cracked several more, whisked them, and set them aside, then started to cook the sausage.

"Am I the love of your life?" the Devil asked.

Ira glanced at him, then poked the breakfast sausage so it would brown on the other side. "I don't know. You're the only love my life has ever had."

"I see."

He poked the sausage again even though he knew it needed to cook more on its current side. He'd rolled his sleeves up to cook and the fresh pink scars shone on his left arm. He set aside the fork and turned to look at Lucifer, leaning on the counter. "I do love you and you are important to me, but I haven't got any stars to give you."

"I don't want stars."

Ira nodded, then chewed his lip. "I feel like we're always doing this."

"Discussing our relationship? That is, generally, a healthy thing to do when in a relationship."

"All the time?"

"As often as is needed."

Ira glanced at the sausage, then turned it again. He took the mushrooms from the Devil and when the sausage had finished, he cooked them in sausage fat and butter. Once they had cooked, he added the eggs and watched them carefully.

When he set a plate in front of the Devil, he declared, "Look, I can cook now."

"I did sort of notice."

"I bought a cookbook last week."

"Ah."

Ira stabbed a bit of mushroom and then a piece of sausage. "I wasn't sure how Becka was going to work out for you," he admitted, more to the fork than to Lucifer.

Lucifer beamed at that but didn't say anything.

After breakfast, as he washed the dishes wearing nothing at all, the bedcovers abandoned as too cumbersome, Lucifer said, "I think I'd like you to come up and properly meet her."

"You would?" The idea appealed to Ira not at all.

"Yes."

"Isn't she going to try to scare me away?"

"I thought we'd be able to avoid it, but she's already stayed for longer than I thought she was going to." He set the last dish aside to dry.

Realization dawned and Ira accused, somewhat disbelieving, "You were avoiding me."

"No."

"That wasn't a question."

Sulkily, Lucifer pointed out, "You were fucking other people."

"*Don't!* Don't do that. Care about it or don't, but don't just bring it up because you don't want to talk about something," Ira warned because he didn't think he'd be able to stand it, not with the way the statement had sent a queasy jolt of pain through his guts.

Lucifer looked immediately reticent. "I'm sorry, love. I'm not perfect, you know."

"I'm not asking you to be perfect."

"It bothers me, but I meant it when I said I wasn't upset with you. If you want to sleep with other people—"

"I don't."

"Then do it. But I've never liked it when people hurt you, whether you've allowed them to do it or not."

"I don't want to sleep with other people."

Lucifer sighed.

Ira got the feeling that they'd had two different conversations, which happened sometimes.

Satan approached Ira and pulled him into a hug. "I was avoiding you and I apologize if that hurt you. Come and meet my wife. We'll sit down for dinner or something. She will try to scare you, but this has got to come out in the open at some point. Better we do it on purpose, I think."

"I will but I don't want to."

"Thank you. Now, give us a kiss."

Ira stretched up on his tiptoes to press a kiss to his mouth. "What should I wear?"

"Mmm, let's go look," he proposed, looping an arm around Ira's shoulders and pulling him to the bedroom.

He pulled open the door to Ira's closet and observed, "Well, it looks like your option is to wear a suit. Would you like to wear an old one or a new one? Whatever happened to those tight breeches you used to wear? I was fond of those."

Ira scoffed and pulled out of his grip. "Rotting in a landfill on Earth somewhere."

The Devil stepped into the closet and ran his fingers over the sleeve of one suit, the burgundy one. "I don't think I've ever seen you in this one."

"I told Imogen I didn't need so many."

"I'll have to start taking you to more formal events," the Devil mused. "Maybe I should start hosting formal events...the cats don't care for it, though. I think Marlow would have a conniption if I let too many people into the palace. We could have a wedding, that would be something."

"Someone's got to get married if there's going to be a wedding." Ira eyed Lucifer's body, which looked somewhat different than it had a few minutes ago. He started to wonder how many of these subtle changes Ira had missed. Had there been other times when Lucifer's physical sex had changed without anyone noticing?

Lucifer stopped looking at the burgundy suit and moved further into the closet, pulling out the darkest of the gray ones. He held it up next to Ira, then put it back, remarking, "It'd be sort of monochromatic on you, wouldn't it? Good for something serious. A funeral. We could have a funeral."

"What about dinner, though?" Ira asked.

"Hmm?"

"Dinner. With your wife."

"Oh. Christ, I think I'm losing it." Lucifer looked back through the suits, then pulled out a teal one. "I like this one."

"You don't think it's a bit much?"

"It's my favorite color."

Ira hadn't known that, but Imogen must have. "I thought it wouldn't look good on me." He reached up to touch his curls, which were dark and had almost a purplish-red cast to them in the light.

"No, it will be lovely," Lucifer promised. He hung the suit on the closet door. "I ought to go and let Becka know how many she needs to cook for. Oh, shit, and Tabby. I should tell her, shouldn't I?"

"Probably."

"Ugh. What if I didn't? What if I stayed here?" He embraced Ira, lifting him off his feet and squeezing him tight. "What if it really could be just the two of us with no one else coming around to bother us? We could go far away and never come back."

Ira got the sense that he meant it. "You're the Prince."

"What if I wasn't?"

"You are."

Lucifer set him down. "I know."

"I'm sorry, love."

"No, you're right. Still, maybe we could have a real day together sometime. There's this house by the lake, you should see it," the Devil trailed off.

"Never been."

"You should. Even if it isn't with me."

"Maybe."

Lucifer groaned again and hugged Ira once more. "Come by for dinner. I need to go get things arranged."

Ira didn't want him to leave just yet. "Could you do me a favor first?"

"Of course."

"Do you think you could come inside of me?"

"I can certainly try."

Ira wound his fingers through Lucifer's hair. "I sort of like the idea of sitting down to eat with her while I've still got your seed leaking out of me."

"Gracious," Lucifer breathed.

"If it's not too much to ask."

"Ask like that and I'll grow a cock every time."

Lucifer scooped him up and brought him to the bed, hastening him out of his clothes and wasting no time getting to the point, moving with a fervor that Ira appreciated. He pushed Ira onto his belly and climbed behind him, leaning close and nipping at Ira's ear.

"Tell me again what you want," Lucifer said, his voice bordering somewhere between a growl and a rasp.

"Come inside me," Ira begged.

"Would you like me to be careful with you?" he asked, his fingers raking through Ira's hair.

"No." Ira had started to quiver all over, anticipation growing in his belly. He wasn't frightened, not really, but it was sort of fun to pretend and it was nice to know that he would never really be in any danger, that he wouldn't get hurt more than he wanted.

The Devil entered him and Ira let out a trembling gasp, aching in the nicest way possible. Lucifer sank his teeth into Ira's shoulder; his nails dug into Ira's skin. They moved together, fast and rough, and finished together, the Devil letting out a hissing cry and Ira unable to make a single sound, his breath caught in his throat and his body tense.

After, though, they oozed together, a tangled heap as they caught their breath.

The Devil kissed the back of Ira's neck then pulled away. Looking almost bashful, he asked, "I wasn't too rough, was I?"

"No."

"You're sure?"

"Yes." Ira wanted to do more to reassure him, but his thoughts were clouded. He put his arms around the other man and burrowed against him.

One skinny finger poked at a tender spot on Ira's neck. "That looks bad."

"Good."

"It looks like I've brutalized you."

"I did ask," Ira reminded, but Lucifer still looked unsure, so Ira kissed him and cooed, "And you do like to give me what I ask for, don't you?"

With a tempted sigh, Lucifer warned, "Don't start with that, I really have got to go soon."

"It could be quick."

"Maybe but I can't go again yet."

"No, me neither," Ira admitted.

They existed together for a few minutes until Lucifer said, "I do have to go."

"I know."

"But I'll see you soon," the Devil promised.

They parted ways with a kiss and Ira wished he could have stayed a little longer. They would see each other again soon, he knew, but he didn't relish the idea of sitting down to eat with his wife.

At first, he was only irritated with the idea, but the closer it got to dinner time, the more his nerves started to jangle. He mangled his tie twice before he gave up and went downstairs, the bit of silk grasped in his hand. He poked his head into Mrs. Spiros' apartment, finding the door open as always.

"Do you think you could do me a favor?"

She jumped and looked up from her game of solitaire, then scolded him for startling her and asked what he wanted. Or so he thought. His grasp on Ancient Greek was bare bones and that was generous.

He held out the tie to her.

She tucked her wings in and approached him. She took the tie.

"I can't do it right," he confessed.

She slipped it around his necked and teased him, though he knew by her tone and not her words. When she finished, she patted his shoulder.

He mumbled his thanks and headed toward the palace, feeling conspicuous in the teal suit. Several people catcalled him as he passed, and he almost turned around to go home and change into something less colorful.

He hesitated outside the door to the palace. He was expected and normally when he was expected, he didn't knock. After a short debate, he rapped on the wood.

Imogen opened the door, looked him over, then smiled knowingly. She stepped aside to let Ira in and whispered, "She'll be jealous for sure." In a louder voice, she informed him, "Our Prince and his queen await you in the dining room."

"There's a dining room?"

"Right this way." She gestured for him to follow.

She led him past her office and the kitchen and off to the right of the stairs, through the foyer. He'd never taken much time to explore the first floor of the palace. The Devil's bedroom, library, and study were all on the second floor overlooking the foyer, and those were the things that interested him the most.

Lucifer had assured him that almost all the other rooms were covered in sheets and cat hair.

The walk from the door across the foyer felt longer than he expected; he wanted to joke about it with Imogen, but the odd, formal air of the evening had dried up all his words. Instead, he listened to the click of his shoes against the tile.

They passed the one room off the foyer that he had been in, a parlor that he now realized must have once been a smoking room, as it was located right next to what had turned out to be the dining room.

He voiced this to Imogen, who told him, "He doesn't smoke," which Ira had known. His cheeks grew hot and he forgot to be nervous.

At the entrance to the dining room, Imogen announced, "Ira has arrived, sire."

Lucifer sat not at the head of the table but to the left. Tabitha sat across from him and Marlow glowered at her from where she crouched at the head of the table. There was not even a chair there and Ira wondered what that choice was meant to communicate.

The Devil stood to greet him, his eyes lighting up. He clasped Ira's hands and drew him in for a kiss. "You look beautiful."

"Thank you," he said, though he doubted it somewhat. He was pretty but he wasn't one of the city's great beauties. He wasn't half as handsome as Georg and paled next to the Devil's wife, who nearly radiated. Georg would be attractive even into old age and Tabitha was surely timeless; Ira had the smooth, even features of a youth and his looks would wane when his age started to show.

If it started to show, he reminded himself, recalling that the Devil had made him undying. He wondered if he would now be baby-faced for eternity.

Lucifer kissed him again, still holding his hands, and then touched his forehead to Ira's. He'd donned his crown again, the circlet cool where it touched Ira's forehead. It warmed quickly against his skin. "I've told her that she has to be nice to you, but it doesn't mean she'll listen," he confided.

Ira nodded and let the Devil bring him over to the seat on his left.

Tabitha shooed the cat from the table and Marlow went, but

not without putting back her ears and growling. "It was Noah, wasn't it?" she asked.

"No."

Lucifer rolled his eyes but didn't correct her. He poured Ira a drink and took his seat. His fingers sought his hair, though he confined it to tucking a lock of hair behind his ear.

"I don't think the two of you have been formally introduced," the Devil began.

Tabitha fixed her eyes on Ira and, with a polite smile that did little to soften the boredom in her tone, said, "Tabitha Bonesmith, Queen of Hell and—"

"Don't start with titles, Tabby, no one has time for that," Lucifer interrupted. "Tabby, this is Ira, my companion. Ira, my wife, Tabitha."

Ira nodded, fixated on the terrifying prospect of bonesmithing. The silence stretched for too long and he babbled, "Nice to meet you, though, I've heard about you plenty, so I guess it had to happen at some point."

"I can't say I've heard much about you," she feigned an apology. "Just that my husband's been carrying on with a few others while I was away."

The first course came, a thick, smooth soup made of root vegetables and a lot of black pepper. Ira swirled his spoon in the soup, waiting for it to cool.

Lucifer said, "You can't expect things to be as they were after you've been gone for so many years."

"So many years?" she asked, her voice light and almost laughing.

"Centuries," he reminded. "Without a word."

She shrugged and took a bite of soup. "Oh, that is good. Go on, try it. Clearly, you haven't been eating right. When I left you looked like a man, not a scarecrow."

"The body—"

"Does what it wants," she finished, "I know. But you *can* make it do things. You can still do that, can't you?"

"It's...itchy, though, making it take a shape it doesn't like."

They ate in silence for a while until, out of nowhere, Lucifer asked, "But where have you been?"

"All around."

"That isn't an answer."

She said, "I've been wherever I wanted to be."

"Then why come back?"

"That's obvious, isn't it? Because this is where I wanted to be."

"But *why?*" Lucifer demanded, his voice losing the cool boredom he maintained around her.

She didn't seem impressed by the edge in his voice. "Curiosity. A new star, our daughter imprisoned, Mylas beheaded, an angel on Earth seeking an anti-Christ...I thought maybe you were up to something interesting."

Lucifer's face remained smooth, but Ira saw him adjust his silverware to lay more neatly.

"But instead I find you playing the same games you always play." She turned to Ira. "Where'd he find you? Tucked away in some corner of the library, your sweet little face buried in a book? Strumming a harp in a pub and making doe-eyes at your love of the week?"

"In a brothel."

She laughed. "Buying companionship, Luci, is that the best you can manage? Making me sit down to meet someone you're paying like it means something? Or was that supposed to be a secret?" She looked over Ira, but barely. She never seemed to really look at anything. She glanced at people as though she could glean everything she could possibly want to know in a few seconds. "You don't look the whoring sort, though."

Ira could only think to say, "Whores have got all kinds of looks to them, I guess."

"How'd a thing like you end up in a brothel, anyway? You hardly look old enough to sell yourself."

"My parents sold me."

Her face darkened and he wondered if he'd misspoke.

"It's not slavery," Lucifer clarified.

"No?" she asked.

"No, it's technically indentured servitude."

"We weren't called slaves then, either, were we?" she challenged.

The Devil let out a long sigh, the sigh of one who had heard this argument already and lost it just as many times.

She asked Ira, "Has he told you how we met?"

"No," he said, then softened it with, "Not that I recall."

"He came to our camp to make sure the warboys were hunting souls and not just raiding other clans. I watched him ride in, tall and strong and *beautiful*, really, his mount as pale as he was and feistier than anything other riders could have handled. I thought he looked like a man who would never let his wife be stolen. That was my whole world at the time—I'd had five husbands in as many years. First, the one who'd paid my brideprice, then the one who'd slain him and then the one who'd slain him...each one stronger, more bloodthirsty than the last."

Ira didn't know what to say. He had frozen with a spoon halfway to his mouth and thought that it would be rude to eat, so he set the spoon back down.

"But this one, Husband Five, was cruel and I'd realized the mistake as soon as I'd goaded him into killing Husband Four. I was one more hearthwife to him. Do you know your history?"

Ira nodded.

"So what do you know about hearthwives?"

He hesitated to answer, looking at Lucifer.

"Don't look at him, I'm talking to you," she warned.

"Hearthwives were for keeping camp and making meals. Cleaning armor and saddling mounts and feeding the hounds. Warwives got the glory and the honors."

"Husband Five thought hearthwives could be used however he wanted. And who would stop him? He wasn't some warboy, he was chief, and I was *his*. So I thought it would be best to find Husband Six and I'd been keeping an eye out. Who would be better than the king himself? I watched him carefully when he broke bread with us the first night. And the second. I watched as he inspected the soul pens and praised Husband Five for keeping them so full."

Lucifer continued eating, ignoring her almost completely.

"I tried to catch his eye or his ear, I tried to get him to make a claim on me." She grinned then, almost fondly. "But the king didn't have any interest in me. Just another hearthwife to an ill-tempered husband. I should have been more cautious, he told me. That's what happens when you depend on others to guide your fate. Only death would rid me of Husband Five and his claim on me and he'd never been bested in a fight."

"And you asked if I could best him," Lucifer chimed in, his bowl the only empty one. He'd started watching her at some point, drawn into her retelling.

"You assured me that you could have—"

"I could have."

"If only you'd had any interest in his things."

Ira wanted desperately to eat something and decided to risk

rudeness and take another mouthful of soup before it got cold. Tabitha didn't seem to notice.

She continued, speaking more to Lucifer now, "I killed him at the feast that night. You saw me then."

Lucifer grinned. "The ax stood as tall as you did."

"After that, I knew I wasn't about to be anybody's property again. That I wouldn't waste my time trying to find a husband to raise me up or keep me safe or throw his dirty armor at me."

"But you got what you could out of Husband Six," Lucifer reminded. The warmth between then snapped like a twig underfoot.

"I never asked—"

"But you didn't say no, either, you took it all and you left."

"It doesn't matter what you gave me. I was never yours, I didn't *belong* to anyone."

"Fuck off, Tabby, I never wanted you to belong to me! I wanted you to love me."

They eyed each other across the table, their silence awkward and hostile.

"I couldn't," she finally told him, not sounding heartbroken or apologetic. "Not the way you wanted. You wanted something I wasn't made for."

"Should I go?" Ira murmured.

Lucifer shook his head.

"I couldn't stay, not with you. Not with you always wanting...wanting to stay in bed all morning and following me around and letting our girl twist you around her little finger...Luci, it was like being shackled. So I left." Tabitha shrugged, then added, "I thought you would get over it quicker," as though their marriage had been a youthful tryst and not a partnership spanning centuries.

"Has there been a Husband Seven?"

"No more husbands, no. I don't hold with that sort of thing anymore. People should be free to come and go as they please."

Lucifer nodded, then cleared his throat. "I." He stood. "I'll be right back."

He left Ira and Tabitha to stare at each other.

Ira rubbed his nose, took a spoonful of soup, and found it cold. He set down his spoon with a sigh. "You never loved him at all."

She looked offended and insisted, "I am fond of him."

"Fondness and love aren't the same."

"And you love him, I suppose," she sneered. "You love all the things he gives you or the money he pays or throwing his name around to impress people."

He didn't feel the need to correct her. "Why'd you come back?"

"You haven't got to worry about losing your meal ticket. I thought he might be up to something interesting and he isn't. I'll see if I can get a little fun out of my visit. See if I can't get him going...he always was so eager to please. Is he still? Like a little puppy if you let it lick between your legs."

Ira couldn't work up the level of shock she must have been looking for. He sipped his drink.

She looked up as Lucifer returned, a smile spreading across her face. "Do you remember how to use your tongue the way I taught you?"

The staff came in with trays and served a little roast fowl to each of them. Ira started to pick the crispy skin off his.

Lucifer sat without answering her question, so she left her seat and came around to their side of the table. She slid her palm against his cheek and murmured into his ear, "Maybe I came back because I missed you, Luci, maybe I've had my fill of hard men with thick cocks and hairy chests and no brains between their ears."

Ira savored the skin, liking Becka considerably more than Oris by virtue of that skin alone. He sucked a bit of grease off his thumb and watched Tabitha slide onto Lucifer's lap. She pulled up her skirt to do so, exposing an expanse of thigh.

"No one's ever lasted like you could," she told him. "Do you think your little pet could keep up?"

Lucifer melted against her, his thin chest moving shallowly as he stared up at her. She nipped at his ear and he gasped, his hands settling on her waist.

"Does he listen as good as you do? I always loved the way you listened."

Ira, having eaten all the skin, picked up a fork and dug it into the flesh, tearing off a piece. He thought about telling Lucifer to eat before it got cold; he also contemplated sinking the fork into the lovely length of his wife's bare thigh.

"Just tell me what you want," the Devil pleaded.

Her hands slipped inside his shirt, at first eliciting sighs of pleasure as she told him that she'd known he could get hard for her. She undid the buttons on his shirt, gyrating on his lap and though Ira couldn't see the results her movement had elicited, the way they groaned made him guess that she had managed in getting him hard. The shirt slipped off his shoulders and Ira saw that she had his nipple caught between the points of her nails.

Ira reached over to steal the skin off her little chicken and thought about leaving.

Lucifer gasped, sharp and high. A sweet, breathy noise he made in bed, one that made Ira's stomach flutter painfully. Before Ira could gather himself to leave, the Devil grunted, the sound rough and abrupt.

That sound drew Ira's attention better than the sounds of desire.

Lucifer whimpered as she pulled at his hair and dug her teeth into his shoulder.

"Don't," Ira said, too quiet.

She didn't stop.

Lucifer had reached up to try to disentangle her fingers from his hair. "You're hurting me."

She purred, "I know," her teeth finding a home on his throat.

"Stop it," Ira said, his voice stronger now, but shaky. When she didn't, he grabbed her by the arm and pulled, not enough to dislodge her from the Devil's lap, but enough to get her attention. "Leave him alone."

"Your pet is jealous." To Ira, she said, "Maybe when I'm done, he'll have something left for you."

Ira could see where she'd broken the skin on his throat. He tightened his grip on her arm.

She seized his wrist and yanked him close, her hand like iron. Her face lost any hint of amusement. "It's time for you to go."

He shook his head, meeting her eyes. "Not if you're hurting him."

Lucifer said nothing. He barely moved.

Ira didn't know if he could or if he had shut down completely.

"You think you know him so well—"

Ira cut her off, "I know he doesn't like this. I know he didn't even want you to come back."

She dismounted the Devil, standing toe to toe with Ira, and stared down at him. "You're his whore, but he's *my* husband—"

"And it's my star," Ira snapped. "You can have his hand in marriage and the palace and you can be the queen of Hell and whatever else, but that's *my* star in the sky. If you look at him and tell me *that's* what he used to look like when you fucked him, then find me a mirror and I'll show you a rapist."

She blinked a few times, then looked at Lucifer. He still hadn't moved, and his breath still came quick and shallow; a few tears had slipped down his cheeks, from pain or fear they couldn't know.

"He isn't well, and you *aren't* what he needs," Ira insisted.

Tabitha shoved him, and Ira thought she meant to do him harm, but she only stalked out of the dining room.

Ira moved in closer to the Devil, putting a hand on his shoulder. "Darling, I'm sorry if I overstepped…"

He shook his head, the movement barely perceptible.

Ira took up one of the cloth napkins and pressed it over the oozing bite mark on Lucifer's shoulder. He evaluated him and found droplets of blood were welling up all over his chest and neck. He reached out to smooth back Lucifer's hair because his circlet sat askew and his braids were badly mussed.

The Devil flinched.

Ira dug his teeth into his lip to combat pain that lanced through his chest. He bent to pick up Lucifer's shirt and handed back to him; the Devil took it, his fingers barely gripping it.

"Go on, dear, get dressed, you'll feel better," Ira prompted.

Lucifer didn't move.

Ira topped off his drink and held it out to him. "What about something to drink?"

He still didn't move so Ira set down the class and looked around. He headed out into the foyer and found Marlow sulking around the stairs. He snatched her up and braced himself to be scratched bloody, but she was surprisingly docile, if not exactly content. He brought her back to the dining room and set her on the Devil's lap.

She stood up on her back legs and put her paws on his chest, scraping her face against his jaw, purring loud enough that Ira could hear.

Lucifer reached up to stroke her head. Moments later, he began to smile, though barely.

Ira smiled, too, and extended his hand, palm up with his fingers crooked, a clear offer if the Devil wanted to take it.

He did, placing his hand in Ira's and bringing it to his mouth to kiss Ira's knuckles. "What about that drink?" he asked.

Ira handed him the wine glass.

After a few swallows, he set it aside and pulled on his shirt, leaving it unbuttoned. Undeterred by the movement, Marlow settled on his lap.

Ira lifted his plate and held it out to him. "You should eat."

He took the plate and did as Ira had, plucking off the skin first.

Marlow chirped, her nose twitching. The Devil fed her a sliver of meat. When he'd picked a little more than half the meat from the bones, he wiped his hands on a napkin, then patted Marlow's haunch.

She leaped onto the table and went at the rest of the carcass.

"I should talk to her," Satan said.

"You should stay the fuck away from her."

Lucifer shook his head.

"Can I at least fix your hair?"

A bit of color crept into Lucifer's cheeks and he nodded his acquiescence.

Ira removed his circlet, setting it on the table, then finger-combed his hair so it lay neatly again. He grabbed the circlet and Lucifer took it out of his hands; instead of donning it, he placed it on top of Ira's head.

"Don't go anywhere, there's still dessert coming," the Devil told him, resting his hands on Ira's shoulders and guiding him back to his seat. He kissed his forehead then left.

Marlow watched him from the table, eyeing him but not glowering. While he waited, Ira picked at Tabitha's untouched dinner and offered Marlow one of the legs. She snatched it out of his hand.

"Do you like me now or do you just hate me less than her?"

The cat ignored him, gnawing at the leg.

Someone came to clear away the dishes, entering hesitantly and pausing altogether when he saw the other two missing. The manservant who must have been hired to replace Gila reached for a plate then paused. "Should I wait?"

Ira shook his head. "Go ahead, clear it."

He nodded.

"I don't think we've met."

The other man shook his head.

Ira leaned forward and offered his hand. "Ira. You?"

"Hasbani, sir." He shook Ira's hand.

"Oh, I'm no sir. I love your name, though. I've never heard it before."

"It's where I was born."

Ira didn't know of anywhere in Hell by that name, not in the

Eighth or the Ninth, which might not have meant much. It could conceivably be a place outside the city walls.

"It's on Earth," the other man told him.

"Oh!" Ira exclaimed, unable to help his surprise. The manservant had fair brown skin and wavy dark hair, but his hazel eyes had narrow, vertical pupils, so Ira didn't think he was human, at least not fully.

"My mother," Hasbani provided.

"It's none of my business, you don't have to tell me," Ira assured him. "Unless you want to, I'm all ears. I'm just waiting for those other two to come back. Did you grow up on Earth?"

He nodded. "My mother passed away. A couple of weeks ago, so...here I am." He shrugged and looked around the room. "My father thought it would be a good fit for me here. He pulled a few strings...It's what I did at home anyways, though I think I like your fellow better than the Brits."

"Who's your father?"

"His name's Marius, uh, Marius malak ha-satan, I think is the whole thing."

Ira turned so quickly that he almost knocked over his wine glass. As he steadied it, he exclaimed, "Marius! I didn't know he had any kids!"

Hasbani nodded.

Ira grinned at him. "I work for him, you know. Isn't that something! Have you been down to the house, yet? You should meet Georg, he's wonderful."

Hasbani stared, then started to gather up the plates. "No, not really."

He didn't talk much after that.

Ira thought he must have scared him. Of course, life in a new realm really had to be something that required adjustment and, considering that his mother had died, he must have felt terribly alone in the world.

Hasbani took off with the plates, his eyes lowered.

Lucifer and Tabitha returned not too long after that.

Ira gave the Devil an affectionate swat. "You didn't *tell me* that was Marius' son!"

Lucifer stared vacantly at him, then opened his mouth halfway. "The manservant."

"Oh, oh, right, yes. You know, I think Imogen mentioned it but, well..." He made a vague gesture with his hand.

Ira nodded.

The Devil swooped down to kiss his cheek.

Tabitha returned to her seat across from them, setting her elbows on the table and resting her chin on her hands. "He tells me he isn't paying you."

Ira pressed his lips together. He wouldn't have even taken the time to spit on her if it had been up to him, but Lucifer nudged his leg with his knee. "So?"

She shrugged. "You led me to believe—"

"I didn't. You went ahead and *decided* without even asking."

Her eyes narrowed slightly. "He's asked me to be civil with you—"

"And he hasn't asked me to do a fucking thing," he spat. He turned to the Devil. "I don't know why you wanted to do this!"

"I didn't know," Tabitha said before Lucifer could answer him. "I didn't come here to traumatize this...*thing* that used to be my husband. How was I to know that he can't even tolerate a bit of playing around anymore?"

"You ask," Ira said.

She glowered at him.

He met her eyes. "It's easy. Should I show you? Do you think you can keep up?"

Lucifer put up his hands. "Let's not play the game of mounting me to try to upstage each other, I don't think I can take it."

He sounded jovial, but Ira heard the note of panic. He reached out to pat his hand and assured, "No, love, I wouldn't." He gave Tabitha half a glance. "I don't need to."

Lucifer put his hand over Ira's. "And to answer you, I asked you here because I wanted to get this out of the way. And I certainly didn't want it to happen unsupervised. Now really, let's be adults about this, I'm incredibly certain Becka's made us chocolate cake and I've been thinking about it for hours."

"I am being an adult," Ira muttered.

He sulked, running his finger up and down the stem of his glass until Becka came in, her platter laden with a carafe of coffee and thick slices of chocolate cake. He tried to persist in his pouting but couldn't, not with the two of them chatting about days long gone and a beautiful piece of cake sitting in front of him.

"I feel like I shouldn't eat it," Lucifer declared after he'd had the cake sitting in front of him for about a minute.

Tabitha reached over and dragged her fork through the glossy ganache frosting, marring its perfection.

"Do you hold nothing sacred?" the Devil demanded.

She beamed at him, a broad, fond smile that seemed surprisingly genuine. "Now stop fussing and eat it. You are peculiar, Luci, you know that, don't you?"

He nodded, using his own fork to smooth out the frosting a little before he took his first bite.

"Positively queer," she pronounced.

He didn't seem to mind her judgment.

Ira poured himself a coffee and looked around for the milk, finding it next to Tabitha. Rather than ask her to pass it, he sipped it black, doing his best not to grimace at the taste.

Lucifer reached across the table and snagged the little pitcher, then placed it in front of Ira.

He splashed in a bit of milk and sprinkled in a touch of sugar. He found it much more palatable then.

The Devil finished his cake, scraped all the frosting off his plate with the edge of his fork and then stood, leaving the two of them alone, surely heading to the kitchen in search of another piece.

"I thought he needed reminding," Tabitha shared. "About how we used to be."

Ira sipped his coffee, trying not to frown at her.

"What was I supposed to think?" she asked. "He goes on telling me he can't get hard instead of telling me he doesn't want to fuck me."

"He probably does want to fuck you," Ira told her. "He just doesn't want you to hurt him."

She rolled her eyes. "He could have told me."

"So you would leave again?"

"I thought he didn't want me to come back."

Ira set down his mug so hard that coffee sloshed over the sides. "Don't you understand anything about him?"

"Apparently not."

"He waited for ages hoping you'd come back and just when he's started to put it behind him—"

"It? You mean our marriage."

Ira sighed and rubbed his face. He raked his hands through his curls and his fingers caught on the circlet. He'd forgotten about it entirely. He tossed it on the table. "Can you go a single fucking minute without contradicting yourself?"

"Do you know what it's *like* to care about someone like him? Someone who wants to give you the entire world and all you want is to live your own life? And I do care about him, but...I can't give him what he wants. So I left and that was wrong. I've come back and now that was the wrong thing to do, too, wasn't it? What am I supposed to do with him?"

Ira didn't get the sense that the question was rhetorical, but that she had asked in earnest. "Be honest."

They fell silent as Lucifer came back in, an overlarge hunk of cake on his plate. Ira almost teased him about it but then changed his mind, glad to see him enthusiastic about something and feeling that he deserved a little bit of indulgence right then.

"You can keep talking about me," he told them.

"The two of you ought to talk to each other," Ira advised.

Lucifer shook his head. "I've always known she didn't love me. What else is there to know?"

Tabitha protested, "I care."

"Rest assured, I feel very cared about."

"Luci," she said.

"Tabby."

She came around the other side of the table and crouched beside his chair. She took his hands into hers and clasped them to her breast, over her heart. "I didn't come back here to coerce you. If you want me to go, then say so."

His brow knitted and his tongue flicked out to wet his lips. "You'll be angry."

"No."

"You will. You're always angry with me."

She sighed. "I'm not angry..."

"No, I suppose not. You have to care to be angry."

She released his hands and stood. She clapped him on the shoulder. "I'll go. I never meant to stay for long. I'd sort of hoped that I'd be around enough to see a Revel."

Ira watched an expression of disappointment flit across Lucifer's face. Ira knew that tactic well, presenting himself as worthless in the hope that someone else would assure him that he wasn't. Ira didn't think he did it on purpose, he thought that Lucifer slipped into periods of really believing that he lacked value and badly wanted someone to tell him otherwise.

He didn't think Tabitha understood what the Devil had done. He doubted she'd ever wasted a moment thinking she was worthless, not since she'd gotten a real sense of agency and killed her last husband.

"I should probably head home," Ira announced.

Lucifer's head snapped around to look at him, plainly wounded, though it showed for only a second or two before he threw that mask back on. "If you want."

"Watch yourself with that," Ira warned him, "I can't do the work for both of us."

When Lucifer didn't ask him to stay, he walked out.

The Devil caught up with him before he'd gotten halfway across the foyer. He snagged Ira by the wrist. Ira turned around, scowling, but his mood softened when he saw Lucifer's face.

"I need help," he confessed, "For a little while. Please."

That was all that Ira had wanted, really. He spread his arms and the Devil almost collapsed into his embrace. "Of course, I'll help, darling, you haven't got to ask twice."

Tabitha breezed by them towards the stairs, not even looking their way.

Ira stepped back, tucked a lock of hair behind Lucifer's ear and, keeping his voice low and one hand on Lucifer's face, inquired, "You don't want her to go, do you?"

"No," he confessed, his voice thick and his face twisting. "I want her to love me."

"She can't."

"But I want her to. I want her to stay, I want...I want things to be like they were in the beginning, before she hated me."

"She doesn't hate you. She *can't*, though, Lu, you've got to understand that. She doesn't love like you do."

"I know." Lucifer swallowed. "But it doesn't stop me from wanting it."

He wanted to ask if it mattered at all that Ira loved him, but he knew that question wasn't fair and wasn't what Lucifer needed to hear. Instead, he told him, "Go ask her to stay for a little longer. As a friend. You two could probably manage to be friends, couldn't you?"

He nodded and looked towards the stairs. "Will you stay, though?"

"I will," Ira promised, though he didn't know where he was going to sleep, not if Tabitha had reclaimed her space in the Devil's bed.

"Thank you."

Ira rubbed his back and nudged him towards the stairs, watching as he climbed and disappeared through his bedroom door.

When he couldn't see him any longer, Ira went to Imogen's office and demanded to know all the details of Tabitha's stay thus far.

"I've been busy, you know. Gathering the details of their relationship hasn't been my priority," she informed him, "We are dealing with an insurrection. He's hardly been here."

"But what do you think of her?"

"I think the sooner she's gone the sooner he'll stop acting like he's on the verge of a nervous breakdown."

"I think he might be."

"He's welcome to have one once we get rid of these dissenters," Imogen said. "He showed me the letter you wrote. We need to know more about them."

"I know." Lucifer might not have wanted Ira poking around, but Ira had little intention of letting the in he had with this reiteration of the Raven Company go unused. If Astrid associated with them, and if she didn't hate him now, he could find out as much as they needed to know. "Once this is done with, I'm going to take him away for a while. He mentioned this house on the lake. He'll finally be able to get himself together."

"Get their names, find out how many there are."

"I will."

"If you can do that, I can have them...removed from the equation without needing him to exert himself too much."

He nodded, then, not knowing what else to say on the topic, told her, "New staff seems to be working out."

"I'm pleased with both of them."

"Did you know Hasbani is Marius' son?"

"Marius approached me about his employment, yes."

He loitered in her office for a while longer, the two of them not saying anything until he cleared his throat and said, "Well. That's all."

"Goodnight, Ira."

He gave her half a smile and wandered upstairs, not sure where to go or what to do. He passed by the Devil's bedroom and caught a snippet of their discussion. Lucifer reminded Tabitha that there had been things they'd enjoyed doing together, things outside of the bedroom and she asked to know if he did any of those things still.

He admitted that he didn't.

Ira stopped listening, going into the large bathroom. He selected a volume from the bookshelf and made himself comfortable on the settee there. He wondered how long it would be before they were done talking and what Lucifer intended to do for the rest of the night.

An hour or so passed before Lucifer came into the bathroom and admonished, "I was looking all over for you, I thought you'd left."

"You asked me to stay."

"Tabby's gone to stay with Siobhan. She promised she'd come back, though, once she's had time to think about things."

"You believe her?"

Lucifer said, "She wouldn't bother to promise if she didn't mean it."

"Are you alright?"

"I don't know."

"You should get some sleep," Ira advised.

"I don't think I can."

"I'll lay down with you."

In bed, Lucifer wrapped around him and buried them both with enough blankets to make Ira worry about suffocating.

IRA KNEW what he needed to do. He spent the morning with Lucifer. They woke late then shared the last bit of chocolate cake and took a long bath together. Lucifer asked him not to go but he promised that he'd be back that night, saying that he needed to check in at work. It didn't feel right, lying to him, but he knew his task was necessary.

When he left, the first thing he did was go home, put on one of his older suits, and then headed to work.

Georg lounged in one of the armchairs, chatting with one of the other workers. "I need to borrow you," Ira told him. "The back room."

The young man followed, worry scrawled across his face.

Ira closed the door and asked, "Where does Astrid live? Which residence?"

"Why?"

"Doesn't matter."

"I'm pretty sure she's in Fenbrood Hall."

Ira clapped him on the shoulder. "Thanks. Hit me."

"What?"

"In the face."

"What the fuck, Ira?" the younger man demanded.

"I've got to make Astrid think Lu and I are done."

Georg crossed his arms. "Why the *fuck* would you want to go within ten feet of her?"

"Because I think she knows who's letting souls out. I need to get to them and convince them that I'm not loyal."

"That's a stupid idea."

Ira threatened, "Hit me or I'll pick a fight and I'd rather not do it that way."

Georg heaved a sigh and uncrossed his arms. He rested his hands on his hips. "And what does our Prince think of all this?"

"Hopefully he won't know about it until it's over."

"This seems like an incredibly bad and stupid idea."

"Maybe it is, but he needs help. You've seen how he is...I'm worried and I need to do *something*, I can't just watch things go to shit. Georg, please, I don't have anyone else to ask."

"Fine," Georg huffed. "Fine, alright. Close your eyes."

"Why?"

"Because I can't hit you if you're looking at me."

Ira closed his eyes and held his breath, waiting for the blow to come. He grew antsy when it didn't. "Georg!"

"I'm sorry, just...give me a moment."

A few seconds later, a shock of pain rocked Ira. He clapped a hand to his jaw, cursed, and opened his eyes to find Georg staring at him, his hands over his mouth.

"I'm sorry," Georg whispered. "Ira, I'm so sorry."

"Once more."

"Ira."

"Please."

This time Georg hit him hard enough to blacken his eye, then let out a ragged sob. "I won't do it again, don't ask me to."

"No, darling, I think that was perfect."

Georg embraced him hard enough to knock the air from his lungs.

"Thank you. Remember, as far as you know, Lu did this to me."

"Be careful, Ira. This is so stupid."

"I've got to do *something*."

Georg gripped him tighter. "Promise you'll be careful. You're the only real friend I've got. I don't want to lose you."

"Ah, he made me undying, remember? Nothing to worry about," Ira assured, though he didn't think he sold Georg on his lack of concern. Maybe he wouldn't stay dead, but a violent death didn't seem like a wonderful thing to experience. "When all this is done, I'm going to take him somewhere quiet for a while."

"The two of you deserve that."

"You could come with us."

Georg stepped back, licking his lips. "Maybe."

Ira took his hand. "I think we'd both like that."

Georg nodded, hesitant at first, but then smiling as he said, "I think I'd like it, too."

"Good." Ira smiled. "I should go get this done."

He left Georg and thoughts of a pleasant vacation behind as he walked over to the university. He knew the way there by now. He tried to work up a façade of distress, something that would convince her that Lucifer had ended things and made it ugly. The closer he got to campus, though, the less he had to pretend to be upset.

He didn't want to see Astrid. The thought of her made his stomach hurt. He doubted he'd be able to insinuate himself into the group enough without her. He could certainly sell them information but if he wanted to know their plans, he needed to appear committed to their cause.

By the time he made it to her residence hall and up to her room, he had real tears streaming down his cheeks. He forced himself to knock on her door. When she answered, he let out a sob at the sight of her.

She stared, then embraced him, which only served to further upset him.

He wanted to shove her away, but instead, he wept, "I'm sorry."

She shushed at him and cooed that it was alright, holding him close and making his skin crawl. She pulled back to look at him and gingerly touched the bruise on his jaw. "What happened?"

He shook his head. "It's done. It's over and..." He had to force the words from his mouth. "You were right."

"Ira, I'm so sorry. I am."

He couldn't stop the tears or even out his breathing.

She brought him into her room and settled him on the bed, rocking him gently while she rubbed his back, telling him a lot of nonsense about being here for him, about making things better.

He fed her a made-up story about a fight between the two of them, mentioning that the Devil's wife had returned and that he'd been set aside for her. He said that Lucifer had put him aside like he was nothing and had hit him when he'd refused to go quietly.

She called him brave.

He felt disgusting for casting their Prince in such a poor light. "I hate him. I never wanted him to hurt you, either, I didn't. Astrid, I swear..."

She kissed him gently. "I know. I know how hard it must have been for you, Ira, but it's done now. He won't hurt you again."

"What if he does?" he asked, "What if he...what if he comes back for me?"

She shook her head emphatically. "He won't, we're going to get rid of him."

He made himself look shocked, widening his eyes the same way he did when a bragging customer thought himself particularly well-endowed. "How? He's...he's the Devil, no one can stop him."

"There someone who can now. Come with me, tell her what you know."

"If he finds out..."

"You haven't got to be frightened anymore. She's an angel, she can hold her own against him."

He nodded. "If...if you think she can help."

He wondered if this angel would remember him, if she would be suspicious, but decided to risk it. He looked weak and people never took him for someone that was particularly smart. She knew him as a whore and she would be willing to believe that a whore would go where the money was, just as she would believe that the Devil would brutalize him. She had called him a foul beast, after all.

Astrid took his hand and they walked like that through the Ninth and into the Eighth. The whole time he could only think about the clammy feeling of her hand in his.

She brought him to a boarding house in the Eighth. Ira got the feeling that this sort of establishment saw a lot of hourly renters, in addition to the usual crowd of workers that preferred to rent a room instead of wasting their pay on more space than they needed.

On the third floor, she rapped on a door, once then twice more.

The door opened and the silver angel frowned at her until Astrid pulled Ira forward and told her, "I brought someone—"

"I wondered how long it would take," the angel said, speaking to Ira instead of Astrid. She took Ira by the chin and examined his bruises. "What happened here?"

"I thought he was done with me. I was wrong. I'm done with him, though, I-I don't want...I was stupid. I thought he loved me, but he can't. I was never anything to him but a thing to use."

She nodded, her sympathy seeming real. She opened the door wider and allowed them into her room, which lacked any personal touches. She motioned for them to have a seat on the bed. She pulled over the room's single chair and placed it across from them.

She crossed her legs and folded her hands on her lap. "What do you have to tell me?"

Cagily, he returned, "What do you want to know?"

"Everything."

"I don't know everything," he said.

"Tell me about him."

Ira looked at Astrid. He hadn't thought this through enough, apparently, because he didn't know what he was going to tell this angel. "Tell me about you first."

She tilted her head to the side, her skin shimmering in the candlelight. "About me?"

"How am I supposed to know that you won't be worse than he is? You're an angel."

"That's why you should trust me."

He shook his head. "Maybe if I was human but this is Hell. Relations between our realms have been...less than ideal for a few millennia. But I don't even know your name. I don't know why you've come here."

"I've come to the Pit to make it what it should have always been."

He stood and took a step to the door. "If you can't give me your name—"

"I don't have a name."

The question staggered him, and he blurted, "Why not?"

"The first angels were all given names. The ones made to replace the Fallen? We were not all so lucky. Rumor says that He replaced His favorites by hand, with care. When it came to the petty angels it was enough to make...groups. Sixty glittering golden foot soldiers, ten beautiful black watchers, one hundred lovely purple domestics—"

"I thought you were going to keep up with the alliteration," he quipped, the words slipping out before he remembered that he was supposed to be a distraught, abused lover.

"And two dozen silver notaries."

"You're a notary."

"The Pit needs to keep its affairs in Hell. There are souls here that need to be cleansed for their assent Heaven not corrupted into demons!"

He sat back down. "You should get a name. You can't just be Queen Notary."

They sat in silence for a while.

"Rivka," she pronounced.

"Hmm?" Ira asked. He had been busy contemplating the pain in his jaw, focusing on not wiggling a molar that had loosened slightly. It proved to be difficult to leave the tooth alone and the experience had brought back the memory of being fourteen and wiggling his last baby tooth, a stubborn molar that hadn't wanted to go.

"Rivka. You can call me Rivka."

He nodded. "Fine. You have to tell me what you want to know, though, because..." He scrambled for a reason, "Because I was just his whore."

"You're more than a whore," Astrid assured him.

He wished she hadn't, but he allowed her to take his hand and give it a comforting squeeze. He told the angel, "What I know probably isn't going to help you. But you said something about, uh, seeing things. Tell me what I was supposed to be seeing."

"We've gotten reports that he faints."

"He does."

"Often?" Rivka asked.

"Since he was poisoned a little more than a year ago. Most people don't know about it."

"Poisoned?"

He nodded. "By an angel. One of those golden soldiers you mentioned. He's been getting better but..."

"But cleaning up messes in the First and the Third has worn him out?" she guessed and when he nodded, she smiled. "We hoped it would."

"Is that your plan? To make him tired?" Ira asked.

Rivka corrected, "To exhaust him. He caught us off guard in the Third, though. I lost a lot of supporters that day."

If a dozen was a lot to her then she couldn't have had that many.

"What else?" she asked.

"His wife came back," Astrid answered for him.

Ira could have strangled her.

Rivka's face contorted. "His wife? She's been away for centuries."

"Well, she's back now," Astrid confirmed. "Ira says she's at the palace with him."

"This isn't good." Rivka stood, almost too tall for the room.

Ira watched her, feeling that he'd done something terribly wrong. "Why isn't it good?"

Rivka said, "Wives support their husbands. Queens support their kings. We need him isolated and weak if this is to succeed. And he did that to your face, so he's...regaining some of his vitality."

"He seemed out of sorts," Ira insisted.

The angel ignored him. "We need to move now. Tonight. Astrid, go to the Ninth, gather Ravens there."

"I don't know if they have what they need from Falco yet," Astrid shared.

Rivka nodded, then said, "We'll manage it without him if we must. I'll organize here. We meet at the chancery."

"Which precinct?" Astrid asked.

Rivka didn't answer, her mouth drawn tight. She didn't look so kind and lovely then.

Ira had overplayed his hand. He should have listened to Lucifer and stayed away.

"Where do I tell them to meet?" Astrid asked, grasping the sleeve of the angel's shirt.

"We must run him ragged."

Realization dawned on Astrid's pretty face. Her wide, blue eyes grew even wider, making her look alien and terrified. "But the Seventh...those souls are dangerous. They're *actively evil*, not just some confused bugger. The Fourth—"

"We don't have *time* to dally. Get Davos, too, he'll help you rally the Ninth," Rivka ordered.

Ira started to panic.

The angel addressed him, "We'll need all the hands we can get, Ira. I don't imagine you've ever worked with the souls?"

"No," he whispered.

"I hope you're a fast learner. Go."

Astrid took him by the hand and brought him out into the hall. She retrieved someone from the next room over, a stocky purple demon who must have been Davos. She introduced Ira then told Davos that they had to rally the Ravens in the Seventh tonight.

Davos took the news with a nod and headed out of the boarding house at a brisk walk. Astrid hurried after him.

Ira had to get away, but he didn't know how without arousing their suspicion. With the looks Davos shot him, Ira worried that arousing suspicion would get him killed or incapacitated, which would make it impossible to warn their Prince.

He went with Astrid and Davos, knocking on doors, catching people as they came home from work, even finding people at their evening meals in restaurants throughout the Ninth. When they went to get Tycho, he whispered to Astrid that Tycho had been a customer and he couldn't bear to see him.

She looked like her heart was going to break as she put a hand to his cheek and assured him, "Of course you can wait, my love, I can't imagine how hard it is...We'll be right back."

Ira remained outside as she went into the house, but Davos didn't follow her. Ira fidgeted and put his hands in his pockets to hide their nervous tremble. He found a few coins and couldn't stop fiddling with them.

He searched the streets and finally spied a raggedy beggar girl stationed on a street corner, her eyes clouded and sightless. He took the coins out and approached her as she piped her sad tale, asking for something to feed her baby brother, a skinny toddler that languished at her feet.

Wretches like this came to beg in the Ninth, knowing that in the Eighth they were more likely to get clouted for their trouble.

He put the coins into her upturned hand and whispered, "If you love your Prince, you'll go to the palace and tell him that there will be trouble in the Seventh tonight and you'll be quiet about it. He'll grant you a boon for your help."

She only thanked him for his kindness, her fist closing around the serpents.

He hesitated then headed back to the stoop, his hands in his pockets again. He stood beside Davos, his mouth dry and sticky.

Davos grunted and huffed, "She pulls in more doing that than anyone does working."

"Drip a bit of acid in your eyes and see how much you can pull in begging, then," Ira suggested.

The demon graced him with a burning looking but said nothing else.

As he waited outside the chancery in the Seventh for the Ravens to gather, Ira could only think that Lucifer would be worrying. He'd promised to come back and he hadn't. He hoped the blind girl had loved her Prince enough to head to the palace. He assured himself that to get from the Eighth to the Ninth, she had to possess reasonable skills of navigation.

Astrid had her arm around his waist and her head resting on his shoulder as they waited.

He wanted to flee.

She must have felt him shaking because she pressed a kiss to his cheek and hugged him tightly. "Don't worry, Ira, all we have to do is unlock the doors, not open them. In the Seventh, they want to get out. We'll have time to get out and then we'll be safe at home."

Falco arrived, having apparently joined their cause, and let them into the chancery. He handed out keys for the cells in different wards in the Seventh. Tycho's group got the key to A ward, Davos' group received the one to B ward, someone Ira couldn't name ended up with the key to C and so on.

As the groups got their keys, they headed out. By the time Falco got to the last set of keys, only Ira, Astrid and half a dozen others, including the angel, remained. The souls must have been finding their way out by now.

Ira kept looking out the window, praying for the Devil to come and put a stop to this.

Astrid took the last set of keys and headed outside, but she stopped dead. She grabbed on to Ira's arm, her fingers biting into his flesh. "No," she gasped, "No, it can't...!"

Tall and lanky, the Devil approached, his pace even and unhurried. He carried an unsheathed sword in one hand and Ira recognized the blade. It had hung in the foyer, unused, for as long as he'd been visiting the palace. Imogen had once mentioned that it was the sword that he'd wielded in single combat against the archangel Michael.

Lucifer stopped in front of the chancery, not even looking at Ira.

"Should I come in or will you come out?" he called.

Rivka exited the building. She stood almost as tall as he did. "Is that part of being the Devil? Knowing when things are amiss?"

"I'd be a poor Devil if I didn't know where my souls were."

Ira thought he was lying.

"Go on, then," Rivka taunted, "Go clean things up."

"Not yet."

Cries start to ring out through the Precinct, coming from the direction of A ward. Whoops of delight and bloodcurdling battle cries.

The Seventh was the smallest Precinct but these souls would be harder to wrangle than any of the others. If Lucifer didn't go to get them, Ira couldn't fathom how arduous the task would be.

Rivka frowned.

"It won't be easy, cleaning them up, but I'll deal with that later. After I deal with you." He shifted his grip on the blade, then swung it.

Rivka dodged the blow and it seemed Lucifer had expected her to because a small smile played on his lips.

Astrid clung to Ira.

The demons that remained watched, crowded around the fight in a wide circle.

Rivka danced away from the Devil, drawing a long dagger from her waist. The blade lacked the sickly green-silver color Ira had seen in other Heaven-forged weapons; when the Devil struck at her again, she parried the blow.

They traded blows for a while and Ira thought that Lucifer would win, that he would have to win. He drew blood twice and offered to let her go back to Heaven unscathed if she put down her weapon.

"After all, I admire a rebellion," he told her, grinning his biggest, widest smile.

She didn't answer, lunging towards him, feinting to one side. It looked like she would land a blow, but the Devil stepped aside and smacked her in the back with the flat of his blade.

It looked like he was playing with her. It looked like he would win. He even smiled and hope dared to take root in Ira's chest. He would kill her soon, drive that blade into her chest or throat or lop off her head, Ira knew he would, and he seemed to know it, too.

Until.

Until blood started to dribble from his nose.

The Devil touched his nose, examined his fingers, then wiped his face with his sleeve. No one else appeared to notice, they were all too busy looking at their would-be queen as she stumbled forward.

She spun and Lucifer started to circle around. He moved closer to Ira's side of the circle and glanced towards Ira, their eyes meeting for just a second.

He was going to faint and they both knew it.

He would pass out and Ira wouldn't be able to do a thing to help him.

The flow of blood from his nose grew heavier.

When Rivka struck at him again, he knocked away the blow,

but it was sloppy, and she noticed. She moved again, harder and faster this time.

He barely managed to keep pace with her, large gaps growing in his defense until she managed to slip inside and drive her blade into his chest.

He stayed on his feet for a few seconds. When he fell, he grabbed onto Ira and dragged him down.

Astrid screamed as she lost her grip on him.

"Traitor," he accused, his voice all venom and hatred. His hand wrapped all the way around Ira's throat. He pulled him closer and the others rushed over to help in.

Lucifer kept his grip on Ira, pulling him even closer, his mouth next to Ira's ear. "Don't let them know," he whispered before the others freed Ira from his grasp.

His nails scraped against Ira's skin.

The others gathered around to watch him die.

Ira bit his tongue hard to hold back his tears and screams; they couldn't see him crying, no matter how badly he wanted to drop to his knees and take the Devil into his arms so that he wouldn't have to die alone. No one couldn't doubt that this was what he wanted.

He can't die. Not really, Ira told himself over and over again. He would be back soon, and Ira would find a way to get rid of this angel.

Things would be alright. They had to be. He must have told himself that a hundred times as they waited for their Prince to die.

Rivka ripped her knife from his chest and that seemed to be what did him in, sending a gout of blood spilling on to the ground as he sputtered.

Ira put a trembling hand to his mouth and realized that he'd smeared blood all over his face. "Should we bury him?" he asked, his voice no more than a whisper.

Rivka shook her head, putting a hand on her shoulder. "Of course not. I don't have any intention of letting him wiggle out of this."

"Oh."

"I owe you a boon, Ira, for getting my reign off to such an auspicious start."

He tried to smile.

"Tell them to stop unlocking the doors," she commanded.

Several demons bolted off towards the different wards, shouting at the top of their lungs that the Devil was dead, to get the cells locked again.

Ira stared down at the Devil's body, more ungainly in death than it had seemed in life.

Blood sluggishly pattered from the blade in Rivka's hand, leaving behind a trail wherever she went.

"Your knife..."

Rivka glanced his way. "Hmm?"

It didn't feel right that such precious blood should be left to mingle with dirt and trash. She should clean the blade. Someone needed to clean all this up.

"What about my knife?" she asked, fixing her eyes on his face.

"It's silver."

"It's steel, actually." She gave him a funny look. "Picked up from a shop in the Ninth. Why?"

He shook his head.

With real concern, she inquired, "Are you well?"

"I've never seen anyone die before."

"Neither have I."

When the Ravens had all reconvened at the chancery, Rivka sent most of them off to spread the word that there was a new queen.

"And pick him up," she added.

Ira hurried to be one of the people lifting him. Someone else helped with the arms, two more grabbed the feet. "Where to?" the woman at the feet asked.

"To my palace."

People came out of their houses to watch as they carried the Devil's body through the streets. Some cheered, some wailed. Many did nothing but look, stone-faced and silent.

They found the palace in a state of nervous chaos, the staff debating what to do. The gardeners argued with the cat keepers, Becka kept insisting that she had hardly worked for him at all, and Hasbani said nothing.

Imogen could not be found. Her office had been emptied hastily, drawers left opened and her chair knocked on its side.

Ira helped bring the Devil down into the dungeon and lock up his body in one of the cells, knowing that he would be sick later.

Several of them spat on his corpse as they left.

When he came upstairs Astrid kissed him. "I thought he would kill you," she simpered.

He nodded, out of words.

By the time he was able to get away from her and their celebration, the sky had grown light. People were still out in the streets, talking about the coup, the souls from the Seventh, arguing about what to do.

He went to his bathroom, intending to wash up, but instead climbed into the bathtub and sat there, not knowing what else to do, not sure if he would ever know what to do again.

About the Author

Dan is an author and educator who has lived in Connecticut for their entire life. They received a degree in education and later wrote their Master's thesis on representation of women in same-sex relationships in contemporary Spanish literature and cinema.

What Everyone Deserves
2017 Rainbow Awards **Honorable Mention**
"Although the story deal with some real 1950's issues – discrimination, homophobia, interracial couples and hate crimes – it did it in a way that perfectly suited the characters and the story." - **Divine Magazine**

In this 1950s period drama, Junius is a New York City fertility demon with a crush. Ever since falling from heaven he's been alone. Except for the mothers and children he watches over.

James Kelly Rosenburg, a black soldier with snowflakes in his hair, walks right into his life with a big problem. James Kelly, turned vampire during the war, is new to New York and its prohibition against vampire killing in city limits.

Junius offers to teach him to overcome his bloodthirsty instincts and live a proper Manhattan life. Their growing friendship leaves them both conflicted as they explore a city both welcoming and alienated by their kind.

That Doesn't Belong Here
"I liked the ... atmosphere that he created, alongside the paranormal creatures that roam the street. I liked that he wrote characters I could emotionally care for. If Ackerman writes another LGBT fiction, I will give it a try for sure."
- Ami, **The Blogger Girls**

That Doesn't Belong Here begins when Levi and his friend Emily discover an impossible creature in an abandoned pick up. The thing is wounded, frightened and the two friends cannot leave him to the mercy of rubberneckers and tourists. This novel explores what it means to be a person, as the creature, Kato, begins to display not mere intelligence or friendliness but what can only be explained as humanity. The question of who we are allowed to love arises for Levi and Kato, as they are not just crossing the boundaries of gender or sexuality, but of species.